THE CUT OF THE WHIP

Daniel Port is driving through Texas when the other car appears out of nowhere. When Port eventually wakes up, he finds a ministering angel named Jane and her father, Carl Heering, the richest man in town. Heering admits that it was his son, Robert, that ran into Port and that the kid has run off with important business papers. He offers Port an easy grand to bring his son and the papers back. But when Port tracks the kid down, all is not as it seems. The business papers are love letters, the Heering heir is kidnapped, and Port finds he must solve the mystery and rescue Robert before he himself is implicated in the plot and put in prison for kidnapping.

BRING ME ANOTHER CORPSE

He could go it alone, or he could do it with the knowledge and help of a big organization. He didn't like either alternative because it would be too much like going back, like starting all over in the kind of a life about which he no longer had any illusions ... All those surface satisfactions that used to make life spin around with a speed that made you think, Sure now—you're going someplace.

"I'll try it your way," he said to Lubinski, "and I hope it's the fast way out."

Lubinski smiled at Port. The smile lasted a second, and then Lubinski opened his briefcase and drew out the usual folder.

"It can be fast," he said. "A lot of it is already set up."

"Where do I fit?"

"You go to Cleveland," said Lubinski, "and you hire out as your own killer..."

TIME ENOUGH TO DIE

Port thinks he's escaped his problems. Time moves slowly in the Mexican coastal village of Guanadera, and that's just the way he likes it—the sun on his face, a beer in his hand and nothing but Maria on his mind. So when Maria asks him to help her find her missing neighbor, an elderly gent named Kiamoto, he doesn't give the project much thought. How could he know that d'Ortega and his henchman Capo were also looking for Kiamoto? They figure that an American gangster—and why else would Port be living in Guanadera?—must be in on the caper. Because Kiamoto is much more than he seems. And pretty soon there are American agents in on the game. Just when Port thought he was out of the rackets for good, he gets pulled into a

PETER RABE BIBLIOGRAPHY

From Here to Maternity (1955)
Stop This Man! (1955)
Benny Muscles In (1955)
A Shroud for Jesso (1955)
A House in Naples (1956)
Kill the Boss Good-by (1956)
Dig My Grave Deep (1956) *
The Out is Death (1957) *
Agreement to Kill (1957)
It's My Funeral (1957) *
Journey Into Terror (1957)
Mission for Vengeance (1958)
Blood on the Desert (1958)
The Cut of the Whip (1958) *
Bring Me Another Corpse (1959) *
Time Enough to Die (1959) *
Anatomy of a Killer (1960)
My Lovely Executioner (1960)
Murder Me for Nickels (1960)
The Box (1962)
His Neighbor's Wife (1962)
Girl in a Big Brass Bed (1965) **
The Spy Who Was Three Feet Tall (1966) **
Code Name Gadget (1967) **
Tobruk (1967)
War of the Dons (1972)
Black Mafia (1974)
The Silent Wall (2011)
The Return of Marvin Palaver (2011)

**Daniel Port series*
***Manny DeWitt series*

As by "Marco Malaponte"
New Man in the House (1963)
Her High-School Lover (1963)

As by "J. T. MacCargo"
Mannix #2: A Fine Day for Dying (1975)
Mannix #4: Round Trip to Nowhere (1975)

Short Stories
"Hard Case Redhead" (*Mystery Tales*, 1959)
"A Matter of Balance" (*Story*, 1961)

DANIEL PORT OMNIBUS 2

The Cut of the Whip
Bring Me Another Corpse
Time Enough to Die

Three Novels by
Peter Rabe

STARK HOUSE

Stark House Press • Eureka California

DANIEL PORT OMNIBUS 2: THE CUT OF THE WHIP /
BRING ME ANOTHER CORPSE / TIME ENOUGH TO DIE

Published by Stark House Press
1315 H Street
Eureka, CA 95501
griffinskye3@sbcglobal.net
www.starkhousepress.com

ISBN: 1-933586-66-4
ISBN-13: 978-1-933586-66-3

Book design by Mark Shepard, WWW.SHEPGRAPHICS.COM

First Stark House Press Edition: July 2015

FIRST EDITION

Contents

The End of Daniel Port

by Rick Ollerman

Peter Rabe ended his six-book saga of Daniel Port with 1959's *Time Enough to Die*, a novel that both Rabe himself and Donald Westlake liked. In Westlake's more or less well-known critique of Rabe's work (and I disagree with much of what Mr. Westlake has to say about many of the individual titles) he says that this last book is "the only good one" in the series. From Westlake: "The plot is tricky without being artificial, and for once Rabe has surrounded Port with strong and interesting characters. *Time Enough to Die* is the last of the Port novels and the first of Rabe's final cluster of five excellent books."

Westlake refers to Daniel Port as an inferior version of the Ned Beaumont character in Dashiell Hammett's *The Glass Key*. But Port is much more than a Ned Beaumont knock-off in the first book of the series. He's much more fleshed out than Hammett's character, invaluable as a fixer to the Stoker mob, whereas Beaumont's involvement is just sort of hinted at. Indeed, the first Dan Port novel, *Dig My Grave Deep* (1956), is one of Rabe's best precisely because it shows the control, power and influence that Dan Port held in the organization. That's important because, when Port leaves the mob it begs the question: where does he go from here?

In an interview with George Tuttle, Rabe tells him, "I intended to write a series, but I didn't intend to write Daniel Port as a series. I picked up on that being 'the series' simply because it came along at that time. In other words, it was an arbitrary decision–it didn't grow out of my considerations of the character or of the themes I was pursuing then. It wasn't conceived of as a series. I simply decided at one point that I'd use this as a series character."

And I think that "arbitrary decision" helps understand the character arc that Rabe put Port through during the series. Rabe was notoriously and unjustly dismissive of his own work, and he was facing some serious health problems while writing the middle books of this series. At one point Rabe's test results were mixed up and as a result Rabe was told he hadn't long to live. His medical treatment led to a separation from his wife, from which the relationship never recovered.

After *Dig My Grave Deep* the now-free Port is called upon to help an old man protect himself from a penny-ante crook in *The Out is Death* (1957). Rabe shows us the first cracks in Port's self-esteem or self-image, as the low-level crook doesn't show Port any of the respect Port had in his former position.

Then we had *It's My Funeral* (1957), where the restless Port finds himself in California and has a chance run-in with someone he used to know when he was still in the life. This guy wants Port to come in on a scheme but can just as easily use him as a scapegoat. So Port's name means something again, only it's not what Port would like think.

What Rabe has done in this first trio is give us a strong character in Daniel Port, then take away the circumstances that made him what he was, while Port is still trying to function the way he was used to doing. This is, of course, doomed to failure. If Port's power and reputation came from his position in the mob, what does that leave him with when he's out of it? He gets the job done, but he's slow to learn that things will no longer work out the same.

From the Tuttle interview with Peter Rabe, referring to *It's Your Funeral*, Rabe says: "I found that book oddly difficult, but that had nothing to do with the book. Instead, it had to do with the fact that I was physically not well at the time. So I couldn't give you a good answer. It would be entirely contaminated by the physical circumstance I found myself. I had the fascination for the theme. A fleeting one, it wasn't a particularly deep one. But I was so preoccupied with my own difficulties at the time that I can't really give you a great answer to the question you asked.

"The Port novel I liked much better was the one that moves him to Mexico. I don't know the title. *The Chinese Millions*, or something like that."

What Rabe referred to as *The Chinese Millions* was titled by the publisher, *Time Enough to Die* (1959). But we'll get there in a minute.

The latter three Dan Port books begin with the least of the stories, *The Cut of the Whip* (1958). This came out as half of an Ace Double, the flipside being a book by someone named Robert H. Kelston called *Kill One, Kill Two*. Not much appears to be known about Mr. Kelston and he may only be remembered because of the fortuitous pairing with Peter Rabe.

"It was rejected by Gold Medal. I think it was Knox Burger. It wasn't that bad of a book that they should have rejected it.

"Some of the rejections I suffered were very much a function of neglect in writing. I, by temperament, write very fast, which made it very easy to jump the line and get very sloppy. Plus, I never read again, what I have written, in many instances, and from a professional point of view that is unforgivable."

This is typical of Rabe's opinion of his work, but I think it actually applies only rarely and usually in small doses. Unfortunately, coming during his medical issues, it probably is as fair an assessment of a particular book that Rabe ever gave himself.

The Cut of the Whip, while not a major Rabe work by any measure, starts with a chance hit-and-run accident involving Port, who's in the midst of essentially finding something to do with himself. He ends up being asked to do a favor for a man with the wealth and resources to know more about Port, his past–and how he escaped it–than is really adequately explained.

Port agrees to the task but it turns out there is more to it than he originally thought. The normal complexities of plot in a Rabe novel aren't really here; instead we have a bit of Dan Port being Dan Port. His character and abilities are certainly central to the plot, so Rabe was clearly writing another entry in the series. Perhaps because he doesn't have to define Port, explain who he is and how he became that way, show us how he knows how to do what he can do, the plot comes off as a bit too simple, almost as though Rabe were writing an outline for a Port novel but ended up with just enough of a finished product instead.

There's a romance, though it lasts about a page instead of the book-length element we usually see from Rabe. Things are a bit too easy this time out for Port, as well, and though there are shades of Rabe's psychological influences in one of the characters, it isn't until the end of the book that Rabe's background in this area really manifests itself in not only the characters but the plot itself. This makes the ending the best part of the book, but it is marred with a coincidence or two and an unexplained occurrence. "Sloppy," to use Rabe's own word.

There is a plot and a double-cross and a double-double-cross but it's not enough to make the book deep enough to stand up to Rabe's better work. Port also fails to grow as a character in regards to the series. He's just Port for the sake of being Port.

In a way, though, the book fills a certain function in the series: since leaving the mob, Port has taken to the road, helping people he knows or wants to know, crossing the line of what's legal and what's not as it suits him. Is he finding satisfaction doing this? If he did in books two and three, the events in this book probably leave something of a bad taste in Port's mouth. Which sets him up for the fifth book....

1959's *Bring Me Another Corpse* gets the series back on track, meaning it's a mob book through and through. There's a girl involved from beginning to end, off and on anyway, a sort of romantic tease of the sort that Rabe was fond of using, a huge improvement over the stories from other authors that gave us a supposedly hardened man and an equally jaded woman falling in love before the bartender delivers their first drink.

In any case, this book starts out with a literal bang and Port is suddenly pulled back into the life he had worked so hard to leave. The insurance policy he left behind for himself back in the first book—in which he names names—backfires on him when the wrong person finds out about it and figures out a very clever way to use it to their advantage.

After the first book in the series, when Port was *the* man, the second banana with the real power, the fixer's fixer, the one who got things done, each book after his "retirement" shows a Port every bit as self-confident as he was when he still worked for the Stoker mob, but less and less effective with each book. Why? At first Port thought he could rest on his old reputation but he found that dumber crooks could still get over on him because they weren't as cowed as he thought they would be when encountering the one and only Dan Port. He'd given them too much credit. One of them just wants to cash in on Port's reputation, and doesn't even need Port's abilities. Port could be the smartest man in the world but with a gun pointed at his face he's as ordinary as the man behind the trigger. At least until Port can get the gun pointed in another direction.

In *Corpse* Port finds out that after all his time out of the life, it actually takes very little to get him back in. This shocks him and leaves him a bit disoriented by the end of the story. Who was he really? This realization seems to shake him somewhat.

If *The Cut of the Whip* was not on the same level as other Rabe novels, it does seem to serve a very important place in the series: it's the one book out of the six where Rabe is the most ordinary. Sure, a powerful man somehow knows about Port and his past but that just makes him want to hire Port to do a job for him. To do this job, at least to the degree the employer expects, Port doesn't need to be Port. The fact that he is who he is probably saves his life at the end, but no matter the plot, weak or strong, the character of Port is ultimately still Daniel Port.

The series thus far could be summed up like this: the first book is excellent, one of Rabe's best, and it gives us a Daniel Port that is a very special and talented man who outwits the entire mob.

The second book is interesting, as Port tries to help an old friend, and counts on his reputation as being a major factor in his ability to do so. He finds out how limiting and ineffective that can actually be.

In the third, what is interesting is that once again Port is forced to help an old acquaintance. Again, the fact that a third-rate crook can strongarm Dan Port is almost incredible to him, and it's his own ego that compromises his abilities.

The fourth book shows what Port is like without that ego, without the self-confidence or exaggerated sense of his own abilities needed to get him through his situation. Sure, they kick in at the end, but he's certainly far less exceptional than he ever thought he was before.

The fifth book continues Port's loss of influence over the events of his own life. He agrees to a job, and never really gets a handle on it. Again, he gets it in the end, but the superman Dan Port of book one certainly seems like a changed man.

Finally, the sixth book, *Time Enough to Die* (1959), seems to take Daniel Port and get him as far away from the old life as possible. It's almost as though, if he can't be Dan Port anymore–if other people won't *let* him be Dan Port anymore–he'll just fly further afield.

The book is a fitting farewell to Danny Port. After having cooperated with the government in *Bring Me Another Corpse*, Port felt he had been pulled back into the world of organized crime that he'd tried so hard to leave behind. Again. It disgusted him, and the last book opens with Port in the very remote Mexican village of Guanadera. He thinks he's there to sunbathe and make love to the beautiful Maria, but once again, despite how far he's gone to get away once and for all and for good, he gets pulled back in....

It's also a book that's moved 180 degrees from the first one, where Port was in control and in charge and too valuable to be allowed to leave. He stayed longer than he wanted because he'd made a promise to a fragile old man for whom he held a certain affection. In the books that followed, Port tried to trade off his reputation, then his abilities, and finally in *Time Enough to Die*, he's almost a bystander when he's pulled in by people who may be aware of his past but clearly find it meaningless.

Throughout the Daniel Port series, Rabe built up his character into a supremely competent and confident, powerful man. Through definite but gradual changes, Rabe deconstructs his creation so that while Port wants what he always wants–to be left alone, to not be told what to do, to not be held under the sway of men he neither liked nor respected—he is slowly stripped of his ability to make this so. He can run, which he's done since the end of book one, but he can't hide. And by getting lost amidst the jungles of western Mexico he's run very far indeed.

When Port destroyed the organization he'd once been part of, he never seemed to realize that he'd destroyed himself as well. Within the mob he was a feared and powerful figure. Without the mob he was a reputation to be used or to be discarded, a man with a past to hide, and in the end, a man who no longer had anyone to care about who he once was. In a way, though very much alive, he causes his own "death." Even thousands of miles of travel can't bring him back to himself.

The reality is that after the first book, Dan Port could never again be Dan Port. How could he? He himself destroyed that what had made him so. He was a dead man walking, though he didn't know it. He certainly never found more than disappointment and increasing impotence as the series progressed, though Rabe never comes out and tells us this. Was Port happier for getting out of the mob? Was he smart enough to know he never could be entirely free, that he just needed out to keep his sanity? Or did he really believe he could make a new life for himself with so many people knowing his past, even in the barely civilized wilds of western Mexico, and really be happy? Without the big cars, the fancy apartment, the respect, the power, could Dan Port even *be* Dan Port?

It seems that Rabe is telling us that he can't. Port had risen to his greatest heights in the framework of the mob and could never quite gain any traction outside of it. Perhaps he needed a goal, and that aimless traveling didn't suit him; his past wouldn't let him, and he, himself, couldn't stop being Dan Port long enough to find out.

As Rabe said, "Yes, if I would have continued the series it would have been a turning point for him, far from his roots on one hand and with a new beginning on the other. But I didn't continue." I think it's clear from reading the series, one through six, that Port has a clear evolutionary arc. Rabe didn't continue, so the start is much more in focus than where Port ultimately finds himself in the end.

One has to remember that Rabe wrote nineteen–yes, nineteen–novels in five years. The first Port novel appeared in 1956 and the last in 1959, and he wrote more than the six novels in the series during that time span. He actually wrote twelve books in those four years, including *Kill the Boss Good-by* (1956) and *Blood on the Desert* (1958), two of his best books. This, despite his very serious medical scare and the break-up of his marriage. What an escape writing must have been for him.

As for Daniel Port? We can only imagine. Maybe he's still in Guanadera keeping house with the lovely Maria, sunbathing and maybe doing some fishing on the side. Or, what is probably more likely, he's moved on to another locale, with another girl, trying to live the life of Danny Port, a man that he himself had eradicated, no matter how much he tried to tell people otherwise.

March, 2015
Littleton, NH

Sources:
"A Too Brief Conversation with Peter Rabe," George Tuttle,
The Big Book of Noir (1998), ed. by Ed Gorman, Lee Server, Martin H. Greenberg
"Peter Rabe," Donald E. Westlake, *Murder Off the Rack: Critical Studies of Ten Paperback Masters* (1989), ed. By Jon L. Breen and Martin Harry Greenberg

The Cut of the Whip

by Peter Rabe

Chapter 1

The difference between the town of Heering and other small Texas oil towns was that Heering seemed more regimented. Since it was planned, built, and operated by the man whose name the town bore, there were only straight streets, uniform houses, and everything built very close together. Heering looked gray from a distance and it looked gray from close.

Dan Port slowed when he came into the street which went straight through the town and looked for signs. There were no signs except the kind which had to do with the oil fields. Field Three Depot, they said, and an arrow, or Field One, Truck Entrance; but nothing that showed Port how to get out of there. Maybe the town wasn't even on the map, he thought, no more than a factory would be on the map. Port stopped his MG by the curb and got out. He had obviously lost his way.

There were few lights on at this time, except for one gate light over a wire fence and the light in a diner. Port went into the diner.

The counterman looked Port up and down, not because he was something extra large, extra heavy, extra ugly or handsome or something like that, but only because Port was new in the town. Dan Port displayed no peculiarities. He wore a dark suit and had very black hair. His face—the most a description could tell—was quiet.

"Coffee?"

"Black," said Port.

The counterman had nobody else in the place, so after he brought Port his coffee he stayed close and kept looking. Port sat, waiting for the coffee to cool, and lit himself a cigarette. The match made the only sound in the place. Then he said, "I'm getting self-conscious. You're staring."

The counterman smiled and kept looking.

"Why?" Port asked.

"You're new here."

It was a good answer, thought Port. None other would have been as true.

"Well," he said, "have your fill. I'm leaving soon."

The counterman looked disappointed, and, as if to get the most out of his short opportunity, he started to ask Port any number of questions. Having driven all day Port didn't mind. He said yes, he had been driving all day; no, he had not meant to come here; yes, this was his first time in Texas; no, he was not in the oil business.

"So what are you here for?"

"I'm going fishing," Port said. "I was heading for the Gulf, but I think I lost my way."

"That's a fact," said the counterman. "That most certainly is a fact."

"Can you show me the right highway out of here?"

"There's but one way out of here," said the counterman, "and you take that. Take the street this way," and he pointed. "Five miles or so, and you catch the highway south."

Port nodded and started to sip his coffee. It was lukewarm by now, which was the way he liked it.

"Getting dark," said the counterman. "Maybe you ought to stay over."

Port didn't think he would like to stay over. The small town was depressing. It did not feel very much like a town to him but more like just houses, put there for no other reason than to be close to the rigs. And that, Port thought, was a hell of a reason for putting up a house.

"Maybe you don't like our architecture?" said the counterman. He didn't sound proud or anything like that, but mostly resigned.

"It all looks very efficient. Like a company town."

"And cheap. You forgot to say cheap."

"Why are you staying?" Port asked him.

"Because it's a company town, feller. That means I owe Heering. Everybody owes Heering."

"The town?"

"The man. His name's Heering too. Ever hear of Heering?"

"I don't remember."

"Ever hear of oil?"

"Sure—"

"Then you've heard of Heering," and the counterman folded his arms.

Port nodded at his coffee and then he said, "You don't like him," just to be saying something.

"Don't like him? Every time I drive by his house I get an ulcer attack," said the counterman.

"He lives here? Why here?"

"Because his first field is right here, and that way Mr. Heering reminds himself of his humble beginnings."

"Not a friendly picture," said Port and got up. He said it to agree with the counterman and to finish the conversation. He was not really interested and wanted to leave.

It was dark outside when Port got into his car and there were lights on in several places; in houses, a few on the street, and on the field which ran parallel to the main street. But most of all there were no people. The middle of a shift, thought Port, but it only explained part of the impression. It did not explain the mean look of the place, the grimness of the sight which showed silent houses and silent machines in the background. It must be because he was getting tired, Port thought, and because of the counterman's peevish talk. Port drove down the street and when he saw the end of it he speeded up. It would be good to drive in the open again, and old Mr. Heering was probably a very nice man....

As soon as Port was out on the highway the wind was noticeable. It made a noise over the dark plain and pushed at the car. It struck Port as odd that there should be a wind at night. Then he came to the fork in the road. Port didn't remember the counterman mentioning a fork. The size of the two roads seemed about equal but the one on the right was in better condition. There were no road signs. There was a point to driving back into town and asking which fork to take, but Port didn't feel like turning back; he turned right, down the better road.

It started to wind and then it climbed, straight towards a black mass which seemed very large. Then the headlights picked it up. Rock. High, solid rock from one side to the other. The road seemed to end at the outcropping until the headlights picked out the gap which had been blasted to let in the road. The passage was short and when it was over the road leveled out, like on the top of a plateau. And suddenly there were trees. Port couldn't make out what they were, except they were all needle wood, short, thick needle trees which did not seem native.

Port slowed. It wasn't the right road. Everything looked too well tended and the road wound too much, but before he decided to stop and turn, a big car shot around the next bend and the tires screamed.

It came without lights. The driver would have seen Port's car by now, the headlights at any rate, but did not seem to care. With a wild lurch the car tried at the last moment not to hit head-on, to try and get past as fast as possible—if possible. Port jumped. His top was down and he didn't wait any longer, just jumped.

With a loud crash and tearing the MG seemed to fly out from under him and the rush of air from the big car hit Port in the face. But it was harder than air, a terrible jolt that cracked into him without pain, but with great force.

A strange feeling—more surprise than anything else—came over Port. He knew he was on the road and soon he'd start hurting. He lay there and waited. The other driver, a man, was in front of him now. A young, surprised face, an expression that seemed strangely in a hurry—and then the man ran away. Port heard the big car roar and squeal. Then it was gone. Port closed his eyes and passed out.

The coming to was easy and had something classic about it. That was the first thing which crossed Port's mind. The next thing was a pain. His hands hurt, where he had scraped the palms, and the back of his head hurt, where he could feel the bump. Port kept his eyes closed for a while, to get used to himself, and then he opened them slowly. He still saw the same thing. A large room, dark where the glow of the bed lamp didn't reach, a four-poster bed, and he was in it. The walls of the room were paneled, there was heavy furniture on a thick carpet, and the windows were tall. It was night outside and Port could hear the wind.

He sat up and winced. A weight seemed to shift inside his skull, hitting the back of his head. He moved more slowly and got out of bed. There was just the sound of the wind and his own breath coming carefully. Nothing else. It struck him that a hell of a lot had happened since he had left the diner but he hadn't seen a soul since that time. Except for the man with the large car, some foreign make, a Benz, thought Port. There was something gratifying in knowing that it had been a person who had hit him on the road. The thought helped to balance the impressions now, the soundless room, the time spent unconscious—how long had that been?—the impersonal comforts of the clean bed, the small patch on the back of his head—and all of this without any persons involved.

But there would be an explanation. Port walked slowly to the chair where his clothes hung and where his suitcase was standing. Everything was still there, the things in his pockets, all his clothes. There was a long rip in one trouser leg and his shirt had some blood on the collar. Port started to dress from his suitcase. When he came to the tie he started to think what he should do next, besides walk out of the door. Call for somebody? Walk around carpeted corridors in a large house which seemed empty? When he put on his jacket a phone rang.

It rang very gently, not like any other phone Port had ever heard, and it took him a moment to place the sound. On the third ring he saw it on the bedside table, and when he picked it up he hesitated a second, with something like anticipation. I'm sure, he thought, this will be a human voice.

"Mr. Port?" it said. "Are you awake?"

"Yes. I'd like—"

"May I come in?"

"I wish you would," he said, and then the phone clicked in his ear.

She came into the room only a few minutes later. She was a girl with large waves of black hair and a small face, a very beautiful face, except for the tension Port saw. She wore a house robe which showed how well she was built, in spite of the fact that it reached from her chin to her feet. She closed the door and came towards him quickly.

"I'm so glad you're up, Mr. Port. But you shouldn't be dressed—"

"I shouldn't?"

"I mean, the doctor advised..."

"How long have I been out?"

"Two hours. You had a sedative. Are you dizzy?"

"No. I'm not dizzy," said Port. He would have liked to sit down, because of his aches, but the girl kept standing.

"That's good," she said. "The doctor didn't think the bump was too serious, but if you were dizzy or had trouble seeing..."

"I don't think I cracked my skull," said Port. "Just the bump hurts."

He watched her stand by the bed and Port thought that she looked concerned, but it was a distracted kind of concern, as if she didn't know what to worry about—as if she were not too much disturbed.

"May I use your phone for a moment?" she said.

"Of course. I thought it was yours."

She didn't answer and dialed a two digit number. Then she said, "Father? Mr. Port is up... Fifteen minutes? Very well," and she hung up the phone.

"Everyone here seems to know my name," Port started.

"We looked in your clothes. The driver's license—"

"...but I still don't know yours," he finished.

"I'm Jane Heering," and she started to smile but then dropped it. "I'm sorry I didn't—there's been so much—"

Port smiled at her because she seemed so distraught. "If my accident has upset you," he said, "the damage is nothing that can't be replaced. Rip in the pants, dent in the car maybe, and for the rest," he touched his head, "you've been very attentive."

But she didn't return his smile. She just nodded. "It sounds simple," she said. "It would be nice if something very simple would happen sometime."

They looked at each other for a moment, but then it went. Jane Heering straightened a fold in the bedclothes and Port turned to look out of the window. There was nothing to see. "Tell me," he said. "Who hit me?"

She didn't answer immediately. Then she said, "That was my father before, on the phone. He'd like to see you."

"*The* Heering?"

She was at the door, holding it open, and then Port followed her down a broad hall. It led to a staircase which curved into a center hall which had the square area of an average house. The floor was stone and the ceiling had a peak. It was a cold looking hall. Then Port saw Heering.

Port's first impression of the man was formality. Heering was slight and pale, of medium build and medium height. He stood by a tall door and looked up to the stairs. His eyes had very little movement.

Heering and Port shook hands and Jane Heering made the introductions. Not counting the man's eyes, Port thought, Heering might look like some elderly shipping clerk. Not that it meant anything—J. P. Morgan would have looked right tapping beer in a neighborhood tavern. But counting the eyes, and going back about two hundred years, this Heering looked like a witch burner.

"Thank you, Jane," said Heering and made a small nod with his head. He kept looking at her until she left. She had not wanted to leave, thought Port.

Heering took Port into an unlit room and for a moment, before the light was turned on, the long frame of the window showed the moon coming up at the end of the plain, the black derrick skeletons silhouetted against the sky. Then the light snapped on and the windows turned blind.

"Sit down, Mr. Port. And you may want some of this." Heering came back from the liquor cabinet and brought a small glass. "It's *Schnaps*. Quite bracing." He gave the drink to Port without any gesture of friendliness or the companionable air that should go with offering a drink. The *Schnaps* was a medicine and that's how Heering gave it to Port.

The room looked heavy and Victorian, everything showing craftsmanship, quality, and no beauty. There were two large chairs facing each other and Heering and Port sat down there.

"Did you see who hit you, Mr. Port?"

It seemed very abrupt. It seemed important to Heering to get that part out of the way.

"Did I see? I saw him, but I don't know who he was."

"Did you see him well enough to recognize him again?"

"Yes," said Port. "I'll recognize him."

Heering looked down at his hands. He sat like that with his lids lowered over his eyes and, since his eyes were the only alive thing in his face, it now seemed that he was hardly there. His eyes were not closed though. He was looking down at his fingers, rubbing their tips with the thumb.

"Well?" said Port. "You ask as if it makes a difference."

Heering looked up and said, "It does." Then he obviously changed the subject. "You will of course be reimbursed in full. Your car, in case you don't know it yet, is a total wreck."

Port hadn't known it. This would delay his leaving, of course, but then it struck him that his leaving was not such a matter of importance at all. To fish in the Gulf? A diversion, a way to kill time because he had nothing else to do. It had been like that for some time now....

"It makes a difference for this reason," said Heering. "If you had said no, you didn't see the man's face, I would have reimbursed you for your damages and then bade you a good night."

"But?"

"You saw him, well enough to find out who he is."

"This is important?"

"He's my son," said Heering.

Port sat back and waited. Heering had told him very little, but enough to show that something in Heering's affairs, something very important, might now involve Port.

"I would like to offer you a job, Mr. Port."

"What?"

"It happens I know who you are."

Port looked at Heering and then he looked at his empty glass. He got up, went to the liquor cabinet, and poured himself half a pony of the *Schnaps.* Then he came back and sat down.

"You know what, Mr. Heering?"

"You are the Daniel Port who was affiliated with the Stoker organization up North."

"There is no more Stoker organization."

"And I know that you were responsible for its collapse."

Port shrugged. These polite facts could have been known to anyone who had read the right papers. They were very polite facts, because Heering had not called the Stoker organization by its right name, a syndicate branch, political on the surface, criminal in almost everything else.

"I know," Heering went on, "that you were Stoker's right-hand man, that you left because of disagreements, and that in the process you ruined—or exposed may be the proper word—the entire set up."

"You do know more than the papers," said Port.

"I have my own investigative organization," said Heering. "I was particularly impressed," he went on, "with the unique way in which you have stayed alive."

"Not working, you mean?"

But Heering was not in a joking mood. "I mean the threat of a sweeping exposure, for which you have arranged in the event of your death."

"Well," said Port, and his surprise was genuine. "And do you know the details of that exposure, too?"

"No. I've only had a few hours. And besides," said Heering, "what I know is sufficient."

"For what, Mr. Heering?"

"To hire you."

"You want an ex-hood?"

"Not necessarily; but I know for a fact that you functioned more as a businessman. I will tell you that I have only respect for a businessman who can maintain himself on the other side of the law. I want you," said Heering, "for three reasons. First of all, you are discreet. You could not have maintained yourself as you have, if you were anything else. Second, hiring you saves me from exposing my personal matters to additional people, since you saw my son anyway, and could have learned his identity sooner or later."

"Not even your own police force would do?"

"They are not a police force, Mr. Port. They are a legitimate, investigative branch of my—"

"All right, let it go," said Port. He disliked Heering's righteous manner. "I would like to know," he said, "what the job is."

Port was not especially interested in Mr. Heering. He even disliked the man slightly, but Heering's presentation had been so circumspect that it had piqued Port's curiosity. And there was the girl Jane, who seemed so concerned. And Heering's son, the one who had rammed him; in retrospect the young man appeared to Port as if driven by furies.

"You may or may not know," said Heering, "that I am engaged in some Near East negotiations concerning oil."

"I've read that Pan-Continental Oil is."

"One of my companies. Now, basically, you need no further information on the subject, except for an emphasis on the delicate nature of this kind of business."

"How delicate?"

"As delicate as personal feelings, Mr. Port. So that a delay in a conference, displeasing publicity, any number of little things could throw the balance for or against my enterprises."

Heering had not said very much yet. But Port knew that all this was leading up to something highly important and he should not forget it.

"My negotiations have been completed," said Heering. He looked at his fingertips, as if nothing were quite so important. "However, at this point nothing has been acted upon. And a contract, as you may know, is only as good as the good will behind it."

This time Heering began rubbing his fingertips, the way he had done once before. He did it slowly, too slowly, which was his way of guarding his tension.

"My son has stolen a packet of papers which bear upon my negotiations. He will attempt to pass them into the wrong hands. If this should happen," and Heering looked up, "I would expect grave difficulties."

It was a delicate way of putting things. Port wondered why the man wasn't able to come right out and say, "If those papers get out, I'll be ruined!"

"All this time," said Port, "your son is running."

Heering's answer showed a great deal about the man. "After Robert left the house—which was when he ran into you—I phoned the town police to determine which way he was going."

"Why didn't you ask them to stop him?"

"I thought I explained to you, Mr. Port, that no one is to be involved beyond—"

"I'm sorry. I forgot."

"I learned," said Heering, "that the Mercedes Benz he is driving took the right turn at the bottom of the plateau. That road leads nowhere except to join the highway to Lamesa. There is nothing in between. Tomorrow I will have you flown to a spot where you can intercept the Benz easily."

"You talk as if I had taken the job already."

"You will be paid, of course. The job should not take you more than one day, the way I'm arranging it, for which effort I will pay you one thousand dollars."

Port hadn't been thinking about that part of it. He had been thinking about how little Heering had really said. He had spent a great deal of time impressing Port with the secretive, delicate nature of everything, and he himself had arranged it so the job would take no more than a day. All Port knew about Robert Heering, the son, was that he had robbed his old man, smashed into Port's car while running away from the house, and that he looked frantic. A thousand dollars for one day's work catching a truant rich boy? Port didn't believe it.

Port did not know exactly why, but he had already decided to take this thing on. Perhaps because he felt suspicious of Heering, because of the way the girl Jane had acted, the way young Robert had looked....

"One question," said Port. "Why did your son steal your conference papers?"

The evasion, which was sure to come, would be smooth. But Heering said, "Because my son is unstable."

When they were through Port went back up to his room and found Jane Heering waiting for him in the hall. "Father asked you to find him?" she said.

"Yes. Why so worried?"

"I don't know you at all," she said, "but I think you'll find him and bring him back without harm."

Port wondered what she might be like without the worry and without the regard for her father. He nodded and said, "How sick is your brother?"

"He's my half-brother," she said. She didn't explain more but took up Port's question. "If you mean is he crazy, he isn't."

"Your father said 'unstable.' "

"I'm sure whatever father has told you is correct."

"He told me that Robert stole some business papers."

"That doesn't make him crazy, does it, Dan?"

She did not seem to have noticed that she had used his first name. It had been the natural thing to say, the more personal thing, when she pleaded.

"I know the papers mean money," she said, "but I don't know if that was his reason for stealing them. Robbie is not very responsible. Father says he did it out of spite. I don't know."

"Where is his mother?"

"He hasn't had a mother for a long time," Jane said, but then they didn't talk any more because Heering came up into the hall and pointed out that it was late in the evening and that Port's job would start early. Port touched the girl's arm and smiled at her.

"Don't worry. When I come back, afterwards, maybe things will be simpler?"

It was the first time that she smiled back at him and only Heering's presence spoiled the moment a little.

Chapter 2

Port was at Heering's private airport at five in the morning. By seven in the morning the Benz would have gone a maximum of three hundred miles. It would put the car about fifteen miles this side of Heering's Station Ten on his Low Shelf field. The copter would land there as if on business, Port would find a car at the station, and would then drive back toward the Benz, which he should meet somewhere on a stretch called the Red Plateau. In all likelihood Port would meet the Benz and nothing else.

The helicopter took off on schedule, and it was just a little after six A.M. when it landed in the parking area in front of Number Ten station. There was just a pickup and a new station wagon. There wasn't a soul anywhere.

Port and the pilot got out of the copter and went into the pump house. A big Buddah Diesel sat in the middle of it, filling the bare room with a low roar. Still not a soul anywhere.

"The office is this way," and the pilot walked across the cement room and around the big Buddah.

There was less noise in the office, just a vibration. It shook the geranium on the small desk and the coffee pot on the hot plate seemed to be trembling.

"This is the man Heering called about. To pick up his station wagon," said the pilot to the man at the desk.

The man nodded his head and looked Port up and down.

"You one of them men from back East?"

"I just came to pick up the car," said Port.

"There's two of them Dallas men out there now, see 'em there by the rigs? Can't make up their minds about that fault we got here. You know about that fault, I guess."

"I just came to—"

"Want some coffee?"

"Sorry," said Port. "I haven't got time."

"Too bad," said the man. "Here's the keys," and he handed them to Port.

Port took them, nodded good-bye, and went out to the station wagon. When he closed the door to the pump house he shut off the drone from the Buddah and the landscape seemed that much more deserted without the raw sound.

Port spun the car out of the parking lot fast and a gray jet of dust shot up from the rear end until the car hit the hard-top. Port turned towards the plateau, racing the car all the way. He gunned the car up the plateau, cursing himself for being ridiculous and cursing himself for the cold-blooded job he had taken on—cold-blooded because he couldn't muster enough feeling about it to give him an interest.

He saw he was driving a flat road now, on top of the plateau. The terrain was rocky on both sides and the road started to swing so that Port couldn't see very far. If the Mercedes Benz should show up now and going the same speed... The road suddenly dipped and Port could see miles ahead. The road went down and across the flatlands. And there was the Benz, like a small, shiny bug scooting along the band of road.

Port hit the brakes hard, then reversed so fast that the gears gave a loud clank. The pilot's shenanigans had almost cost him his chance and even now there wasn't the time to pick the best way to handle this thing. Port drove in reverse with his head out of the side window. The motor whined with a high, urgent sound and the rear of the car swung back and forth in sharp jerks when Port started maneuvering through the curve. He hoped that the man in the Benz hadn't seen the maneuver. He hoped that nobody would come from behind and crash into the station wagon. A pile of junk on the highway would stop the Benz, but then what? Port was out of the curve and could see across the plateau. No one from that end... He braked, swung the car towards the ditch, then headed back into the road and stopped broadside. He turned off the motor and sat for a moment. He noticed that he was sweating.

If nobody came from the other end this should work fine. Port got out of the car, left the door open, and walked off the road. He stood there, where the Benz would see him last, and listened for the sound of the car coming up to the plateau. With no one else coming, this whole thing could be over in minutes. Except for the drive back, of course, with young Heering who was a little bit crazy.

Maybe he should have brought a gun, just for the effect...Then he heard the motor.

The Benz didn't look like a bug any more but like a missile. The square grille seemed to rear off the road and the black body seemed the size of a bus.

He's going too fast! He sees the wagon but he isn't stopping—

The Benz was rocking wildly and the brakes screeched but a little too late. What stopped the Benz was the station wagon.

If the crazy bastard has killed himself, or is hurt bad... Port didn't think further and ran to the cars.

The station wagon had one sprung door, a deep dent in the side, and trim bent off the body. The Benz, big and black, showed no damage at all. The man behind the wheel was opening the door and Port could hear him mutter. Port coughed, low in his throat because this was it. Talk to the man. Try it smooth and civilized first.

The man came out of the Benz and Port stopped walking towards him. This was not Robert Heering.

Chapter 3

They stared at each other for one dead moment and then the other man made a slight move which broke the tension.

"Who in hell are you?" Port yelled at him.

The other man was young and shaggy looking. He didn't understand what Port meant nor was he listening to the words, just the tone of voice Port was using. He yelled right back:

"You got no better place to park that wreck than smack in the middle of the highway?"

"It wasn't a wreck until you came driving, or rather flying, along here! And I asked you a question. Where in hell—"

"Wait a minute—wait a minute!" and the young man leaned his back against the station wagon. "Gimme a chance, willya? I'm getting the shakes." And he stood there, breathing deeply, his eyes closed, while the shock of the accident caught up with him.

Port lit two cigarettes and gave the man one of them and in a short while they both stood by the sprung door of the station wagon, looking at the damage.

Port was thinking of something else though.

"I know this car," he said. "Where's the guy that was driving it?"

"I was driving it... He said he was tired. Jeez, I wonder what—" he stopped in the middle of the sentence and in the middle of turning around. The only thing Port was sure of was that it hadn't been the young man who had cracked him on the back of the head. And then he passed out.

The first thing Port saw was the big sky and then he noticed something nice and soft under his head and he didn't want to move at all because he knew how it would feel.

He gritted his teeth and sat up.

"Boy, am I glad to see you up!" said the voice, and then, "Listen, you got an idea where we are?"

Port closed his eyes and said, "Wait up a second, will you—" and he waited for the pain to simmer down in his head.

He was sitting among the rocks, there had been a musette bag under his head, the highway was empty, and the station wagon neatly pulled up to one side. The young man from the Benz was squatting next to Port, anxious for him to get better.

"He's gone," he said, when Port looked at him.

"The bastard," said Port.

He stood up and knew there was no point rushing it. His head might fall apart. The young man helped Port light a cigarette and then took one for himself.

"Listen," he said, "will you explain something to me? All I want to know—"

"Later, later." Port breathed slowly for a moment. "Stop me when I'm wrong. You were hitchhiking, the Benz came—"

"The what?"

"Benz. That's the car you were driving. The car came along and the driver gave you a lift. Then he got in the back and let you drive. You hit my car, then the guy came and hit me, then you pulled the station wagon out of the way and the Benz took off without you. Right so far?"

"Yes. And he throws my musette bag out when he drives off."

"Considerate. Now tell me this. What explanation did he give you for all this?"

"Robby? Nothing. He—"

"You know his name?"

"Just Robby. I don't know the last name."

Port breathed with relief and even the pain in his head seemed less important now. The whole thing with Robert Heering was still between him and his father and Port.

"How long ago did he take off?"

"You've been out maybe ten minutes. Listen, I don't know anything goes on here, but all I want to know where this is. And can you give me a lift outa here?"

Ten minutes only. Port started running to the car.

"Wait a minute—"

"Come on, come on," Port said. "Jump in if you want a lift."

The sprung door stayed open but it didn't slow Port. He raced for the end of the plateau, half hoping he'd see the Benz down below once the road dipped into the flatland. This should have happened earlier, he thought, this little trick of getting slugged from behind. If it had happened to him before he had gone to wait for the Benz on the plateau, there would have been enough good, red-hot intent inside him to handle young Robert Heering and his Benz and his papers with one hand tied behind. Which was the way Port felt now. He knew the heat would go after a while, but he'd still be after the man, and with a purpose this time.

"Look, Mister, I know how you must feel and all that, but would you just answer me one—"

"We're on a plateau. Red Plateau is the name."

"I'm not from around here, so the name doesn't mean anything to me. What—"

"What you want to know is where you're going? Don't ask me, fellow," and Port kept watching the road.

When the car left the plateau Port could see far ahead. There was no Benz anywhere.

The blank sight of the terrain ahead did it. The pain in the back of his head seemed to turn stiff and the rest of his neck and the muscles along the spine grew tense and painful. It was like urgency riding his back but where his aim ought to be, straight ahead, it was just blank.

Robert Heering was crazy! Why else pick up a hitchhiker while running with a million dollar bundle of paper. Or at least a little bit off, though not enough to stop him from going all out to get his way. Not like Port, who'd been standing alone on the plateau worrying about how to act with the man. But that part was all fixed now.

Except for the problem of old Mr. Heering. When he heard what had happened—though that need never come up.

Port raced past the cut-off that went to Station Ten. There was a fork in the road a little further on and Port took the right one, only because of momentum, and then the road forked again. There were now enough dips in the terrain to give only a short view.

Port stopped the car hard and maneuvered around. "You want to get out here? I've got to go back."

"Here? Jeez—didn't we pass a pump station before? Maybe somebody there could—"

"Whatever you say," and Port took off, trying to hold the sprung door close to the body.

The office was full of people when they arrived. There was the pilot, the old man at the desk, and three engineers.

Dallas men, without doubt. They all wore fatigue caps. "Hey!" said the pilot. "What are you doing back here?"

"I got to use your phone," said Port. "This is urgent."

"Go right ahead."

"If you could clear the room for me," he said close to the old man's ear. "This business is confidential."

"About the fault?" the pump man whispered back. "You don't want them Dallas men—"

"That's right. Hurry it, will you?" and then Port watched the old man clear the small room, telling the men that Mr. Heering's special man had to make a call which was confidential. And they'd better be sure about that fault not being a danger because there were other outfits with maybe other opinions and there better not be anything wrong with their figures.

The door shut and he picked up the phone. When the operator came on he asked for the town of Heering, Heering residence, and to push that call through.

It was now forty-five minutes after the time when Robert Heering had met and then left Port on the plateau.

It was one hour and twenty minutes after the time on the plateau when Port finally reached Heering.

No one but the butler had been at the house when Port called and Mr. Heering had flown to the Galveston office. At the Galveston office nobody had ever heard of Dan Port and Mr. Heering was in a conference. The best private secretary in the Southwest kept Port at arm's length without hanging up on him and without causing offense.

"...I understand, Mr. Port. I understand it is confidential, but I am merely trying to point out, Mr. Port—"

"Damn it, man, can't you tell when it's a matter of urgency?"

"I well understand, Mr. Port, but my position..."

"Just give him my name! The reason I'm calling is ten times more important than any conference he's in. Just give him my name, for God's sake, and you're out of it!"

"Daniel Port, you say?"

"Heaven help me, yes!"

There was one minute's silence, and then, "This is Heering. You can get off the phone, Burnett."

The private secretary hung up.

"Mr. Heering," said Port. "The matter went by me. About one hour ago."

Another silence, and then, "Where are you?"

"Number Ten station on Low Shelf. I'm—"

"Let me understand this, Port. You are an hour behind?"

"More now. The matter is still safe, still just between us, but I can't follow it up without more information."

To his complete surprise Port heard Heering curse. Not long, not loud, but completely ferocious.

"The road after here forks several times, Mr. Heering, so if you—"

"I know that."

"The copter is still here; however that would mean taking the chance of making the pilot suspicious."

"Out of the question."

There was a long silence while Port let the other man think it over, then, "Mr. Heering. If you have any idea where this matter is going, some contact point, anything like that, then please consider that nothing can be gained from keeping it from me."

"Yes, of course."

"Well?"

Port heard the other man took a long breath. "It's difficult, the involvement—" and then he coughed to make it seem less of a revelation.

"Mr. Port?"

"Yes."

"Please don't write this down." The voice was no longer charged and Heering sounded impersonal. "The matter is going to Lubbock. The address is 912 South Brandywine."

There was a pause. And then, smooth and controlled now, "You understand that there must be no contact. You understand that the international nature of all this goes beyond my personal business. If you keep this in mind, Mr. Port, you will not have to be told to keep yourself out of this as much as you can; not to be seen, not to be recognized, not to talk to anyone at that address."

Heering was obviously back in command. He had loosened up and had painfully given Port more information, and was now building the wall again.

"You have a gun, Mr. Port?"

"I can get one."

"Do that."

And the less you know the longer you live was the warning behind that exchange....

"Now, if you will get me the pilot, I'll arrange for you to be flown to Lubbock. In terms of distance, contact should be tonight, physical contact. And you will have to be there first, to prevent it. There will be a car for you at the airport."

"I'll get the pilot now."

"About the arrangement between you and myself, Mr. Port, we will of course change that."

"Fine. I'll see you."

"There will be a new arrangement," Heering said and Port got the impression that Heering had said it to himself. Port could see the witch-burning eyes now....

Port got to Lubbock at noon. A Heering employee met the copter to give the pilot a briefcase with papers and to show Port his car. The briefcase was a blind to give the trip importance, while Port had just gone along for the ride. The pilot was instructed to leave right after gassing and the Heering employee had to get back to the office.

Heering had picked a good car, a three year old Chevrolet which looked like a hundred other cars in the town.

Port looked at the Chevrolet for a moment, looked up to watch the employee drive off in a company car, put the keys in his pocket, and then folded his arms.

This felt nothing like on the plateau. This felt like the middle of a two-handed job with a start that was over and an end which was clear. Port started to whistle and stood a while longer. Then he started to move.

First he went back into the terminal and asked for a city map at Information. He got one and left.

Then he drove his car into the first gas station, checked the air in his tires to be doing something, and asked for a roadmap of Texas. He didn't need any gas. He asked for the warehouse district and drove there.

He cruised the streets near the depot until he found what he wanted. He parked in a street with small stores and bars and went into the pawnshop that looked most expensive. He could see five pawnshops from where he was standing, but Port wanted quality.

He picked a Luger because the action was smoothest and the barrel was like new on the inside.

He went to a second hand clothing store, bought a scuffed leather jacket and a cap with a visor.

Ammunition for the Luger gave him a little bit of trouble and he ended up downtown finding a store that carried nine-mm.

Then he had lunch in a restaurant and while his coffee was cooling he figured things out on the Texas map. Heering had been close in his guess. The Benz couldn't possibly make it to Lubbock till eight or nine; any time between eight and ten was more reasonable.

It was two now and Port drove out of town. After a while he left the main highway and found an arroyo where he shot twenty-eight rounds of his ammunition, at which point the gun felt familiar enough.

He had coffee at a truck stop and looked at the city map. He could have asked anyone in the town how to get to South Brandywine, but he still wouldn't have known where the street was in relation to the rest of the map. He wanted to know how to leave there and get out of town fast.

South Brandywine had a chummy look. The street was all residential and old enough to show some individual touches from one house to the next.

Port left his car on Sumner, the cross street at one end of the block, and walked down South Brandywine looking busy. He walked past number 912, which was on his side of the street, but never stopped until he had turned into Pitt Lane at the other end of the block.

He had seen the stamped-iron sign set into the lawn and the name was Powell. *The Powells* it had said. He had seen the neat flower beds, the raked gravel on the short drive, and the car in the garage. Everything had looked very well kept. There had been no toys in evidence. Nothing but neatness.

It took Port ten minutes to get back to his car without going down Brandywine. He sat in the rear of his car, took off his jacket, his tie, unbuttoned his shirt. He came out again wearing the leather jacket and the visored cap.

The alley was dusty and full of the glare of the sun, looking more like a country lane than the garbage road between two rows of houses. From the back, 912 Brandywine was much harder to spot. It lacked the individual touches that marked the front of the house, and if there hadn't been another sign, *H. Powell* this time, Port might have walked by. He was sweating under the leather jacket and stopped to wipe his face. The backyard was as neat as the front, only less attractive and more utilitarian. Garden tools were stacked in a corner and next to the garbage can was a carton half full with empty beer cans. There were also three empty gallon jugs labeled *Muscatel, Very Sweet.*

The screen door in back snapped open and a man came out.

"Howdy," he said to Port.

The man was older than Port but dressed younger. He wore two-tone shoes, highly pressed slacks, and a polka dot shirt.

"You looking for something?"

"Yes," said Port. "Could I see you a minute?"

Heering and his secretive warnings be damned. The only way Port could feel ahead in this job was to know everyone in it. He had known much too little, right from the start.

"Who you with?" asked the man, nodding at Port's cap.

"Are you Mr. Powell?" Port asked. "I'm with utilities," and pulled out a black notebook and a pencil.

"I'm Powell. Come in, feller, come in," and he opened the gate for Port.

Powell was friendly enough. He had carefully combed hair with one spectacular wave, but the haircut gave him a shaved look about the ears, the kind of thing they do in the country. Like a rancher who had moved to the city and in no way meant to go back.

"I'm just counting the lines," said Port. "Maintenance purposes." He was walking towards the house. "Everything all right here, everything shipshape?"

"No complaints here, none whatsoever."

Port looked up the side of the house where the three power lines were attached and scribbled something inside his book.

"Man, it's hot," said Port and wiped his face. "And as soon as I saw those beer cans there I really started feeling hot. Isn't that funny?" and he laughed.

"Hell," and Powell leaned closer, "you want some? I know you're on the job, but you want some?"

"Well, I don't want to..."

"No trouble, no trouble. What's your name?"

"Dan."

"Mine's Herbie. Come on in, Dan," and the two men went through the screen door.

It was cool inside because of a large air conditioner. There were other expensive items. A dishwasher, a washing machine, a dryer next to it, and a garbage disposal unit in the sink. Port heard the sounds of a serial story in the front room and by bending a little he could glimpse the twenty-seven-inch TV set. He couldn't see the rest of the room.

Powell slammed the refrigerator and punched open two cans of beer.

"Mud in your eye," he said and gave Port one of the cans.

The beer was a cool pleasure going down his throat and Port felt like closing his eyes and paying attention to nothing else. He put the can down and nodded his head at the kitchen.

"Nice," he said. "Nice, cool comfort."

"Like it, huh? You're looking at over two thousand bucks worth of conveniences right here."

"I know. I wish I could afford it."

"Wouldn't want to do without it," said Powell. "I can wash clothes, do dishes, cook supper, and grind up the garbage all at one time."

"I can appreciate that," said Port. "I'm a bachelor myself."

"I'm no bachelor," said Powell. "My wife's ailing."

He sipped beer, then put the can down carefully.

"But no matter; if you want something done right you got to do it yourself."

He had, while talking and between sips of beer, wiped the wet rings made by the cans, hung the can opener on its special hook, and washed the rag and put it to dry on a small rack where three other rags hung side by side without touching each other. It was the best way, the neatest, to let them get dry.

"Well, sir," said Port, "it's sure been a pleasure. And I sure wish I could have a fine kitchen like this."

Powell gave a proud smile and put the two empty cans into a trash box.

"But on my salary, hell—" and Port shrugged. "What do you do for a living, Herbie?"

"Me? I'm retired. I used to be in cotton, way back that is, but no more of that for me," and he laughed.

"What did you do, strike oil?"

Powell laughed some more and shook his head but never answered.

When Port was at the screen door he stopped suddenly and turned back.

"Herbie, would you mind if I go out the front? I got the other side of the street and going out the front would save me time."

"Sure, Danny, sure," and he waved Port into the small hallway. When the two men were next to each other, Powell bent close and said, "Don't mind if I don't introduce you to my wife, Dan. When she's listening to those serial shows there's no interrupting the old lady," and then they walked past the living room.

The woman who sat there was an old lady. She seemed close to twenty years older than Powell, sitting there plump and neat in front of the set. When she heard the men she turned to look into the hall and gave Port a friendly smile. She had a friendly pink face, clear blue eyes, and snow-white hair. She seemed to be wearing a housedress, something wrapped around to be loose and comfortable, but then Powell had Port by the door. The only other thing Port had seen was the nicely shaped glass next to her, half-filled with wine.

Chapter 4

As soon as he reached the car Port took off the cap and the leather jacket, threw them into the back seat, and drove off with the vents turned his way so the air blast would cool him. He just drove for a while but then he used the map. He made the run from South Brandywine to the highway going out of town and clocked himself at twenty minutes.

He stayed in a roadhouse outside of town, drinking lukewarm coffee and watching the sun go down towards the horizon. He had three cups and with the last one he started to whistle, not loud, not melodious, but mostly a beat.

When the sun touched the end of the prairie, Port stopped whistling and left.

As soon as the sun had set the air became cooler, and with the wind springing up Port felt suddenly cold. It was eight, but not dark enough. He stood on Sumner where he could see the length of South Brandywine and by turning a little he could see the parallel alley, the one which passed Powell's house. But it wasn't much good this way. If he were in luck the Benz would enter the street, or the alley, from Sumner, and if it were darker Port would even be able to tell when a car swung in from the other end. But if Robert Heering came on foot, Port would know nothing about it.

The wind, Port noticed, had shifted. It now came straight down Brandywine. It was chilly and had an insistent push, reminding him of the wind on the open prairie. The only thing interrupting the illusion was the cars. One after the other they stopped further down the block until the curb was lined with cars for a long stretch. And the wind carried the voices to Port, snatches of loud talk and forced laughter. Powell's next-door neighbor was having a party.

Port could park where the other cars were, sit in the back seat, and no one would pay any attention. It was too dark now to stay at the corner.

When he parked the car up the block he could see anyone coming down Brandywine, and anyone entering Powell's house from the street. But he could see nothing of the alley.

Port felt the Luger under his belt and pulled his jacket into place. There was only one way to handle this. He left the car and walked the few steps down the street. This was the sure way to solve his problem—and the fastest.

The door of number 912 opened after the first ring and for a moment Herbert Powell squinted out into the dark without seeing clearly. Port thought that the man looked much older than he remembered him. In the unguarded moment when Powell was thinking of nothing but to see better than his eyes allowed, his face fell into old lines with the effort.

Then he smiled suddenly, and the retired farmer's face showed again, with the self-satisfied folds around the mouth and the skin tight as if from good health.

A chair creaked in the living room and, "Who is it, Herbie?"

"The utility man, Emmy. Remember the one who was here in the daytime? Come in, uh—Dan, wasn't it?"

"Yes," said Port and came into the narrow hall. He had his hands in his pockets and smiled apologetically. "I'm really sorry to bust in at a time like this, Mister Powell, and maybe I should have waited 'til morning or called up first anyway. . ."

"Who is it, Herbie?" and the chair creaked again.

Powell shrugged and took Port by the arm. He pulled him to the arch leading into the living room so that Mrs. Powell could see who it was.

"The utility man, Emmy. See?"

Emmy Powell looked exactly the way Port remembered her, an impression of pink skin and powdery hair and a housedress on her soft body. Her hair, thought Port, must have turned prematurely. She looked like an elder sister to Powell, but not as old as the white hair and the motherly face might suggest. Besides, Powell had said that she was his wife.

"You're not interrupting a thing," said Powell. "We were just watching TV."

"What a beautiful set," and Port put admiration into his voice. "It's clear like a picture." He laughed at the feeble joke and saw that both Powells liked it fine. Emmy Powell laughed with simple amusement and Herbert Powell laughed like an MC.

"Great," he kept saying, shaking his head back and forth. Then he held still and listened. "The water," and rushed towards the kitchen.

"Maybe this young man would like a cup, too?" Mrs. Powell called after him.

"You want some tea, Danny?" Powell yelled from the kitchen.

"Strong and no sugar," said Port. Then he sat like that for a while, with the television set humming sounds which might have been drama or commercial and with thin party sounds coming through to them now and then from next door.

"If you were about to retire," Port started, but Mrs. Powell shook her head before he was through and said; "No, no, we're just sitting around."

"Or perhaps you're expecting company and I shouldn't take up your time."

"No," she said. "We're not expecting anyone," and kept smiling at Port.

Herbert Powell came back with three cups of tea on a tray and gave one to his wife, one to Port, and kept the last cup himself. The TV kept garbling in dull tones and the only other sound was the light tinkle of the cups. Outside the windows Port could hear the wind. There was a carafe of white wine by the side of Mrs. Powell's chair and she poured some of it into her cup. Herbert Powell took three lumps of sugar and stirred his tea.

Port got the eerie feeling that he was in the wrong house. He was, spending the blandest, the absolutely nicest of evenings there. The big Luger pinched him under the ribs while Mrs. Powell said, "Ah..." each time she took a sip of her tea. And they all sat sipping while nobody had bothered to ask Port why he was there.

"You'll have to do something about the corner screen, Herbie," said Mrs. Powell. "The way that wind shakes that corner screen..."

They all listened to the corner screen rattle in the wind. "Oh yes," he said over his cup. "I forgot."

They all sat, almost as if they were waiting. But then, why had Powell let him in, kept him there with an invitation to tea?

Powell put down his cup and then he chuckled.

"Why, Danny, I even forgot to ask you!" He got up and turned off the TV. The sudden quiet in the room made the wind sound stronger outside. "You came in and wanted to tell me something and never got the chance!"

Powell grinned at Port, waiting.

"Why'd you come back, Danny?" he said.

Port had the answer to that one all ready. "You remember," he said. "I was here with that little black book of mine? The notebook where I take down things on my rounds?"

"You stuck that in your hip pocket when you went out the front door," said Powell.

It surprised Port that Powell should have observed this. Powell sipped tea again, not looking at Port.

"I did?" said Port. "You mean I had it when I walked out of here? Maybe I dropped it on your walk."

"No. I would have found it sweeping up."

Port gave a puzzled laugh, looked from one to the other. They were looking back at him and nothing else.

"Well," said Port. "That's why I came around." He shrugged and got up. "Yours was the last house where I used the book and I thought maybe..."

"You said you were going across the street," said Powell. "Didn't you use the book across the street, whatever you were checking there? You ought to have missed it then."

Powell made sense. He sat with his cup in his hand, watching Port, waiting to hear the answer.

"That's true," said Port. "Except over there the utility survey was about appliances in the house. How many appliances. I use a different ledger for that, different book."

The lie had come easily. Port was aware of this suddenly, now that it was done, and felt the tension catch up with him. Under pressure, he knew, he always lied easily, did things with unthinking ease. Until this moment he had not been aware of the pressure which really existed.

"Oh," Powell was saying, and then he twisted in his seat to look out of the window.

"What time is it?" Port asked. "I went to this restaurant down on Sumner and maybe the book fell out of my pocket when—"

"Eight forty-five," said Emmy Powell.

Powell had turned back to the room and now he said, "It's dark across the way. I figured if they were home you could just run across and see if your book was there. Or maybe they're in bed."

A quarter to nine, thought Port, *and young Heering should get here any time now....*

"How about you, Emmy," Powell was saying. "Don't you think you should go up now?"

"I slept during the day, Herbie, I don't think I could..."

"You're supposed to get your rest," and then Powell turned towards Port. "She hasn't been well."

"My liver," said Mrs. Powell.

"So maybe you'd better go up now."

"But it's Thursday, Herbie. *Hour of Life* is on at nine."

"That's right," said Powell. "I forgot. She never misses that *Life* thing," he told Port.

So Mrs. Powell stayed in her chair, Howard Powell went for more tea, and Port was still standing.

He did not want to leave. He did not know how dangerous any of this might be, what the Powells were doing besides watching TV and drinking their tea, and he had not been able to plan anything for the time when young Heering would come. He knew too little for that and the Powells behaved in an unknown pattern.

Powell came back and brought more tea for himself. He brought none for his wife who was now filling her cup with the wine, and there was none for Port.

"You were saying," he said to Port, "about that restaurant."

"Yes. I thought if they're still open—or I can go there tomorrow, there isn't that much of a rush."

It was feeble, but necessary. Port had again lied himself into a position where his staying at the Powells' house would look suspicious.

"They're open all night," said Powell. "But if you're in a rush about it, why don't you call up?"

It could mean they didn't want Port to leave. It could mean that for a long time now nobody had thought Port was a utility man and that he, Port, was deep in the middle of the Heering affair.

"It's just about nine, now," Emmy Powell said. "Would you turn the set on, Herbie?"

She smiled and hitched herself around in her chair. She looked warm and comfortable.

Powell went to the set and when he clicked it on he said, "What do you say, Danny, you want to go in the kitchen?"

"The kitchen? I thought perhaps I'd better go. . ."

"No, no. Let's you and me go in the kitchen and have a visit. That is, unless you want to watch this here."

Port said that was real friendly of Powell and he'd rather go into the kitchen than watch the program. Watching the program, Port did not feel he would learn anything. It would be best to sit in the back with Powell and talk, have a visit, the way he had put it.

Powell poured his tea into the sink and looked at Port over his shoulder. Then he winked.

"I figure you and me deserve better than tea. I just never drink in the front parlor," and he took a bottle of bourbon out of a cupboard.

They both pulled up stools and sat down by the sink, Port at one end, Powell at the other. Port could see the back door, the arch to the corridor, and the black windows. He could see nothing on the other side of the windows.

"I must tell you," said Port, "that I really appreciate your hospitality. Here we are, hardly knowing each other, and having a friendly drink. I really appreciate that, Herbie."

"Glad to hear it, Dan, mighty glad."

"You do that often, take in strays like you did me?"

"Hell, no," said Powell. "I'm a suspicious man, way down. You just naturally struck me the right kind of person. I'm a sharp judge of character. I can tell."

"Tell what, Herbie?"

"I can tell you're people like me. We work hard, we look out for number one, but we're nice about it, huh, Danny?"

"Sure, Herbie."

"Now you're with the utility people. What do you make, maybe fifty a week, sixty-five?"

"Sixty-five, seventy-eight."

"Ah. You see, I can tell. With that kind of income, you got a feeling for money. I knew that."

Port waited. Whatever Powell might say would most likely be a lie—unless by some weird chance Port had gone into the wrong house—but as long as Powell kept talking Port could see more of the man. He saw already that Powell was also sly.

"That's why I feel free to ask you, Danny, and no hard feelings. Want me to freshen that drink?"

"No thanks. But go ahead."

"Sure, Danny. Now here's what I mean. You utility people got different rates. I mean rates for households, for industry, for different equipment. I know that a man who comes around checking wires and looking at appliances is the man that makes recommendations to the men in the office, telling them what kind of establishment he's been inspecting."

For all Port knew this might be correct. And for all he knew at this point Powell was a retired farmer who had moved to the city, or an international spy in remarkable disguise, or just a grinning fool building up to a touch.

"Now, what would it be worth to you, Danny, to go back to your office and tell those people there I'm running all my appliances here in an establishment like a rest home, or a hospital even, seeing I'm taking care of a sick wife all day long, and have them change my rates to a lower category?"

Port picked up his glass and took a slow drink. He had heard right, of course, and Herbert Powell was no mystery in this matter. He probably got a big kick out of the thousand ways a man can scrounge an illegitimate penny: protesting over the right change, skipping out of a hotel, stuffing a grocery bag after it has been weighed—

"Did you ever get your change for a buck from a cashier and then raised a stink you gave her a five and where's the rest of your change?"

Powell stared for a moment and then he started to laugh, sounding surprised.

"Hey—sure I did! You know, that reminds me of that one time—why did you ask?" and he looked puzzled.

Port had just asked him on impulse and having gotten his answer—the one he had expected—he was no longer interested.

"Funny my asking that, isn't it? I was just thinking of something else." Port coughed and put down his glass. "About this rate business, the electrical rates, I think, Herbie, I may be able to do something for you."

"You mean it?" and Powell's face lit up as if he were five years old and had just gotten a new toy. "You think you can? I'll pay you for it, Danny, I'll make it up—"

"No. Forget it. Your friendship, Herbie, is all—" and the rest got lost in mumbles and little laughs as the two men shrugged at each other and made a show of being embarrassed.

"Tell me this, though, Herbie," said Port. "How come a man, successful like you and retired, has to watch his pennies like that?"

"Don't have to, Danny, don't have to at all. Just habit. The same habit that got me where I am." He grinned smugly and saluted with his glass.

But the air in the room had changed and Port knew that Powell didn't want to talk any more. He'd asked his question had arranged his deal. He was through now.

As if reading Port's mind, Powell said, "Emmy's just about done with her program. That's mostly the time we go to bed in this house...."

Port got up. There was nothing else to do.

"You going to let me know about that rate business, Danny?" and Powell went to the short hallway, then waited there for Port to come through.

Yes, he would let him know.

"Any time," said Powell. "Come over any time, you hear?"

Any time except after ten P.M. this evening. Port got off his stool and put the glass in the sink. What would the Powells do if he refused to go? And why had they kept him till now in the first place? Because Powell thought Port was a utility man, no question about that.

"You going to drop in on that restaurant, for your book?" Powell was saying, "or do you want to use the phone? Might save you a trip."

Port left the sink and when he came up to Powell, who was standing there waiting, Port told him, "I'm a little tired myself. I think I'll check the restaurant tomorrow."

Powell had nothing to say to that and turned into the small hallway. Port flipped off the light in the kitchen, making a click, and then there was a click from the front room where Emmy Powell had turned off the TV; the silence was sudden.

The bell rang, like a shot.

Port saw the man in front of him as a black silhouette but could tell how Powell stopped, startled, and turned quickly to look at Port. The opposite light from the living room made it hard for Port to see Powell's expression; then Powell turned, went straight to the front door. There was no sound from the living room and nothing from Powell. Only his steps, going to the door.

Before he got there the bell rang once more.

Port stayed in the dark hall and his hands were up by the belt. He would draw either way, fast.

"Yes?" said Powell, not friendly.

The man from outside stepped into the light so that Port was sure.

Robert Heering.

"Excuse me, does Mrs.—*Miss* Semmerling live here?"

Chapter 5

"Does who?" said Powell and did nothing when Robert Heering came in.

"Miss Semmerling," Heering said again, and his awkwardness in the delivery looked remarkably genuine.

Port hadn't had a good look at the young man before. There was some resemblance to his sister Jane, mostly the large eyes, except with Robert the largeness was not beautiful but made him look bewildered. And there was the same kind of intensity which showed in his father's face, aimless in this case, as if hunted, and without the hardness of the elder Heering. Robert was blond and a little stooped, but that might have been part of the haste he felt at the moment.

"I forgot," he was saying. "She has a different name now. Are you Mr. Powell?"

"I am. And who would you be, young man?"

But Heering didn't get to answer.

"Herbert!" came from the living room, and Port, in the dark hall wondered at Emmy Powell's voice. "Did someone, did someone ask for Semmerling?" and her chair moved heavily when she got up.

It was the first time that Port had seen her stand. She had crossed to the archway that led into the hall and she was standing there, leaning forward. Her pose reminded Port of a fat little chicken, a very curious one.

"Did you say Miss Semmerling?" she asked, looking at Robert.

But at that moment Robert Heering was the one who drew Port's attention. Powell meant nothing right then, and Powell's wife meant nothing, except for being a little bit strange, but Robert Heering drew all of Port's attention.

His face became loose jointed and even though he actually did not move there was a flutteriness about him. Only his big eyes held very still, looking at Emmy Powell.

Port kept in mind what the elder Heering had said, that his son was unbalanced.

The young man reached into his pocket and slowly pulled out a rectangular packet. It was tightly wrapped with brown paper and a white string around that.

"You're Mrs. Powell, aren't you?" said Robert Heering. "I don't think you know..."

He stopped, swiveling his head, because Port had made his move. It was very simple. He stepped out of the dark corridor, and the gun, with one hand around it, was now in the right jacket pocket.

"That's all," said Port. "Toss it here and that's all."

Emmy Powell cocked her head, frowning, and Herbert looked at Port's jacket with his mouth hanging open. His whole face seemed to hang, making him look very old.

Robert Heering hadn't moved except to tighten his hand on the packet. His forehead screwed up in painful wrinkles and his eyes started to blink.

Then he turned fast and ran.

For a moment Port was too startled to move. Then he started to curse and kept cursing all the way down the street, running, while the taillights of the big Benz nodded at him and got smaller. Then the car turned at the corner and then the motor roar disappeared too.

The car had turned on Sumner, which was good. It had turned left, which was even better, because that's the way Port's car was facing on Sumner. Port could again see the Benz, tearing off in the distance, but by the time he had slammed his door the Benz was gone.

Port had the car in gear when the motor caught and shot off with a high squeal. The sound seemed to sharpen his anger. Port was boiling inside, not knowing quite why and with no time to think about it.

The longer the Benz stayed in the city the better Port's chance. The big car was slow on pickup, a handicap as long as there was some traffic, but wouldn't be easy to beat on an open straightaway. Port went past the first three intersections without letting up on the gas. He had still seen the Benz further on. It had disappeared where Sumner jogged to the right and then cut by two small streets which Port remembered from his trip during the day.

If Robert Heering was leaving town he would do best to take either of the two side streets because both joined the big road out of town; if he didn't know about that he could go on with Sumner and join the outgoing road by going through downtown. In that case Port could be on the highway, waiting for the Benz, before Heering would be there. But Heering would also take Sumner if he meant to stay in town and double back.

Port took Sumner, hoping there'd be no police cruisers around.

There were stoplights along Sumner now, all the way into downtown, and after the first one Port saw the Mercedes' taillights ahead. It went bright and then dim, because Heering had stopped for a light. The traffic was much thicker up ahead and Port lost sight of the Benz for a moment, then saw it again. The big car was traveling a straight line, making no effort to pass other cars.

Robert Heering didn't think he was being followed! He had seen Port run after the Benz, but he had never seen Port get into a car of his own. And not knowing that Port was driving, or what Port was driving, some inconspicuous maneuvering should get Port close to Heering without making the man speed up.

For a chase the drive soon became more like dancing a waltz to a loud rock-and-roll beat. The Benz didn't go fast, so Port didn't go fast.

The Benz swung off Sumner, away from the road that went out of town, and Port swung off right behind him.

Apparently he meant to cruise around for a while, an hour, let's say, and then double back.

A few more turns—Port wasn't closing in because he could have done very little; there were bars now, and theaters letting out—and the Benz started slowing towards the curb. The bastard was going to stop, go into the drug store on the other side of the street, make a phone call, have some coffee and kill time. The big car hadn't stopped yet when Port shot ahead and pulled close. He made no effort to stop, but leaned over to the right window so that Heering could see him.

Heering did. Port couldn't tell what went on in his face but the Benz made an unnatural leap, bucked a few times, but made it. The car accelerated with a clumsy nodding of the big body and Port let it go. He stayed close behind.

Robert Heering wasn't clever at this. He headed straight out of town, leaving the lights and the people, pressing the car ahead with no calculation except to get out. Port didn't know whether Heering wasn't smart enough to do any better, or whether he was just frozen at the controls. It came to the same thing. But later it would make a difference, because the man, Port reminded himself, wasn't completely sane.

A short way out on the highway, Port hit the gas hard. It was time. Any more straightaway and the big car could walk away from him. He came up on the left, forcing Heering to jerk away and waste time in getting his car under control. Port sat right next to the Benz now and studied its side. Both cars were gunning now, and the racket beat hard at Port, making the air excited—when the Benz swung off. It meant a sharp drop in noise, a bare pavement rushing along where the black car used to be, and then Port hit the brakes. He had his head out the window in time to see the Benz careen off the highway. There was a small, rocky road, a wind-stunted tree, and a sharp rise on either side of the road.

Port got the car to stop and turned back deliberately. A strange piece of luck, because Port knew that road. It went into the arroyo where he had tried out his Luger. It went in there and didn't come out again because the arroyo was blind.

Port watched the beams from Heering's lights for awhile, where they danced along the walls of the gulch. He couldn't see the car itself, but it would take Heering at least ten minutes to come back out. Port drove the short way back to the diner, the one where he had stopped during the day, and pulled around in the front so the car headed back in Heering's direction. Then Port went inside. He was not taking much of a chance on losing the man and this might be the only free time he would have between now and getting back to the Heering estate.

Port went to the wall phone inside and dialed long distance. His connection didn't take long and he kept watching the road through the window.

"Heering residence," said the voice.

"This is Dan Port. May I speak to Mr. Heering?" A few clicks on the line and then Heering.

"Did you meet?" said Heering, as if this was the middle of a long conversation.

"Yes," said Port. "I called to tell you we're coming back."

"You have the material?"

"Yes. Actually—"

"When will you be back?"

"By car? Not before the day after tomorrow. If you can arrange—"

"It will have to be by car. You will remember I want nobody else involved and I remind you of Robert's condition. Take nothing for granted with him, discount whatever he may say, and please be aware of the fact that a certain cleverness, rather surprising at times, is part and parcel of his condition."

"All right. I have to hang up now."

"I'm depending on you completely, Mr. Port."

"I know. Don't worry about it," and then they hung up.

Port left the diner and ran to his car. He tore down the highway with unnecessary speed and wished that something violent would happen. As if the whole job ahead were a vague thing and unknown. But this was ridiculous. Hunting Robert Heering into the end of the arroyo was like shooting an animal caught in a box trap.

For the second time Port knew why he felt wrong. To hunt a loser made him feel sick....

The arroyo wasn't long, but it wound back and forth, and Port was sure that Heering would have driven almost up to the end before seeing the dead stop. What Port had misjudged was the time it would take for Heering to come back.

He came through the bend in reverse, the taillights bobbing up and down, closer and closer. Port had come into the gulch with his lights off, and the Benz kept coming at him. Port's headlights snapped on, showing the back of the big car nodding closer, and then the Benz jumped and tore straight towards the hood of Port's car.

Port clutched and ground the car into reverse before it had come to a stop, and with full pedal squealed backwards, throwing stones and loose sand. The Benz shot by and kept going.

It was now very much the kind of feeling Port had waited for, the sharp anger with a real object and the hard action with an aim that wasn't too far away.

Part way up the incline leading to the walls of the arroyo, Port stopped. He couldn't have gone further anyway. He yanked the gearshift into first, wheeled hard, and bounced back on the road after the Benz. The big car was just making a bend, but then it never got quite out of sight. Going forward Port had more speed and more skill, and even if he hadn't reminded himself that young Heering was crazy, he would still have done the same thing.

He gunned hard and rammed the Benz with his right front wheel and kept pushing.

Then he let up. The other car kept going for a stretch longer but couldn't steer any more. The rear end dug into the side of the gulch and the car stopped.

Port stopped and got out. Nothing moved for a moment, except the slow dust moving through the beam of the headlights. There was no wind in the gulch, like on the highway, and the only noise was the long sigh from the cut tire.

And why hadn't Heering moved? Remember, he's off—

The Benz suddenly rocked and the door flew open. Robert Heering squinted into the light, but only a moment, and started to run. It was getting to be a familiar sight, an irritating sight and a useless delay.

"Stop it," said Port. "For chrissake—" But the man kept going.

Port moved to the side of the Benz and looked up at the sky. He could hear the man. Stones falling and sliding sounds.

"Heering—come back here!"

No change in sounds.

Port took up the Luger, aimed for the line where the sky was lighter than the rim of the gulch, and squeezed twice. He couldn't have hit the man!

But the man screamed and screamed, and the sounds from the steep incline were rushing each other, with the screams getting louder.

He was running. He was screaming and running back. When Port met him, Heering did a difficult thing: he swung at Port's head while running, and made it good enough to burn his knuckles on Port's skull.

Port hit for the midrift with the heel of his hand, let his hand slide on up and jar into the jaw.

Robert Heering kept going forward and fell on his face.

Chapter 6

He just lay there, making no move. Port couldn't tell if the man were hurt or if he were waiting his chance.

"Heering," he said, "get up." And then again, "Come on, fellow—up!"

Port moved with a great deal of caution. He stayed well back and reached out to touch Heering's arm. The touch would do something. It would end the stalemate, it would tell Port something.

He took the arm harder now, feeling how tense it was.

All of Heering was tense. He turned on his back and stared up at Port, as if frozen, and Port saw that there wasn't going to be a fast jump, or a kick, or any attack. Robert Heering was in a stark panic.

Port hunched down on his heels slowly and then took out a cigarette. He lit it and smoked.

"Here," he said and handed it over.

The young man, after a while, shook his head.

Port smoked again, waiting it out In a while Robert Heering sat up and his hands were trembling now Port watched, hoping the shakes would run their course and die out.

"Don't be afraid," he said "It's over."

He offered the man a cigarette from his pack and this time Heering took it. Port stayed where he was and let him light it himself.

"Better?"

The young man smoked. There was no need to answer.

Port got up, stretching himself, then flipped his cigarette into the bank of the arroyo. It hit and rolled a short way. Then it lay there and went out.

"All right, Robert. Give me the package"

For a moment a peculiar look came over Heering's face, but then he put down his head and exhaled. The long, breathy sound then became like a cough, or perhaps a laugh, but whatever it was it was all resignation.

"My father sent you?" said Heering.

"Yes."

The young man made the sound again, like a laugh this time. "I didn't think he'd go this far. "

"Far?" Port thought a moment, then said, "The shots were my own idea. He didn't say I should shoot you."

Heering got up. "I didn't mean that." He brushed at himself, doing no good. He wasn't paying attention. "I mean allowing a stranger. He goes far—"

Heering took a deep breath and looked up at the skyline He did this without interest, as if he were through expecting, or looking.

"Give me the package," said Port.

"Oh, yes," and Heering just handed it over.

It was wrapped and tied, the way Port had first seen it, and there were papers inside.

"Is he paying you much for this job?" Heering asked. "Compared to the million he's going to make, no."

"What?" said Heering, and he laughed a little.

Port didn't answer. He walked to his car, past the Benz, and kept his eyes out of the beams. He didn't look back because he could hear the young man following him. The footsteps were unhurried, just walking. Port stopped by his car and opened the door.

"We'll take mine," he said.

"Oh?" said Heering. "That's decent of you, but I'll manage. I'll just change this tire."

It wasn't going to be simple, Port saw. This man didn't grasp anything.

And then Heering came closer, so he could see Port and talk without shouting. He said, "Considering, you've been very decent. Really, I mean it."

"Thank you."

"I feel hopeful," he went on, "asking you just this one favor. It's small, considering, and if you say nothing to father, he won't be concerned."

"Robert," said Port, "there's nothing personal between you and me. That's why I'd like all this to be over as quickly as possible, and the less delay the less friction. Uh—so let's go," he finished off.

He had finished off rather suddenly, frowning over what he had said. Robert Heering, with all his removed manner, had drawn something personal out of Port. It's a thing about crazy people, Port thought to himself. He felt confused.

"You didn't let me finish," said Robert Heering.

"Oh?"

"I just want to have one of the photographs. There are four, I think. Just let me have one."

There was no detachment now, but a very serious wish.

Port tossed the packet into the front seat, and leaned his arms on the top of the open door.

"Robert," he said, "I'm sorry. It's the whole point of my job, you can see that. I can't even give you a photostat."

"I said photo," explained Heering and he too was patient. His growing anxiety would only slow down if he too stayed slow, spoke that way and tried to be reasonable.

"Yes," said Port, not wanting an argument. "Look at it this way, Robert. Think of me as a machine, built for a special job. You wouldn't argue with a machine, would you?" Port coughed, then he said, "I've been sent to get the conference notes and I've got them. And I've got to bring them back. I can't give them to you."

Robert Heering blinked, licked his lips and seemed to be on the point of saying something. Then a small tic, like a short shake of the head, developed. Port took his arms off the top of the door and stood carefully.

"Are you crazy?" said Robert Heering.

Port ran one hand back and forth over his face so that he wouldn't have to worry about his expression. He didn't know what to answer; finally he said, "No."

"Who are you, anyway?" said Robert Heering.

"My name's Daniel Port." He felt somewhat safer.

"Well, you needn't lie to me, Mr. Port—"

"All right, Robert." The young man's agitation was bad now.

"Did my father really send you?"

"Why, of course!"

"My God!" Heering said, and then again, very loud, "My God! Did he tell you *that?*"

Heering had thrown up his arms and then clapped them down again, hitting his sides. He took some fast steps, but not towards Port, walking towards the wall of the arroyo and then back to the car again. "Listen to me," he shouted at Port. "What did you come after me for?"

"Your father hired me—" Port started patiently but Heering was shouting again.

"What for? To do what?"

"To bring you back, Robert, so that there won't be any complications for you, and to bring back the conference notes."

"Conference notes? Oil deal?" Robert Heering's face was glutted with rage. "Is that what the filthy swine said?"

Port felt his teeth clamped tight. He was losing his patience.

"That filthy swine said conference notes? You know what's in that packet, you idiot?"

"All right," said Port and got ready to move.

"Love letters! You hear me? They're love letters in there, from that swine to his illegitimate wife!"

Robert Heering went to the bank and sat down there. He put his arms on top of his knees and kept sitting like that. Now and then he ran his hands over his face.

Port watched him a moment. He lit himself a cigarette but did not offer the other man one. Then he sat down in the front seat of his car, facing out of the open door, and smoked. After a while he reached back without turning and found the brown packet there. He held it in his lap and felt it with his fingers. Then he tore it open.

A dozen letters, perhaps, in their envelopes.

They were very old. They were dated back thirty years. They were written by hand, a steep, angular hand, and they all started, *My darling, Darling Emmy*. The envelopes were addressed to Miss E. Semmerling.

Port didn't read much. Some were stilted and awkward and others showed a free passion. There were musings and plans of how they would live. They were all signed *Carl*.

"What's your father's name?" said Port.

"Carl."

Port folded the letters and wrapped them again. It was a great, deep mess and he wished he had never gotten into it.

Robert Heering got up and walked over. He looked stiff and bent.

"Please, Mr. Port. I ask you this one favor, this *one*—"

"The picture?"

"Please!"

Port opened the packet again and in one of the letters there were three pictures.

"Which one?" and Port held them out.

Robert Heering took one with a young woman sitting on a bench and holding a small child in her lap. He gave back the other two.

Port put them back and wrapped the packet again. "Tell me, Robert," he said. "If you want."

Robert Heering was putting the picture into a pocket and when he looked up his face showed a gratefulness and a relief which took the old lines away. But then it all stopped very abruptly and the face tensed again, because Heering was listening.

"You understand," Port was saying, "that I'll have to see your father again. If you could tell me more, it would help."

Heering waited, showing his nervousness.

"Why did you steal this?" asked Port. "Why did you want these letters?"

"You know who this is?" and Robert Heering held out the picture. "See this woman? That's the Mrs. Powell you saw, back there in that house. It's her, years ago, when she was Emmy Semmerling and she and my father were in love. Can you imagine that? About my father I mean?" Heering laughed, a frantic and heartless laugh, and then, "And this baby here, see this baby? That's me!"

He started to laugh again, but then, at the last moment, changed it into a deep breath and when that was gone he seemed to have lost all interest. Port could hardly hear what he said.

"Do you have any idea, Mr. Port, what it's like being Carl Heering's illegitimate son?"

They had turned off the headlights to save the battery and sat in the dark car in the arroyo. The motor was idling so that the heater would work. The night was very cold outside the car. Port smoked and listened while Robert Heering told the long story.

The elder Heering had met Emmy Semmerling when he was in his twenties. She was the daughter of a pump man and Carl Heering was an engineer. It was the first time he had left the East, his first job in the fields, and Emmy was his first woman. She was soft and simple, and made no demands on him.

He loved the girl with the same sudden intensity with which his new life must have struck him; the raw men, with whom he suddenly felt equal, the gamble of the work, which everyone felt like a tonic, the wildcat fever everywhere. But it went just so far with him and no further. His ordered mind was more inclined to planning, and his temperament to act by plan. His jobs began to change from working in the field to working from the map. Carl Heering began to know Texas and Oklahoma better underground than on the top, and he saw fortunes, big ones, in oil. Except that he had no ante. That's when his father died.

The death meant fifty thousand dollars clear, paid to Carl Heering—if he stayed single till he was thirty-one. It was a revolting form of discipline, but coming from his father, Carl Heering didn't question it. He had three years to go before he got the money and Emmy Semmerling said yes, she'd wait. And Heering borrowed money on his inheritance, he speculated, he made deals, he worked all day and planned all night. And then he wildcatted. He changed. The wildcat fever was the only thing that still reminded of Carl Heering's brief show of life and intensity.

He and the girl made an arrangement. She had the baby and would wait.

It wasn't a matter of money being more important to Carl Heering than his love for Emmy Semmerling; nothing that simple. It was Carl Heering finding his way of life: hard work, long hours, the peculiar thrill of complicated deals, cold calculations, and the kind of singleminded drive without which nobody gets rich or powerful any more. The qualities he showed were nothing new; rather, he had forgotten them for one brief interlude before his father's death.

Not that he forgot about the girl, or the new baby.

Carl Heering paid the girl regularly, so she and the new baby would get along. And then he struck oil, and he paid all his creditors, and struck more oil, and made more commitments, and struck again, and paid again, and so on till his life, like all big business, was one continuous stream of owing and of paying.

"Except," said Robert Heering, "when it came to business he always made more than he owed. Still does. It's the other way around with the rest of his life."

He didn't say anything for a while and then Port prompted him.

"You mean about your mother?"

"On the surface he paid up, don't worry. He put her on an allowance. It's a lifetime thing and very comfortable. Every month she gets this check from a trust company in New York. And when I was two or so, he took me over. To do right by his obligation—"

"Do you remember that?"

"I don't know if I remember," he said, "I just have nightmares."

And then he started to scream. "Guilt and obligation! All my life I've been nothing but his guilt and obligation. I've got to suffer it! I've got to listen to it! I ought to do this, I must not do that—" It stopped with an attack of coughing, like a retch. It racked the man, doubled him over, and when he stopped, wheezing for breath, Heering was limp and weak.

Port moved behind the wheel, snapped on the headlights, then put the car in gear. It might help to drive, to change the mood.

Port maneuvered slowly until the car was out of the arroyo and on the highway. Then he drove fast. He opened the vent on his window so that the wind drummed past the slit and he couldn't hear anything else. He had been driving like that for twenty minutes when Robert Heering said, "I'm not finished. You have to understand the rest."

"All right," said Port. He closed the vent, drove slower. He said, "I understand about your father. I don't think I want to know any more."

"I'd like you to turn back to town," said Heering. "That's part of it."

"All right," said Port.

He U-turned on the wide highway and headed back to Lubbock.

"You got a cigarette?" asked Heering.

Port was out. He said he'd buy some and he'd like a cup of coffee. They found a trucker's restaurant and went inside. It was a change from the arroyo. There was a lot of light, there was steam on the windows, and two truckers were arguing about a brand of fishing tackle.

"Sometimes, like now," said the young Heering, "I think about it and it isn't bad—I mean bad the way it is at home, the destructive kind of bad."

"I don't know what you mean," said Port.

Robert Heering didn't act as if he'd heard. He stared at nothing, slurped his hot coffee without tasting it, and stared. And then Port saw the tense hate come into his face.

"My father makes it that way—what he touches becomes a special kind of bad—filthy with shame. Look," he stared at Port now, never blinking, "I grow up without a mother—all right. Except the swine makes it bad with secretiveness. Is she dead, is she alive, will she come, why don't I have one? Then he got me one, he married. Jane's mother. She was nice, she tried her best—but the swine makes it bad: treat the daughter like a normal child, but watch out for that boy! He's delicate, he's sick, he's got a burden... When I was fourteen my father's second wife ran away, or maybe he sent her away, and I'm sure she gets a monthly check.

"When she left it got worse. She took Jane along—Janey didn't come back until she was fifteen. She took everything along except the duty-preaching swine, the guilty old man teaching me right from wrong and everything was wrong. It was out now, about my mother, so he switched his method and wouldn't let me forget about it for a moment: she was no good, she came from some lowly stock, with bad bred into her, and that's why I'm the way I am, and on and on—" Robert looked up and said, "Did he tell you I'm nuts?"

"Unbalanced, he said."

"It wasn't hereditary. Is a nervous breakdown hereditary? Listen, there's a building on the place, back of the main house—I used to live there. I used to get the best. A private sanatorium all to myself, handlers all to myself, to play therapeutic games, a doctor on the premises, to give me needles—Christ!"

Heering was bad now. He didn't breathe right, his hands were moving back and forth, hunting for specks or smudges on the table top, touching them and pulling back not to get dirty. But he kept talking.

"And later private tutors there, instead of school. It got so I had nothing to look forward to except the nights. I started sneaking out, sneaking around the place, my place in back, the main house—a feeling like I was invisible. That's what I wanted. I started sneaking all over, prying into drawers, closets, that kind of thing. I lived in the main house now, you understand, but I kept this up as if I were a thief, breaking into someone else's place. Anyway, that's how I found the letters. He had the safe open in his room—he'd gone downstairs with something from the safe—and I got in there. I just read one and I ran out of there. I got sick again, maybe a month. A touch of the flu, a touch of fever, a touch of nightmares. I was dying with disgust, that was the real reason."

Robert looked sick, thinking about it. He swallowed some cold coffee and went on, looking at his hands.

"After a while it changed into something else. I don't care what you think about it, but to me it means something healthy. I had to have those letters. I had to have those letters and find the woman they were written to. She was just a woman—a nice, live woman. And she was my mother. I had to take those letters and look at them and then go find her, just see her once in case it turned out awkward, but go and see her and find out she was no monster, and I'm no monster, but flesh and blood. I don't care what you think about it, to me that's right!"

Port nodded, but Robert didn't see it. He was afraid to raise his head. He spoke again, and now he sounded stubborn.

"I'm going to see her. I have this notion everything will be different after that. Or at least one thing. She's flesh and blood. Then I will be too."

They stood outside the diner and had nothing else to say. Robert stood hunched over, as if the wind along the building were too much for him.

"You want the Benz?" said Port.

"What?"

"You're going back to Lubbock, aren't you? I thought you might want the car we left back in the gulch."

"Yes. I shouldn't leave it there."

"Can you change a tire?"

"I think so."

He looked miserable. He wished he could say more, but there was nothing else important. He licked his lips, the way Port had seen him do before, and then he thought of something, something to say to rile himself up, to make excitement.

"Do you know my mother isn't even sure that Carl Heering, this Carl Heering in the town of Heering, is the father of her—of me? He did some kind of conniving, some kind of planting of evidence, to make her think that her Carl Heering was working on a British dam project in Madagascar. And then he made up a rumor about some Carl Heering who died in the Burma campaign. So if she should have it in mind to make trouble, there would be all this confusion. You get what I mean?"

"Your father is very clever. You want to go now?"

"Of course, I don't think she ever tried anything."

"Robert, I'm leaving. I'm taking back these letters, and I'm leaving you to do yours."

"I'd like the Benz back. If you think it'll run—"

Port drove back to the arroyo and stopped at the mouth.

"I wish you luck," he said.

"Listen, Mr. Port, would you help me with that tire?"

He drove up to the Benz, and by the light from the beams showed Robert Heering how to change the tire. Then he said good-bye and drove back to the highway.

He parked not far away, without his lights, and sat for fifteen minutes. The Benz came out then, stopped, the engine idling. Port didn't drive away until the big car had slowly turned into the highway and headed towards town.

Chapter 7

Port drove all night. Once, in the early morning, he pulled off into a stretch of sage and slept behind the wheel. What woke him, so he thought, was the silence. The sky was light now, more white than blue, and the night wind had stopped. Without the wind the air seemed dull as lead. He drove again, feeling too much awake, too sharp, with nothing anywhere to look at, with nothing else to do.

By three-thirty in the afternoon he saw the town of Heering. He must have been driving like hell, he thought. This detail he hadn't noticed.

The feeling of being nowhere got worse when he drove up to the plateau where Heering's place stood. He'd never seen it in the light. The strange needle trees were all one mass, not very high, a thin, green color with the vacant sky overhead. This made the main house look very large. It was of dark brick, a sullen red, thousands of bricks.

Port stopped the car in front of the main entrance and got out. There wasn't a soul anywhere. The windless air made him want to shout.

He rang the bell and waited. When the door opened a man in a black silk jacket was there. He looked as silent as the air.

"I'm Dan Port. Is Mr. Heering in?"

"Ah, of course," said the houseman, and looked past Port to the car.

"Robert Heering isn't with me," said Port.

As much as was possible for him, the houseman showed concern. He finally said, "I see," and stepped aside for Port to enter.

"Mister Heering," said the houseman after closing the door, "isn't here. You were expected tomorrow."

"I know. I hurried."

What else could he say? Disgust with the new delay, with the need to sit uselessly waiting, kept Port from saying more. He would have to wait for Heering, to tell him that his, Port's part of the business was over, and try to explain the rest. It would be useless.

"Your room was kept ready for you," said the houseman. "May I take you up?"

"I'll wash up," he said. "After that, I suppose it's all right to take a walk out there?"

"Certainly, Mr. Port."

Then they went upstairs. He caught himself walking carefully which put him in mind of young Robert, making his pitiful, thieving rounds of the house.

When the houseman left Port at the door to his room, Port remembered to ask something else.

"When is Mr. Heering coming back?"

"Tomorrow. He assumed—"

"Can he be reached? I think he'd like to know..."

"I hardly think so, but you could call his Galveston office. Mr. Heering himself has gone to Anchorage."

"Alaska?"

"Yes. Though he may be on his way back by now."

There wasn't any point in trying.

Port washed and shaved, and changed into one of the shirts that had been put into his dresser. Then he went outside and walked around the house. There was no garden anywhere, just planted pines. Port lit a cigarette, threw it away.

Standing on the veranda he could see the roof of Robert's old house. It would be morbid going there, thought Port, but nothing worse than how he felt already.

And then he heard the car. He hoped immediately that this would be Heering, so the waiting would be over and he could finish.

The low convertible shot up the drive, dipped hard and stopped.

"Dan!" she called. "How good! Where's Robbie, Dan?"

For one short moment Port forgot about everything except the girl. For that short moment, when she came around the bend, then waved at him and called, Jane was the opposite of everything Port had gone through in the last twenty-four hours.

She got out of her car, came over. Port would have liked to see her run, anxious perhaps, but happy. She came over with the concern showing in her face, the same distraction Port remembered from the first time, but this time he knew a lot more about it. He also knew how useless her concern was. . .

"Is—is something wrong, Dan?" She put her hands on his arms and looked up, at his face.

"No," said Port. "I'm just glad to see you," and he smiled at her, meaning it.

"I'm glad," she said. "He's inside?"

Port took her arm and walked her towards the house. "No, Jane. It's a long story. He isn't here."

The main door opened and the houseman made a little bow at Jane.

"Will you and Mr. Port have dinner together?"

Neither of them felt like thinking about food, but the houseman stood there, needing an answer.

"Is there some soup? Could I just—"

"Of course, Miss Heering. And Mr. Port?"

"Whatever you have will be fine, thank you," and then they went into the dining room because they had to eat.

They talked very little during the meal. All Port said was yes, he had seen Robby in Lubbock, and yes, Robby was all right. And all Jane said was that she didn't understand all of this, but either Port or her father would have to explain things to her later. They could both go to her room, she said, when they were through, because none of the servants came up there unless they were called.

What Jane called her 'room' was a small apartment. She had a living room with thin-legged period furniture, a bedroom which was light blue with white trim, and a large bathroom beyond that. After they were in her place, she closed the door and started to talk immediately.

"What went wrong, Dan? Please tell me everything. Father said you and Robby wouldn't be back 'til tomorrow and—"

"Jane," he said. "I'm a little puzzled by you. Tell me, do you know your brother well? Are you two close?"

She took a deep breath and leaned forward with her arms on her thighs. It made her full hair fall forward along the sides of her face and Port could not see her.

"It isn't easy to be close to Robby. Perhaps once or twice, I remember, we started to be warm, really warm with each other, but—" She sat up again and shook back her hair. "He's secretive, and distant. The truth is," she said, "half the time I'm concerned about him just because it's a convention. Brother and sister type convention—"

"You may find it unpleasant to be closer to him," said Port. "That's why I won't tell you anything, unless you ask me again."

"About Robby?"

"And your father."

"You sound as if you know this family's most well-guarded secret."

"How many people," he asked her, "know about your father and his first wife?"

"They were never married!"

Her tone showed him her loyalties, and that her version of how Heering had deserted the Semmerling girl must be something tragic; the evil Semmerling girl, the suffering Carl Heering, paying terribly for his once-in-a-lifetime mistake.

"I don't care if they were married or not," said Port. "I'm asking about your father's secretiveness. On one hand he seems willing to fight heaven and earth to keep his secret hidden, and on the other hand I find that both his children know about this."

She looked very cold and said, "You are being insulting. We are his family."

"Ah. And Robby?"

"That's why father suffers even more. Robby must have told you about this, didn't he? He finally did let it out."

"Yes."

"You are," said Jane Heering, "the first outsider who ever knew."

"And heaven help me once your father finds out, is that it?"

He was sorry he had put it that way, even though it had been Jane Heering's meaning. It created an awkward and hostile air between them now, the opposite of everything Port might have wished for with Jane.

"And your mother? She and your father didn't part friends. Doesn't your father worry..."

"You are going too far," said the girl. "My mother is not vindictive. When a person has breeding—"

"All right. I'm sorry. And Emmy Semmerling? He isn't worried about her?"

"She is a drunk," said Jane. "She is somewhere in California, I think, and by the description I—"

"You don't know her?"

"Certainly not."

The old Heering had surrounded his guilt, and his secret, with three powerful safeguards. He was safe behind three of the stiffest conditions: good breeding, blind belief, and stupidity. The chink had been Robert Heering, and then he had pushed him too far.

A lot would collapse for the old Heering.

"You asked me where your brother was and whether something is wrong. Robert is with his mother, and as for the second, a hell of a lot is wrong."

And then he told Jane Heering everything he had seen and how he himself felt about it, and he watched how the girl, at a cruel pace, changed through a spectrum of strong emotions. She was hostile, angry, then stubborn, then weak; she showed fear and disgust; she became anxious with her confusion. She opened up, after a while, to the whole impact of Port's story, and when he was done she closed her eyes and her only movement was breathing.

The light was all gone now. Port killed his cigarette and looked at the low table for a moment. He stood up, rubbed his face, and wished he were walking somewhere in the open, and whistling maybe.

"Please," said Jane, "Don't put the light on—not yet."

Port hadn't known that he had been about to turn on the light. He pulled his hand back and turned to see Jane. Her voice had been different from any other time, without any intentional meaning, without trying for anything; as if she were through.

Port sat down next to her and put his arm on her shoulder. He held her face with the other hand and made her rest against him. It was too dark to see her, but he felt how she leaned close to him and drew together, as if for warmth.

They sat for a while and he stroked her arm.

"It's bad," he said, "isn't it?"

"I'm confused. Everything is so much more confused, so terribly complicated—" and then, by her movement, Port knew she had started to cry.

In his way, Port felt as badly as she, but no longer about the filth in the Heering affair and not about anyone except Jane. He wished they could have been this close for other reasons, for sheer joy of closeness and not fear of being alone and confused.

They held each other close with the warmth and the need growing in them, and then reasons didn't matter at all.

"Dan," she said, "I want something simple to happen. I just want something to be very simple...."

He took her through the dark room and into the dark bedroom. They undressed each other, staying close, neither wanting to lose the touch of the other.

Chapter 8

After breakfast the next morning, the houseman told Port about Heering. The Galveston office had called to say Mr. Heering was due back in the afternoon; that Mr. Heering—still airborne and on his way back from Alaska—had radioed the Galveston office for this information: is Mr. Heering's son, Robert, back at the house?

"What did you tell them?"

"I told them," said the houseman, "that Robert Heering was not here." Then he added, "I believe that was the extent of my duty," and left for the kitchen.

The houseman, thought Port, felt it too: the tension growing and the unfinishedness....

Four hours later, Jane was upstairs in her room, napping, and Port was sitting in the empty front hall. Outside something changed. The wind noise dropped away and did not come back. It was as if a vacuum was left. This held for a short while and Port sat there, pulling on his cigarette, listening, straining into the silence, when the big door opened and Carl Heering came in.

The older man, Port thought, moved like a cat. It had not struck Port before. And another thing Heering did, he said "Good afternoon," nodded, and at the last moment he smiled.

It was gone very quickly and Heering had passed to walk towards a door. "Will you come with me, please?" and he held the door open.

Port walked in and Heering followed. Port thought he must have been mistaken about the smile. Carl Heering does not smile. He has a nondescript face, a mouth as impersonal as a line drawn with a ruler, and the only thing about Heering's face are his eyes.

But Heering was going across the room with his eyes downcast, it must be, because they showed nothing. He sat down at his desk, looked up at Port, and his eyes still showed nothing.

He put his briefcase on top of the desk, pulled out a folder, a letter, more folders, and then he left everything there.

"Now then, Mr. Port," he said and waited.

Port stood up and handed the brown packet across.

Heering took it and laid it on the couch next to him.

"It's been opened, Mr. Port."

Port kept standing. He put his hands in his pockets and looked straight into Heering's face, so that Heering had no doubt about the way Port felt.

"I'll make it short," he said. "I did only half the job. I brought your package back but not Robert. That makes your bill half, five hundred bucks, which I'll take in cash. Or your check will do. Then I'm out of it."

"Not so quick, Mr. Port," said Heering. "I would at least like to hear why you failed with Robert. Where is he?"

The behavior was puzzling. Heering was much too conversational—unless the control the man had over his emotions was really fantastic. Port said, "Robert is with his mother."

Port did not expect any great change in Heering's behavior, and he was right. Heering gave no response, except to raise his eyebrows a little. So Port said,

"I believe you know, or suspect, that Robert told me what was in that package."

"I know it," said Heering. "I saw that the package had been opened."

"It changes only one thing," said Port. "Instead of conference notes I returned your letters. I see no point in more talk."

"But you forget about Robert," said Heering and the venom crept back into his voice. "And I assigned you to bring him back."

"That's out. We don't have to discuss it."

"But we do, Mister Port. I'm saying it for the third time: Your assignment was to return Robert and—"

"Once more," said Port. "And so you understand what you're up against. I believe Robert. I've seen the wreck you've made out of him with your poison. I've heard about the house in the back, that sick-maze you built, and it—with you—reeks of intentional murder. I've known a man who killed in cold blood. He's dead now himself. He killed in cold blood and all alone. You, Heering, you're worse! You don't do your killing alone but make somebody else do it. You make the victim do it!"

"I'll see to it, Mister Port—"

"The hell you will," said Port and walked to the door. The sheer impact of the high voice stopped him and he turned around, looking at Heering. The man was livid now.

"I will force you! I want Robert, and you are the—"

"How?" said Port, and he felt so removed by now he could almost laugh.

But when he turned to the door again he still caught a glance of Heering. A white rage was trembling all over Heering's face and his voice was close to a shriek.

"Here!" and he held up a letter, as if ready to strike. "Here's how! *My son has been kidnaped!"*

It was typewritten and started, *"Dear Mister Heering, Sir."* All through the letter backwoods phrases kept showing up, the way sugar is used to cover a poisonous taste.

Your son Robert is here now and feeling all right now. I figure that's only natural and his mother does too. I'm proud to know the boy and we're in this little old place here, just resting up where nothing can harm the boy or be of bother, because he deserves the best. We all think so and our Mister Port too who helped the boy out when he was so wore out and near loco from fretting himself over what was the right thing to do. Well we got him all safe now and not to worry. I'll let you know more by and by. I know you'll want to hear, being his father, and being so well set up you will want only the best for Robert.

It was signed, *Herbert Powell.*

There was no return address and the letter had no stamp on it.

"Well?" said Heering.

Port put the letter back on the desk and nodded.

"I think you're right. And the next letter will be the touch. The first touch."

"I thought you might know how it goes," said Heering.

He was going to start all over, thought Port. The man didn't give up. As a matter of efficiency, and to keep his secret confined, he had decided that Port would handle this thing, until Robert was back and Heering took over himself.

Port didn't look at Heering. He knew how the other one felt, how his eyes sat in his face and what the expression would mean. And at the other end of the scale were Port's feelings about Robert Heering. His first free swing out of the black rut where he had been kept most of his life, and the swing snapped back in his face.

"I'm not part of it," said Port. He almost sounded tired.

"I didn't mean that you were part of the kidnaping," said Heering. "I was referring to your criminal background, that it doubtlessly gives you some familiarity with this sort of thing."

"You're only half right. I wasn't in on this, and I'm—"

"Of course not," and then, for the second time, Heering smiled, very briefly. "I know you quite well by now. You are not too, easily predictable by the usual standards, but your impulses, I notice, are quite consistent."

There was no point standing any longer, nor was it wise to leave now. Heering, Port felt sure, was building up to something that mattered. Port sat down and said,

"You mean, with my clean-cut impulses and with your clean-cut instructions, I'm now going forth and rescue the lost Robert?"

"You mean, no?"

"No."

"Well, then—"

"Discounting pity, which never goes very deep, Robert means nothing to me."

"You're right," said Heering, and for a moment he could not keep the high look out of his face, smug and well-satisfied for having understood this much about Port, and for being prepared. The last thought gave him the most satisfaction.

"You will do what you can, Mr. Port, because I have this." He held the letter up and then, from that height, let it drop to the desk. The letter fell down with a smack.

"You are one of the kidnapers, Mr. Port."

Port put his hands back in his pockets, and very slightly he started to rock on his feet.

"That, Mr. Port, is how it will look. Your name mentioned affectionately in this letter. Your presence here, to negotiate. The amount of money—considerably larger than five hundred dollars—which I am transferring to your account. The car outside, which you used to chase Robert." Heering sat down behind the desk and looked at his hands. "You didn't know that my Benz was picked up in Lubbock, parked illegally somewhere? My office was called by the police about that. One fender is dented. And the car you drove shows the paint. You must have chased the boy hard. And then the story of some young man, a hitchhiker who works at one of my pumping stations—" Heering looked up, shook his head, "He's not working at Low Shelf any more. I can imagine what you might do to one of my witnesses. And then," Heering went on, "the entire complexion of your movements after your arrival here. My employees—the copter pilot, pump station supervisor, Lubbock office, my Galveston secretary—all instructed to aid your progress but no reasons given. You can see how that can be cast—"

"I don't doubt you can do it," said Port. Then he put his hands on the desk and leaned slightly.

"And then," he said, "when I get on the stand, Mr. Heering, how long do you think your secrets will stay secrets? How long do you think it will take me to undo your twenty-five years of hard effort?"

Carl Heering was a narrow man, built smallish, and most of the time nothing changed that impression. He stood up now, standing less high than Port, but none of that mattered. A fantastic strength moved into him, or moved to the surface of the small man so that it showed everywhere. This reservoir of strength made him so sure, it made effort unnecessary. His voice was low and quiet.

"That way," he said, "you could wreck me. And in that wreck I'll tear down everything in my reach. I'll wreck you, my children, anyone who gets within reach. Believe that, Port. I don't win, no one else will either."

Port moved away from the desk, went to the window, and stood there for awhile, looking out. He couldn't see very far because of the light, but heard the wind again. It was starting again with a whisper.

"All right." He turned around and looked at Heering. "I'll get Robert," he said.

Heering had been sure of it. He did not have to relax, or feel relief when he heard Port give his answer, because he had been sure. He had known that his strength was greater than any.

But he did not know why Port agreed—what made the switch possible; that every move Port made, from now on, would be a move against Heering.

Chapter 9

Both men were finished with their decisions and the rest was cold details. It was business now and a concrete job. The two men, on this level, worked well together.

Port sat down on the couch again and asked if he could have a cup of coffee. Heering rang for the coffee and asked for two cups. Until the houseman came back with the tray Heering did things with papers on the top of his desk and Port sat on the couch, arms folded. He had his eyes closed part of the time and every so often he made his monotonous whistle sound.

The houseman poured Heering's cup half and half with a lot of sugar. Port asked for his black. When Heering came over to sit opposite, Port started asking.

"How did you get that letter from Powell, since it didn't come through the mail?"

"It was in my Galveston mail. Delivery by the mailman is made on the ground floor, into a mail bin. The slot to the bin is accessible from the Information office—somewhat like a mailbox."

"I could walk in there and drop a letter?"

"Yes. It happens rarely, but sometimes outgoing mail is dropped there by mistake. Even though the slot is clearly marked."

"Are you sure this is from Herbert Powell?"

"There is no question."

"You know his handwriting?"

"By sight."

"I don't understand, why?"

"This—this Mrs. Emma Powell," said Heering, "receives a monthly check. From a New York—"

"I know about the check you send her. Quit being so secretive, dammit."

Heering said, "Some of those checks have been endorsed by Herbert Powell. The signature on the letter is the same."

"Any idea when that letter was dropped?"

"Today."

"Today when?"

"After three P.M. At that time the three o'clock deliveries had been cleared out and this single letter came through. The clerk forwarded it to my office immediately."

"Last night, at about ten o'clock, Powell was in his home in Lubbock. Your son Robert couldn't have identified himself there until about twelve, or even later. He left me, to go to the Brandywine address, after eleven. And today, less than twenty-four hours afterwards, you get this letter. How far is Lubbock from Galveston?"

"About five hundred miles."

"I don't know the roads down there. Can a man drive that distance in fifteen hours?"

"No, I gave you air miles. By highway the distance is quite a bit more. Both Abilene and Austin constitute major swings of direction on the main highway. And secondary roads are no saving in the central part of the state."

"And Powell had probably less than fifteen hours..." said Port. He thought a moment, then said, "And airmail is out.

"Naturally it's out. I told you—"

"What you told me doesn't stop Powell from sending a letter to a friend in Galveston and having it dropped at your building in a plain envelope. Anyway, there wasn't time. Even if the letter got there the same day, it wouldn't be delivered 'til the following. Which would be tomorrow."

"Robert is in Galveston!" Heering said suddenly.

Port shrugged. "He's with Powell and Powell flew there from Lubbock and dropped the letter?"

"Of course! I fly from Lubbock to Galveston in less than two hours. I don't know what commercial planes do on that run, but—"

"It makes sense," said Port, but he didn't move. He kept sitting still, fingering the rim of his cup.

"A short while ago," said Heering, and there was an edge to his voice, "you were in a great hurry to—"

"The more I can figure out sitting here, the faster can I move once I leave," said Port. And then, "Do you know of a detective agency which—"

"The chief reason, Mr. Port, why you are working for me—"

"I know, I know," and then Port took a deep breath. "Look. I want some leg work done. You can disguise the assignment all you want without cutting in on some efficient leg work which an agency can do better than I."

"I first want to hear what you want. As far as investigations are concerned, I have my own organization, as a part of my enterprises."

"Yes," said Port. "I'm sure." Then he lit a cigarette. He started to talk while the smoke was still in his lungs. "I want to know if Powell left Lubbock, and if so when. Any clue where he, or he and Robert, might have gone, and if Mrs. Powell is still at her address on Brandywine. By the way," said Port, "do you know where that Benz was found?"

"I don't know. I can find out."

"Yes. And I'd like a little background on Powell. There may not be time for much, but something about what he does, whom he knows currently."

"I can help you with that myself," said Heering, and for the fifth or sixth time Port realized that Heering usually knew a great deal about anyone even slightly involved with him.

"Can you reach your private police now and give—"

"They are not a private police, Mr. Port. As a legitimate branch of any enterprise as large as mine, an investigative branch is both necessary and ethical."

"Can you call them now and ask them for a fast job on this?"

Heering got up and went to his desk. He sat down behind it and asked Port to repeat what he wanted and wrote it down on a pad. Then he picked up the telephone, and in a short while: "This is Mr. Heering," he said. "Connect me with Ebberhouse. If he isn't in the building, try his Houston office. If he isn't there; ring his home, a Galveston number."

Ebberhouse was 'in the building,' which Port guessed was the Heering office in Galveston, and got his instructions. In the end Heering asked, "How long?" Then he nodded and hung up the phone.

"Some of it will be phoned in as early as this evening, late this evening," said Heering. "The rest, with any luck, will be available tomorrow forenoon." Heering came around his desk, soothed down his jacket. "It is dinnertime. Will you join me and my daughter or would you prefer to eat in your room?"

"I'd like to hear about Powell," said Port. "You said you had information on him."

Heering looked at the watch he had in his vest, then sat down opposite Port.

"We eat at eight," said Heering. "In fifteen minutes. What I know won't take any longer. Would you like the coffee heated?"

"No. This is fine." Port put his cup down, put his arms on his knees. "I'd like to know how much money Powell has."

"Money?" said Heering. "He has none."

"None?"

"Why the question?"

"I was wondering why a man, retired in his forties, pulls a kidnaping stunt."

"He isn't 'retired,' in the approved sense of the word. He is living on his wife's stipend. I mentioned to you that a New York bank sends her—"

"Yes. You told me. Now, something else. Where did he live before he came to Lubbock? He mentioned he was a cotton farmer in the past."

"Before he married the Semmerling woman," said Heering, and Port had to marvel at the anonymous way in which Heering spoke of her, "he lived in various places; Fort Worth, Houston, Galveston, New Orleans, and in Laredo and Brownsville, on the border. Those are the main places. He was brought up in Dry Waters, a small place near the New Mexico border. In the panhandle that is."

"They raise cotton there?"

"Certainly not. Nothing grows there. The town only exists because it used to be on the trail—one of the trails—into former Mexican territory."

"Then why did he say—"

"Yes, about the cotton. The only contacts he's had with cotton are some shady warehouse deals in which he's been involved. They had to do with buying, hoarding, selling, with undercutting legitimate concerns in the buying transactions from farmers."

"Powell did this?" Port was surprised. "Doesn't that take a great deal of money, buying on speculation?"

"It wasn't large scale. What money it did take came from someone else. Powell was just one of the underlings."

"Who else?"

"Some local person, Joseph Flynn. He's been involved in some border manipulations, dollar-peso transactions, wetback running, some minor black marketing during and after the war—"

"Local where?"

"I meant Galveston. I don't know exactly how Powell got involved with him, though that wouldn't be difficult. Any drifter around the Galveston docks usually runs one or two errands for that Flynn person at one time or another. All this, by the way, predates Powell's marriage which occurred over eight years ago."

Powell made much more sense now. A thin kid in the windy plains country of northern Texas, shy of work, sick of the home town with one beer parlor and movies on Saturday, he runs to the big cities and starts hunting, like a scavenging dog. He starts with the filthy jobs that take no training or pull, but he's hungry, always hungry for the big buck that comes for nothing. He finds company with that way of thinking. He worms himself into the dead-end orbit of some local operator, running errands, taking his gaff, living on promises.

But the biggest deal, the easiest buck, comes from somewhere else and has nothing to do with the one thousand small plans Powell must have been making over those years. Unexpected! Like in the movies, and the way this sort of thing ought to be. He marries a woman with a permanent income, rich even, a simple woman with no mind of her own. She likes to drink wine and watch television. Or maybe Powell started her on the habits....

End of the hassle, easy street. Except that kind of end never takes care of the inside greed. Powell feels big, as if all this was earned in some grand, special way, earned through his special qualifications, except he has never proven it. He sits in his automatic kitchen and knows what a hot operator he really is, but how to really prove it...

And so the Heering bonanza.

There was a knock on the door and the houseman came in.

"Yes," said Heering, "I'm ready. Mr. Port?"

"I'll eat in my room, if you don't mind."

"Two places," said Heering to the houseman.

"Miss Heering," said the houseman, "asked to be excused. She isn't feeling—"

"One place," said Heering, and walked out of the door.

The first phone call from Ebberhouse came at ten-thirty that night. Heering took the call at his desk while Port sat in the next room reading maps of the state and of some of the big cities. Heering called Port to his desk and gave him the phone.

"Port?" said Ebberhouse. A deep voice, but mostly anonymous.

"Yes, Mr. Ebberhouse."

"Mr. Heering says to report directly to you—"

"I'm listening."

"The employee—"

"What did you say?"

"I'm talking about this Herbert Powell. The employee Mr. Heering talked about."

"Yes. Please go ahead."

"He left the Brandywine address at about eight this morning. This came from a neighbor. And he was carrying a bowling ball bag."

"With a ball in it?"

"Seems not, and the next information bears that out. Checking all public transportation we find he bought a ticket—"

"One ticket?"

"One, yes. One ticket on a northbound Greyhound leaving Lubbock at ten-five A.M. That's according to the ticket man's seating chart, which ought to be verified by the driver's chart and maybe his personal report. We haven't got a hold of him yet. He's still on the road."

"Going where?"

"The driver?"

"No. The employee."

"Ticket was made out to Fort Gander, changing at Amarillo. Now that in itself, Mr. Port, doesn't mean—"

"Where's Fort Gander?"

"Western panhandle. Last town of any size in that direction. In Texas, that is. Now, we weren't instructed to check destination, Mr. Port, but if you want me to—"

"Just tell me this. Do you know a town by the name of Dry Waters?"

"You say Dry Waters?"

"Do you have a large detailed map there? If it's just a road map I don't think it'll do."

"Just a minute..."

Port heard the turning of pages and then the phone being put down on the desk. Ebberhouse seemed to be walking across the room. His footsteps came back and he said.

"I found it on the wall map we have. Just a burg, you know. Couldn't have found it without the index."

"Where, Mr. Ebberhouse?"

"About sixty or so miles from Fort Gander."

"Thank you: Now, if you'll—"

"Would you hold it a minute, Mr. Port? The other phone—" and Ebberhouse was inaudible again.

"Mr. Port?"

"Here."

"That was the report from my man covering the bus driver angle. The bus driver says he checked off Powell at Amarillo."

"Anybody else?"

"Eight other passengers."

"All from Lubbock?"

"Just a minute... Three from Lubbock. You want their names?"

"Give me their names."

When Port said this he glanced up to see Heering. The man was now holding one lip in his teeth and his hands were very still on the edge of the desk. Heering, Port saw, was sweating blood. He had followed the conversation well enough to know that passenger names were going to be mentioned.

"Mrs. J. Gomez, Mr. Herrick Ross, Mr. Saul Rostoff."

"Which one," Port asked, "sat next to Powell?"

"Ross did, by the chart. Now that doesn't mean—"

"Hold it a minute, Mr. Ebberhouse?" and Port looked at Heering. "Whom does Robert know by the name of Ross? Anyone?"

"First one that comes to my mind," said Heering, "is a Dr. Jacob Ross. For a certain time he was my son's attending physician."

Port nodded and then he said, "Robert was with Powell on that bus. They both left at Amarillo."

"How do you—"

"He gave a false name, so don't worry. He picked Herrick Ross, his own initials reversed. Many people will do that. He picked the last name for familiarity."

"He did not like Dr. Ross."

"That's all right," said Port and turned back to the phone. "What else, Ebberhouse?"

"Mr. Heering asked about his Mercedes Benz, where it had been found. That was, according to the police, half a block from the Lubbock Greyhound station."

"Fine. Do you know where Mrs. Powell is?"

"At home. According to my man, Mrs. Powell was reluctant to answer the bell. He could see her through the window."

"Why? Reluctant, I mean."

"She was watching television."

"All right. Did you find out anything else, something about Powell's associations in Lubbock, friends, that sort of thing?"

"Not much, Mr. Port. Bowling club, poker friends in the neighborhood—maybe something will turn up by morning. I don't think I can promise much more before then."

"You've done fine, Mr. Ebberhouse."

"I hope to be able to have some kind of rundown for you in the morning. Sometimes phone records tell a lot when it comes to leads, but we got our instructions a little late to do much before morning."

"You have access to telephone company records?"

"Why of course, Mr. Port."

"One more thing. When did that bus get to Amarillo?"

"On schedule. Five in the afternoon. It wasn't a direct bus. Had a lot of local stops."

And that was about the end of their conversation. It meant to Port that Robert and Powell were heading into the vicinity of Powell's home town, not an uncommon decision when a man suddenly wants to hide. It also showed that Powell wasn't very experienced with this sort of thing. And it meant that Powell's letter to Heering had been dropped at the Galveston office building by someone unknown.

Powell, it seemed, was willing to take the risk of letting someone else in on the caper. Or maybe he didn't feel big enough to pull it alone.

"There's one more thing I'd like to do tonight," Port said to Heering. "I need some bus information from the Lubbock depot."

"Please," said Heering and waved at the phone, "help yourself."

A passenger arriving in Amarillo at five would miss the last bus to Fort Gander by forty-five minutes, Port learned. Such a passenger could catch the first bus to Fort Gander at seven A.M. and would get there at noon. Another bus that was strictly local and not Greyhound franchise. That same line had a scheduled run from Fort Gander to Cuevas, Dry Waters, and New Sevastopol at two in the afternoon. If that bus ran on that day it should reach Dry Waters at maybe five-thirty.

"There's time for tomorrow's phone call," said Port and then went to bed.

Heering, at nine in the morning, had made one phone call to Galveston, but Ebberhouse hadn't been in. Port and Heering sat in the same room, not talking, ignoring each other, which was how they played it.

Port took out a cigarette and looked up.

"Can you spare me a plane?" he asked Heering.

"To go where?"

"I can beat Powell to Dry Waters," said Port. "It would make things easy that way."

"Can you fly?"

"No."

"Then I can't give you a plane."

"It's a gamble by car," said Port.

"I have no holdings in the Dry Waters area. I could give the pilot no reasonable pretext for taking you there."

It was hard to tell, sometimes, what was most important to Heering: to get back his son as fast as possible or to observe his secretive habits.

"I can get you a State trooper's car," Heering said. "With markings, light, siren. You can make the distance in five hours easily, traffic or no traffic."

"And let everybody in the Dry Waters area know I'm out hunting?"

"I'm sure you can handle that some way," said Heering, and then the phone buzzed.

Ebberhouse's men had been active. They knew that Powell shot pool for money, making small bets winning more often than not; they knew that everybody thought he was a retired cotton man and that he was liked well enough, mostly, it seemed, because he never tried to strike up any close acquaintances; that he doted on his wife and only talked about her in pleasant platitudes. They had also learned that he paid his bills regularly, that his monthly bills were from normal to low, with the exception of his electric bill.

Port knew why that was. And, Ebberhouse's men had found out, his telephone use had jumped suddenly.

"He called Houston twice and then Galveston," said Ebberhouse.

"When?"

"That's it. All one after the other and in the middle of the night. That was night before last."

That was when Robert had gone there.

"You know whom he called?"

"The first Houston number was in the name of a Joseph Flynn. There was no answer. The second Houston number is listed as Antonio Martinez, realtor. We happen to know who that is."

"Who?"

"He runs three whore houses. The call was person-to-person and Martinez answered."

"Would you know what was said?"

"No. I'm sorry. We got this information from the records and the phone company doesn't listen in."

"Maybe you know how long the call took?"

"Yes. Twenty minutes. And the next call right after that, to a Galveston number. That call lasted just about half an hour."

"To whom?"

"The Gulfboat Park. That's a dance hall, sort of, with an all night restaurant right on the water and a golf link on the other side and a yacht harbor. This isn't a country club, you understand, but more like—"

"Who owns it, Mr. Ebberhouse?"

"Joseph Flynn."

"Was the call person-to-person?" Port asked.

"No. Just the number of The Gulfboat Park. We don't know who answered."

Port thought he knew who had answered and had talked for half an hour: Powell's old hero and one-time boss, the operator who was big with the bums at the docks, Joseph Flynn.

"Do you happen to know," Port asked Ebberhouse, "when there's a flight leaving Lubbock for Galveston?"

"Two. Seven-thirty and eleven, all in the P.M. I've taken them often enough," Ebberhouse added.

But it didn't fit.

"Do you know how long a fast train takes to the same destination?"

"Let me check," said Ebberhouse, and it took almost five minutes. He came back and said, "The fastest is the one they call Black Crow, but you'd miss it, I'm afraid. It runs once a day only, ten A.M. Gets to Galveston at three in the afternoon. Practically nonstop."

"Thank you," said Port, "I'll try it tomorrow."

They hung up after that and now Port knew one more thing.

"How far is your Galveston building from the railroad station?" he asked Heering.

"A five minute walk, I'd say."

"That comes out right. I think I know how Powell got his letter into your mailbox while he was on his way to Dry Waters in the opposite direction. He sent it along with somebody who went to Galveston on the Black Crow, some acquaintance most likely, or a poolroom friend who got a bill out of the errand, and it's likely that Flynn met the man at the station to see everything came off. The train gets to Galveston at three, your building is five minutes away, and the letter was dropped there, by your report, a while after three."

"Why," said Heering, "this hurry to deliver the letter?"

"Has nothing to do with hurry," said Port. "The main thing was, Powell wanted to mail it from someplace where he wasn't. That it got there so fast was chance, and our luck."

Heering nodded and said nothing else until he had reached for the phone.

"I'll arrange for the highway patrol car," he said and picked up the phone.

"Don't bother," said Port. "I'm going to Galveston."

Chapter 10

But before leaving, Port wanted to see Jane.

It was part of everything Port was doing. It had nothing to do with love. The way Port had decided it when Heering had forced him, there was just one motive left, till it was over, and the old Heering was all of it.

Heering stood in the big hall and looked up. He watched Port come all the way down the stairs and then said, "The car is ready."

"I know," said Port and was looking elsewhere.

"My daughter," said Heering, "is no longer in the house. I'll say good-bye to her for you—when I see her."

They looked at each other and Port held his teeth together, because he was thinking, *You sonofabitch, you lousy sonofabitch, you got one jump ahead of me.*

"I thought it best," Heering explained, "considering the damage you have done already."

Port came down the rest of the way and said, "I haven't seen your daughter since you came back."

"I have. I saw her last night." Heering picked up a coat he had lying on one of the chairs and then his hat. "My daughter and I have never been very close, however we haven't been enemies. The car is waiting, Mr. Port," and Heering stood by the door.

She wasn't in the house—no point staying. Fly to Galveston with the old bastard and do what you can...

"You sent her away?" Port asked when he walked down the outside stairs.

"Don't bother trying to pump me, Mr. Port. You will have no further contact with her. Do your job, deliver my son, and then leave my family. You do that, Mr. Port," Heering stopped beside the car, waiting for the chauffeur to open the door, "and I may well leave it at that."

What I'll be leaving you is going to be more like a mine field, thought Port. He kept thinking about this while Heering got into the car, and it helped.

But when Port started into the car the chauffeur suddenly slammed the door. Port, it seemed, would sit with the help.

Heering was inside the car and Port and the chauffeur stood outside, close together. The chauffeur talked low and fast. "There's a mineral springs resort fifty miles from here. Blackwell. You should call her there, any time. Blackwell Hotel—" and then the chauffeur opened the door again, apologized audibly, and the rest of the trip—from the house to the airstrip, from the airstrip to the Galveston field, from the Galveston field to Heering's building—was silence between Heering and Port, each with his own plans.

There was a parking space in front of the building reserved for Heering's car. They stopped and got out.

"Wait in the basement garage," said Heering, "until word is sent down to furnish you with a car. And as I see it, there is no point in your calling me before tomorrow."

"I'll call you when I've got something," said Port.

And with the organized logic which made Heering the man that he was, he accepted this, keeping apart in his mind the man Port whom he hated and the man Port who had said he would deliver his son and therefore would do so.

Joseph Flynn wore a cheap suit which didn't fit his big body and the striped shirt he had on showed a frayed edge on the collar. Because Flynn was fat he kept the collar open and the necktie was pulled down which made it show the wrong side.

But his shoes cost sixty-eight dollars and he wore silk underwear with a monogram in it. Since none of that showed, it was all right, and when Flynn wasn't in Galveston he didn't wear the same clothes.

He sat like that at his old desk in The Gulfboat Park, said nothing. He had a can of beer next to him on the desk and the beer had been standing there going flat. There was a long line outside the room, an especially long one which went all the way to the end of the corridor and the last man in line could look down the stairs. He could see the big dance hall, the floor-waxing machine going back and forth, then only the cord which snaked across the big hall; and the man was still standing there when the lights went on down there and the waxing machine was turned off.

The change in sound made everyone in the long line stop talking and they wondered why Joe wouldn't open the door. One time this had happened, the line not moving, and that day there hadn't been any hand-outs. They hadn't known it, but Joe hadn't even been there. And they hadn't known why, until Joe Flynn got out of prison thirty days later, and that day had been the only day the line had been longer than now.

They stood in line, worrying. The door stayed closed.

"I don't know any Dan Port," Flynn said. "I know everybody who might be thinking he wants to muscle in here, Tully, and there's nobody wants to muscle in here."

Tully and a white-haired man, Bill, nodded at that because Flynn was waiting for it. But nobody talked. They had talked this thing back and forth for a long time and it hadn't helped. There was just this man, Port, talking like a damn foreigner, toting a gun, and threatening to shoot everyone in sight if he didn't get in to see Flynn.

"Maybe he's crazy," said Flynn.

"Then why don't he use that gun?" said the white-haired man. "He's so crazy, why don't he shoot, instead of just threatenin'?"

"That's right," said Tully. "At least shoot in the ceiling! Now if I was crazy—"

"Shut up, Tully," said Flynn. He felt disgusted and a little bit dizzy. Hadn't eaten enough that day. And now, this. He pushed the warm beer can around a few times and said, "I may not know this Port, but he's sure gonna know me."

The two men in the office with him picked up their heads and listened.

"Tell you what," Flynn continued. "You go on downstairs, Tully, and round up some of the fellers—you know who to pick. When you got six or seven together, have 'em take ahold of this crazy man and bring him up to me. Open the door now, Tully."

Tully got up from his chair and walked very carefully toward the door.

"And tell those bums to keep their britches on, or else," Flynn called after him.

But when Tully opened the door there was nobody left in the corridor, no line, not even one grifter. Only Port stood there. He nodded at everyone and then he walked in.

"Close the door, Tully," he said.

Tully closed the door. The man with the white hair just gaped, and Joe Flynn, a fat hulk behind the old desk, mottled a little.

"Where—where," he got out, "is the bums?"

"I sent them away. You and me, Flynn, want privacy."

"You sent them—"

"Yes. A little trick I have," and Port took out a policeman's badge. "I flashed this and they ran."

"Mary and Joseph!" said Tully and he kept looking from the door to Joe Flynn and back, since one or the other would be his answer.

"You like it so much," said Port, "let me give it to you." He walked over to Tully. "See? It says, 'Junior Deputy, Eat Your Oaties,' " and Port put the badge into Tully's hand.

"You're no cop!" Flynn managed.

"Clever," said Port.

He walked to the desk, sat down on a chair that he found there, and crossed his legs. Flynn shifted his weight, and with a great moaning of springs let his swivel chair tilt back at an angle. The new posture, with feet dangling above the ground, gave Flynn the look of a sleeping boy.

"Before anything else, let's hear your story," he said. "I'm fair. Start with that."

"First you send out your sidekicks, Flynn, and then you and me will get this over with."

"And what if I don't?" said Flynn. "What'll you do then, Mr. Wiseguy?"

"I'll explain it right in front of them. I'm talking about Heering and Powell..."

"What's he saying?" Tully came up. "You mean you do know this guy?"

Flynn was sore, suddenly, and had to give it to somebody.

"Get outa here," he said to Tully. "Get the hell outa here and don't show your face 'til I call you! And you too! Now git!"

They did this quickly, closing the door behind them without any noise.

"Now you!" and Flynn looked at Port. Flynn was still sore and in no mood to hide it. "Now let's have none of that gun waving with me! That don't count for nothing with me here alone. You got that?"

"Of course," said Port.

"So what's this gaff with Heering and whoozit? Start with that!"

"When you say whoozit, I assume you—"

"Yeah, yeah, yeah. I mean Herbie. I mean that Herbie Powell bastard."

Instead of relieving himself with his shouting, Joe Flynn only became more upset. He grabbed for the can with the warm beer, and not until he had taken a gluttonous swallow did he remember how lousy warm beer is. He hefted the can into a corner and spat out what he had in his mouth. He cursed, wiped himself, and walked to a door which didn't lead to the hall.

The adjoining room was nothing like the one they had just left. There was a small bar, with built-in refrigerator, leather chairs and a leather couch. And whoever had done the decorating had felt that old hunting prints were the right thing to have around Flynn. Those prints were arranged all over the walls, and in one corner was a stuffed fox.

"You like riding to the hounds?" Port asked.

"Shut up. You just sit down there and talk."

Port sat and watched Flynn get cold beer from the refrigerator. Flynn got one can, opened it, drank most of it standing. After that he took off his jacket, got a silk robe out of a closet and wrapped himself in it, picked up his beer. Then he sat down in a leather chair and kept his eyes closed while the cushions sighed. After that he opened his eyes and looked at Port. Joe Flynn, so it seemed, was somebody else now. He looked right and comfortable inside his fat, and inside that fat was a sharp brain.

"Go ahead," said Flynn, waiting.

"You delivered Powell's letter?"

"Powell never sent no letter to me," said Flynn. "How come you know Herbie Powell?"

Port sighed. "Herbie Powell isn't very smart. All he had was the setup. I found out about it and rigged up this snatch."

"Snatch?"

"Kidnaping, Flynn."

"Go ahead."

"That means fifty-fifty for me and Herbie. I'm down here to find out where in hell you come in."

Flynn, too fat for fast bending, put his beer can down very slowly, but when he came up again his face showed a different mood. Flynn was suddenly boiling with rage, and he started cursing with a filthy violence.

"...suck me in on a sucker deal, will he? Get me to jumping in the middle of the night with a telephone call! Too big to come down here and set this up right. A telephone call in the middle of the night and yammering at me and moaning about all this loot coming his way and me, old buddy Joe, call up old buddy Joe for old times sake and to give him a cut. Fifty for you!" he yelled at Port. "Then where in hell's fifty for me?"

Up to this point, then, Port had figured it right. Flynn was in on the deal.

"That's why I'm down here," said Port. "And I apologize."

"What's that?"

"For thinking you were a chisler. Powell's the chisler."

"Ahh..." Flynn said, and let himself sink back into the chair, face turned up toward the ceiling.

"Better get Powell down here," said Port.

And now Flynn was himself again. "Get him down here?" said Flynn. "You sound like you're doing me a favor."

"I wouldn't dream of it, Flynn."

"Then why get him down here. Why aren't you wherever Herbie is, huh? That makes only two of you, that way."

"You know where Herbie is," said Port. "Could I maneuver up there and find him, if he decided to hide?"

"City boy, huh?"

"Dry Waters," said Port, "is the moon, as far as I'm concerned."

"It is," said Flynn. "Just exactly like it, up there."

Which showed Port that Flynn knew where Powell was.

"The truth is," and Port told the truth, "I'd be lost chasing him all over his home territory, but down here I can maneuver."

"Why would you be chasing him? I thought you and him—"

"Don't you know about Herbie yet?" said Port, sounding weary. "He's a chisler, I told you."

"I see that. I can see that good."

"And stupid. Take for instance that letter to Heering. You dropped that letter for him?"

Flynn nodded, because it had sounded like an aside, and admitting that part seemed of little importance.

"You got that letter off a guy at the railroad station, isn't that right?"

"That's how we set it up."

Port was happy to hear he had figured it right.

"You know the man who gave you the letter?"

"Some buddy of Powell's. Some salesman buddy from the bowling club, and he was coming down to Galveston anyway. We both wore a carnation," said Flynn.

Port almost laughed, but kept it down.

"That shows you, Flynn, what I mean. A thing like that letter, as important as that, and he sends it down here with some stupid drummer! A guy who could have got drunk on the train, or maybe get himself rolled by some hooker he picks up on the way—"

"Yeah," said Flynn. "Yeah, yeah..." and he was thinking about it.

"And the same thing with that stupid stunt of going up there in the wilderness, that Dry Waters place. All out of touch, so few people up there he's bound to attract attention. And maybe that Heering kid suddenly gets impatient. Maybe he doesn't believe all of a sudden that Powell is doing this thing for his own good. He starts smelling a rat, he doesn't like sleeping in some windy shack, eating cold beans and so forth. Why, man, here's a million bucks or so riding on Powell's half-ass planning, a million bucks teetering out of sight because that dumb stumble bum up there!"

"Yeah! And I argued with him! Over the phone I was trying to tell him!"

"And here he goes to the trouble," Port kept it up, "to get you into the thing, to help handle this thing, and then what does he do? Use you to deliver a letter, for God's sake!"

"Damn his hide, yes!"

"And you know why, Flynn? For the same reason he left me with my mouth hanging open. He gets the best out of me he can, and then skips. He gets the best advice out of you and then he tries it alone. He needs you like a hole in the head, is Powell's opinion."

It worked. It worked so well Port got impatient with Flynn's lengthy cursing. But when Flynn had calmed down and sat still again, he said, "Maybe you got other reasons for wantin' him here. Like you said, you can't move so good in a place like Dry Waters. But down here..."

The whole thing was a stall, Port figured. At one time or another, Powell would come down to Galveston anyway, or wherever the hide-out was going to be, because that would have been part of the plan whether Port pushed or not.

Port's main reason for working through Flynn was to make the job clean. If Port caught Powell and Robert Heering, up in some shack in the panhandle, he might manage to get Robert away, but not Powell, not two men at the same time. And then Powell would still run around with his tongue hanging out, and more so, Joe Flynn. There wouldn't be anything to keep them from trying again.

They had to get burned, and both of them.

Port got off the couch and walked over to Flynn. He put his hands in his pockets and stood in front of the man without saying anything for the moment. When Flynn started to frown Port started to talk, as if this was the last thing he wanted to do.

"I guess you know Powell's angle. Do you?"

"About Emmy Semmerling? Sure I do."

"So you know," said Port, "that it all depends on her."

"No problem. I met her once. And she's Herbie's wife."

"Did you know she's a wino?" said Port.

Flynn hadn't known. The thought was disturbing.

"You know about winos then, about how unreliable they are."

"She's still the mother of that Heering kid, drunk or sober."

"Who says, Emmy herself?"

"Powell says! That's what the whole thing's about!"

"The hell with Powell!"

Flynn hoisted himself around in the chair, very uncomfortable. He hated looking up, and Port was still standing in front of him. And he hated to see things get complicated.

"So come on," he said. "About this angle. Start with that."

"Emmy Semmerling, or Mrs. Herbert Powell, she doesn't remember so good. Those winos, you know—"

"Come on, dammit, get to it!"

"I know this from talking to her, when I was with Powell. Now, if she leaves home, if she goes out of reach, and old Heering should get to her, how long do you think it'll take him to get a deposition out of her, signed, sealed, and paid for, that she never slept with Carl Heering, never had a son, and maybe is even a virgin? How long, Flynn?"

"Good God—"

"Then Robert Heering wouldn't be worth a red cent."

This time it really worked.

"I'm gonna pick that sonofabitch up myself!" and Flynn wrestled himself out of the chair.

"When you going to be back?" Port asked him.

Flynn went to his closet, took off the silk wrapper, and put on his coat. He gave Port one sideways look but didn't answer.

Port lit a cigarette and talked very quietly.

"You might as well face it, Flynn. You don't shake me. Nobody does."

"All right. But we got to talk this whole thing over yet, about the split."

"I'm willing to split."

"We'll talk about that when I get back."

"I'm willing. When will you be back?"

"You mean you aren't coming along?" Flynn said this hopefully.

"Not if you tell me where and when we're going to meet."

"Trusting, aren't you?" Flynn put on his hat.

"I can afford it. I can take Powell's wife up to Heering myself."

Flynn almost choked on the picture of that, and then he just nodded. He didn't open the door, the way he had planned, but came back and explained.

"You know Route 87, from here to Port Arthur?"

"Like the palm of my hand."

"Once you're off the Bolivar peninsula you come to Route 124, going north. Where it crosses the waterway—"

"What waterway?"

"Intercoastal waterway, for pete's sake, the canal!"

"All right. The canal."

"Right there, over the bridge, you come to the maintenance road that goes off to the right."

"It's open?"

"No. But you go there just the same. You drive down there after five-thirty and there won't be anyone at the maintenance sheds. You go to the second way-house, not the first, the second, and that's where I've got it set up."

"No cops, no canal men, nothing?"

"Taken care of," said Flynn.

"When?"

"I'm flying up as far as I can. Amarillo, I guess. I'll rent a car there or take the bus, I don't know yet. And the same way back. Figure the second day."

"Okay," said Port and watched Flynn go to the door. He let him go so far and then stopped him.

"One more thing."

Flynn turned, his heavy face dark and way off.

"Maybe Powell won't want to come. Maybe once he sees you and finds out I got to you, he'll start snowing you, the way Powell knows how."

"I remember about Powell good. Don't—"

"Get this, Flynn. Tell him, first off, that he's made me sore. That I'm switching to Heering's side and I'm after him, hot and bothered. So he better hightail it down here with you, where it's safe. Got that clear?"

"Don't worry," said Flynn and opened the door.

"Just remember this," said Port. "If you don't show up the way you explained it—because you changed your mind, because Powell changed it for you—then remember I'm going to get Emmy Powell. You can start with that," said Port, and then they both left the building without saying any more to each other.

Now Herbie Powell could talk his head off once he heard about Port. Whether Powell believed Flynn or Flynn believed Powell, it would come to the same thing: Port was in.

He made two phone calls. He called Heering to lend him a plane, and he called Jane, to tell her to meet him.

Chapter 11

It was completely dark when Port got to 912 South Brandywine. The street was empty and the nightwind funneled against him, cold and unpleasant. And Emmy Powell, or Semmerling, would be sitting in her warm room, the flowery housedress wrapped around her body, the wine warm inside her, cloudy and comfortable.

It would be an unpleasant visit, but he knew of no other way. The image of Heering was riding him.

It took her a while to open the door, but then she stood there and smiled.

"Mr. Port! Did you find your little black book?" and she stood there hoping he had. "Come in, Mr. Port. Herbie isn't in right now, but come in."

He came in and while Emmy Powell sat down in her chair, Port stood by the television set. Then he said, "Do you mind if I turn that off?"

"Why—why, yes, go ahead," and she smiled uncertainly.

Port snapped off the set and sat down on the hassock close by her chair. Sitting the way he was he had to look up at her and she smiled back at him.

"You want to tell me about Robert?" she said.

Perhaps she was much less of a wino than Port had thought, and much less confused.

"He told us how nice you were, what a nice young man..." She was looking off now, at the wall. Then she looked at Port again, smiling politely. "What I don't understand yet is you being a utility man here in Lubbock, and also a friend of Robert's. I don't see..."

Emmy Powell, and what she knew, would be no help. Port took a deep breath and then took out a cigarette. "You mind if I smoke?"

"Oh, no. Go right ahead, Mr. Port. Herbie smokes. Herbie isn't here, you know, but if you'd care to visit a spell—not that I expect Herbie tonight any more."

"That's all right, Mrs. Powell."

"They left the same night, you know. Robert was so grateful—I'm not sure they should have left, but then they both said it was best."

Port wasn't sure of anything. Emmy Powell was much too vague.

"How was it, Mrs. Powell, finding your son again after all these years?"

She looked at the wall again and said, "Well, it's hard for me to say. But I had to cry..."

Port saw she was smiling when she said this, though the meaning wasn't clear.

"But then," she went on, looking at Port, "with all the time since the baby, and everything since then, he was mostly a young man to me. A very nice young man..." She reached for her wineglass and took a sip. "I don't mean to shock you, Mr. Port. And he's such a nice young man."

Port wasn't shocked. He thought Emmy Powell's admission was the first clearly sane thing she had said.

"It couldn't be any other way," he said. "Though perhaps it shouldn't have happened."

"Oh? But I loved having the baby. I remember that."

It was a cruel thing to see what had happened to the woman since then.

"Mrs. Powell," said Port. "This young man, Robert Heering. You keep calling him a very nice young man—"

"Yes. Except I thought he was terribly shy, you know what I mean? And upset."

"Well, considering the circumstances..."

"I mean altogether. Not just because of him and me meeting like this."

"Yes. Which is why I've come back, Mrs. Powell. Why I've come back to ask you a favor."

"I don't think his father treated him right," she said, half to herself. Then she took up her glass again and sipped.

"You felt this, or Robert told you about it?"

"Well now, he did tell about having this trouble, not getting along with his father. That's why Herbie took the boy along, you know, to find him a place where he can get a rest and not be bothered by anything. But I felt it. If he hadn't said so, I would still have felt it." She sighed to herself and looked at the wall.

Emmy Powell, Port thought, was very much the same woman she had been a long time ago; a warm, simple female, with feelings about people. Only the alcohol had been added.

"Would you like to see Robert again?" Port asked her.

"Again? Why, of course. He said he'd like to see me again."

It was shallow, thought Port, but what else could he do. At least it was genuine.

"It would mean, Mrs. Powell, seeing Carl Heering again."

This was the point.

This was the way it would have to be, to break the old Heering, or to break his lie, and Robert would be there to see it.

"You mean—Carl? After all these years?" And in a while she said, "I don't know... Maybe he doesn't even remember me."

"Carl Heering? Listen to me, Mrs. Powell—"

"And I think I'm a little afraid of him."

"Carl Heering," said Port, "is afraid of *you.*"

It was close to an hour now, and Port kept listening for sounds from outside, hoping that Jane would come soon.

"Afraid of *me?*" said Emmy Powell.

Port considered the woman and how much he could tell her without confusing the issue. He told her how Robert had lived, how the old Heering had taken it out on the son, and that Robert was close to the end of his rope. Port left out the part Herbert Powell was playing, to stay with one thing at a time.

"It means so little to you, Mrs. Powell. It just means something to Robert Heering. And he's a nice young man—"

"I wouldn't know what to do, Mr. Port."

"Nothing. Just be there, Mrs. Powell," and Port thought of the contrast she would make, sitting there in a chair and Carl Heering opposite.

A car drove by outside and Port looked at his watch. An hour had passed.

"I don't think," she said, "Carl would like it. After all these years gone by..."

Time was pushing him, and more so the failure; how to move this woman, budge her through the fog.

"Look," he said. "I'm talking to you because I have two reasons for pushing. One's my own. Frankly, I don't like Mister Heering. I started with that one. It's the reason that got me in. But the other one's growing on me. I'm not saying I like Robert, I hardly know him. But he's down and out. And that means something to me." Port felt better now. "And that part, I mean Robert, can mean a great deal more to you—"

"Is there someone outside?" said Emmy Powell.

Port hadn't heard anything, but Emmy Powell was more used to the noises of the house and the wind outside. Port got up, turned the light off in the hall, then opened the door. It pushed into his hand, because of the wind, and then he heard the sound from the corner, a high-powered roar, and the convertible shot into the street. It slowed then and came along the street in low gear.

Port knew the car. He stepped out on the street and waved at it till the girl behind the wheel saw him. Jane stopped where Port was and got out of the car.

"Dan—" Then she looked at the house behind him. "Is that where she is?"

"Yes. You must have driven like a demon," he said. "I thought you would get a plane."

Jane paid no attention to the remark. Instead she asked, "Does she know yet, about coming along?"

"She knows, but I don't know if she's willing."

"But her own son!"

They walked across the street and went into the house.

Emmy Powell stood in the arch and smiled when the two people came in. She looked from Port to the girl and waited.

"Mrs. Powell," said Port, "this is Jane Heering. She—"

"Oh yes!" and Emmy Powell held out her hand. "You're my son's half-sister. He mentioned you," and then she waved them into the room. "You look a little bit like him," she said when Jane passed her.

Neither Port nor the girl said anything right away. Emmy Powell—and they both had heard it—had called Robert her son.

"I've been thinking," said Emmy Powell, "if I don't have to go alone, I'd like to do what you said, Mr. Port."

If it had been any other time, they would have sat down now and talked, some tea maybe, and some of Emmy Powell's wine. But Port didn't think that Joe Flynn would let this go by, knowing about Emmy Powell, and the threats Port had made. He got up, looked out of the window, came back.

"You won't be alone," he said. "Jane is here, to go along, and I'll come with Robert. And while you're with Jane, she'll explain more to you. I'm afraid there isn't time now—"

Neither of the two women knew why he was rushing them. They looked up at him and Port had to spend time explaining more. Flynn or his man could have been here half an hour ago. Port walked back and forth, making it urgent. He told Mrs. Powell that they had to leave now, that the old Heering didn't want any of this to happen and he might send someone to stop Jane from taking her. He didn't think he had to make too much sense for Emmy Powell, that the sense of pressure would be enough to convince her. And Port counted on Jane to take the cue. She knew, since his phone call, what had happened to Robert and what had happened in Galveston.

"I can't believe..." Emmy Powell was saying, when the taxi drove past the house for the second time.

Port stepped away from the window and the change in his voice was enough.

"Is there a hotel in this town?" he said to Jane.

"Well, there's the Jefferson. It's not the best—"

"Never mind that now. I want you to take Mrs. Powell and go there immediately. If you can't get a room—"

"I can get a room," she said, which reminded Port that Heering owned a good part of Galveston and probably more of Lubbock.

The taxi was gone, not that it meant anything. While Emmy Powell and Jane got into the car, Port kept looking around. Maybe the cab had stopped before disappearing, and left off a fare

Two headlights swung into the street, came slowly closer. "Don't go yet," said Port. "Hold it," and he put his hand on the steering wheel of Jane's car.

The headlights kept Port from seeing too well, so he didn't know that the car was a taxi until it was almost up to him.

And then the taxi stopped abreast.

It was empty, except for the driver.

"My mistake," said the driver. "I thought you were somebody else."

"Your fare?" said Port.

"Uh-huh," said the cabby. "I guess I keep cruising." But when he started up Port leaned into the window and the cabby had to stop.

"Your fare coming from that house?"

"Yeah. He still in there?"

"He'll be right out," said Port. "Why don't you pull up to the curb," and when the taxi had moved Port turned to Jane.

"Just do what I say now. Drive off slowly and allow the taxi to follow you. Circle around and bring him back here. Don't let him catch up! Just make him follow and stop here again, got that?"

"I—all right," she said.

"First, put up your top."

Emmy Heering understood very little of this, and Jane didn't understand very much more. But she did what Port said. While the convertible top hummed up and over the car Port walked away. He didn't go fast, not wanting too much distance between himself and the car, or it would mean his man might make a rush. But Port kept walking, hand on his gun, and then Jane's car took off in the opposite direction.

Port was in the shadow enough to risk turning around. Jane's convertible was halfway to the end of the street, the taxi was standing, when the man came running across. Port couldn't see who it was, but he came from the back of a house, Emmy Powell's house, maybe, and jumped into the cab. The cab followed Jane's car.

Port pressed himself flat against the side of Powell's house and waited....

Chapter 12

First one pair of headlights swung into the street and then the other. The two cars were not far apart. The first car, the convertible, started to slow, and for a moment it looked like the taxi was going to pass it. But now the first car was pulling over, meaning to stop, so the taxi stayed behind, quite close now, and just followed suit.

Port waited. He felt himself shiver, knowing it had nothing to do with the cold.

The convertible stopped, but the headlights were still on. He should have told Jane to turn off her lights once she stopped. A door opened, the door of the taxi, and Jane's headlights were still on.

The taxi door slammed.

"Just hold still, lady..."

The headlights went off.

"I'd just as soon break the window and drag you out, lady. And that wouldn't be all—"

Port sprinted.

He didn't know if the man had a gun and he didn't care. He heard the convertible rock on its springs and then heard the door fly open. The man sounded angry.

"And just for that, lady, I'm gonna give—" when the word became a hoarse push of air coming out of his mouth, with the Luger barrel knifing his kidneys and Port's arm choking his neck, yanking the head up in the air.

"Drive!" said Port. "Come on, you know where to go! For heaven's sake, Jane, jump to it!"

She roared off, finally, closing the door while under way and forgetting to put on the headlights till she turned the far corner.

The man wasn't Flynn—not fat enough. Port let go suddenly and with a fast trip at one shin helped him fall down.

"Tully!"

Tully stayed on the pavement, not moving, because he saw the gun and he knew about Port in general.

But all this was new to the cabby and unexpected. He came out of the cab and started to holler, but he could see the gun well enough and shut his mouth when the muzzle turned his way.

"Come here." Port had stepped back to watch both men. The man came closer, like a doll on a string.

"Hop in your cab," said Port, "and drive like hell."

"Yes, sir!"

"And I'm taking your number. Any cops show up here, or anything like that, and you'll be too dead tomorrow to do anything else."

Port heard feet scrambling, door thumping shut, and the cab taking off like a streak.

"Get up, Tully."

Tully did. Port grabbed his arm, and together they made their way up the steps and into the Powell house. Port snapped on a light in the living room, drew the shades, and told Tully to lean against the wall. In Tully's clothes he found one gun, one spring knife, a sap, nylon cord, and a wad of cotton which could be used as a gag.

"Sit down, Tully. In the couch there."

It was a very soft couch and Tully sank into it. He rubbed the sweat in his palms and glared at Port.

"How come you're in on this, Tully? I thought Flynn was keeping the help out of this thing."

"Noo Yorker," said Tully after a while, which was the worst insult he could think of at the moment.

Port sat down on the hassock and started to toss the Luger from one hand into the other. "Where's Flynn?" he asked suddenly.

The question caught Tully unawares, and all he said was "Huh?" Port asked him again and this time hit the man over the nose.

But it didn't make Tully talk. The slap had startled him and then he sat rigid while the slow wave of pain traveled all through him. It left him exhausted and even his impulse to jump and hit back wasn't there any more.

"Where's Flynn?" Port asked again, but Tully just sat there, hunched over. His fear of Flynn was still greater than his fear of Port.

"Look, Tully," Port said, and now he was caressing the Luger, rubbing it gently between his palms, "I need information. If you won't give with it, you're no good to me. And if you're no good to me, then from my point of view, you're better off dead." With this, Port raised the Luger in his hand, sighted right between Tully's eyes, and said, "Well, might as well get it over—"

That did it.

"I'll tell you, I'll tell you! But Jeez, put that thing down!" and Tully's face was frightened now.

Port lowered the hand with the Luger, sat down on the hassock. "Okay, Tully. Let's start with question number one. Where's Flynn?"

"He said he was going up to Amarillo some place. Honest!"

"I believe you, Tully."

"He isn't going to Amarillo itself. I thought you know he was picking up Powell up there."

"Yes," said Port. Then it occurred to him. "You know where, outside of Amarillo?"

"Place called Margarita. That's where Powell is staying."

"Not Dry Waters?"

"That's where he wanted to go but Flynn told him nix. I wasn't there when Powell phoned. I didn't even know from nothing 'til just today."

Port thought this over. First of all Flynn had lied to him, bothering to lie over a little thing like Dry Waters versus Margarita. Not so little. Margarita was closer to Amarillo, much closer probably, and then Flynn had said he'd be two days.

"When's Flynn coming back with Powell and company?"

Tully wiped his mouth and sat back.

"Tomorrow. The canal place was to be ready tomorrow."

Port sat on the hassock and lowered his head. That way Tully couldn't see his expression. Port was cursing himself for the near-slip, and the new pressure. Tomorrow!

"Now, listen, Port. I been square with you, haven't I? Wouldn't you say—"

"Yes. Thank you."

"What I mean is, if you're done now, no more questions or anything, why not call it quits here and now? You know, I been square with you, and now you just forget about meeting me—I won't say a word—and let me go, huh, Port? I'll just blow—"

The question now was what to do with Tully.

"Come on," said Port and went to the front door.

Tully jumped up from the couch. He was even smiling. He ran over to where Port was waiting and meant to open the door for Port. One good turn—

Port clipped him over the ear with the Luger and watched him sag to the floor. He was going to have a long sleep....

Chapter 13

Jane answered the phone almost immediately, and Port could feel the hysterical edge in her voice. She asked if he were all right, if she'd done all right, if it were safe now, and Port said yes each time she asked a question, letting her talk it off for a while. The strain on her, Port knew, would get worse.

"Now, Jane. Listen to me."

"Yes, Dan, yes."

"How is Mrs. Powell?"

"Fine, fine. She's gone to bed, Dan. I bought her some wine and she had some of that and went to bed a little while ago."

"Asleep?"

"Yes. I can hear her. You know—"

"Jane. Listen to me."

"Yes, Dan. What?"

"Is the Jefferson Hotel large enough to have a nurse in attendance?"

"Well, I imagine they can call someone in from the hospital..."

"Then get a nurse or somebody to stay with Mrs. Powell, Jane, and come back here. You understand?"

"To that street?"

"Yes. I'm here. I need your car and I need you to come with me."

She hung up in the middle of saying good-bye, much too excited, and Port smoked three cigarettes while he waited for her in the front hall. Tully was on the floor. Port had taken the man's jacket off and draped it over him. On top of that he had put a blanket.

When Jane had stopped at the curb she ran up to the house. Port held the door open for her and she came into the hall. The first thing she saw was Tully on the floor.

"Oh, my God—"

"He's alive, Jane. Come here. Don't stare..."

"Oh, my God," she said again and Port had to turn her around forcibly. He turned her towards him and put his arms around her back.

"How much longer," she said. "How much more of this, Dan?"

"It's almost over."

"And all this," she said, "and all this because thirty years ago—"

"No. Nothing's that simple. Listen to me, Jane. About now."

"Yes," she said and moved out of his arms. "What happened to him?"

"I hit him back of the ear with the Luger. He needs a hospital."

She could look at the man now and just see what was really there. A man passed out, with a welt on his head. And she had caught the rush behind Port's words, the pressure to finish.

"Open the car door and I'll bring him out."

They committed the man to the Heering Memorial Hospital, private room, and gave instructions not to let him out. Miss Heering herself would come back in the morning, with further instructions. The whole thing, she explained, was a delicate matter.

Then they drove to the airport.

"Tomorrow," said Port, "if he listens to reason, just let him be. He's got to stay there at least two days. If he tries to get out, if he acts too healthy or you're worried in any way about what he might do, call the police. Have him charged with breaking and entering, on 912 South Brandywine. I don't care if it sticks, but he mustn't show up in Galveston between now and day after next."

"It'll be over then?" said Jane.

"I don't know. But by then Robert will be back home."

Port got out of the car, nodded at the girl, but did not try to smile. He just nodded at her and walked to the terminal. It was worse than being strangers...

Port took a room in Galveston and slept eight hours. He got up at ten in the morning, ate breakfast, and thought about the rest of the day. Flynn and his investment wouldn't come to the canal house till after five, because before then the maintenance shed would still be busy. And Flynn would go to the house because he had told Tully the same thing, would expect Tully there with Emmy Powell.

It would help, Port thought, to look at the place.

He still had the old leather jacket from the time he had cased the Powell house and he put that on. He left his tie in the room but took the visored cap with him. Then he went out to rent a pickup truck.

The rental agencies wouldn't do him any good because their trucks were marked with the agency's name. He found what he wanted in a garage. The pickup was olive drab, dusty and dented. There was an old battery in the back and a five gallon drum with a grease pump attachment. Port left all that on the truck and drove out of Galveston.

He didn't get to the canal road which Flynn had described until two, and at first he missed it. The road left the highway where one big tree and some bushes kept it from view, and then it followed the side of the canal. The canal itself was straight but the maintenance road wound back and forth. Port drove into the yard of the maintenance shed without having seen the buildings come up.

There were dump trucks, three grades of gravel in separate bins, and one big dragline, with the long arm lying flat on the ground. Three men were working on a pinched cable.

"Hey!" said one of them when he saw the pickup bounce into the yard.

Port needn't have gone into the yard. The road itself curved around and continued ahead. But the three men were looking now and Port's pickup was not official.

"This is state property, you know," said one of the men, coming towards the pickup.

Port had slowed, and when the man was close enough he thumbed at his load in the back and said, "Garage service. The guy called from the house further in—"

"How come he didn't call here? We got—"

"Beats me," said Port. "You know how it is, though," and he drove off again.

To the left of the yellow dirt road was scrub country and to the right was the canal. Port couldn't see the canal itself because the bank here was as high as his head. The high ground made a straight skyline without anything growing there. Further ahead, squatting on top of that line, sat the first way house.

Port stopped and climbed up on the bank. The house was a brick square with no windows. There was a steel door facing the road, and another one facing the canal. They were both painted green and both were locked.

If the other house looked the same it wouldn't make much of a hide-out. There was no cover of any sort and boats coming down the canal would be about on the same level as the small house.

Port got back into the truck and drove three miles to the next house. It looked exactly like the first, except here the door facing the canal was open.

The inside of the brick square was packed with a dull heat. There was little light just what came in through the door, and the vague light which filtered through the vents up under the roof. The roof was raftered, with angled timbers and horizontal timbers from wall to wall. Some of the beams were boarded over, forming a platform under the roof, and wooden steps led up to it.

For the rest, there was nothing, just an empty square. The heat pressed into Port like a physical threat and the windowless walls made it worse. Robert Heering—or anyone else for that matter—could go mad in there.

Port stayed in the way house, squatting by the crack of the back door. He smoked, blowing the smoke out into the open because inside the house the air didn't move. They would come later and smell the smoke. From where he sat he could see four of his butts floating in the canal. At first they had all stayed together, circling a little and turning brown, but at one point they had suddenly moved. Perhaps a lock was sluicing things around, or the tide had changed or they had launched a ship... Port stayed with it as long as he could, because the time was dragging.

At five o'clock Port moved. First he drove the pickup deep into the brush, where it would be well hidden, Then he closed the door to the canal, opened the one which faced the road. They would come after five. He hoped soon after five.

They didn't come until ten.

They came into the house in the dark and Port, squatting on the wooden platform, could only tell by the sounds what was happening. The front door made a metallic snap, then one pair of footsteps went to the other door and there was a rattle. Both doors were closed now, and for a moment Port just heard breathing.

"Get one of the lights."

If he sees me, I'll shoot him now. I don't care who—

"Got it," said the man almost into Port's face.

Down below, they used several matches before they had the lamp lit and then the three foreshortened men stood around the lamp on the floor, with their shadows huge. They stood like that for a moment as if they didn't know what to do. Powell, Flynn, Robert Heering. They stood like that looking from one to the other, because there was a lot of unfinished business between them.

Then Robert Heering couldn't stand it any longer. He ran one hand over his mouth and cleared his throat. "I want—I think I should have an explanation! Herbert," he said to Powell, "ever since this awful man—"

He never finished the sentence. Flynn hauled out one fat arm and with his open hand smacked the young Heering across one cheek. The force made Heering stumble, and, still off balance, he got an ugly kick from Flynn which threw him against the back door.

The steel made a hollow sound. Robert Heering sunk down there, and stayed, drawn together. It wasn't the pain that cowed him, but the fat man's dislike.

Now they started haggling like animals, Powell with a screech in his voice and Flynn bellowing.

"You push him around, Flynn, and you're pushing around what's mine! I don't go for your interference and I don't go—"

"You'll go to hell, Herbie-boy, mark my word! You don't double-cross me and get to heaven, not on your sweet life!"

"Double-cross? You're the one tied in with that Port! You're the one what's not needed and don't forget that!"

"Needed? I got this rich-boy right here, and I got his mother sewed up in the bargain! You keep forgetting that, Powell. You keep forgetting that Tully's got your old lady—"

This got Powell so mad he made a wild swing at Flynn, who just stepped back. Powell swung once again, maybe just to be swinging, because in the middle of it he started yelling again.

"You think I'm waiting around for that Tully to show up here? You can have the old lady! Take her! Keep her!" and he kept following Flynn, who was edging along the wall.

This was the chance Port had been waiting for. He picked up a hurricane lamp which he'd found on the platform and threw it towards Heering.

It made a frightening crash against the brick wall.

Powell spun around and Flynn moved very fast. He had his gun out of his pocket, ready for Heering, and for the moment both men didn't worry about each other, but just went at the young man by the back door.

It meant that the stairs were behind them.

The double fright of the crash and then the two men coming at him was almost too much for the Robert Heering. He froze with such an intensity that his jaw trembled. Flynn raised his gun high, maybe to rake the young man over the head.

"Hold still!"

The leap had brought Port in back of them, but only Powell stopped dead in his tracks. Flynn was too crazy mad.

He swung around with the gun, so Port shot him.

In the dead quiet they all watched the fat man weave. When he fell, if there was any emotion about it, it was relief. Powell exhaled, Robert Heering sprawled out on the floor, and Flynn let out a thick sigh.

"Stay where you are," said Port, and Powell stopped moving. The gun on the floor wasn't far from his feet. Flynn rolled a little and groaned.

"He's alive?" said Powell.

With the light and the range it had been an easy shot. There would be a big stain under Flynn's fat shoulder now, and if he kept moving like that it would come through his jacket.

"Robert," said Port. "Get up and get that gun. Robert!" The young man got up then and went toward the gun. Then he hesitated, looking at Powell.

"Step back, Powell," said Port.

There was no problem now about picking the gun up, but Robert Heering didn't do it well. He moved slowly and when he straightened Port saw what it was. The man was afraid. He had the gun in his hand now, and he made a gesture with it, towards Port, and said, "Here. Maybe I should look at—at this man's wound?"

"Keep the gun," said Port. "And hold it this way."

"Why? Aren't we leaving?"

"Go up those steps," said Port, "and see if there's some rope up there."

It must have been the noise Robert Heering made as he went up the steps, but Port didn't know a thing until he felt the cold draft. And then when he swung around he stopped midway in the motion, not because Tully was there in the doorway with his gun held out, but because Jane was with him.

Chapter 14

Tully had a bandage around his head and a smile on his face. His arm was around the girl's waist, pinning her tightly to his side.

Port let his Luger drop to the floor, and said, "I give up."

This made Tully happy. He even let go of Jane and gave her a push into the room.

"Shoot, damn you! *Shoot!*" Port yelled.

Tully spun back and forth, but no one else moved, and there was no shot. And before Powell could shout a warning, Joe Flynn's gun fell to the bottom of the stairs, fell down with a smack and lay there on its side.

Tully watched Robert Heering come down the steps and the sight made him laugh. He reached back to close the door and he was still laughing when he looked back at Port.

Again Port said, "I give up," and now he leaned against the wall looking tired.

"Our bread-and-butter family stand right over there," said Tully, pointing to Robert and Jane, "and the Danny Port invasion stay right there leaning against that wall." Then Tully craned his neck and said, "You all right, Joe? Something wrong, Joe?"

Joe Flynn answered with a stream of filth and invective, and very carefully raised himself to a sitting position.

"Jeez!" said Tully when he saw the stain.

"You gonna leave those both guns lie there and rot?" Flynn bellowed.

Powell went to get Flynn's gun and Port's when Flynn said, "Not you, Jackass!"

"Herbie's out, too?" said Tully.

"Him, too."

"Ah..." said Tully and waved Herbert Powell to stand by the wall with the Heerings.

Then he picked up Flynn's gun and thumbed at the cylinder. The cylinder wouldn't spin.

"No wonder," he said and then looked at Robert Heering. "You shouldn't have dropped it," he said. "You should have brung it."

Robert Heering said nothing. He looked down at his hand where his sister was holding it, and Port could see she was holding it very hard. She had one arm through Robert's and was holding his hand in both of hers.

Tully picked up the Luger and Flynn said he'd take it. He held it in his bad hand, on the side where he had been shot, and with the good hand he jackknifed the slide open, to check like Tully had done. A shell sprung out of the chamber and rolled on the floor. It showed Flynn that the gun was good and he put it into his pocket.

"And now?" asked Tully.

"Wait 'til I get up."

They all kept still and waited while Flynn worked himself up off the floor. Another minute passed while he guided his bad arm so the hand would rest in his jacket pocket, and then he came over to Port. While Tully covered, Flynn kicked Port in the shin.

Port did nothing. The gun was too close. He arched with the pain but did nothing else.

"And now!" Flynn turned on Tully and yelled at him. "How'd the dame get in this, and where's Powell's old lady?"

"This is Heering's daughter. She was with him, see," said Tully, "and he got there before I did, just like you figured—"

"I didn't figure he'd get there before you did," said Flynn. "What happened, he break your head?"

"No," said Tully. "He just slugged me out."

"And this dame here? How did she get in?"

Tully explained how Jane got in, how she took Emmy Powell some place and how she came back and drove him to the hospital; that he couldn't get out of there because of instructions, but how the girl came in the morning and then he, Tully, snowed her but good.

"I lie there and I figure the only way I can get out is by her say-so and the only way I can make her budge is by telling her something went wrong with her brother, see? After all—"

"Come on."

"So I tell her the only reason I'm after this Emmy Powell is because we slipped up with Robert and he's no good to us any more."

"Like what?"

"He got shot, see? *Escaping*. She believes this!" and Tully laughed. "And he's dying fast," he finished off.

Flynn just nodded.

"Clever, huh?" Tully prompted.

Flynn said nothing. His arm and his shoulder hurt badly and he was listening to something else.

Then they all heard it, a low thumping noise outside, coming closer.

"Take your gun," Flynn said to Tully. "That must be the boat."

Tully took his gun and Flynn got out the Luger. Then they had Powell open the door, and Port saw the canal water, heaving a little and sparkling.

The boat was an old tug which would attract no attention. It slid into view very slowly, with just the one forward motion, so that it looked for a moment as if the frame of the door was moving and not the boat.

Tully herded them over the plank and then below. Something clanked topside, something scraped, and then the big Diesel started puttering. They sat in the engine room, which was almost entirely taken up by the Diesel, and when it really started roaring the sudden noise of it almost split their heads.

It settled down in awhile and just rumbled. This sound didn't hurt the ears any more, but there was an annoying vibration. Then the Diesel fumes got bad and Tully started looking green.

But he kept sitting there. They all sat, and the thicker the air became with the fumes, the more tension started to show. Powell, who sat on the floor, had a twitch in his face. Robert Heering, his eyes nervous and small, started biting his lip, and Jane took deep gasping breaths.

Port sat very still, holding back an urge to spring up. He had only one thought: how to time it. There was more than one way—a thousand of them kept chasing around in his mind—but only one was the best.

It had to do with the Luger.

"Hey," he said, "How's your stomach feel, Tully? Squirmy?"

"Shut up, you bastard—"

"Rolling over in there, isn't it? Feels like it's gonna crawl right up to the roof of your mouth."

"Shut up, shut... up..."

"What was that, Tully? A cramp? Sometimes it's like a tight gag traveling up and down your gullet, huh? Squeezing—"

"Joe!" Tully yelled up through the skylight. "Joe, for God's sake!"

Then Flynn came down the stairs fast. He saw how it was with Tully, stepped aside to let him pass up the stairs.

This wasn't the time yet. Flynn was holding the Luger and Tully wasn't quite gone. But once he was up there, once he was hanging over the railing, retching himself weak—

Port suddenly laughed. The sound wasn't very loud next to the Diesel but they all saw how Port laughed, and how he got up off the floor, stretching a little.

"Stop moving around!" Flynn yelled,

"Louder," said Port. "The Diesel, you know."

"I said, get back to—"

"I can hear you," said Port, and then he started to walk. He walked towards

Flynn, with no rush in his movements, just walked towards Flynn and enjoying the sight of the fat man.

At first Flynn gaped, and then he went rigid, slowly, until in spite of the fat in his face the jaw muscles showed there.

The Luger had crept up with each step Port took, so that it kept pointing at the same spot all the time. Right at the belly. The muzzle trembled a little, but that wouldn't matter.

"Point blank," Flynn said, hoarse now. "I'll rip you open point blank—"

"Go ahead."

So Flynn, inches away, pulled the trigger.

It went *tick*.

And then again, *tick, tick, tick*.

"You need this," said Port, and took the Luger clip out of his pocket.

Flynn sagged when he saw it, and then he realized what had happened. No wonder Port had been so willing to drop the Luger on the floor—he'd taken the clip out! And Flynn, had ejected the only shell that was left in the gun, the one in the chamber, to make sure that the gun was working right!

"All right!" Port moved fast now. He waved Flynn to the wall and he looked over at Jane, a quick smile. He nodded at Robert to get over to Flynn.

"And Powell," he said, "get in there."

Powell crawled where he was told, in the small space between the Diesel and wall. It would take him minutes to get out of there.

"And Robert, if Flynn doesn't stay put just knock his shoulder. He'll faint." Port smiled reassuringly at the boy, and then bolted up the steep stairs.

He saw Tully first, but Tully was mostly in shadow, and because Port didn't think he'd have to shoot that way Tully got his shot off first.

It missed, in spite of the light on Port, because Tully hadn't taken the time to aim. He threw himself after his shot, disappeared out of Port's view for a second, and when Port was up high enough to see what had happened, he saw Tully down on his belly and halfway into the open skylight.

Tully stayed there, with no intention of moving, because right below, right under his gun, were Joe Flynn, Robert Heering and Jane.

Port remained where he was, halfway out of the stairwell. He could save Jane, or he could save Robert, though he didn't know which it would be. He was glad that he didn't have to choose, though the thought was meaningless now.

"Go on down there where you was, Port, and throw that gun down there ahead of you! I'm counting to three..."

Perhaps he could move like a cat, or fast, like a mouse scooting down a hole.

"I'm watching for that gun, you bastard. And I said now!"

Tully was watching two places! The end of the stairs down below, and the three people by the wall! If something distracted him, if something moved

"One!"

Not Jane, please not Jane—

"*Two*, you bastard!"

Robert Heering looked like he was going to be sick! His face worked, his throat worked, and his eyes were too wide open. And Port saw the sweat on his face, a sick wet shimmer.

"Three!"

Flynn screamed and fell over the girl, and the target—the best target was Robert—was no longer there. The shot rang and bounced hard in the small engine room, and not till Port was down the stairs did he see clearly what was happening.

Heering jumped right at the gun, couldn't have done it better if he had meant to jump right into the muzzle. Now he had Tully's wrist with both hands, and he was yanking and twisting the gun.

Tully lost his balance, and Robert Heering, like a beast, stepped back, waiting the second it took the man to fall; then he yanked him up by the same wrist, and pistoned his free fist into Tully's face. Before Tully collapsed he did it again, grunting with the force of his swing, and then let the man be.

Heering took a deep breath and stepped back. He saw Tully's face, saw that the jaw was broken. But it meant nothing to him, no queasiness in the stomach, no wish to go over it again, to try it differently. He was done.

He took his sister's arm and nodded at Port.

"All right," he said. "Let's go."

Chapter 15

They got to Galveston in the morning and went directly to the Heering Building. The elder Heering was not in and he was not expected. He was at Low Shelf and could not be reached. Robert Heering left word that he was going home and when his father contacted the office he should be given that message. Then he arranged for a company plane.

They had not had any sleep. Port thought that Robert Heering must be tired too, but he didn't act it. He was moving on an impetus which had not been there for years and he didn't want to stop. He talked most of the time while they flew towards Lubbock and sometimes there was true conviction and sometimes he faked it.

"He's through," said the young Heering. "I'm done with him."

"What will you do," asked Jane, "when you see him?"

For a moment Robert Heering did not know what to say. What would he do? Then suddenly he put his hands in his lap, a relaxed gesture, and he smiled. "I'll show him his lie. My mother—to show him it's finished. And then I can leave. I can go anywhere."

Jane and her brother kept talking about that, about leaving the house, about taking trips, and for a while the talk was happy and animated. It ran out after a while. Jane was too tired and Robert's wakefulness became brittle and jumpy.

"You're worried," said Port, "they'll involve you?"

"I was thinking about that," said Robert.

"Don't. The more they talk about you—which they won't—the closer they'll get to a kidnaping charge. They'll talk about the shooting to the cops, blaming it on each other."

"It's a good thing they hate each other's guts." Then Robert dropped that and in a while he kept still altogether.

They picked up Emmy Powell in Lubbock and Robert was polite with the woman, thanked her for coming along, made flat small talk that kept him away from her. After a while nobody talked. It helped that Emmy Powell was a good-natured woman and without need for approval or flattery.

When they reached the large house, the old Heering, of course, was not there.

It relieved Emmy Powell but it tightened up Robert. He called Low Shelf, he called Galveston, and when he finally learned that old Heering had gotten the message and was on his way, his state became bad.

"Let's take a walk," said Port. "You can't sit still anyway, so let's walk."

"Let's do. Big place here. Whole plateau planted with those crazy trees, did you know that, Port?" They walked out and Robert kept talking. "By the way, you know that place down there? Let me show you the place I mean, or did I ask you before if you knew that place down there. End of this path. Very interesting."

Robert Heering was much too brittle. Once the hardness broke—if it should—Port wondered what would be left underneath.

As they walked up to the square house, the male nurse came around the corner, a half-smile on his face.

"His name is Swen," said Port. "He's a kind of male nurse."

"Ah..." said Heering, watching the triangular muscle shape come towards the gate.

"Well, Mr. Port," said Swen, smiling his big smile, holding his hand out. "You up at the house again? Oil business or something?" Then he nodded expectantly at Robert Heering.

But Heering said nothing. His face didn't move.

"You a colleague of Mr. Port's?" said the male nurse. "Uh—my name's Swen," and he held out his hand.

Robert Heering didn't take it. He nodded his head and said, "I'm Mr. Heering's son. However, I'm not your patient. You may stay here, stay by the phone, because I may need you up at the house. If you're needed, I'll call you."

It was so collected, and so cold, the male nurse gave no answer. He nodded, said, "Yes, sir," and went quickly back to the square house.

Robert Heering lasted just that long. Then he started to shake.

"The effort," he said. "The effort—"

"But you did it," said Port. "You did it very well."

"But the effort—not to scream at him like a maniac. It shouldn't be that hard!"

Port took the younger man's arm and they walked back up the path.

"You're asking too much at one time," said Port. "Don't force it."

Then they heard the car.

The young Heering stopped. He listened for the sounds which told him that his father was getting out of the car, walking up the stone steps to the house, going inside. They heard the big door click shut.

"What did you mean," said Port, "when you told that nurse he may be needed up at the house?"

"I don't know. Perhaps I'll kill him—"

"Don't be an idiot!"

Robert Heering gave a small laugh, but it was over quickly. He turned to look at Port and held his arm. "What'll I say?"

"You're leaving, Robert. Tell him you're leaving."

"Leaving. Why didn't I leave? Why come back?"

"Don't you know that the worst is over?" said Port. "You've gone through everything."

"Yes."

"Your mother will help you."

"She?" and it sounded ugly.

"You're here to confront him," said Port. "And that's why she's here."

The thought of that part of the meeting seemed to do Robert good. He took a deep breath and they walked to the house without saying more.

The butler opened the door and said, "Your father wishes you to join him in his workroom."

"And where is my sister and the lady who is with her?"

"In the morning room."

"Does my father know?"

"Miss Heering asked me not to—"

"All right. Thank you."

The butler left but Robert Heering kept standing. He did not know which way to go first.

"See him first," said Port. "I'll go with you."

When they opened the door, the old Heering stood at a window. He did not turn until he heard the door close and then he turned slowly. He waited for his son and Port to cross the large room and then he sounded almost conversational.

"Thank you, Mr. Port. I'll take care of matters from here on." There was silence and the old Heering waited. Then he said, "You may leave, Mr. Port."

"He stays."

The old Heering looked at his son. He gave a slight cough. "Robert," he said. "There will be a great deal of time for us to discuss—"

"Like hell!" said Robert, and when his voice cracked at the end he had to keep talking or choke on it. "There'll be no time! You understand that? I'm leaving. I've come back to tell you I'm through here and I'm leaving!"

"You are through in more ways than—"

"Shut up!"

Not until then did the older Heering show any emotion. A sharp line appeared on his forehead and his eyes became jumpy.

"If you can't muster the manners to—"

"Manners? I can't afford manners," Robert yelled, and the desperation squeezed his throat, his eyes, so that he had to talk with a scream and tears stood in his eyes. "I can't afford them! It's your manners that made you kill me off, your manners that made you kill off my mother, your manners that made you force the lie down my throat, your lies that—"

"Are you out of your mind?" and Heering was roaring. "Are you forgetting just exactly the kind of sick stock that's been crippling you? And my efforts? My patience?"

Heering kept on like that, the witch-burning hate coming out of him, the destructiveness. His son said nothing. He stared at his father, as if mesmerized, and perhaps that's what was happening. Port held his lip in his teeth, not knowing if Robert would come through.

"I had thought," Heering kept on, "that helping you would be possible, that it would be possible here. An environment designed for your illness, here, close to home. But that seems too benign," said Heering. His voice was getting hoarse. "You force me to a repulsive extreme! There are state institutions which—"

He stopped, because Port had turned and was going to the door. It was time, thought Port. Robert wouldn't do it alone....

When Port came back through the hall with Emmy Powell, he could hear the old Heering before they got to the door. And then he heard Robert. He was cursing his father, because that was all that seemed left to him. He was still cursing when he came through the door, and only stopped when he reached Emmy Powell and grabbed her hand.

"You tell him," he said. "You stand in front of him and tell him what I can't say!"

"But I don't know what you..." She let it trail, because Robert was pulling her into the room and she had to walk fast.

She seemed breathless when her son made her stop, but she tried to smile at the old Heering.

What the old Heering saw was hell. A dumpy woman who wished she could smile at him, a young man who wished only the worst—

Then he did not see them any more. He knew that his eyes were open but they could no longer focus on the pest that stood opposite him. He reached for a chair, but the pain darting through his chest stopped him. He crumbled to the floor.

A few days later, in one of the rooms, Robert Heering stood by the window and watched how the needle trees moved. His back was towards Port and his sister but he kept talking with the light monotone which for the last few days had been his manner.

"Did I ever tell you about the meeting I had with Mrs.—with my mother?" He turned and looked at Jane. "Where is she, by the way?"

"Upstairs, packing."

"Oh."

"What about that meeting?" Port asked.

"Oh..." and Robert Heering sounded as if he were trying to remember. Then he said, "Well, it was awkward. Very awkward."

Port got up and walked to the door. He stopped halfway there and turned back.

"I'm sorry it was like that. I thought it might have been important."

"Yes." But then Robert Heering said nothing else.

"Have you decided?" asked Port. "About leaving?"

"There's no decision to be made," he said. "It's out of my hands. Father's heart attack, and what the doctor said about his recovery. I hardly think—"

"Perhaps later," said Jane. "Later, things will be more simple."

She looked after Port when he left and then she looked away. She felt he must be thinking the same thing as she, that the moment of a simple decision had passed.

THE END

Bring Me Another Corpse

by Peter Rabe

Chapter 1

When the road flattened out toward Albany, Daniel Port started to drive faster. For a short while this distracted him, but there was an unpleasant stiffness down his back, and his hands were too tight on the wheel. At moments the fast driving was like running away, though Port didn't know what he was running from.

When the light was almost gone it started to rain. The rain was thin and cold, but it put a veil over the late-fall landscape.

Dan Port slowed a little and lit a cigarette. The rain produced a feeling of shelter inside the car. This feeling grew as it got darker, and when he reached the outskirts of Albany Port felt easy enough to think of stopping and stretching his legs. He slowed for the next gas station and rolled up to the pumps. Then he got out.

The pumps sat in a big orb of light through which the rain showed like driving mist. The rain felt cold and wakeful and Port stood by the hood of the car while the station man let the gas hum into the tank. It was very quiet under the rain. The orb of light over the pumps illuminated a small area only, leaving the highway dark. A few cars passed there, each with two eyes of light and their tires writing signatures on the wet black asphalt.

The next car was just a murmur and a wet sound, because it went by so slowly. For a moment the gas station man thought the car meant to turn into the station, so he looked up. He saw his customer standing by the hood, smoking, hunching a little because of the rain—and then he saw the cigarette spray up in the air. There was a sound like a whipcrack or a sharp rap with a stick on a wooden box, and the man spun suddenly, trying not to fall.

But Port began to bleed almost immediately. He dropped on the cement with a hard slam, which he didn't feel at all.

He woke up carefully. He opened his eyes and saw green, first a green ceiling, then walls in the same light green oil paint, the kind that seems standard in public buildings. And he was lying in bed. He did not feel any pain—which worried him for a moment—until a big ache started in his head. He thought for a while it would spread to the rest of him, but it didn't. The pain stayed in his head, boring there and wavering the way an open fire weaves back and forth. Port felt the thick gauze patch on the top of his head. He wondered how much hair they had shaved away.

"You keep moving around like that," he heard, "and I'll sew your tongue to your lip."

"Now listen, doc. I don't want you to crochet up nothing that don't absolutely need it, on account of my appearance when I go face my friends after—"

"Stop breathing on me. I got to keep a steady hand."

There was a hospital screen next to Port's bed, and on the other side of it Port could see the drunk sitting on a chair and a young intern who was sewing a long gash in the drunk's face with needle and thread.

A big nurse came through the far door, and before she closed it Port saw the sign, *Clinic, Emergency Room*. She said to the intern, "Why—Dr. Lehman! You're almost done!"

"Purl two and an anchor stitch," said the intern, "and that's it." Then he snipped off the thread and sighed at the job he had done.

"But the patient never got his anesthesia," said the nurse. "I just came back to give—"

"He's had it," said the intern and got up. He stretched and lit a cigarette. "He's had it for years."

The intern went to get the cup of coffee he had left on an autoclave, and the nurse put a piece of plaster across the drunk's face. After that the drunk left.

Port sat up in bed slowly. Before the next case came in, or before they decided to start in on him, he wanted to be out of the hospital. His head seemed to have a large drill in it, one that was spinning.

"Well," said the intern. "Feels like hell, huh?" He hung one arm over the screen and stood there, watching as Port moved very carefully.

"Thank you, yes," said Port.

"What size bullet was it?" asked the intern.

The question irritated Port because the other man was offensively casual. The intern knew nothing about the shot and neither did Port, but for Port the sudden attack at the gas station was not something clinical. It was unexplained and therefore bad.

"You mean you didn't take it out yet?" he said, and started to dress. He didn't expect an answer.

"You'd be dead," said the intern. "Just a scratch up there. Juncture of temporal and occiput."

Port grunted and worked slowly into his clothes.

"How long have I been out?"

"Two hours maybe. Feeling dizzy?"

"No."

"That's good."

Port suddenly closed his eyes, to wait till a wave of pain went away.

"If it's just a scratch," he said, "why did I pass out this long?"

"Because you got a sensitive nature," said the intern. "Tense personality." He slurped his coffee in a way that set Port's teeth on edge.

If the intern were shot in the head, he thought, he would probably not only stay conscious, but would be able to probe for the bullet himself.

They didn't talk any more while Port dressed. Port wanted coffee badly but didn't feel sure he could keep it down. For a moment he concentrated on that, but it wasn't the important thing. He was puzzled and worried. He thought about the shot, trying to be very precise about it. First the car, slowly, then the shot, then the car screeching off when he fell. That station had been a good choice for a hit. The whole thing had been very professional, except for the miss. Why? Why any of this? His hands started to shake, and he took a slow breath. Think later. Not yet.

The intern kept standing by the screen, watching Port. He felt the man should actually be in bed. If he had been a personal patient, the intern's own patient in his own practice, he would be in bed. This man was no different from the drunk with the gash in the face, except for his importance. He might even be so important that he was dangerous. Why four policemen? Why the instructions not to insist on the usual paper routine in cases of gunshot? Even the contents of the man's pockets were removed by an officer before the hospital routine could get hold of them. And no one was to question him about anything.

"I'm leaving," said Port.

"Of course." The intern stepped away from the screen and watched Port walk—steadily enough. "There's somebody waiting for you," said the intern.

"And he smokes a cigar."

"No. But he is a detective."

That stood to reason. Port's pockets were empty, meaning they weren't through with him, and there had almost been a murder, meaning— Port stopped by the chair where the drunk had been sitting. There was some dried blood on the floor.

"Do you know this detective?" he asked the waiting intern.

"Never seen him before. We never get any important patients."

"How do you know he's a cop?"

"He doesn't smoke a cigar," said the intern—and he sounded irritable, "but he's got one in his breast pocket."

The intern probably hadn't slept in forty-eight hours, Port thought.

He rubbed his face because his skin felt clammy. The whole thing could just have been a mistake. The police would want to know about the attempt, and they would be glad to find out it was a mix-up of some kind.

The man in the corridor got up from his chair and walked toward Port. He touched his finger to his hat and said, "You all right now?" Friendly enough. He even took out his badge and showed it to Port. "I'm Fields," he said. "We'd like you at Homicide."

"I'm not dead yet," said Port. "You got my things?"

Fields patted his pocket where Port could see a manila envelope, and then he took Port's arm. "Patrol car's right out that door. We can walk slow."

"Thank you," said Port. "Very nice of you." He did feel grateful to the man and for the arm holding him, but the sentiment seemed to make Port feel extra weak. He had to breathe deeply in order to clear his head. If Fields had asked at that moment, "Tell me, Port. Why did you shoot yourself?" then Port might well have answered that he didn't know what had come over him and he was sorry to cause so much trouble.

A uniformed cop stood by the police car and helped Port into the seat. Fields drove and Port sat in the cold blast from the open window. The air whipped a kind of fake life into Port, the kind of wide-awake state which made everything look overly simple. Detective Fields was a kindly man giving Port a lift, the shot at the gas station had been some kind of a bad mistake, the police wanted Port to come over so he could pick up his car. And the thing about the shot could be cleared up right now.

Port looked at Fields behind the wheel, and that glance took all the tired simplicity out of Port's thinking. This was a cop who was driving Port to the station because there was a hell of a lot unexplained.

Nothing had been a mistake. Only the miss.

"You got my cigarettes in that bag?" asked Port. "I need one."

"Can you wait till we get to the station?"

"I guess so," said Port. The thought of smoking had suddenly made him feel ill.

The detective didn't say anything else. He didn't try questioning or anything like that. Saving it for the station, official and serious. Nobody thought that any of this had been a mistake. Port didn't either. There had been those nervous moments, three of them over a short span of time, each one a little bit more disturbing than the last. They had not made him suspect the sudden thing at the gas station, but they had built, one after the other, an ugly feeling of something ominous.

He had spent two weeks at Elks Lake, for the fishing. A day before leaving, the desk clerk at the hotel had said, "Did Mr. Donnaly reach you?"

Port didn't know any Donnaly.

"But he inquired about you, Mr. Port."

"What did you tell him?"

"That you would be here two more days."

"That's what he wanted to know?"

"And what your previous address had been because, he said, he wasn't sure you were the same—"

"But you didn't have one to give him," said Port.

"Of course," said the clerk. "I explained to the gentleman that we don't ordinarily give out that kind of information."

Actually, Port had not thought about this Donnaly much, but he had left a day early. He had suddenly felt that the hotel was an eyesore in the Maine landscape and that the guests talked about fish too much.

He had gone to the coast to watch the beechwood turn color from the early frost. The hotel had been almost empty because it was past the season, and there had been a warm, pleasant coal fire in his room. The maid had come once a day to straighten the room and twice more to shake down the fire.

On the third day, when Port came back from a tramp over the cranberry bogs, his room hadn't looked right. The bed wasn't tucked properly, his suitcase was in the wrong closet, and the flaps on his jacket pockets were pushed in. Port remembered that the maid had pulled them out nicely when she had hung up his clothes.

Nobody had asked for Port. Nobody had even been there to ask for a room.

Port had left the same day, even though he had meant to stay an extra week. He remembered the incident at Elk Lake. That and the search of his room had started to get under his skin. He had headed inland. He hadn't known where he was going and he hadn't known what he was running from. But when he took the turnpike going south he kept watching behind him.

On a long turnpike trip how can you avoid seeing the same car more than once, maybe several times over a long period of time? But Port didn't reason like that any more.

He had wanted a city, any large city—maybe because it would be more crowded, maybe because it would feel like familiar ground. He had not thought about it more definitely, because nothing definite had really happened.

That had changed now, for the worse.

Port thought he wouldn't be at the police station for long. He didn't know enough. Perhaps the police knew his background, which might hold him up some. The point was, thought Port, to get out as quickly as possible, either to lose whomever was following him or to find him. But first, to get rid of the police.

Port drew up his shoulders, feeling cold and tired. He rolled the window shut and, like Detective Fields, said nothing for the rest of the trip.

Chapter 2

But by the time they reached the station the silence had become worrisome to Port. It was as if Fields was keeping things to himself and Port was the only one in the dark. Port tried to shake the feeling, but it didn't work. There was a sergeant behind a counter in Homicide who nodded at Fields but hardly glanced at Port. Port waited for Fields to say something but nothing was said. They just stood by the counter in silence, and Fields started nibbling on one of his cigars. Perhaps they were waiting for him to say something. Port put his hands on the counter and said, "I'm Daniel Port. I'm here to report a gun shot."

"We know," said the sergeant. He didn't look up at Port but looked at a clock on the wall. Then he said to Fields, "Should be any minute now."

Fields just grunted.

"Listen," said Port. "Lemme have one of my cigarettes."

"Oh." Fields pulled the brown envelope out of his pocket and smiled at Port as if he had forgotten he was still there. He waved for the sergeant to come over and then tore the envelope open. Everything was there: driver's license, car registry, an insurance receipt, paper money, coins, a pencil stub, matchbook, the cigarettes.

"Sign this receipt, Mr. Port."

After Port had lit a cigarette he signed the paper the sergeant had put on the counter and then took his things.

A door opened in the back of the room and a man in a blue uniform with gold trappings came through. Nothing less than a captain, thought Port, and he worried about the importance of it.

"We're ready," said the captain to Fields.

The room in back looked impressive. There was a good, polished table, leather chairs, and a glass cabinet full of fat law books. There were a great number of people in the room, men in uniform and in mufti, and none of them looked at Port or said anything of much importance. They said things like, "You want these notes?" "Just in case," "See you for coffee," and "Glad to have met you." Then everyone left except three. There was Fields, there was a thin man with glasses, and there was the third man, who made no impression on Port except that he sat with his arms wound into each other and that his face was expressionless.

The thin man came toward Port, shook hands and smiled nicely. His smile moved his glasses down his nose, and he pushed them back up with a practiced gesture, almost like a tic.

"Mr. Port, I'm glad you are better. My name's Lubinski." Then he waved Port into a chair.

The silent man was not introduced and kept sitting there as before.

"Maybe you'd like some coffee?" asked Lubinski.

"Very much."

Fields went to the door, opened it, and said he wanted three coffees. Then he came back. Everyone sat except Fields, and there was another silence. Lubinski had a folder in front of him which he opened. When he looked down his glasses slipped and he pushed them up as before. One lens glinted.

"You're dropping your ashes on the floor," said Fields.

The tone of voice made Port look up. Fields wasn't friendly any more. He was still standing, he had the cigar in his mouth and—as if playing the part to the hilt—his hat was still on and pushed back on his skull.

"That's all right," said Lubinski. He smiled and moved a glass ashtray toward Port. Then he pulled something out of the folder and held it for Port to see. "Not many of these around," he said, "if any." He smiled and stabbed his finger at the bridge of his glasses.

It was an 8x10 photo, high gloss, obviously an enlargement. It showed Port down to the waist, facing the camera, with a group of people—some of them sliced by the print—not one of whom Port cared to remember.

"Here's the coffee," said the sergeant from the door.

Fields went to take the tray from him and brought it back. There were three mugs of coffee, one for Lubinski, one for Fields, one for Port. The silent man just sat as before.

"That was some time ago," said Port, nodding at the photo.

They knew who he was or had been, and who he had been seemed the important thing. The picture had been taken about four years earlier, and Stoker was shown standing next to Port. It had been an outdoor shot, taken from some distance, apparently, and the occasion had been a political rally. The picture-taking had been an oversight because neither Stoker, who was dead now, nor Port had favored that kind of publicity.

"Why don't you drink your coffee?" said Fields.

Same voice as before, with an unfriendly edge. The coffee had cream in it, which Port didn't like, and it was much too hot.

"Mr. Port," said Lubinski, "drinks his coffee lukewarm." Then he smiled at Port as if for approval.

Port frowned because Lubinski was right. Lubinski seemed to know a hell of a lot, even the unimportant things.

"Well," said Lubinski, "let us begin." He sighed and added, "I'm from the

F.B.I. Out of Washington."

Not even local, thought Port. It no longer looked as if he'd get out very soon.

"May I ask—" Port started, when Fields interrupted him.

"Why don't you wait, huh?" said Fields.

"Am I being detained?"

"We can arrange that, Port. We can make any arrangement—"

"Please, just a moment," and Lubinski held up a hand, as if apologizing. He smiled at Port and sounded warm. "Of course you're not being detained, Mr. Port. Nothing of the sort." When Port didn't answer he looked down at his folder again and started to hum.

Fields stood next to Port's chair now and folded his arms. Port could hear him breathe with a soft rattle of phlegm. The silent man stayed silent.

This was the pattern, and old as it was it had been working on Port. The heckler, that was Fields, the nice one, Lubinski, and number three was silent doom. The more Fields would needle, the sweeter Lubinski got, and with the dark threat of doom at the table it wouldn't take long for the victim to talk—and to talk to Lubinski in this case, who was the only friend left.

"You can break up your combo," said Port, "and tell me what you want."

"We know your background," Lubinski said. He coughed and kept looking down at his folder. Then he recited, "You were the wonder-boy of the Stoker machine. You did every illegal thing in a legal manner, tightroping yourself and Stoker's organization from vote-juggling and appropriation-fixing to such niceties as trade extortions, gambling, and who knows what else to make undeclared income. You ran the organization up to a fine peak and then knocked it over."

"I severed relations," said Port. It sounded formal and funny.

"Yes. You did that. You must have figured you'd made enough."

"I had my belly full," said Port, and his meaning was serious.

Lubinski looked up and sighed. He pushed at the open folder flap and watched it close. It wafted shut very gently.

"We have nothing on you since you left Stoker."

"You have nothing on me, period," said Port.

"True, Mr. Port." The way he said this showed that Lubinski was obviously not finished.

"Then why am I here?"

"Because you were shot at this evening."

Port leaned on one arm and bent over to blow at the coffee in front of him. There was no other sound in the room. Port kept waiting.

"We know something else about you," Lubinski said. "We know why nobody tried gunning you down before."

Port took a cigarette out and held it in his teeth. "Because I'm a gentle man," he said.

"Look—" Lubinski leaned forward a little. He had the build of a nervous man, long boned and spare, and the methodical way in which he had handled things up to this point was beginning to wear on him. "You weren't so gentle when you broke loose from that syndicate outfit, Mr. Port, what with the exposures you peppered into the organization at the time you left. We are grateful, of course, for the assistance you—"

"That was self defense," said Port.

"Please. Let me make my point. The point is, you are still alive. You are alive because you've let it be known that your death would get them more of the same. Much more of the same."

"Yes," said Port. "I have that kind of a testament."

"And you've furnished a copy of it," said Lubinski, "to the big ones who'll get hurt the most." Lubinski started to wave his hands. "They know exactly why you should stay alive. They know exactly how much better off they are as long as you stay alive!" He took a deep breath but barely finished it. "Can you explain to me, Mr. Port, why, in view of all this, somebody set you up for a hit tonight?"

Port looked at Lubinski, then at Fields, then at the silent one. They said nothing and showed nothing, and Port didn't know the answer. Lubinski had built up to his point and had made it big. He needn't have done it that way. The point was big all by itself.

"Suddenly," said Lubinski, sounding quiet now, "you are in danger."

The point: it made no sense to kill Daniel Port. *Why* then?

Port took the cigarette out of his mouth, looked at it. He still hadn't lit it. He lit the cigarette with forced slowness, hoping that something would come to him by the time he was done. He exhaled and said, "I don't know why it happened."

He looked at Lubinski and could tell that the other man believed him. But then Lubinski just nodded. It struck Port like the blank stare of a schoolmaster who wants to encourage the dumb student to go on but doesn't wish to say that the dumb student is doing fine. Port felt suddenly irritated.

"How do you know it wasn't one of those new-type delinquents pulling off a dare? Maybe the gun was a zip-gun and he was really aiming at the lightbulb ten feet over my head?"

"No," said Lubinski. "We know it wasn't."

"Huh?" Port was beginning to feel that this whole session was at least as weird as the attempt on his life.

"I said, we know it wasn't. We even know who shot at you."

"*What?*"

"Bankroft. Do you know Bankroft?"

"Who in hell is Bankroft?"

"Bankroft, alias Bink the Bouncer. Usual thing: hot number in the Golden Gloves—long time ago, of course, fade-out into wrestling, then bodyguard for some minor operator, next bouncer in a few sleazy clubs. And," said Lubinski, "an occasional job of enforcing. At the present, he does that work exclusively."

"I never heard of him."

"Let me finish." Lubinski got up and walked back and forth in the room. He kept stretching his back while he walked. "You get the picture that this Bink is by no means the best kind of professional. He missed you."

Lubinski was saying something else but Port didn't hear it. He had closed his eyes and was leaning back in his chair, hoping with that calm gesture to get something like clarity into his head. He felt as if Lubinski was talking up a bizarre kind of joke—knowing who had done the shooting, quizzing Port instead of the killer, giving some cheap punk's biography. He felt he might go out of his mind with his headache and the incomprehensible tack Lubinski was taking. He felt his mind beginning to go blank, something he mistook for a feeling of calm, and that's when he started to talk. It wasn't calm, though, but pure anger.

"You know the gun that did it? How come you know? How come I get hit and the next minute you show up, with an ambulance probably, with the whole force here oiled to give me a reception, with that folder all ready there and full of old history? How come all this mixed-up jazz in the middle of the night in the Empire State capitol, a town I myself didn't know I was going to pass till this morning? Am I going off my nut or are you playing some private game and I shouldn't know the rules?"

He was tapped on his shoulder at that point, lightly but insistently, and Fields leaned down and said, "Port. Shut up a minute, Port."

"All right!" Port knocked the finger out of the way so he wouldn't have to feel that poke any more. He half hoped that Fields would try tapping again, try anything of the sort that would deserve a hard swing square in the middle of his teeth, but nothing like that happened. Fields wasn't playing the vinegar part in the inquisition trio any longer but was nice again, the way he had been in the car, looking a little concerned. That sobered Port. He kneaded his hands together and leaned his arms on the table. Then he said, "Go on," and nodded at Lubinski. "But clear. Something I can follow."

"Ask me."

"How come you were here when I came to Albany?"

"Because we've been following you."

"How come you know about Bink or whatever?"

"We learned he was being hired," Lubinski said.

"By whom?"

"We don't know the man, we just know the group."

"A syndicate group?"

"That's what's puzzling us."

"Puzzling *you*?"

"Yes. And since we have a common—"

"Where's that son of a bitch now?"

"Who?"

"That Bink!"

"On his way to New York. Highway Nine."

"You're *letting* him?"

"He can't make a move without our knowing it."

"Like blowing my head off a few hours ago? You knew all about that before it happened?"

Lubinski came back to the table, sat down, and folded his arms.

"Bankroft's attempt is part of a plan. The group that hired him sits in Cleveland, Ohio. What we picked up is this: there's a shift in authority going on in the Middle West, line of command kind of thing in the big organization. We don't know the details, only that your name is mentioned, your name and that you might be important, and then Bankroft is hired.

"Then Bankroft does research—where is Port, what does he look like, what is he doing, what are his habits. You realize what he was up against, finding you. There are no photos of you; the men you used to work with are dead, in jail, or on the West Coast; and you haven't been mixing with your former—uh—associates for over four years. So, Bankroft, digging around, comes to our attention." Lubinski took a deep breath. "He's been under surveillance since Cleveland. That's how we found you."

"And you're telling me all this," Port said, "in line with protecting a citizen, is that it?"

Lubinski tried laughing but gave it up. "Not entirely, Mr. Port," he said, "We would like your help."

Port put his hands over his face and looked very tired. He moved his head up and down, rubbing his palms over it. He could have been tired—or, by the deliberateness of his motion, he could have been on the point of blowing up. He stopped moving and looked at Lubinski.

"Are you serious?" he asked.

"Look at it this way, Mr. Port, in this simple way. There's a shake-up in the

Middle West. That's primarily our interest. You, without having known it yourself, have been made a part of whatever goes on there. The attempt on your life makes that clear, and that's *your* interest now. Don't you see, that we've got a common interest here?"

All Port said was, "Go ahead, Mr. Lubinski."

"Uh—yes. The point is, Mr. Port, as I said, we can use you."

Lubinski was about to say more, to explain more fully, when Port blew up. He smacked his hands down on the table, and his voice would have been louder if it hadn't hurt his own head so much. "Use me like you did? Setting me up for a hit so you can use the crime for a wedge in some very fancy and legal way?" He got up and kicked his chair back behind him. "To hell with you!" he said, and he walked out of the room.

They argued with him for a while longer, all the way through the outer office, down the corridor, through the front hall to the steps leading down to the street, but it didn't do any good. Port wasn't thinking about it any more, and perhaps—with the pain and the tiredness—he wasn't thinking at all. He paid no attention to anything they were saying but got a taxi and asked for a hotel, any hotel.

He started to think about the affair while he was riding, not very much but enough to remember Lubinski's point about having a common purpose in all this. It struck Port that his stake in the vague plot they had explained was really the greatest. The FBI was doing a job which was run-of-the-mill business to them. He, Port, was involved in the same thing—but for his life.

Then he dropped the thought and got off at the hotel. They gave him a room for the night, and a bellhop took Port upstairs. He felt so dull now he even forgot to tip the boy. And he had forgotten to ask the desk to send somebody to pick up his car at the gas station on the outskirts of town.

Port took the elevator back down to the lobby, found the bellhop, gave him a tip and apologized, and asked the desk to pick up his car. Then he went back to his room.

His door wasn't locked. Port was sure he had locked it when he had left. He stood back and let the door swing open slowly. From where he stood he could see part of the room and the open door to the bathroom. Through this door Port saw a long metal box by the sink, like a plumber's tool box, and a man crouching by the sink.

Lubinski had said that Bink was on his way to New York and the man by the sink was wearing overalls—but Port left the room anyway. He left the door open the way it had been and ran down the long, softly carpeted corridor. Port went down the steps, hoping they would not lead to the lobby. But he did end up there. He stood by the door for a moment, feeling the sweat under his shirt.

"Mr. Port?"

He turned his head too fast, causing a wash of pain to start swirling around inside his skull.

Lubinski was there, and the silent partner.

"He's a real plumber, upstairs," said Lubinski.

Port just breathed hard and then he cursed, which was like relaxing.

"Get some sleep," said Lubinski. "We have a man watching you."

Port felt weak and a little bit dizzy.

"Will you come down and talk with me in the morning?" Lubinski asked.

Port felt that Lubinski was sweet and considerate. He said, "Yes. I'll be over," and then he allowed Lubinski to take him back to his room.

Chapter 3

Lubinski was there along with the quiet man with the sullen face and Dan Port—there were no local police this time. The three men met in Port's hotel room. The room looked anonymous and the window looked out on a gray wall with smooth plaster and, above that, the gray sky. The grayness outside produced a milky, even light in the hotel room, leaving nothing to focus on except Lubinski.

"We're not thinking of you as a walking target, Mr. Port. I'm sorry I gave that impression last night."

"Then why do you want me?"

"Because you're acquainted with the type of thing you'll be dealing with—and, frankly, because you have a personal stake in succeeding."

"For that, Mr. Lubinski, I don't need you."

"You don't think so?" Lubinski smiled. "Last night, who saved you from a panic?"

Port nodded. "Yuh," he said. "The FBI."

"We did, you know. It was just a little example of a little service, but you know that we can do more."

And then the silent man talked for the first time. "You might even learn," he said without moving, "that there's some satisfaction in working on the side of the law."

Port looked at the man and didn't like him. He didn't like the righteous tone. The man might use the law to excuse his worst faults.

"The point I was trying to make, Port—" and Lubinski looked a little bit worried— "the real point..."

"I know. It makes sense," said Port. He walked to the window and stared at the smooth wall opposite. It was so smooth that no grain of any kind showed, but Port wasn't trying to see anything there. He could go it alone, or he could do it with the knowledge and help of a big organization. He didn't like either alternative because it would be too much like going back, like starting all over in the kind of a life about which he no longer had any illusions—the disregard for right and wrong, the fast scramble for a buck and a free hand no matter who got broken in two, the loud thrills of grabbing a kick with a bought female, a bought bottle, anything paid for in advance. All those surface satisfactions that used to make life spin around with a speed that made you think, Sure now—you're going someplace.

He turned away from the window, went to the bed, and sat down.

"I'll try it your way," he said to Lubinski, "and I hope it's the fast way out."

Lubinski smiled at Port. The smile lasted a second, and then Lubinski opened his briefcase and drew out the usual folder.

"It can be fast," he said. "A lot of it is already set up."

"Where do I fit?"

"You go to Cleveland," said Lubinski, "and you hire out as your own killer."

For a moment Port's mouth stayed open. He felt the impulse to laugh. The impulse had a frantic edge, which had nothing to do with laughter but brought back the real feeling that went with all this—that somewhere somebody was sitting at a desk, somebody who didn't know Port at all except as a gimmick in a big plan which was set up and run like a machine, and Port would get killed for it.

"Okay, you've got Bankroft tagged," he said. "Can't you ask him who hired him?"

"We don't think he'd know the head man, the man who really wants to kill you."

"And the one who'd know what the Middle West shakeup stacks up to?"

"Same one, we think." Lubinski opened his folder. "So Bankroft goes free. We need him that way. When he gets to New York we've got a trail laid out for him that'll take him out of the country. You, Daniel Port, took a powder to France. That's what Bankroft finds out in New York."

"And when he's out of the way?"

"We'll have him held in France, which is beside the point. The point is, he reports back to Cleveland that he's looking for you in France. Now. You ever hear of Don Paducci?"

"Paducci—" Port tried to remember. "Paducci—a long time ago. I'm not sure I remember—"

"Not too long ago, but I don't think you knew him. Professionally, your work had no call for him."

"He's a gun," said Port. "I remember. High-priced gun."

"And you'll be him."

"*What?* First of all, Bankroft and Paducci were acquainted. Second, Paducci went to South America over eight years ago. And he's dead now."

"You look interested, Mr. Port," said the quiet one. It seemed that he only opened his mouth to say the wrong things.

Port looked at him and said, "What's your name?"

"James O'Day. FBI."

"Takes all kinds," said Port and ignored him.

"Uh—to go on." Lubinski got up and started walking around. "You'll be Don Paducci in Cleveland. We'll discuss the details, but the point is that you know Dan Port."

"It's a relief," said Port, "that at least some of this is true." But nobody thought that was funny. Then Port said, "Somebody might recognize me—"

"Yes. But the risk—"

"—or know that I'm not Paducci."

"What makes it less of a risk," said Lubinski, "is that both you and Paducci have been gone for a while and have never been in the limelight. In addition, we got a fair list of people who knew either of you."

"Only fair?"

"We'll check it out with you—your part, at any rate—and we'll see to it that nobody who knew you or Paducci gets a close look. Somebody like that shows on the scene, we'll take care of it."

"Jeesis Christ," said Port.

O'Day stretched himself in his chair. "In an emergency, and for the best interest, Mr. Port, we can arrest anybody."

And O'Day, thought Port, would enjoy that assignment.

Lubinski got up and closed his briefcase. "Well, Mr. Port?"

"This is big," Port said.

"This is big. Yes."

Then Port nodded, and they all got up. The only other thing they did was to arrange for the briefing sessions. Then the two agents left. Port stood at the window again and looked at nothing. In a short while now, the rat race would be with him again, and he'd be back in the rottenness he had thought he was done with. In more ways than one, he felt, he would go out as his own assassin.

In Cleveland, that part of fall had started when it looks like it will rain but doesn't. Port looked out from the door of the hotel and thought it fit—the coldness, the rushing just to be fast, and nobody looking at anyone else. The whole thing was, in miniature, the way Port remembered his life in the past and the way he pictured what he would do now. But maybe it wouldn't last long.

Then he went to Central Avenue. Some of the lights were going on, but for Port's business it was still too early. He walked down the street and smoked. Grocery stores, barbershops, junkyards, barbecue joints, wine bars, and night clubs. Only the night clubs looked different. They didn't look makeshift, and they didn't look drab.

Club Sassafras had a long, black glass front, and all the windows in the facade—picture windows with curtains and table lamps—were fake. Port looked at the billboards in the windows—a sweaty face killing itself with a trumpet, a dramatic grin wearing a tuxedo, a lot of white flesh with a veil down the crotch and hands holding two breasts.

Port stopped on the other side of the street, and because he was early he leaned against a brick wall and smoked. Then he started to whistle. He had a low, heatless whistle that slid around with no tune in mind. It gave an impression of thoughtlessness, or of thoughts wandering. But he was thinking of only one thing—that he should now start acting the part of Don Paducci or of someone like him at least, with the cold greed, the quick smartness, the hard shell. He wondered whether he had been a lot like that, and the thought made him angry. He flipped his cigarette into the street and pushed away from the wall. When the time came, when he walked into that club and from then on in, he wouldn't think of Paducci or of anyone else. He wouldn't need to. All he needed was to feel the climate he was going to breathe and know that somebody in it was hatching his murder. That was enough. It was better than trying to masquerade. It would make his face quiet and his walk smooth, and to an outsider it would mean nothing.

Chapter 4

He walked into the Sassafras at eleven o'clock. The dark room was crowded and thick with blue smoke. The round bar was in the middle and a combo of three was beating a tune to death so hard that nothing but the rhythm remained.

Port found a two-man table which was big enough for an ashtray and two glasses. As jumbled and dark as it was he attracted a lot of attention right away. First the waiter in black—Port ordered rye and water. Then a waitress in white who recommended the Southern fried chicken. Port said no to that. Next a young girl who was wearing mostly her body. She had blonde hair in a high bun, a penciled face which kept her own very well hidden, and a corset which pinched her waist, squeezing the breasts up and the hips out. She legged her way up to the table and put her camera down.

"Would you care for a photograph?"

Port smiled up at her and shook his head. He kept unconsciously shaking his head because of her looks, and when she noticed this she started to laugh.

"I should have taken that picture right then and there," she said. "You know what you looked like?"

"No."

"I can't tell you." She seemed good natured about it, or perhaps bored. Then she said, "Mind if I sit down a second?" and sat down before Port could say yes.

She put the camera on the table, crossed one leg over the other and took off a spike-heeled shoe.

"Your feet are killing you," said Port.

She put on the same straight face he had and said, "So is your humor," but then she laughed.

They suddenly got along very well. They hadn't said anything else, and nothing visible had happened between them, but they smiled at each other across the small table and knew that it wasn't a customer-client thing any more. It was so plain to them that the girl had to say something.

"I like people fast," she said.

Port looked down at his glass and spun the ice cube around. "If you're looking for a rabbit..."

"You didn't get it. I mean, I'm a fast liker or disliker. It happens bang, just like that—" and she made a dangerous swipe with her spiked shoe.

"And if it happens slow?"

"Then something's no good. If I feel something fast enough, then it means I got through to you."

"You sound dangerous," said Port. "And I wish you'd put that shoe away."

She put the shoe back on and sighed. "You have the time?"

"Eleven-twenty."

"Gad. Over two hours yet. Could I?" and she reached for his glass.

Port nodded and turned to look for the waiter.

"Don't buy me a drink," she said. "It won't get you anywhere and I just want the ice cube." She fished it out of the glass with the mixing stick and put the lump into her mouth.

"You look like a monkey," said Port, "or a toothache."

She couldn't smile without losing the ice, so she cracked it between her teeth, making it smaller. The sound went through Port like a rake.

"Sensitive, aren't you?" she said.

"You did that very well. Sort of like a wolf cracking a bone."

"Better than you looking like one. I'd be bored."

Port grinned at her and put his arms on the table. He leaned closer and looked at her, but before he could say anything she got ahead of him.

"And now," she said, "you're going to ask what a girl like me is doing in a place like this."

"I know why," said Port. He wished she hadn't taken that cold, clever tone. "It's a job. Right?"

"Right."

"Is it a good job?"

"Sure. I mostly take pictures. I don't have to sleep with anyone I don't like, except maybe once or twice during a month."

"It struck me," said Port, "that you wouldn't sleep with anyone you didn't like."

"Job security, that's all. And I'm on the way up."

"Don't sound so damn callous," said Port.

"Why not?" she said. "It's good for survival."

"You know," said Port, "I'd like to see you sometime when you're not struggling for survival."

"Christ," she said, "when would that ever be?" and then she got up. He watched her walk away between the tables. She was a tough little cookie, but with a nice taste, and if she weren't tough—just as she had said—how soon would she be eaten up?

He had passed half an hour since coming in. He could have asked the girl with the camera about a number of things, or he could have cut short talking to her and attended to business instead, but he was glad he hadn't done either. He wouldn't have wanted to miss the way she had looked—and he had to laugh to himself over the way she had managed that ice cube. Like an icebreaker. She'd been a lot like an icebreaker, in a number of ways.

He lost sight of her around the bend of the bar, and suddenly Port felt ill-tempered. The waitress in white came back but left when she saw Port's face. The waiter in black returned, but Port didn't want a refill. "The manager," said Port. "Bring him."

"The manager, sir? If you have any questions about the drink—"

"I got no questions. Just bring him."

The waiter went toward the door where a handsome, wide-shouldered Negro was smiling at some customers. The Negro wore a plaid tuxedo with big checks, but they didn't look big on him. They looked just about right.

He came over and put both hands on the table. They about covered the top. He smiled down at Port and said, "You were asking for me?"

"I wasn't asking for you. I was asking for the manager."

"I don't wish to argue with you, sir, but I'm the manager. Or were you thinking of somebody else?"

"Molnar. I'm thinking of him."

"Ah. You see? He isn't the manager. He's the owner."

"You know where he is?"

"Why?" said the Negro. He was smiling all the time and being polite, and Port was sure that the man wasn't angry. He was just like glass that nothing could penetrate. This was his job.

"I'll tell him," said Port. "It's that important."

"Is there a complaint?" said the Negro, and Port noticed that the smile went across the room. And back there, behind Port, would be the bouncer.

"The sooner you go," said Port, "the less complaint. Tell Molnar Paducci is here. Me. Don Paducci."

Maybe the Negro didn't know who Paducci was, but from the way Port had said it perhaps Molnar did. And another reason why he went without arguing more—he might have had a prejudice that all Italians were hoods, which made Paducci important.

He smiled his way across the room and disappeared through an arch with drapes.

Molnar, thought Port, must be in. Molnar was a slow start for Port's business because his only established importance was the fact that Bink the Bouncer, or Bankroft, had worked at the Sassafras between other assignments. Lubinski had told Port to start that way, because Port, as Paducci, wouldn't be likely to know about anyone else in the gang.

Then the Negro came back. Port saw him come through the drapes, put on his smile and weave past the tables. Port also saw that two waiters, built like matching meatballs, stood around not far away.

"Mister Molnar," said the Negro, "doesn't know you."

"I don't know him either." Then Port leaned closer. "You know Bink?"

"Bink? He isn't here."

"I know. Tell Molnar I got a message from Bink."

The Negro left as before and, passing through the drapes to the corridor, walked into Molnar's office.

"Any trouble?" said Molnar.

"No. But he's still here."

Molnar gave the Negro a brief look to tell him that was his department. He heaved himself up behind his desk, and when he looked up he frowned. Molnar had a thick head and thick gray hair. He looked short-tempered and rugged. He was surrounded by a cloud of perfume, but he looked rugged just the same.

"What in hell you standing around?" he yelled at the Negro. "Get rid of him. I don't talk to every grifter comes here and wants—"

"He's got a message from Bink."

"Bink," said Molnar. He didn't look any less short-tempered but he seemed to be thinking. "What message?"

"I didn't ask. I'm sure he wouldn't tell me, when it comes to that."

Molnar gave the Negro a look which showed his dislike for the man. He didn't like his good looks, his fine figure, the manners he had. Molnar had the sudden wish that the Negro would wear perfume because then there wouldn't be any question about it—the bastard would be a fairy and he, Molnar, would can him on the spot. The bastard, true, brought in a lot of the trade, but if he were a fairy out he'd go. Molnar turned away and tried to think of the other annoyance. Paducci, he mumbled to himself, Paducci...

"I think I remember Paducci," said the Negro. Molnar turned around. "I mean, I've heard Bink mention the name."

"Only names Bink ever mentions is somebody important. This guy out there looks important?"

"I don't know," said the Negro. "Depends."

"Depends on what, damnit?"

"Just depends. Depends on who introduced him, how he acts, that kind of thing. Or the clothes. I couldn't tell how good his suit was." And he smiled at Molnar. The Negro smiled because that was exactly the kind of shallow thing Molnar would go by and Molnar, knowing this would be annoyed that they both had had the same thought.

Molnar said, "You stupid sonofabitch," and went to the phone. The Negro only smiled.

When Molnar got an answer he didn't mention any name but said, "Is he in? This is Molnar." When he got his man he said, "Listen. A guy walks in here and says Bink sent him. Message from Bink."

"What's the—"

"Listen. He says his name is Paducci. You know any Paducci?"

After a little silence, "I know of him. He's a gun."

"Like Bink?"

"No. More expensive. What does he want from you?"

"Me? How do I know what he wants from me?"

"I thought you said—"

"I haven't seen him. Leonard here—" Molnar gave the Negro a disgusted look—"he comes in and says there's this guy—"

"You said that. Molnar, you sure about what you're saying?"

"Huh?"

"Paducci is supposed to be in Brazil or some place."

"Brazil? I'll throw him out! I can't have—"

"Shut up, Molnar!" There was a silence of thinking. Then, "Bink knows him. One of the big shots he brags about."

"I should talk to him?"

"You better, if he's got a message from Bink. You know what Bink's doing."

"I know what he's supposed to be doing," said Molnar. "So find out what's what. And check if he's Paducci for sure."

"I never seen the guy! How in hell am I—"

"I think Canning knows him."

"He's in jail, for chrissakes."

"I know." And then the voice explained to Molnar how they could have Canning, who was in jail, check on the Paducci in Molnar's club.

Molnar banged down the phone and said, "Leonard!"

"Yes, sir," said the Negro because he knew it pleased Molnar, and he enjoyed making Molnar react as expected.

"Uh—good job, Leonard. Keep it up. Go out there and keep Paducci company for ten minutes, and on your way send Gracie in here."

"If you want," said the Negro, because he knew the tone would annoy Molnar. He smiled to himself as he left. Port saw the Negro come back and killed his cigarette in the tray. Molnar would see him. The Negro had stayed away long enough.

"Mr. Paducci?" the man said when he came back to the table. Port noticed the friendlier tone. "My name's Leonard. I've just come from Mr. Molnar's office."

"He'll see me?"

"He'll see you."

"Good." Port started to get up.

"One moment." Leonard put out a big hand, doing it casually, but holding the hand so that Port couldn't get up any further without pushing his face into it. "I just want to greet a customer over there. You understand," and the Negro walked away to another table.

Port sat down again. The customer, Port saw, wasn't new in the club. He hadn't just come, and Leonard had stopped at that table before. Then Port saw the half-dressed girl with the camera. She came out of the back exit where the drape was hanging and wound her way past the tables. She didn't look around to promote a customer until she was fairly close to Port's table. She talked to somebody at a nearby table, smiled, laughed, held up the camera. When the flash went off the lens was looking at Port.

"I'm sorry I took so long," Leonard was saying. "You understand—" But Port was already getting up. He said, "Yuh, I understand," and walked toward the back, Leonard following. The camera girl was going the same way.

In the corridor behind the drape Molnar's door was first, with a few others toward the back. Way in back was the darkroom with a red bulb over the door. The girl headed toward the darkroom, made a high-heeled click with each step, and her good-looking rear swiveled this way and that with the rhythm.

"This is the door," said Leonard, and Port said, "That's good. Open it." But while Leonard opened the door Port walked past, after the girl.

Leonard didn't catch the maneuver right away, not expecting it. But before he could say anything, Port was quite far down the corridor. Port heard the man call after him, and then he heard the long steps, but he had the girl's arm now, and he grinned at her. "I couldn't wait any longer—"

"My!" she said. "My—"

"Please—" Port was suddenly serious—"please open the door."

She raised her eyebrows at Port and said, "And what if I don't?"

Port didn't answer her, but the girl had the feeling she shouldn't have asked. Leonard was very close now, and Port looked unfriendly. She unlocked the door. When they were halfway into the darkroom Leonard was behind them, grabbing the door handle.

"Mr. Molnar—" he began, but he didn't get any further.

"Let go of the door, Leonard. The light's getting into the dark room," said Port, and he put his arm around the girl's waist.

Leonard's duty was to bring Port to Molnar. What Port did on the way didn't worry him too much, and getting to the office late was all right too, because Molnar would be irritated. Leonard smiled and closed the door with a small bow.

The room was a windowless cubicle with black walls. Its only light, a red bulb, turned their lips dark and gave their skin a reddish tan. They stood very close.

"You can let go now," she said.

"No reason."

"You look like a ghoul."

"And I've never had a girl with orange hair."

But the banter didn't hold up, didn't please them. The girl knew why Port was here, and Port knew that the time and the place were against him.

But they didn't let go. He held her and she held him, and for a moment they stood very still.

"You know what I told you—" She talked low.

"Yes. A fast liker—"

"I can't help it."

"Come here—"

The corset was hard between them, like a husk on a soft fruit. Her bare thighs felt warm against Port. Suddenly she pushed him away.

Port saw the painted face again and the calculated outfit. The girl sounded irritated now. She sounded callous as hell.

"I don't like it standing up," she said.

"Yuh," said Port. "And in a darkroom yet." He smoothed down his jacket and looked at the camera. And then he thought of the corridor outside with the big Negro waiting like a tolerant chaperon, maybe giving them a few moments before breaking down the door and making everything else break in on Port again—such as a present matter of life and death. He hadn't forgotten about it, he just tried to hold it off for a little. Port stepped back from the girl and smiled at her briefly. A hard little apple, but sweet. Then he picked up her camera. He just held it for a moment and said, "I'd like to see you some other time."

"To let me down easy?"

"No. Without business." He hefted the camera.

"That's right," she said. "You want the picture." She took the camera out of his hand and opened the back. "You must be very important, what's-your-name."

"Don."

"How important are you, what's-your-name Don?"

"I'm just careful." He took the plate from her and broke it on the edge of the sink. Then he ran hot water over the pieces, ruining the emulsion. "I was asking you," he began, but then they both heard the racket outside. Molnar had come out of his office and, seeing Leonard in the hall, had started to yell for an explanation. Leonard and Molnar were both talking at the same time.

"Before you go," said the girl, "you might at least ask my name." Then she said, "Gracie. Will you remember?"

"Are you free tonight?"

"No. Not tonight. Business," she said, and then they heard Molnar banging on the door.

Gracie raked her hands through her hair, shook it, then smiled at Port. "I'm ready. Looks good?"

"Good and disreputable." Then Port opened the door.

What Molnar saw was what he was meant to see—Gracie stepping away from Port and the quick gesture to straighten her hair. The man whom he knew for Paducci was the kind Molnar didn't like. He couldn't be typed by his clothes or his manner, because both looked very quiet. But he had a straight, unimpressed look in his eyes—brazen, the way Molnar saw it—and that was what rankled Molnar the most.

It would be easier to yell at the girl. "Come here," he barked at her.

She came out of the darkroom and stood in front of him. Molnar made a display of looking her up and down insultingly. "You got the darkroom," he told her, "because you're supposed to be a photographer. Not because you're a whore."

Gracie put her hands on her hips and started tapping one foot. She didn't say anything. Port didn't say anything. He folded his arms, and since he wasn't there to act like a gentleman he tried to blank out about everything. He just whistled a little, mostly breath.

"So where's the merchandise?" Molnar pushed past the door and into the darkroom. "And that mess here in the sink. What the hell!"

"That's the merchandise," said Gracie and enjoyed the way Molnar's face changed. But when he started cursing at her she didn't like that. Molnar did it with too much relish.

Gracie looked at him like a snake and said, "Closet queen!" Molnar's face snapped shut like a door. He gave everyone a vicious look but didn't say any more. Port wondered why Molnar kept her in the club.

Then the three men walked down the corridor to the office.

Leonard closed the door, and Molnar got behind his desk. He watched Port get closer and sit down in the chair next to the desk. "All right," Molnar said, "Besides laying my help, what do you want?"

"I want you to understand something, Molnar." Port lit a cigarette and let Molnar wait. Then he exhaled and said, "You try taking a picture of me again, and I'll break more than your girl Friday's camera."

Molnar leaned back and said nothing right away. He wondered what Port was like, how to handle him. "Afraid of something, Paducci?"

"Of course."

"I never heard of no gun being afraid."

"Then you don't know any live ones."

Molnar thought that Port was a smart-aleck bastard and liked him even less.

"You wanted to see me," he said. "What is it?"

"Same reason that made you decide to see me, most likely."

Molnar said, "Huh?"

"You checked on who I was, and you were even anxious enough to try and check further. With a photo. I've come to see you, Molnar, because you're anxious."

"I'm going to ask Leonard here to throw you out. That's how anxious I am, Paducci."

Port just laughed at the bravado. He looked at Leonard to include him in the gesture, but he saw that Leonard wasn't making a move. Leonard was smiling.

"I met your man Bink," said Port. "That's why I'm here."

"I hear you and he met years ago, so how important can it be?"

"I met him in New York, a short while ago. And he gave me a message."

Molnar started rummaging for a cigar on his desk which pleased Port, since it showed that the introduction was working.

"And he gave me a message. He said he's leaving for France on the job he was doing, and would I please let you know. You'll hear from him, he said, once he knows what's what in France."

Port saw how Molnar relaxed, and that too was a good sign. It showed that Molnar had heard about the trail leading to France from Bink himself. Port's mentioning it here seemed like a confirmation of the truth.

"Which is partly the reason I'm here," said Port. He had to smile at Molnar's renewed suspicion. Each time Molnar got tense he shifted position, such as leaning a little or stretching himself, and each time that happened, Port caught a whiff of perfume. He could have sat there with his eyes closed and still have known when Molnar was getting excited.

"Like what?" asked Molnar. "Like maybe Bink told you to come all the way down to Cleveland because that Gracie bitch outside was a sure thing?"

"How would you know if she's a sure thing," said Port, and he gave Molnar a half look which was an insult in itself. Then he went right on talking to take advantage of Molnar's state. "I'm here because Bink is looking for that Daniel Port."

Molnar tried very much to hide his feelings on this, but he suddenly started to chew on the cigar. He was not a cigar chewer, Port had noticed; he sucked on them instead. He was the type who held the cigar in his mouth, turning and twirling it and loving it with his lips. He now chewed on it and then started to spit out some pieces. Then he said, as though half listening, "I don't know what you're talking about."

"Bink and I are good friends," said Port. "Bink and Paducci, a close buddy team."

For the moment Molnar was startled only because this seemed to confirm

Bankroft's bragging. Any time Bankroft talked about anyone big, it was usually hot air—except this time.

"So," Port went on, "he told me he was looking for Port."

"And then he told you why," said Molnar, trying to get back into the conversation. He was also hoping to trip Port up.

"No," said Port. "Since when does a gun know any whys?" And he smiled as though the remark was a private joke. The only reason he himself was turning gun was to learn all the whys—why the shifts in the organization, the thing that Lubinski was worried about; why the attempt on his life, which was his standing interest. And who was behind it. Molnar?

"Lemme make a phone call," said Molnar, and he reached for the instrument.

Molnar, thought Port, was not it. He said, "You got nothing to call about, yet. I haven't told you why I'm here."

"Maybe you've told me too much already," said Molnar, "and that's why I'm calling," but he just left his hand on the phone and sat waiting.

"I know where Port is," he said. "Bink doesn't."

It had the right kind of effect. Molnar said, "You're blowing hot air," showing that he thought it important enough to cover his interest.

Port shrugged, got up and turned to the door.

"Just a minute, uh—Paducci."

Port turned around. "You're buying, Molnar?"

"All right."

"You're not buying," said Port. "The top man is buying," and he nodded at the phone.

Molnar started to curse. He was the top man, he started to say, but suddenly looked as if he might want to bite off his own tongue. He blustered and ranted a little while longer, while Port stood there, frowning. It was as if Molnar might be the man behind this but had suddenly remembered that it wouldn't be wise to say so aloud. But all Port knew was that Molnar must be in deep.

"Sit down," Molnar said. "You don't walk out." He was suddenly holding a gun on Port, a big dull automatic. Then he nodded at Leonard. Leonard, with the manner of greeting a guest, came over and frisked Port from behind.

"Clean," he said.

"Paducci without a gun?" and Molar grinned from behind the desk.

"Why should I have a gun?" said Port. "I'm not working yet."

"You asking me for a job?" and Molnar put the automatic on top of the desk.

"If you want Port dead," said Port, "you better consult me about it."
"Tell Gracie to wait," Molnar said to Leonard. Then he made his phone call.

Chapter 5

The plan was very simple. Port had to find out who was head man in the area and the rest would follow.

At two-thirty A.M. he stood on the curb in front of the dark Sassafras club. Leonard was on one side of him and Molnar on the other. Central wasn't dark or deserted, but the people walking on the street were through for the night. When they laughed they worked at it too hard, and when they kept still it was because they were exhausted. The night air was very cold.

A big Chrysler rolled up and stopped in front of the club. The chauffeur got out and stood with the men. He didn't open the door for anyone but just waited with them.

"He say anything when you left?" Molnar asked the chauffeur.

"Nothing. Just to come over. Here's the dame," and they all turned back to the club where Gracie was coming out of a side door.

She was wrapped in a fur coat and carried a small overnight bag in one hand. The chauffeur opened the car for her, and she sat down in the back. Then Port got in and Leonard next to him. Molnar sat in front with the chauffeur.

They drove up to the Heights where there was no traffic at all and where some of the streets looked like small-town streets.

"Tell me," said Port to the girl, "how is it you can afford this car? Or do you own the club too?"

"No. I just sleep with the Master," she said, and she tapped her fingernails on the small overnight bag. "Once a week."

"Oh."

"Oh what? You didn't believe me when I told you I'm ambitious?"

"I believe you. You're an honest working girl."

"I work and I'm honest," she said. "You're right."

Molnar turned in his seat once to stare at them, but they didn't pay any attention to him. Then Molnar looked front again.

"And tomorrow," said Port. "You working tomorrow too?"

"No. You want to see me?"

"Very much."

"Let's," she said, and they smiled at each other in the dark.

They only spoke once after that. When they were almost there, Gracie leaned over and whispered close to Port's ear. "I don't know what you know, Don, but you got ugly friends. You'll be careful?"

"You get along with them," he said.

"I just work here. But you—" and he could feel her shrug— "you get away with too much."

"Oh?"

"Like getting to see Schenk first crack out of the box. And on *my* night—" Then she let it trail off and laughed to herself because Molnar was staring at them, trying to hear.

It could be concern for him, thought Port, or it could be for herself. He was breaking up *her* night with Schenk....

The man she had called Schenk had a big house on a lampless street in Shaker Heights. The street was lined with large trees, and each house had a four-car garage in back built like a carriage house. The real estate sales were governed by certain delicate restrictions to keep the neighborhood pure. This had given Schenk an added incentive. He had bought the house through money and pressure, and he continued to keep up the latter so his neighbors would not forget about him. What he did was either plain mean or funny, depending on whether you were a neighbor or not. Came dark, and all the lights in the house went on—including a string of colored bulbs from the house to the gate by the street. This raised hell with the decorum of the neighborhood and also showed clearly who walked up the drive after dark. Every night, around bedtime, Schenk had a different girl walk up the drive to the house. He always had the limousine park on the street so that there would be no doubt in the neighbors' minds as to what was going on. Sometimes two girls came, doing a fair amount of giggling and laughing, and they always carried overnight bags. And so there would be no mistake about how Schenk was treating his friends, the girls usually wore mink coats which Schenk had lent them.

This was Gracie's night. The difference was that the mink was really hers, which showed what Schenk thought of her. And the other difference was that Schenk was messing up his night with her by having the meeting with Port. If it was that important, thought Gracie, maybe this night she'd get some sleep. She yawned as the limousine slowed down by the gate.

It didn't stop on the street but turned up the drive and rolled up to the house. None of the lights along the short driveway were lit and there was not one light over the front door.

Schenk opened the door himself. He looked short and strong in front of the light from the hall, and there were bright highlights on his black hair. He puffed on a cigarette as though he were nervous, but he always smoked cigarettes that way. He stood aside while everybody came in and didn't say a word till he had the door shut. Then he said, "Gracie, will you wait upstairs?" He gave her a quick laugh—sharp, thought Port—and then he looked after her when she went up the stairs. "I'll wake you," he said, smiling again, and then turned to the others. He nodded at one of the doors and they all walked into the room. Schenk kept looking at Port.

"There's some fixings in that thing that looks like an altar," said Schenk and pointed to the chest where the liquor was.

"Leonard," said Molnar, "go fix us something."

Schenk laughed again, with the same sharpness. "He's not the butler," he said. "How come you treat Leonard like the butler?"

Molnar got red in the face but didn't say anything. Then he got up and got himself his own drink.

"This," said Schenk to Dan Port, "is called the den. Something, huh? Sounds like pen, almost," and he laughed. Nobody else did.

"I hear you didn't like your picture taken, Paducci." Schenk looked at Port and waited for his answer.

"No," said Port. He got up, went to the liquor chest and mixed himself rye with water.

"Got to check on you some way," said Schenk. "Nobody here's ever seen you, and last I heard about you, you were dead."

"The more people think so, the better for me."

"Lousy reason," said Schenk, and Port saw that it was true. And that Schenk had caught it without any trouble. "Because," said Schenk, "if that's how you want it, how come you gave your right name, Paducci?"

"To impress you," said Port, since this was mostly true.

"Well, you don't." Schenk got up and walked around a few times. "Molnar and me didn't ask you over," he said. "You came bucking in. So you get treated on my terms. Understand?"

"You didn't say anything yet."

"If I want your picture taken, Paducci, I'm taking it." He stopped pacing and leaned over a little. "Like you don't know whether I got a camera right there in that TV box that's sitting there, do you?"

Port didn't think there was, but he thought Schenk's manner required an answer. He swallowed the contents of his glass, dropped the ice on the carpet and threw the glass at the TV screen. There was a sharp crash, and the gray screen had a big, jagged hole in it.

"You make a threat, Schenk, always expect me to have a reaction."

Nobody said anything. Schenk stared at Port and then he sat down. "You sonofabitch," he said. He folded his legs and lit a new cigarette from the old one. "You got a first name, Paducci?"

"Donald."

"Fine. That's easier." Schenk puffed, and then said, "What do you want, Donald?"

"I might want Bink's job." He paused. "I want to kill Port."

There was a sudden silence. Port saw that Schenk didn't like anyone knowing about the Port business.

"I never knew Bink being much of a talker, Donald."

"With me he's different. Anyway, your gun is off on a wrong lead going to France. Port's in this country."

"So?"

Port shook his head. "Maybe you're buying," he said, "but I don't know yet."

"All right!" Schenk got up again and walked back and forth. He was more impatient than angry. "I'm buying! What am I buying?"

"I didn't mean that," said Port. He sat with his hands folded and looked very mild. "I meant I don't know yet if I'm selling to you."

Schenk stopped pacing. He suddenly looked as if he meant to bite somebody. He kept looking back and forth from one man to the other, hoping to get an idea of how to handle that last remark. But nobody helped him. Leonard, who enjoyed everything mostly because he felt like an outsider, stayed by the liquor chest and looked at labels. Molnar had a clear idea of what he wanted to do with Port, but that wouldn't help the discussion. Later, maybe, after Schenk had handled this. Schenk always knew how to handle talk.

It was true, thought Port, that Schenk had a way of conducting a conversation. His fast voice came out like a fist.

"Now listen to this," Schenk went on. "Don't worry about who's gonna buy you, Donald." The way he used the first name was like an insult. "Because so far, you got nothing to sell."

"But I do. I'm selling Port," said Port.

"I don't know nothing about any of that."

"Don't tell me, Schenk, your hired bouncer knows more than you do."

"You keep it up that way, Donald, and I lose my temper."

"I'll help you," said Molnar suddenly. "Wait till I tell you what that sonofabitch did at the club." Molnar was momentarily satisfied at Schenk's puzzled look. He'd give out with the fine piece of gossip later. Like dessert.

Schenk sat down, leaned forward on his knees and started to pick his nails. He didn't look up. "All right, Donald. Where'd you meet him?"

"Port?"

"Who are you selling?"

"I met him," said Port, "around the time I entered the country. I'd known him when he used to be Stoker's right-hand man but he hadn't changed much. There he was, taking a sun bath."

Schenk looked up from his nails but he kept his temper. "You didn't tell me where, Donald."

"I'm telling this to the head man, I told you. I already told you something for free. That he isn't in France."

"But in this country," said Schenk to his nails.

"The sun was shining," said Port, "and there he was, taking a sun bath."

Schenk didn't often get double talk. He wasn't used to it, and he had no intention of getting used to it now. He said, "What kind of a gun do you use, Donald?"

"Little Mauser."

"I thought you guys used something heavy, something that means business, Donald."

Port noticed the tone and that Schenk was getting meaner by the minute. "If you're not a very good shot, Schenk, then you use a big caliber that tears a big hole. If you know what you're aiming for, then a pin can do the trick." Port stretched back in his seat. "More important to me," he said, "is that there shouldn't be too much noise."

If they found a way to check on Paducci, they'd find out that all this business about the gun was true. But Port hoped they would have a hard time checking well. Paducci had been thin and small—and Port wasn't.

"Let me see it," said Schenk.

"I'm not carrying a gun," said Port. "Only when I'm working."

"Oh."

Schenk got up. He put his hands in his pockets and walked toward the liquor cabinet. When he passed Port Schenk suddenly kicked out, cracking his shoe into Port's shin, and before Port was even doubled over with the pain he got a sharp clip to the side of his head, making his ears ring and blurring his vision.

Then there was more. All three of them seemed to be at him now—Schenk, Molnar and Leonard—because there were that many fists and legs.

Port didn't remember landing a single punch, nor was there any real heat in what the others were doing. But it hurt. They got out of the way when he swung or kicked, or else they were too close. The main sensation was always somebody else's clothes pressed into his face and the blow, all the blows, coming from the back or the side where he wasn't protected.

He went suddenly limp, hoping to stop all of it. That was the moment when someone took him from behind, bending his arm at a bad angle and putting the crook of an elbow tight over his throat.

Schenk and Molnar stood in front of him. Schenk's black hair was hanging wild and Molnar had a rip in his pants. Port could see his underwear, a strange rose-color, and perhaps silk. The one holding Port was Leonard.

"If you'll hold still for some questions," said Leonard close to his ear. The voice was low and round from close up, and Leonard didn't seem to be breathing very hard at all.

"You shoulda held still sooner," said Schenk and raked his hair back. Then he stepped closer, working one fist into the palm of the other hand.

He had started to ask his question again when Port kicked out very fast. It didn't break Leonard's hold for a second, but it punished Schenk right between his legs. The man doubled over and groaned.

"Listen to me," said the Negro. His voice was so close it sounded intimate and calm. "You hold still now, or it'll get worse. You know that." He gave Port's arm a small tug, shooting an electric pain into all the bones and joints all the way up to his head.

Molnar helped Schenk into a chair, and Leonard without any transition let go of Port. Not that it made too much difference, because Port felt crippled.

"You can sit down, Mr. Paducci," said the Negro, "while I'm holding this gun on you."

Port sat down.

"If you'll pardon me, Mr. Schenk," the Negro said, "I'd like to say something about this."

"Just keep holding that gun," Molnar said. "Just keep holding—"

"Shut up," Schenk said. Schenk looked at Leonard.

Leonard said, "The next thing you're going to do, Mr. Schenk, is to dream up a fancy way to harm Paducci for the way he kicked you. Isn't that about what you got in mind?"

"Any minute," Schenk started again. "Any minute—"

"And that's why I wanted to point out something to you, Mr. Schenk." Leonard sounded smooth. "You really think that this man here—" and he nodded at Port—"is going to do things your way if you twist his arm?"

By the looks of Schenk he was going to take that remark as an insult, so Leonard kept on talking. "At least you know Paducci by reputation," he said. "You know he's one of the meanest and one of the most accurate guns. Paducci, from what we know, has never made a mistake. He's even alive when we thought he was dead. And he used to cost more than any of his kind, because of the services he provided. Such as—" and Leonard nodded the gun each time he made a point—"never a trace to the source of his jobs.

Never a word to anyone who wasn't in on the job from the beginning. Never cracked even when the Feds tried to railroad his career with some easy, fat offers. He isn't going to talk *this* way—" and Leonard hefted the gun.

"Gimme a drink," said Schenk. He leaned back carefully in his chair and waited for Molnar to bring the glass.

"And if I'm not mistaken—knowing no details—what Paducci's got, Mr. Schenk, you need."

Schenk swallowed his drink and kept sitting.

"There's always later," said Molnar, and there was another long silence.

"I'll talk any time," said Port at last, "to the head man."

Schenk sighed. There was a lot of tension in the air, and suddenly Molnar couldn't stand it any more.

"Listen, Schenk. You want me to call him?"

"You mean Bainbeck?" said Schenk.

Now Port had a name. But only a name.

All the tension melted out of the room when Schenk turned his head and looked at Port. Schenk grinned slowly and then chuckled. It was weird to hear such a comfortable chuckle come out of the man.

"I seen you light up," said Schenk to Port. "How smart are you, Donald? You think I'd drop the name of the head man just like that when I wasn't going to give it to you a minute ago?" Then he laughed.

"There's an awful lot of people in on this thing," said Port. He didn't know what else to say because he didn't know what to think.

"That's how it is with big operations," said Schenk. "Leonard."

The Negro looked over but kept the gun on Port.

"You got a cigarette?"

"Yes, sir."

"Put the gun away and give me a cigarette."

Now the gun was gone, Schenk was smoking, and there would be a talk.

"The head man is me," said Schenk. "You don't know me, same as I don't know you. But I'll show you I'm the head man."

"Go ahead," said Port.

"I'll tell you why I want Port," said Schenk. He nodded at Leonard and waited till the Negro had left the room. "Very simple," said Schenk. "I'm going independent. I'm breaking away. It turns out I can only do it neat if I ruin the other side."

"Whom?"

"Get him," said Molnar. "*Whom.*"

"Callo," said Schenk. "Landsman of yours out of Chicago. You know Callo?"

Port knew him. In the structure of the syndicate the man heading up the territory was an old racketeer by the name of Callo. He was friend of politicians, some financiers, some union heads, and he had run this section of enterprises for a very long time. He had done it well but he was the old order, and Schenk—with any luck at all—might swing things his way. Schenk was an upstart, by Callo's standards, but Schenk also knew what Callo had long forgotten—that any rake-off, when handled locally, rakes more and better than some long-armed system which only maintained itself because it had been there a long time. Perhaps Calla thought that nothing short of a gang war could make him lose part of his territory. Callo was that old.

"The way I'm throwing that sonofabitch," Schenk was saying, "is by killing Port."

"Jeesis Christ—" said Port. It had been involuntary. He kept still then, to hear the rest.

"If you know this Port," Schenk kept on, "you know that his death will do away with his testament."

"I know," said Port.

"That out of the way," said Schenk, "and Callo—not to mention some others—is dead and gone. With Port's information out, the cops of all the known denominations will be over Callo so fast he won't have time to even remember his own name."

"And the field is all yours," said Port. He took a deep breath. "The damnedest trick," he said.

It sounded flat and noncommittal. It was the only way that occurred to Port to cover up the shock he felt. He had broken away from his old ways and had stayed alive afterward—something that didn't happen very often—because of that insurance, that testament, as Schenk had called it, that threat of a big expose. But he saw now that it didn't work any more—in fact, his testament was to be his death warrant. And if Schenk could have thought of this, who else might have?

He looked down at his knees, not caring how it looked. Maybe they would think he was paying homage to the stroke of genius he had just learned about. But he was keeping his head down like that because everything felt suddenly useless. What if he impressed Schenk by breaking his television set, what if he let Schenk break his arm without talking, what if he killed Schenk, Molnar, Leonard, and one nameless man after another? As long as he was Daniel Port that threat which came from knowing too much would be there.

Port sat up. "You sound important," he said to Schenk. He went over to the liquor cabinet and mixed himself some rye, talking without turning around.

"Seeing you're important, Schenk, how come you need Molnar?"

"Because he does what I say," said Schenk.

Port turned around then because he wanted to see how much they liked each other. He could see that they didn't very much. Molnar got mean, then pettish, and Schenk tried to insult him. They may need each other, Port thought, but they didn't like each other. Maybe this knowledge would be useful later.

"All right," he said. He took a swallow, then walked back to the two men. "Hire me."

"Maybe you're too expensive," said Schenk.

Head man?

"One thousand," said Molnar.

Another head man?

"If you know me," said Port, "and if you know your business, you shouldn't have started so low."

"We're broke," said Schenk. "You haven't delivered the big money yet."

"Five thousand," said Port, "or nothing."

They didn't react much. Schenk smiled. Molnar chewed on his cigar. He hadn't sucked on it once since the fight had started.

"Tell you what," said Schenk. "We'll talk about it after you're gone."

A team? Maybe their organization was new enough to have two men at the top.

"And we got to tell Bainbeck about this," said Schenk. The way he grinned when he said it showed Port that the remark was meant to throw him off.

Port got up then, because they had said they wouldn't decide anything now. They hadn't said no, no sale, they had said they might want to talk to the man Schenk kept mentioning, Bainbeck. Perhaps there were three in the team and their outfit was new enough to have *three* men on top.

"And while you're waiting," said Molnar, "I got something for you."

Port stopped and waited.

"Something to occupy you, so we can see how you work." Then Molnar went to the door, opened it, and yelled, "Leonard!"

The Negro stood in the hall, talking to Gracie. She was wearing a filmy thing now which covered more than the corset she wore in the club but which gave life to her body. The shape that showed was all her own—and the way she stood on the stairs, leaning on the banister, made Molnar feel mean immediately.

"What are you doing down here? Get upstairs!"

"I got me some postum," she said and held up the cup.

"Get up where you belong," said Molnar. He watched her as she stood up straight and, noticing how the thin wrapper stretched over her breasts, he felt like spitting at her.

"You can pimp for me," she said to Molnar, "but that's all." Then she gave him an evil grin. "And that's as far as you can get, anyway."

Molnar walked over to her and slapped her across the face.

What left the situation unfinished was Schenk. He called from the room, wanting to know what was going on. Gracie went into the room first and looked at the two men there. They just sat and looked very normal. Then the others came in.

"This bitch," Molnar started, but Gracie got ahead of him.

"He hit me," she said to Schenk. "He's got no business hitting me, honey."

Schenk reacted as expected. He got dark in the face and made like he meant to get out of his chair.

"She and that Leonard," Molnar started yelling, "they were out there—look at her, look at what she's wearing—"

"Shut up," said Schenk.

"Honey—" Gracie went over to Schenk's chair—"you know he suspects everything." Then she looked at Molnar so he'd get the full impression. "*He* can't ever suspect himself, and that's why."

Molnar told Schenk that Gracie and Port had holed up in the darkroom in no time flat, that the smallness of the room and the tightness of her corset hadn't made any difference, that Schenk was an idiot to play favors with a nympho who fell flat on her back anytime a five-minute acquaintance looked at her body, and that she had ruined that chance with the photo for Canning, the only one who could identify Paducci around here.

There was no chance for Port to find out about Canning now. Just another name, so far. That would have to wait, because Molnar had gotten to Schenk with his story. Schenk's face had changed, as if he had suffered a mortal insult.

"Come here," he said to Gracie. He didn't say it loud and he didn't say it low, but he said it with a lot of menace. She came closer, looking afraid, and to make the whole melodrama complete Schenk said, "play me for a sucker, will ya?" And he yanked the girl closer to him by one arm.

"Listen, honey. I never—" and then Schenk gave her a hard push.

Paducci wouldn't have interfered, so Port couldn't. "You just lost the only friend you ever had," Schenk said to her. "Namely, a meal ticket!"

Gracie pulled back one leg and lost one of her mules. When she reached down for it Schenk grabbed it and threw it across the room.

"Now the other one," he said. His excitement was beginning to show.

She gave him the shoe and he threw it after the other one.

"That's eighteen bucks you don't owe me no more. Now comes sixty-five."

Gracie didn't understand.

"Get up!"

She got up and held the negligee close under her throat. She didn't know what else to do. She paid no attention to the four men standing around because that would have made the menace bigger.

"Sixty-five bucks of mine," Schenk said. "Give it here!" Then he grabbed the thin garment at her shoulders and yanked.

She was practically bare now. There were small ribbons over her shoulders holding up the nightgown, and the filmy material seemed to cling to the tips of her breasts by sheer weightlessness. The rest of the gown covered more, but only mistily.

Her yellow hair had come loose and Port was surprised to see how much of it there was. It hung wild and her mouth was open. She shook the negligee off. Perhaps she was angry or perhaps she just wanted to do quickly what Schenk would surely do. Then she put her hands where she was almost naked—an unconscious gesture which was exciting.

"Well?" yelled Schenk. "I'm waiting!"

She tried to say something, but then she couldn't and turned to leave.

"Uh huh," said Molnar. He stepped in her way and pushed her by one shoulder so that the strap came off, "Leave your hands down," he said when she tried to cover herself.

He made no other move to go near her. He kept his hands in his pockets and waited.

Gracie looked down at the floor because she couldn't look at any of the men. What confused her more than anything was her sudden feeling of shyness.

Then Molnar ripped the thing off her because he couldn't wait any longer. He grabbed the gown where it came down to a V, hooked his finger there and ripped. Then the gown fell off and the girl stood there naked.

There was a moment in which everyone looked at her, but it was just out of inertia. When she walked away with a slight sound of bare feet nobody looked after her, but when the door shut with a click they all looked at the closed door.

Molnar got a cigar out of his pocket, and Schenk sat down again. He took a deep breath, as if after an interruption.

"All right," he said to Molnar. "Now what?"

"Yeah," said Molnar. "What I want him to do." He nodded at Port. "I'm thinking of Finkel, on Quincey Avenue. He's due a visit."

"His store burnt down," said Leonard. "That's why he hasn't been paying."

"He's got leave to use numbers money to pay for his lousy delicatessen?" yelled Molnar.

"He hasn't been collecting. That's why there's been no money."

"He's got a quota," said Molnar. He could sound very final. "You take Paducci down there tomorrow and explain to Finkel he's got a quota. And you," Molnar said to Port, "you explain to him afterwards. Don't kill him." And Molnar lit his cigar.

Chapter 6

Port didn't get to his room until close to four, and then he slept badly. He thought that he hadn't slept yet at all when he was awakened by the knock. It was dark outside, except for the blink of a neon sign which hung across the street, and there was a cold draft in Port's face from the open window. Then the knock sounded again.

"Yuh?" he said. He sat up in bed.

"It's me."

Port didn't know who me was. He was still rattled from his lousy sleep, and the words registered but not the voice. He got out of bed, wrapped a towel around his middle and went to the door. "Yes?" he said.

"I'd like to come in."

He opened the door for Gracie and watched her walk past him. She was dressed the way she had been when she had gone to Schenk's house. He hadn't taken the mink coat away from her. That was all Port could see. It was too dark to tell what her expression was. Perhaps the whole thing earlier had been staged. The one who would have planned it would have to be Molnar, because he was the one who could have taken advantage of that scene in the darkroom.

"Don?" she said. "I can't see you very well."

"That's all right," he said. "I'm wearing a towel." He walked past her to the chair where his clothes were lying.

She put her bag down and said, "That's all right."

"Huh?"

"Why dress?" and she put down her bag.

The whole thing, thought Port, was easily set up in advance. The injured female changing beds. He looked at her, and each time the light winked into the room he could see her clear outlines and her frank face. It was a shame.

"There's a draft here," she said.

Port nodded and looked at the window.

"You must be cold. Why don't you get back to bed?"

"Yes," said Port. He dropped the towel and got into bed. He sat there and lit a cigarette.

"I want you to know why I'm here," she said. "May I close the window?"

"Sure, Gracie."

She closed the window and came back to the bed. "I want to sleep with you."

Port smiled at her, but she didn't see it in the dark. She didn't know how he felt. She had her hands on the lapels of her coat, as if wondering whether to open or close it.

"Do you want me?" she asked.

"Gracie, I'd love to have you."

In the dark, and not knowing Port, she didn't catch the simple truth in the answer, but just the flip sound of it. She took that up because she suddenly felt awkward.

"Well—" and she laughed a little— "you've seen me do this once before." She dropped her coat and hoped Port would laugh.

"The difference is," said Port, "this time I like it."

She was glad he had said that. She wished she could see him better.

"You seem nervous," said Port. "You're taking a long time with those buttons."

"Don't laugh," she said. "I am nervous." She took off her suit jacket and dropped it on the chair.

"Why, Gracie?" He had to ask her, though there wouldn't be any way of telling whether her answer would be prearranged or if she really meant it.

"I don't often have a chance," she said, "of asking first."

"You shouldn't have to." He could see her against the window. She was shaking her hips in a soft shimmy to drop the skirt.

"It would keep out the riffraff," she said, "if I could do more of the asking." She put one leg on the windowsill and rolled down a stocking. There was a nice, plump curve to her thigh and an equally beautiful one for the calf. Then she did the same thing with the other leg.

"Why can't you?" Port asked her. "Pretty thing like you." He could see her shrug before answering.

"I'm not a whore, Don. I'm just ambitious."

"Oh. Singer? Movies?"

"No. I just want money."

"How about a husband?"

"I can't find one," she said. "The people I know don't make husbands." She unhooked her brassiere and dropped it. She took a deep breath and rubbed her breasts. "They don't even make love good."

"So leave."

"Sure. That's why I need money, so I don't have to start over in such a great rush." Then she took off her panties. She pushed them down over her hips and then kicked them off her feet. "Can you see me, Don?" She had straightened up, facing him, and he could see her silhouette against the window. It was almost as if she still wore the corset.

"On the next blink," he said, "I could see you good. But don't wait that long."

She slid her hands up and down her thighs. "I'm not ambitious tonight," she said. "I just want to make love."

"Stop standing there," said Port. "Come here."

"Ask me," she said. "Ask me again."

"I'll jump you, if you don't come." He was no longer thinking of her being here meaning anything except the one fact that they would make love.

They woke up when it was light out, but because of the overcast they couldn't tell what the time was.

"That flicker sign across the street isn't on any more," said the girl. "It must be daylight."

"Let's not argue," said Port. "Let's just say that it's morning. Good morning," and he gave her a kiss.

She said, "Now let's say it's noontime. Good noontime," and she kissed him back.

"Good evening," said Port, and they kept that up for a while.

"You know," she said, "I've never gone through a day as fast as this."

"That's because you're a kissing fool."

She rolled over on her back and put her hands under her head. "The fact is, Don, I haven't kissed—just kissing, like we did—in I don't know how long."

"Then how come you do it so well?"

"Oh, I've done it," and she laughed at the ceiling. "It reminds me of high school. This is like that."

"My dear Gracie," said Port. "I don't know what high school you went to, but at present there are many, many teen-aged people who would argue that this, right here and now, is not like high school."

She laughed and nudged him with her hip. "Now is better," she said. "Your hand's going to sleep on my belly."

Her skin was warm under his hand and he pulled her closer.

"Careful," she said. "You made the blanket slip."

"I see that now. I'm very glad you called it to my attention."

"Cover me. I'm naked, you know."

"And so you are," said Port, "and so you are."

She laughed and pulled the blanket up. She pulled it up over their heads and grabbed him so she could bite his ear. After a while she stopped that. She kept holding him, tighter, with her eyes closed and her head thrown back. They didn't let go of each other until they could relax again.

The light outside the window was still the same but they knew it was much later. They could hear the street sounds more clearly, and there were more of them, as if the city had grown while they were asleep. They stretched and looked at each other, but there wasn't much else to say. Gracie sat up in bed and threw her hair back.

"Sounds busy down there, doesn't it?"

"Yuh," said Port. "It sort of breaks everything up."

It was true. It felt that way between them. As if the two people of last night didn't have time to look at each other now.

"What'll you do today?" Port asked her.

She shrugged and kicked the blanket off. She looked at her knees and rubbed something there.

"I haven't thought yet."

"You'll be in the club tonight?"

"No," she said. "I lost my job."

"Oh. That's right." He sat up, next to her, and looked at her back. It was smooth and soft-shadowed. He suddenly wished that either she weren't here, naked next to him, or that this wasn't the day it was. "You'll find a new one," he said. "Won't you?"

He wished he had said something else, or something more, but the light in the room was a cold daylight and the day would be rotten. He put his hand on her back, just a little, and made small movements. But his manner was absent.

"Yes," she said. "Got to be ambitious." She looked at her toes and moved them.

Then he felt that she was moving a little, leaning her back on his hand more. She did this and turned her head, looking at him. It was just for a moment but seemed long, because neither of them said anything. She turned away and got out of bed in the same movement. She stood by the window, looking out. Port heard how she took a deep breath, or she tried to, but everything was unfinished now.

"I wish I could help you," said Port.

"I didn't ask you."

"I know. Same as I didn't ask you to come." And he wondered again if Schenk had sent her. He hated himself for the thought, but there it was. The same coldness was over both of them now.

She took a cigarette and started smoking it while she walked around. Port watched her, wanting her badly again.

"Listen," he said. "I'd like to see you again."

"But you're busy."

"Just for a while."

"But you'll squeeze me in."

"Jeesis Christ, Gracie. Don't take that tone."

"It sounded just like I felt, you know? It sounded just exactly like I felt!"

They both knew that the irritation had nothing to do with the way they had felt during the night. That made it worse.

"I'll tell you something," said Port. He got up and went to the bathroom door.

"You'll take the bathroom first. Right?"

"Just shut up for a minute." He smiled at her while he said it, trying to change the mood. She didn't smile back. "What I wanted to say—" he started over— "perhaps I can help you."

For a moment she almost listened, but then she went hard again. "What?" she said. "Give me money?"

"Why in hell not?"

She looked at him and her face had an expression like a mean bird. "Bastard—" she said.

She watched him go into the bathroom and close the door. That was good. That was at least something definite. Now she wouldn't have to apologize or to keep on like before. She didn't know which was worse. She threw the cigarette into a waterglass and then she poured water on top of it. That gave her satisfaction. Then she stood by the window and looked down on the street. If someone looks up now they'll see me standing here naked. I wouldn't budge. I'd open the window and spit down on them and then close the window again. Done with it. She felt ugly and thought, why not? I had a good night. What a good night! And how long is a short-time tonic like that supposed to last? It doesn't. She thought about everything very clearly now—having lost her job, being out in the cold, probably finished around here, and it did start with him there, Donald short-time-tonic who was now taking a shower and probably dying to sing but feeling constrained because she was here. To hell with it all.

When Port came out of the bathroom she went in. His arm brushed her when she went by. She drew back, put one hand over her breast, and went past him and closed the door. Port looked at the closed door for a second and then he got dressed. He had a notion to leave, so they wouldn't have to go on the way things had developed, the worst of it being now that he thought about her and Schenk without any compunction. And if she did come because Schenk had sent her, he thought, what had she done? What had she learned? What, actually, had the girl done to make him suspicious? He knotted his tie automatically and listened to the shower.

If the interruption had come at some other time and by someone else, Port wouldn't have felt as much anger. The door from the hall opened and O'-Day came into the room.

"Don't you knock?"

O'Day ignored him. He closed the door and looked unpleasant. "You were supposed to show at the office yesterday."

"There wasn't time."

O'Day heard him and at the same time looked across the room at Gracie's underwear. Then he looked at the bathroom door where the shower was making a noise.

"There wasn't time?" he said. "How come there was time for this?" He nodded at the bed.

O'Day better leave, thought Port. The best thing that could happen would be if he left, right now.

"And just because you're on government expense, feller, don't think you can write off the price—"

"Get out," said Port.

The shower had stopped, but O'Day wasn't done. His square face seemed to get squarer, and he folded his arms. "Now you listen to me, Port—"

He stopped and looked past Port to where the bathroom door was opening. The girl was looking out.

"I'd like my clothes," she said. She was holding a towel in front of herself and she held out the other aim, waiting for Port. He gave her the clothes. She looked from one man to the other, and then she closed the door.

Port couldn't look at O'Day. He didn't want to look at him because he didn't want a scene. He stood by the window, his back to the room, and rubbed his hands over his face. Then he started to whistle, a nervous rhythm with no melody. He heard the door close behind him and was glad O'Day was gone, but that didn't solve a thing. Now everything was worse.

Before Gracie came out all dressed, O'Day was back. They were a silent group in the room. The girl stepped into her shoes, put on her mink and picked up her empty overnight bag. She looked completely blank, but then she looked at Port when she said good-by. "Maybe I'll see you," she said and left.

Port stood by the chest of drawers with both hands flat on the top. First he said, "Christ," very low, and then he said it again and slapped his hand hard on the dresser top. "You lousy, stupid, sonofabitch!" he said to O'Day. "You half-assed flatfoot!" he said, louder.

O'Day took it, or rather, he didn't react. He said, "All taken care of. I'm having her followed. Nothing to worry about."

"If she heard you use my name, following her won't help me any!"

"Leave that to us."

"She knows Schenk! She knows Molnar! Christ—" Port stopped for a second, because it cost him effort. "Have her locked up!"

"That would draw too much attention to what's going on."

"*That* would draw too much attention? The only kind of attention I'm worried about, you stupid bastard, is the kind she can throw on me now!"

"We're taking care of that not happening," said O'Day.

In the meantime, Gracie knew that she was being followed. First, because the man had looked at her in the hotel lobby, and she was always sensitive to that. And second because, feeling blank and empty when she sat in the taxi, she looked at everything with eyes that wandered, looking for nothing. That's how she spotted him again.

His car following her taxi made her angry, and she told her driver to double back around the square. Their cars were separated by two lights. She then told the driver to pass the taxi stand in front of the Terminal Tower, and when they passed the Tower she leaned into the cushions so she wouldn't show in the back window.

Two yellow cabs were pulling up Euclid, and two turned to the right, going to Prospect. The man who had been following her now was following the wrong cab.

Gracie told her driver to head East on Carnegie. The place she lived was in that direction, and so was Shaker Heights. Her face was sullen because she felt alone and undecided. She didn't know where she should go.

Chapter 7

Port had his breakfast while O'Day had his lunch. Port ate in the hotel while O'Day went somewhere else, and later on they met in the Federal Building. They had figured that Port's going there should attract no attention because the main post office was on the ground floor and the FBI was just one of the offices on an upstairs floor. Port did not think that he had been followed by anyone.

O'Day looked up when Port walked into his cubicle as if displeased with the man for overstaying his lunchbreak. "So let's hear all about it," he said. "What went on yesterday?"

Port told him.

"I was wondering how easy it would be for you, getting back into the swing," said O'Day.

"I'm not doing it for pleasure, O'Day. If you know a better way for me to stay close to those bastards, believe me, I'd be grateful to hear it."

"No," said O'Day. "You do what comes natural," and he looked at Port, hoping the man would make the mistake and swing at him right here in the office.

"I'll be there with Leonard, the one I told you about. I won't be able to fake it too much."

"We'll take care of it," said O'Day.

"How? That's the third time you've said that. Don't keep secrets from me about how you're running this whole thing!"

"You just do what you're told, Port. Don't sit there and tell me how we're going to run this thing, because the less you know the more careful you'll be. You're running this thing for us, understand? You're running this thing like anyone else whom we hire!"

O'Day couldn't have given Port a better twist. This was why he had left the Stoker outfit, no matter now that he was on the official side of the law—it was the same thing, being a faceless part in a big machine and not knowing a thing about anything. As if making the job meaningless made the work that much better.

Then O'Day's phone rang. He kept his face dull and he said *hum-m-m* a few times. When he hung up he surprised Port with an explanation.

"You ought to know this," he said. "So you watch yourself." O'Day seemed to enjoy it when Port was on the edge of his chair. "My man lost that woman you had in your room."

"Christ—"

"We'll take care of it," said O'Day, watching Port when he said it. But then he explained. "We've got Schenk's house under observation—he's home right now—and we're watching the club where she worked."

"How do you know she worked at that club?"

"We got our sources."

"You knew her when you saw her in my room?"

"No. I checked later. Now, if there's anything else important—"

"I want to know," said Port, hating O'Day. "You knew her first name and you saw her once. You must have somebody planted close to where I'm doing my work. I can't keep tapping around ..."

"We've got our pigeons," said O'Day, "but I'm not telling you about it. Now—anything else?"

The less contact with O'Day, the better, thought Port. After this was over, maybe O'Day would make a mistake and open his mouth to Port just once too often.

"I told you about that photo bit in the club. The man they would send that to is called Canning. Can you—"

"We took care of that."

"Tell me about it."

Perhaps O'Day was tired of playing his game because he answered. "He's a con who knows Paducci from California, years ago. Was close enough to Paducci to be able to tell you're not him."

"And?"

"He's in for fifteen years, armed robbery, down in Columbus. I guess they were going to send the picture to him. He's being transferred."

One load off Port's mind. Let them take their damn picture.

"If Schenk isn't your man and if Molnar isn't—"

"Maybe one of them is."

"How come you don't know?"

"Schenk came from Cuba, not long ago. That's how come he never saw you, even though he was big down there, casinos and so on. We don't think he's the head because he doesn't know local matters as well as he should. He was brought in the way you bring in an outside organizer."

"By Molnar then."

"Doubtful. Molnar has never been bigger than the Cleveland gutter circuit. You saw his club. If he had brains he would have shown them long ago."

"Unless the two of them, together now, make the perfect team. Molnar at least knows a lot about the locale here."

"Maybe you're right. That's why you're here, playing with them."

"Last night, they kept mentioning Bainbeck. To tell Bainbeck and so on, as if he might be somebody big."

O'Day laughed. "He's big," he said. "He's a senator."

"*What?*"

O'Day stopped looking amused. He turned serious. "This is one instance, Port, when you need confidential information." He leaned back in his chair and looked like an executive. "Senator Bainbeck, whom those racketeers mention so freely, is a crusader. We like such men. On one hand, it's true, he is publicly known to have underworld connections, even to the extent of having obtained political advantage from that connection."

"And financial?"

"Certainly not. On the other hand, Port, Senator Bainbeck has served as a constant source of information to us. He is a man with the burden of a double life, a dedicated man."

Port felt like saying, And so am I, you lousy sonofabitch.

"For example all the information which led us to the investigation of this regional syndicate affair, all that came from him."

"Including your knowledge of the plot on my life?"

"No. We dug that up ourselves. Bainbeck wouldn't be in a position to know such details."

Port made no comment on that last. Just O'Day speaking.

"So Bainbeck's out."

"Definitely," said O'Day.

"And Schenk and Molnar, they're out. Perhaps there's somebody else?"

"We think so," said O'Day. "Which is why you are here." He got up, to show he was through talking.

So was Port. He had no other questions, and he had no other information. He left with a nod and walked home through the rain.

He woke at seven and got to the Sassafras Club at eight. The sleep had helped. He made a concentrated effort to think of the Finkel visit as very short. He went straight into the club without looking around, so he didn't see the man with hands in his overcoat pockets and the big-brimmed hat.

There was a new photography girl in the place, wearing the same nothing as Gracie had worn, and looking much cuter than Gracie. Gracie, Port thought, didn't look cute at all. She had just been damn attractive, all the time. Even after they had had the scene that day, she had been attractive. She hadn't changed till O'Day had come.

"Not the same girl, is it?" said Leonard.

He wasn't wearing a tuxedo but had on a regular suit, very quiet, as if he was on his way to a business conference. What else? It *was* a business conference. Think of it that way and about how short it would be, and that Finkel was a very unpleasant bastard because how else would he be part of this rot?

"Gracie isn't here any more?" said Port.

"She isn't here any more."

"Because of last night, I guess."

"You saw it."

"Yuh."

Then Leonard said, "Are you ready to go?"

"Yuh. Tell me, Leonard, you know Gracie's address?" Leonard told Port what the address was, and then he asked him again if he was ready to go.

"Where's Molnar?" Port wanted to know.

"At home. You want his address too?" and then he gave it to Port without waiting because he was afraid that Port might not have liked that last remark. Leonard didn't want any friction.

"Would you like a drink before we go?" he asked.

"No. Let's go."

They went out by the front and then walked the one block to Quincey.

"I forgot to mention it," said Leonard, "but I brought you a gun."

"For this job? Listen—"

"Pocket Mauser, wasn't it? Little smaller than .32 caliber?"

He slipped a small box into Port's hand and Port had to take it. He dropped it into his pocket and grabbed Leonard's arm. "Listen, you sonofabitch. I carry a gun when I decide to carry a gun."

"Please," said Leonard.

Port could feel the big muscle in Leonard's arm roll under his fingers.

Port let go and pushed the box back at the Negro.

They had stopped, and there was enough hesitation between them for Port to notice what was down the street. Hands in the overcoat pockets, big hat. The brim was so big that the face was in shadow.

"Let go," said Port and pulled the box out of Leonard's hand. That surprised Leonard, but Port started walking immediately so there was no more talk. But then Port opened the box and threw away the lid.

"Don't," said Leonard. "Better keep the box."

Port threw it away.

"I just want to tell you, Paducci, the concealed weapons charge is one of the heaviest in this town. But if you keep the gun in a box—"

"Where's the clip?" Port asked. "This damn gun hasn't got a clip in it!"

Leonard felt around in several pockets, and then he found the clip. He had forgotten about it. He gave it to Port without any explanation.

When they turned into Quincey Port didn't see anyone following. The man with the hat wasn't there any more.

"That's the place," said Leonard, but Port didn't bother to look. He held the gun in his hand, inside his pocket.

They went around to the back, and Leonard knocked on a door that was under the fire escape. Then they stood and waited, and Port hoped very hard that Finkel would show and that he would be something brutal and big.

Something ugly to hit.

"A minute," a voice said. The lock was rattling.

Then Leonard said, "Hello, Mr. Finkel," and pushed past the man, who was small and bent and wore thick glasses.

Leonard and Port were in the living room, and Finkel had not come into the light yet, but his footsteps sounded small and nervous. Then he came into the room, and when he looked at the two men his bald head started to sweat.

"Leonard," he said, "sit down, will you, Leonard? And this gentleman, too. I don't think I've ever met this gentle—"

"We'll stand, Mr. Finkel."

"No, please." And Finkel moved around touching chairs, patting furniture, trying to plead with his smile. "Maybe we can talk better, talk more sense, Leonard, if we sit down. And you too, sir."

"We're not going to sit down," said Leonard, "because we won't stay long. Just long enough to say this."

"I know what you come to say, Leonard. And I been telling you all the time, every time you came here, all the times you were here after the fire—"

"I'm not to bring back any more excuses." Leonard started to look over at Port.

"Sir, one moment—uh, I don't even know your name."

Port went toward the man, biting his lip. It must have looked fierce or dangerous to Finkel because he didn't know how Port felt.

"—never in all the years I been handling this," Finkel was saying, "was there ever any cause for complaint. Isn't that right, Leonard? You know that, Leonard!" He was edging around the furniture in the small room, and the sweat was on his face too now, thin and watery. "I want to explain—please, sir!"

Port took him by the lapels.

"Sir! If you'll listen—if you'll please—"

Port was holding the lapels, and then his hands slid down, letting go.

Finkel was crying, "I'll tell you what I can do, what I'll do—"

"Shut up. *Shut up!*" Port yelled suddenly.

He thought he must have pushed Finkel because the man staggered back and fell on the couch. He lay there stiff and looked up with the breath stuck in his throat. His Adam's apple jerked up and down.

Port looked away. He thought his own face would crack with the tension. Leonard stood by the door saying nothing. His arms were folded, his face looked calm. He just stood there, waiting.

In that moment, when nothing moved, Port started thinking, What happens next—so that the first crash at the door was a relief.

Finkel never moved in his fright, but Leonard turned to look. He just had time to unfold his arms when the cops swarmed in—two, three, five.

At first when they grabbed him Port meant to resist, and he felt his muscles jump for it, but then he gave in. They had him—they had all of them good. He gave in under the pushing and went exactly the way they wanted it. Leonard was in front. They had Leonard almost out in the open, and then Port. Get out in the open. Get there and drop that gun before they were lined up by the wagon and frisked.

But when Leonard and Port were lined up where the wagon had pulled into the drive, two of the cops still had their guns out and the rest stood in the way. Port started to tremble from holding still. It wasn't a visible tremble, but something that went all through him and lay under the skin.

Then it was Finkel who caused it. He started yelling and pleading and tearing his arm away as if he were facing his execution. There was a sad, comic note in this, and perhaps that made the cops relax. One went to help his buddy who was leading Finkel, the two with the guns out put them away, one opened the back of the wagon, and the fifth made a face at the spectacle. That was the one Port hit.

Two jumps and he was in the dark. After a few more Port saw that three were coming after him, but the number didn't matter to him one way or the other. He ran. He hit boxes, jumped fences, scared chickens and made a racket when he raced through one cluttered-up end of a junk yard.

Two blocks away he tried to walk like a normal human being. He was still winded, but that didn't bother him. He was still in the same kind of white heat that had made him run but which was well focused now. He raked his hair with his fingers, hung his coat straight the way it should look, and then he pulled the threads off where he had lost a button. The street was lined with dusty ups-and-downs, and big trees kept the lamplight off the sidewalk. Since this was a residential street there was no one out—the nights were too cold. At the end of it Port saw a light and traffic, and behind him the length of the street was empty. No man with hands in his pockets and a big-brimmed hat.

At the light Port caught a taxi and gave the address. The cabby wasn't pleased when he heard it, and five minutes later Port knew why—he could have walked there. It was a big new apartment building in a field of waste, next door to a secondhand car lot, with a construction shack on the other side. Port paid, went through a lobby that was silent with carpets, took the push button elevator to the fifth floor and found 505. The building was so well constructed that Port couldn't hear a thing. He rang the bell. When the door opened he kicked it right out of Molnar's hand.

Molnar was square and heavy but perhaps his feet were too small, because Port gave him one tap in the belly and the big man stumbled far back into the room. Then Port closed the door quietly.

The apartment was small and expensive, and the furnishings were a mixture of hunting lodge things and boudoir gimcracks—crossed muzzle-loaders on the wall, porcelain figurines on the lowboy, rope woven chairs, silk pillows. A big Capehart was swilling mood music, and the record folder on the floor depicted a smiley man surrounded by bubbles. On the coffee table were two pink drinks. Then the toilet flushed.

"You hold still," said Port and showed Molnar the snout of the Mauser.

A young tower of muscle came out of the bathroom, blond hair combed into a shiny nest on top of his head, wearing a black shirt and very tight pants. The boy started to smile but then dropped it.

"Get over there with Mother," said Port.

The boy looked at the gun and then at Molnar.

"Please," said Molnar, "listen to me, Donald. The boy doesn't know a thing, you understand? Whatever you want, the boy doesn't know a thing!"

Port understood. He himself didn't want any audience. "Let him go, Donald. Just let—"

"Don't talk nonsense," said Port and walked to the middle of the room. "Step closer," he said to the boy.

He did. He was taller than Port, had more of a reach and was conceited enough not to feel any fear. Port wasn't sure how to handle this. "Turn around," he said.

"Donald! Will you for God's sake—"

"Shut up."

Molnar was like a mother hen, and Port wasn't sure how long he'd hold still. And the boy was big for a sure clip with the gun. It would have to be a one-blow thing because in a fight Molnar might jump in.

"Get that bottle of bourbon over there," said Port. The big blond got the bottle and brought it back by the neck. He smiled at Port while he held it that way.

"No," said Port. "Put it down on the table. Then you sit there, and you, Molnar, next to him."

Port kept standing. He put the gun back in his pocket and took a cigarette out of a box. The other two watched him and got tense again. Port lit his cigarette and exhaled.

"Drink it," said Port.

"Huh? You mean the liquor?" said the boy.

"From the bottle."

The boy laughed, saluted Molnar and drank. Then he put the bottle down and gave a long sigh.

"Drink some more," said Port.

"And then you *are* going to shoot me, aren't you?" He tipped the bottle again and then smacked his lips. "You kill me," he said to Port and smiled.

"Molnar," said Port. "You see to it that kid keeps the bottle up till I say otherwise." It was all very serious now.

"Donald—" Molnar blinked from one man to the other —"you realize what a quart of that stuff can do? My God, a pint taken in five minutes can kill a man!"

"He'll choke before then," said Port. He looked cold and mean, and his tone was hard.

The boy continued to drink. He drank in short, fast swallows and kept his eyes closed. He gasped for breath, and Port began to move up closer. Molnar, sweating, took the end of the bottle and kept holding it up. The boy couldn't swallow fast enough, and the brown liquor ran down his neck. He slumped down on the couch and kept sliding lower while Molnar, sweating hard now, held the bottle for him. The boy had his eyes wide open now, but they seemed torn wide open. He could see Port's face over him, and the gun—and especially the drawn face. The boy drank like a machine. When Port said, "That's enough," only Molnar heard it.

"How much did he drink?"

Molnar held up the bottle and looked at it. "Half," he said. He looked up at Port and some of the spirit came back into his face. "If something happens to him, Paducci, I'll cut you apart."

"Make him throw up," said Port.

The boy suddenly started to sing, his eyes wandering around in his head. Then he got up before Molnar could grab him and fell lengthwise across the coffee table.

"Better hurry up," said Port, "before he goes to sleep."

Molnar pulled himself together and came around to lift up his friend. He dragged him into the bathroom, put his head over the toilet bowl, and started to pat him on the back. The boy kept singing into the bowl.

"You're patting the wrong side," said Port. He lifted the toe of his shoe and tapped the boy in the stomach, once lightly. The boy threw up for a lengthy time. He was asleep when Molnar pulled him away.

"Put him on the bed," said Port.

Molnar was a strong man and carried the boy over to the bed. He put him down and put a blanket over him. He started to take off the shoes when Port said, "Now your turn, you bastard," and he took his overcoat off, threw it over the coffee table and put his Mauser on top.

There was nothing of the mother hen about Molner now. His hands were hanging down, and they moved a little. There would be a fight, the bearhug type, with sweaty muscles and harsh breathing into each others faces. The prospect was like a tonic to Molnar.

"I've been photoed," said Port, "and followed and set up and put down. You listen to me, Molnar. I'm sick of it!"

Molnar was chewing his lip and grinning at the same time. He didn't say anything.

"The next time I find that torpedo of yours sneaking after me I'll break his legs. And for that double cross with the cops tonight, I'm jacking my price."

"Cops?"

"You were the one who pushed that job in my lap, you sonofabitch, and Schenk's too smart to pull a jackass stunt like tonight. That wasn't brains behind that move, Molnar, that was peeve!"

"Paducci," said Molnar as if he hadn't heard a word, "I'm gonna wrench your back for this, Paducci." While he was still speaking he kicked at the coffee table so it sailed fast at Port's legs.

Port jumped aside, but too hastily to keep in balance, because by the time he regained it Molnar was already grabbing his waist.

And he wouldn't let go. He kept his head down so Port couldn't get at his face, and he kept his legs in the way so Port couldn't knee him. Port grabbed the man's ears but they were too small and sweaty to hold. Then he aimed his foot down, trying to break the other man's arch. At that instant, Port heard a noise behind him. Before whirling around, he rabbited Molnar in the neck. Molnar fell to the floor.

The next thing Port saw was the big forty-five looking at him and the big hand that held it. Leonard closed the door to the hall and came into the room.

"Are you trying to kill him, *Mr. Port?*"

Port froze. Then the shock which had stopped the breath in his throat ran out, and he sighed deeply. He went over to the couch, sat down and rubbed his face slowly.

"Put the gun away, Leonard, will you?"

"I did already." When Port took his hands away from his face Leonard was standing over Molnar, checking the damage, and his gun had disappeared into a pocket of his jacket.

There were a hundred explanations for all of this, but Port didn't care to think about them. It was very hard to think right now, and besides nothing looked much like an emergency. Molnar was passed out on the floor, and

Leonard was quietly smiling as he did most of the time. Now he was pouring himself a drink, a casual enough act for a man with a big gun and a knowledge that could kill Port before morning. Leonard held the glass in his hand and walked around a little, looking at the apartment.

"Did you know there's somebody else sleeping here?" he said from the bedroom.

"Maybe he's dead," said Port. "Better check if he's dead. I'm not sure of anything any more."

His Mauser was still on the table. He picked it up and slipped it into his pocket. And he kept his hand there on it.

"He seems to be drunk," Leonard said.

"He's quite a boy."

Then Leonard came back. He was sipping his drink casually, with one hand in his pocket.

"If you let go of your gun, Mr. Port, I'll let go of mine."

They looked at each other for a moment, and then Port laughed. After they had both taken their hands out of their pockets the atmosphere in the room relaxed.

"Who said I'm Port?"

"I'm not certain I should tell you."

"Who put the torpedo after me?"

"Torpedo? Hard to say."

"Yuh. And how come you got out of jail so fast?"

"I have connections."

"The way you answer, Leonard, I'm reminded of somebody else," said Port. Then he got up and went to the phone. He didn't feel tired any more. "I'm going to make a call," he said, "but for your and my peace of mind, Leonard, what do you say we put the guns over there—on that chair, for instance—and then there won't be any nervousness."

"Are you going to call Mr. O'Day?"

Port didn't think his face had changed at all, but Leonard emitted a low laugh. "You're going through a great deal in one evening. Perhaps you should call Mr. O'Day."

"So you're his contact."

"I appreciate your choice of words, Mr. Port. Really I do."

"Are you with the FBI?"

"No. I have no ties. That's why I can do what I do."

It sounded a little bitter, the kind of tone that comes from doing something without conviction. Leonard was probably neither dedicated nor a true opportunist. Port felt that he was not an ally for either side.

Then Molnar made a sound on the floor, and Port picked up the phone.

O'Day knew who it was right away. "I go to the trouble," he said, "of sending the police over there to save you embarrassment, and you go and cause me all kinds of difficulties with your self-styled—"

"Get together with me on your plans ahead of time, O'Day, and you save yourself trouble. And me. I just accused Molnar of fingering that raid on Finkel, and, I don't have to tell you, he didn't know a thing about it. *That's* trouble, O'Day. That really puts me in a helluva spot."

"Careful," said Leonard from the room. "He's coming around."

Molnar turned painfully and his eyes trembled open. Port couldn't talk any more without tipping everything.

"You almost broke his neck," Leonard said. "Look at the swelling."

Port heard him but didn't answer. Then he turned back to the phone.

"O'Day? Get an ambulance over here for Molnar. He needs hospitalization. He's in the hospital because he's sick, see? It's a police matter because I charge him with assault."

"Where?"

"His apartment."

"His place? Don't you know you don't have a leg to stand on with that charge?"

"He'll hold still for it. Just threaten him with prosecution for pederasty. Molnar will take the lesser count."

O'Day left the phone for a moment to arrange for the pick-up. When he came back he wanted to know why Port wanted all this done. Port told him in such a way that Molnar, in case he was clear headed enough to listen, wouldn't understand.

"I'll have one out of the way. Understand?"

"If Molnar's important, you mean, his absence can narrow your field."

"Yes. It needs it." Port thought about two things which needed clearing right away. "Are you having me followed?"

"What?" O'Day sounded surprised. "You're on *our* side, aren't you?"

"Without the jokes, yes or no?"

"No. Why the hell should I?"

"You should've. Now tell me this. Did you find the girl?"

"Yes. At home."

"She hasn't been near Schenk, or the club, anything like that?"

"No. But she's got a phone in her place. She could have used it."

She could have. The thought made Port feel terrible. "About that shadow," said O'Day. "We can run that down for you. What's he look like?"

"Plain beige overcoat, hands in pockets, straight walk, five-nine maybe, hat with a big brim. I never saw the face. I lost him this evening."

"I should think so."

"But you should be able to pick him up at my hotel in the morning."

"We'll follow him," said O'Day, and Port could hear him tear off a sheet of paper. "And since he probably came straight from Gracie, or because of her information, Port, you're going to get a bodyguard of your own. We want you to live until the job's finished."

"Jokes," said Port and hung up.

Chapter 8

Molnar didn't know Port was Port, but maybe Schenk did. And if Schenk knew by now, that would also indicate who was the important one in the setup. He hadn't bothered to tell Molnar about it.

From Molnar's place Port went to Schenk's.

On his way to the Heights Port didn't think he was followed, and when he got out of his taxi at Schenk's place nobody was there, either. No reason for a shadow there, since Port was going into the house anyway.

All the lights were on, as usual, and Port wondered if the night's girl was still expected or was already there. It turned out that nobody was there. A young kid opened the door who didn't count because he knew how to say only one thing, that Schenk wasn't home.

The kid had the chain on the door and peeked through the crack. He wore pegleg pants and narrow suspenders, and he had a big head of hair, artfully brushed. Port saw only one half of him but he got the full picture. The boy was sort of an apprentice. Port also saw the magazine in his hand, showing half a female, mostly naked. The other half would be the same.

"And you don't know where he went?" Port asked.

"Can't help you, feller, so you better leave." He left the door crack open, watching.

"You don't know who I am, do you, kid?" Port asked him.

"That's right."

"Paducci. Don Paducci."

"Man!" said the kid. "Man—" He had met his hero.

"Can I come in and wait a while?"

The kid unchained the door, swung it open, and seemed willing to offer the whole house as a gift. "I'm sitting in the den," he said. "You wanna sit in the den, Mr. Paducci? Or maybe you wanna sit—"

"The den will be wonderful," said Port.

After the boy had chained the door again he rushed ahead of Port to receive him in the den. The TV set had a new tube and was playing. There was a radio on the bookshelf, and it was playing. A bottle of whisky stood next to a glass, and all the lights were on in the room.

"You alone in the house?" Port asked.

"Yeah, yessir. I take the phone calls. You know, sometimes there's important phone calls in Mr. Schenk's absence and I take 'em. You here for something important, Mr. Paducci? How about letting me offer you a drink? I was just gonna make myself—"

"Go ahead. I don't want any." Port stood near the bar while the kid became very busy mixing exact proportions. Ice, ginger ale, whisky, and a stiff extra shot of the ginger ale when Port wasn't looking.

"Some layout, huh?" and he waved the glass at everything. "That Mr. Schenk sure knows how to live, huh, Paducci?"

He was getting familiar already, thought Port. No more mister.

"Yessir," he went on. "Nothing but the best for him." The kid threw in a few more platitudes that mixed right in with the garble from the radio and the TV set. "And speaking of the best," he said, "lemme show you something."

He put his glass down, untasted, and leafed through the magazine with the posed female pictures.

"You see this one, huh?" He was pointing out a black-haired one, face painted so it would mean temptress, posture suggesting she was ready to leap anything. "And Schenk knows her *personal!*"

"Gee," said Port.

"That's something, huh?"

"That's something," said Port and smiled at the picture. Then he shrugged and said, "You'd never tell from that, would you, that she's no good in bed."

"Her? This one here? Stacked like that here?"

"Strange, isn't it? But Evelina just hasn't got it."

"Evelina? It says here her name's Kitty."

"Well, of course. That's just put down there to disguise her real identity, kid. You know how it is. It protects the reputation, not calling her Evelina."

The kid was off Schenk now and admiring Port again. He went and turned off the TV set and the radio, and then he asked Port to sit down.

"Tell me something, Paducci," he said. "You know her good?"

"You're *interested*, after I told you how she is in bed?"

"No, of course not, not if she's no good in bed."

"It so happens," said Port, "she's got a sister who's good in bed."

"Man!"

"Funny you don't know about her. Just hit town, recently."

"What?"

"Tell me," said Port, "maybe you'd know where I can reach Schenk. We been sitting around here almost half an hour."

"Schenk?"

"Yuh. You know."

The kid looked away from the picture and said, "He's in the Flats, in the place there where they got meetings sometimes."

"Maybe Schenk didn't get my message. Maybe I better go there."

"Yeah. Maybe you better go there. Uh—"

"I don't know where that is, kid. I'm new in town myself. Like Evelina's sister."

Then the kid told Port where to look for Schenk in the Flats, whatever that was. There was a truck terminal by the river which ran through the Flats—Trans-Roadways, Inc. was the name, and you couldn't miss it. Then, "You were telling me about this Evelina..."

"Her sister, you mean," said Port and got up. He told the kid what number to call and to ask for O'Day—the pass word was Evelina's sister.

"Can I mention your name?" the kid asked at the door.

"Better not. It'll jack up the price." And Port left the house to look for a taxi.

The cabby seemed to know what the Flats were and that the Trans-Roadways was open twenty-four hours. The trip from the Heights took almost an hour which Port spent thinking about O'Day. It relaxed him to think of nothing important. It was going to get serious soon enough, and except for general intentions there was nothing he could solve in advance. He knew what he wanted to find out. Did Schenk know that Paducci was Port? Was Schenk the top dog in the setup? He could have asked Gracie a few questions, but not now. She would lie, or if she didn't it would mean he was involving her more than she had already been involved.

But Port wasn't calm about walking in on Schenk. There was a meeting—and the way things had been going, it was more than likely that the meeting was about him.

Downtown, the cab swung down a ramp and the landscape changed. No tall buildings, no big lights, no streets with traffic. The first thing that struck Port as the cab went down the ramp were the black girders and bridges. There were more bridges rearing out of the dark than Port had ever seen in one place. The bottom of the ramp ended in the Flats, a stretch of land lower than the rest of the town, a stretch that smelled of boats on the river, of streets with small factory buildings of dark brick, of the black junk yards and the fat storage tanks for gas and petroleum. And every so often the massive bulk of a bridge arched high over everything, including the buildings.

"See the lights there?" the driver asked.

Port saw the lights, a lot of bluish neon which looked strange in the old gloom of the street.

"That's Trans-Roadways. There's two entrances I know of—"

"I'll get out right here," said Port, "and walk."

For an inconspicuous meeting the place was good.

Port went by the long loading ramp and then past the office part of the building. Most of the offices were lit up too. Then came the unlit parking lot, behind which he could see the river. There were a number of cars parked there, belonging to the men who worked at the truck terminal. If there were any belonging to Schenk and company, they couldn't have been in a better place.

Port walked slowly along the row of cars.

"Just stand there," somebody said.

The light from the ramp didn't reach to the lot. Port stopped and waited. If the man was a watchman, it would be no good.

"I been watching you, feller. You don't work here."

"Neither do you," said Port.

The man had a blue-jawed face, and his ostentatious clothes had cost a lot of money. He looked Port up and down, trying to decide what tone of voice to use.

"Blow," he said. "Scat." And to show what he thought of Port he waved his hands at him as if scaring a bird away.

"Listen," Port said, "I've got to see Schenk."

"Schenk? You?" He would have laughed except Port was losing patience. When the punk grabbed Port by the front, Port pushed the flat of his hand into the man's face so hard that the impact made a sound against his nose. The man staggered back and then reached under his coat.

"I'm Paducci," said Port, and the man stopped reaching.

It was good to know that the name was important by now. It meant less work.

Then the punk took him over to a side entrance which led into a corridor. They went into one of the offices there. The tables in the office held covered typewriters, and there were two more men like the one who had found Port. One was pecking a keyboard, denting the roller, and the other was smiling into a telephone. They both acted interrupted when Port and his escort came in.

"Where's Schenk?" Port asked them. He poked one man in the back with his finger and the other one stopped in the middle of a sentence because Paducci, *the* Paducci, would poke with nothing less than a gun.

"Who wants him?" said the one at the typewriter.

"Just get Schenk," said the one with the finger in the small of his back. "Come on, now. You got to make a production of everything?"

Port was relieved. If Port-Paducci was the topic at the meeting it wouldn't do to have advance notice. He told the two men in the office to stay where they were because he and his friend here would walk right in. His friend began to walk immediately. He walked to the back of the office, where a section was partitioned off by glass. In that cubicle was another door. There was light behind the door, and voices.

"Do we knock?" Port asked.

"We better. If you know Schenk then you'll know—"

"Just knock."

After the knock the conversation behind the door stopped abruptly. Then Schenk yelled, "Who is it?"

"Me. Davy."

"Why? What in hell is so important it can't wait for a while?"

"Paducci," said Davy through the door before Port could prevent it. So instead, Port opened the door to find out what was going on.

Schenk was sitting at a table with two other men. They had some ledgers and papers in front of them, and the big office window at the back looked out on the river.

"This better be important," said Schenk. "Come in."

They came in.

"Not you," said Schenk and jerked his head at Davy, but the man didn't move right away. Then Port showed him his hands, with one finger out, and said, "It's safe, Davy. Don't be scared." Davy left.

Then Schenk nodded at the younger of the two men at the table, and that one put down his pencil and left too.

Schenk worried his cigarette like he always did, waiting for Port to talk. He was angry, and the other man, paunchy and bald, was puzzled. He wore rimless glasses and a very white shirt, all of which made him look important—but small-town important.

"This is Senator Bainbeck," said Schenk, and then to Bainbeck, "this is the one I was mentioning. He's Paducci."

Bainbeck's face covered itself with a professional smile. Love me, it said, and vote for me. He held out one hand and put the other one into the armhole of his vest, country lawyer style, except that he was too bald for the standard impression.

"Why, Mr. Paducci," said Bainbeck through his smile. "We were just talking about you."

As soon as the man talked the Honest Abe impression was gone.

Port and the senator shook hands because the senator was the kind one shook hands with, and then Port looked from one to the other. Whether the senator was going to be in on this would be up to Schenk.

"I reorganized your team a little bit," Port said to Schenk. "Molnar's in the hospital."

"What?"

"I beat him up."

Schenk got out of his chair as if stung. He looked at Port, at the door, but then Bainbeck put in a word.

"Perhaps," he said, "Mr. Paducci should have a chance to explain himself." He put on a soothing face.

The remark could have meant that Bainbeck was in the habit of controlling Schenk, that he just tried to smooth out any conversation he happened to hear. Port didn't know which it was.

"I got jumped when Leonard and I went to Finkel's," said Port, "and the logical one for having set up that timing was your buddy Molnar."

That explanation was as good as any, since it had been the reason why Port had gone to Molnar. Port couldn't explain that O'Day was behind the raid.

"Where's Molnar now?" Schenk asked. He looked suspicious and mean.

"Call the police. They'll know."

Schenk called the police. They gave him the hospital, and the hospital told Schenk he couldn't talk to the patient. The patient was being put in a cast, and besides he was in no shape to talk. Schenk hung up and didn't say anything for a while. His next steps, thought Port, would show how important Molnar's removal was—and how important Schenk was.

"Senator," said Schenk, "I think you better leave."

"Would you like me to wait so we can—"

"Yeah. Wait."

This made Schenk look important again.

When Bainbeck had left the room Schenk still didn't start talking. He picked up the phone again. He called several people and gave instructions. Port didn't know the names, but it sounded like Schenk was the general and the others were lieutenants. With Molnar out for a while, Schenk was reorganizing. Maybe they were little steps that had to be taken because the top man, or one top man, was incapacitated. Maybe they were big steps. Port couldn't tell. Then Schenk hung up abruptly and lit a cigarette.

"Bad thing, Paducci," he said. "Bad all around."

"I hope I didn't topple your empire," said Port.

But Schenk didn't take it up. He said, "They raided Finkel's?"

"I told you."

"And Molnar did it?"

"He says no."

"He wouldn't," said Schenk. "He knows better."

"Your setup couldn't afford it?"

"I told you we're new," said Schenk, and he sat thinking.

It looked now as though what O'Day had pulled could well be the stupidest stunt yet, because Schenk was clearly suspicious. He knew as well as Port did that Molnar wasn't idiot enough to raid his own operations, and that meant he would start looking.

"There hasn't been a raid since I'm in," said Schenk. "You get it? We have good relations." He kept eying Port. Then he said, "If it wasn't coincidence, Donald, it might have been you."

"With my record?"

Schenk got up, looking like he was bored by all this. Then he said, "There's one way, Donald, my boy, you can show me you're right."

"I tell you how right I am, Schenk. With Molnar rubbing me wrong like this, and with you stalling, the ante just went up. I want ten thousand."

"One way you can show you are right," Schenk said again. "Show me Port."

There was a silence. Schenk wouldn't move because he wasn't sure about Port-Paducci, and Port wouldn't move because he wasn't sure who was head man. He didn't know what to say next, but that lull didn't last long.

"How's Gracie?" Schenk said suddenly.

Port didn't answer.

"I got a call from Gracie, you know that, Donald?" Schenk smiled to himself. He started to walk around the room, and Port sat back a little, his hands in his pockets now.

"Wants to see me, she said." Then Schenk came back to the table and grinned. "You couldn't have been much good, Donald." He laughed. "I knew she'd come around."

To keep himself clearheaded and not hear more than Schenk had really said, Port said nothing and tried to breathe without effort. What Schenk had said could mean the worst—or it could mean nothing. It could mean that Schenk was just talking about a lay.

"I bring it up," said Schenk, "to make something clear to you, Donald. There's nobody here likes you any more. Gracie don't sound like she likes you any more, Molnar we don't have to discuss—and me Donald, *I'm* getting fed up."

Nothing was going right. Port wasn't finding out a thing. He should have walked in here with some better plan. It wasn't enough to watch as Schenk phoned instructions after he heard that Molnar was out. It might not even be enough to have seen Schenk send the senator out of the room because of business that was none of Bainbeck's affair.

Schenk was over by the door now, and he opened it unexpectedly. "Cover him," he said to the men outside.

Port felt he could have gotten the first one, anyway, but then what? Maybe they wouldn't have shot back, or, more likely, they would have shot back and tried not to kill him. Then there'd be a long mess of ill temper, anger and needless harm. Port felt almost tired, sitting there in his chair and watching the three hoods come into the room, running like commandos. Davy from the parking lot was first, with a face right off a pulp cover.

"Just cover him," Schenk said from the door, as Davy hauled out his gun.

So three men with guns stood around Port's chair, and Port sat there, not even curious. Then Schenk came walking back, and the senator peeked through the door. He came walking in after a while, very curious but not upset. He now looked like one of those bald men at a burlesque, showing interest but no excitement, because that wouldn't be nice.

"You got a gun on you, Donald?" asked Schenk.

"Right jacket pocket," said Port, but was careful not to make a move.

"Doesn't even show," said Schenk, puffing on his cigarette.

"That's the way I carry it."

Then Schenk nodded and one of the three men with guns took the little Mauser out of Port's pocket.

"Like I was telling you before," Schenk said, "nobody likes you any more." He sat down on the edge of the table and looked at Port as though he were thinking. Then he sighed and said, "Which would be no problem, ordinarily, but maybe it is now."

"What makes you think so?" asked Port and looked at the three guns around him.

"I just heard from Bink."

Who was supposed to be in France, Port remembered, who was supposed to have met Paducci but never did, who was supposed to be hung up with the law by now and no trouble to anyone.

"You did?" said Port.

"I did. He went to France, remember?"

Port just nodded.

"The jackass went to France," Schenk said with some temper now, "and is stuck in jail there—for hopping a broad!"

"In France?" said Davy.

"For doing it without benefit of marriage! And in France!"

Then the comedy dropped right out of it again because Schenk was concerned with other matters.

"So I'm stuck with you," he said to Port. He started pacing while he lit a new cigarette. "Bink arrested—awful lot of arrests lately. All of a sudden nobody around what knows Port around here—or you, Paducci," he said to Port. "And now Canning too." He turned to everybody. "You ever hear of anybody getting transferred out of Columbus and in stir for ten more years? And nobody knows where?"

"Maybe I can help there," said Senator Bainbeck. He came all the way into the room, and the smile said, I am anxious to please.

Schenk looked at Bainbeck for a while, thinking, and then he just nodded. "Go ahead," he mumbled. "Try it." He turned to Port and spoke normally again. "And you, Paducci, I want you out of the way for a while."

"Listen, Schenk—"

"Shut up. With that cop raid I want you out of the way, just because you skipped out from under them. They might still be looking. And because they pulled that raid in the first place. That needs looking into."

Port felt himself sweat now, hoping that O'Day had tied up his connection good and secure.

"And a few other things got to be straightened out," Schenk was saying. "So you stay away till I'm all cleared up."

"Shandor's place?" asked one of the hoods.

"No. Out of town. Best thing would be out of town." Schenk thought about it for a while, not knowing just where.

"Uh—if I could make a suggestion," said Bainbeck, and Schenk looked at him. "I'm not using my place in Hudson."

"Hudson where? *On* the Hudson?"

"I forgot you are new here," said Bainbeck, and his smile forgave Schenk. "There's a small town called Hudson a few miles out of the city. Respectable town, respectable house, which I use summers sometime or for a week end in the winter. It would attract no attention to any one of us."

"All right. Fine." Schenk threw his cigarette away. "Hudson is fine."

Then there were instructions on how to get down to Hudson, and a discussion about the senator lending his car for appearances and about who would go along. Davy would go along. Senator Bainbeck, for the night at least, would go—and of course, Port.

"My appearance at the house," Bainbeck explained to Schenk, "would make everything that much less suspect. And I'd be within reach," he added, "since we didn't finish this business."

All he meant by that last comment, it seemed, was the business they had been conducting before Port had come in, because Bainbeck nodded at the papers on the table and then watched Schenk put on his coat. "Unless you would like to continue now..."

"Naw. I'm not in the mood." Schenk let one of his men help him with the collar, and then he reached for a new cigarette. "Got something else now," he said through the smoke.

The feeling in the room was the same as when a party breaks up—something finished.

"Can I give you a lift?" said Bainbeck.

"No. Phone me a taxi, Walter," he said to one of the men.

Bainbeck was putting papers together and closed a ledger. "But I could easily—"

"Never mind," said Schenk. "I'm just gonna see Gracie." He looked at Port when he said it.

"Why, of course," said Bainbeck and smiled. "I remember the little lady. How is the little lady?"

"Ask him." And Schenk nodded at Port.

"You know her too, Mr. Paducci?" Bainbeck tried on various smiles, one after the other. "I had been under the impression—"

"She's free," said Schenk, "As of twenty-four hours ago."

"Really," said Bainbeck. He was putting on his coat and wasn't looking at anyone.

Feeling the way he did Schenk suddenly snapped at the senator. "You want her?" he said, and then he laughed.

"Well—as a matter of fact—uh—does she know how to type?"

"I don't know if she types. I never used her for typing," said Schenk. He kept looking at Bainbeck, disliking the old man for his roundabout ways.

"She types," said Davy. "I happen to know that she types."

Schenk laughed, but he didn't take it up any further. He wanted to leave. The important thing of the evening had been handled, putting Paducci on ice for the moment. He didn't want Paducci around, but he felt sure he could use him later. The most important thing of all hadn't been accomplished yet—killing Port.

Chapter 9

They did take Schenk along in the end and drove to Gracie's apartment. Port sat in back with one man on each side of him, and Bainbeck sat in front with Schenk, who was driving. Port just sat still because there was nothing else he could do now which made sense. It made sense to hold still for a while and let Schenk make his moves. Once Port was in the house out in Hudson, with only the senator, who didn't count, and perhaps two men to watch Port, it would all be much more in his hands again. But the ride to Gracie's was bad.

They let Schenk off at her apartment, and Schenk never said a word all that time. One off his men got out with him, and only Davy stayed to watch over Port. The senator moved over to drive the car.

"Schenk," said Port from the window.

"What?"

"All my things are in my hotel. Ask Leonard to bring me some underwear."

"Why Leonard?"

"Because I got to know him a little."

Schenk didn't answer. He went into the apartment building. Port had no way of knowing if the message would get to Leonard and from him to O'-Day. On the drive to Hudson he wondered if it would.

Gracie had finished two drinks when the bell rang, and she heard voices on the other side of the door. Why hadn't Schenk come alone? She opened the door, and there was Schenk with one of his men. He came in, and the other man stayed outside.

"For protection," said Schenk. "If he hears me scream, he'll come in and save me."

So far, he was just being sarcastic. Gracie said, "Hello, honey. Come in."

"I'm in. Close the door."

She closed the door and watched him sit down on the couch. He had kept his coat on.

"You want a drink?" she said nervously.

"No. But you want one."

She went and got herself another drink. That was number three. That was the one, she thought to herself, to give her the courage to sell all she had.

She sat down opposite Schenk with her drink and said, "Don't you want me back, Billy?" It didn't sound very clever.

"No."

She looked into her glass and felt herself getting mad. Then she took a quick drink.

"You and me were okay, weren't we?" she asked.

"Sure. So were a lot of people."

Why was he staying? To have his game, she thought. To put her through the mill before taking her back.

"You don't want me," said Schenk. "You want your meal ticket."

"That's right, Billy."

For a moment she was afraid she had said too much, but then he was laughing because it had sounded funny to him. It's all right, she thought. He likes me candid.

"I been treating you pretty good, haven't I, Gracie?"

She nodded at him, not knowing which way he was going to go. To make really sure of her interests, she should go over and sit next to him.

"I buy you things, I give you money, I don't wear you out with demands, right, Gracie?"

"I know," she said. She should move, go over there, but she sat still. She felt she was getting drunk in the wrong way.

"And you'd like all that back, huh, Gracie?"

"And you too, Billy," she got out.

"Sure." Then he changed his tone of voice. "How much you been saving, Gracie?" He didn't wait for an answer. "How much more time do you need?" He grinned at her.

She suddenly got angry. She was ashamed that she had been that obvious.

"What?" she said to him. "And maybe I haven't been giving you a thing? Nothing you couldn't get elsewhere? Then why me? Answer me! Then why'd you come over?"

"For kicks."

"For kicks? I'll give you kicks, Bill Schenk!" Then she wanted to say what she thought would be her best point for getting back in.

What did she know? She knew that Paducci was something imported and that Schenk didn't import unless it was big. And she knew that Schenk was up to his neck in some business, some kind of big business, so delicate it would maybe make a difference to him to know that Paducci had another name. What in hell was that name now? Pod? Port, maybe. If she weren't so rattled now in the head with the lousy drinks and with Schenk's lousy manner she'd know how to bring this thing up, bring it up the right way to see if there was a sign of interest. After all, being ambitious meant she was smart, so smart she could forget about that bastard in the hotel bed a few days ago.

"Come here," said Schenk. "Come here and sit down, Gracie."

She went over and sat down because it was so easy. He put one arm around her and worked his hand on her shoulder.

"Mad, aren't you?" he said. She could feel his face next to hers, and from the way it moved she was sure he was grinning. With his other hand he unbuttoned the blouse and then opened it up.

"So mad," he said, "you forget all about the reason why I'm here..."

She just sat there with him and said, "Why are you here, Billy?"

"To teach you a lesson." He kept holding her with one hand on her shoulder and one hand in her shirt, but that wasn't anything new to think about.

"Hey!" he called suddenly. "Come on in!"

The door opened, and his man came in. Schenk was still holding her.

"Close the door, stupid," said Schenk. "You wanna compromise the girl?" While the man closed the door and Schenk laughed to himself, he started to take off her shirt.

All of a sudden she was very sober. She wasn't feeling ambitious or too far removed from the things that were going on so she hauled out with her free arm and clipped Schenk hard on the side of the face. The blow made a loud smack and rocked him back into the cushions. Then she jumped up.

She began screaming at Schenk but then she heard Schenk yell at his man, who went out of the room, closing the door.

She saw Schenk get up. She was now terribly afraid of him. He could beat her now, and her face would never be the same. He could hurt her now, and she would not know what to do about it. If he asked her now about Paducci, she'd tell him all she had heard.

"Get in the bedroom," he said.

She went immediately, almost laughing, because it had never occurred to her that he would ask the simplest thing of her. She went into the bedroom ahead of him, unzipping and unhooking herself on the way. It was such a familiar thing.

He was done with her in a very short time, not liking it much. And not liking it angered him.

"Get up," he said, "and get dressed."

She did what he told her.

"Get ready with some stuff to wear," he said. "I got an idea."

She was hooking herself and didn't look up. She had thought she could take almost anything, but now that he was going to tell her that she had her meal ticket back, it all seemed very flat. As if all this had only happened to spite Don Paducci but Don Paducci didn't give a damn.

"You have an idea?" she said, to be saying something.

"Yes. I want you to blow town."

"You want me to blow town," she repeated.

"Yes, honey. Because you're through."

That revived her. It was a hopeless feeling, actually, but at least she felt something now.

"Before I do that," she said, "let me tell you something."

"Is it important?"

"I don't know yet."

He caught the difference in her tone and stopped at the door. He waited with his cigarette unlit in his hand. "What's that, Gracie?"

"You interested in Paducci?" she asked.

Schenk came back into the room and sat down on the bed, expressionless. "I'm waiting," he said.

"It'll cost you."

"Sure. Go ahead."

"Go to hell," she told him.

Schenk sighed and decided to handle it better.

"You mean, first I pay, then you tell me."

They were now talking business, and there was nothing else between them. It made their conversation clear and much more to the point.

"Not even that," she said, "because I don't know yet if I know something."

Schenk respected that attitude, and he listened.

"I first got to see him again," said Gracie. She hoped it sounded businesslike because suddenly it wasn't altogether that.

"All right," said Schenk. He got up and buttoned his coat. "But tell me anyway, what *aren't* you sure about with Paducci?"

"First I got to see him again."

He didn't think he could argue her out of it, nor was there any reason to. Anything she could say about Paducci would be something new. Too much had gone queer since Paducci had shown, and anything would be a contribution. Maybe Paducci had plans of his own for the territory? Something like that. It would have to be something like that.

"I'll send you out there," said Schenk. "To Hudson. I'm holding him there, while I check on a few things."

"All right," she said. "Fine."

"You listen to me how you go there. You don't go there to see him, or he'll smell something. You go there and see the senator."

"You mean that politician?"

"It's not a dirty word, Gracie."

"I don't know him. I never saw him."

"Can you type? If you can, you're in."

"He sounds like he drools."

"He does, honey. You just tell him I sent you."

She wrinkled her forehead but didn't say anything. It had to be this way. There was no point acting as if this was beneath her.

"And what with you and your ambitions," said Schenk lightly, "*there's* a meal ticket for you, Gracie. The senator."

Chapter 10

She had an overnight bag with her, and Senator Bainbeck was carrying it. He put it down in the hall, where Port greeted Gracie with surprise. Then Bainbeck shooed her upstairs so she could freshen up, and while she was gone he paced around the living room, smiling and talking.

Port wondered about Gracie and the senator. Had she come to roll in bed with him? He was really surprised to see her here. It was crazy and ugly, and Port didn't like it. But then she had said often that she was ambitious. But what were her other reasons for being here? The grey man with the big hat had showed up soon after that time in the hotel room—coincidence or not?

The bright sun disappeared suddenly, and shortly after it started to blow outside, changing the atmosphere in the room. There had been a garden-room atmosphere in the place, with the sun coming in through the long French windows, but now, the gray light outside made the old furniture look more prominent and the fine rug on the floor seem thicker. When Bainbeck said he would light a fire, that was exactly the one thing the room needed. There was a coal grate in the fireplace, and after a little bit of fussing the fire started up with a roar. Except for Davy on the couch with his eternal gun, there was a deceptive air of comfort and ease.

"I think I'll go up," said Bainbeck, and when nobody answered him he looked as if he wanted to say it again. Then he snickered to himself, saying, "Uh—I'll see if she needs something," he went upstairs.

"What she needs," said Davy, "he ain't got. Huh, Paducci?"

"Why don't you shut up," said Port.

They could hear his footsteps upstairs and a door opening, and then voices. Sometimes the conversation was very low and even, and a few times—when Gracie said something—it got very high. She also laughed, sharply enough to be heard clearly downstairs.

When they came down the steps Bainbeck was still talking to her, laughing at his own remarks, and then Gracie laughed too, a hard and nervous sound. She stopped laughing when she came into the room.

"It got dark in here," she said.

Nobody answered except Bainbeck, who said that there was no telling the weather. Then nobody spoke at all. Gracie sat down at a library table and looked at the fire, and Bainbeck went back and forth from the hall to the room a few times. He still looked the same, oldish and bald, but his manner reminded Port of an adolescent very nervous about his first date.

"I tell you what we could do, my dear," he said the next time he came into the room. "We could take a nice walk. There is some of the loveliest—"

"It's too cold," said Gracie, "don't you think?"

"Ah, of course. Well, we can use my car. I can show you the loveliest—"

"Listen, Mr. Bainbeck," said Gracie, "I feel tired." She gave him a wilted smile.

Bainbeck gave up then and excused himself all around. He explained that he, at any rate, would take a brief walk into the village. Among other things it would show the people in Hudson that there were no strange goings-on at his house but that he had simply come down, with some friends, to spend a short week end. Everybody nodded and thought that was a good idea. After some business of finding galoshes, scarf and heavy overcoat, Bainbeck left.

Port smoked, and Davy looked as if he would like to sleep. Gracie still sat at the library table, leafing through a magazine.

"Davy," said Port. "I'm going to sit closer to the fire."

"Why tell me about it?" He acted as if he had been woken up.

"Because it means I have to get up, and I don't want you to shoot me while I'm doing it."

"That's right," said Davy. "Now you're learning."

Port got off the couch and went to the library table. He sat down opposite Gracie, his back to the gunman. She looked up from her magazine and said, "Hi, Don."

"Hi."

"And I don't want you to sit there making time with that dame," said Davy.

"Just conversation," said Port. "You know, one says hello, then the other one says hello. That kind of thing."

"All right. But loud, so I can hear it."

Gracie leafed through her magazine but kept looking at Port because she wanted to talk. She wanted to say something to him, but even with Davy not there it would have been difficult for her.

"I didn't really expect you here," said Port.

"I asked to come."

"Bainbeck?"

She said yes, so Davy could hear it, but shook her head. She moved her hands around on the table, not knowing what to say next. She could have touched him so easily, she could even have leaned her face over the table close to his face, but none of that was possible. Perhaps even if Davy hadn't been there it would not have worked.

"You remember the last time?" she said.

"Yes. I do."

"Now wait a minute," said Davy. "I told you a minute ago I don't wanna hear nothing I don't understand. What's all this about last time?"

"She means," said Port, "that we met once before."

It was going to be difficult, even not counting Davy.

"Let's put it this way," said Port to the girl. "Considering adverse circumstances, can you formulate matters in a complex way?"

She understood what he was trying to do. He was trying to talk over Davy's head, but things were difficult enough as they were. She said, "I hardly know how even without the circumlocution."

"Now wait a minute, wait a minute!" Davy made the couch creak as he waved the gun. "I'm sitting here and hearing every word, you understand? So watch it! Just watch that language!"

"All right," said Port. "We won't talk."

He opened a magazine and leafed through it. Then he took out a pencil and gave it to the girl. She wrote on the magazine.

I lost out, on your account.

I'm sorry, he wrote back.

That's no help.

But my feeling.

She read that and bit her lip. They were sitting so close, too close for the way they had to handle this. She wished very much that she had no problems but could just go on being ambitious. And Port's face showed her nothing. In a while she wrote again.

I'm here on business.

Schenk's?

Yes.

With Bainbeck?

With you.

Port looked at her, but she looked away. All he wanted to know now was how close she was to all this and who else was in on it.

This is the wrong place, he wrote.

So was the hotel.

Not all of it.

Then he turned a leaf to make a sound for Davy. After that he didn't know what else to write. He wished she wouldn't sit there, staring out of the window, but make the next move. Then she did.

Who are you?

He didn't answer that right away. He wished it were a simple matter with her, a simple response the way it would have been if Schenk or an idiot like Davy had asked the question. In either case things would not have been complicated because there would only have been one thing to do—to fight or lie out of it. Which was why he was here. He wrote,

You're not sure?

No.

Who else isn't?

Just me.

Can you wait?

Just me, so far, she wrote as if she hadn't read his last question.

Schenk wants to know, or you?

Both. Badly.

Why you?

She hesitated for a moment, and then she wrote, *Do you want me?*

Port sighed before he answered her, but she misunderstood it. It stayed that way because the front door opened, and Bainbeck came back in, stamping his feet for no reason. His scarf was wrapped up to his nose, but they could tell he was smiling. He waved at them like an uncle, and Gracie got up.

Port had no time for anything now but to pick up the magazine and take it to the fireplace. He tore out the pages they had written on and put them on the fire.

"Hey," said Davy, "what are you doing?"

"I'm making a fire."

"Oh." He sat down again.

Gracie went to the arch that led into the hall, and she and Bainbeck exchanged a few pleasantries.

Bainbeck said a hot cup of tea would be nice now and asked if he should make enough for all present. Gracie said yes.

Is she with Schenk, thought Port, or me?

Chapter 11

It was a very long day. The wind stopped after a while, and rain pattered briefly against the long windows. Then it was just gray again. Sometimes Bainbeck and Gracie were around, and at other times they would disappear upstairs, but always before long Port would hear conversation or Gracie laughing that forced laugh. Then she would come down the stairs. Not that the senator was trying too earnestly at this point, but it certainly seemed he wanted to prepare the ground properly for the night. He and Gracie stayed in the living room in the later afternoon, playing cards. To avoid additional partners he had at first asked Gracie if she knew how to play chess, and when she said no he had offered to teach her the game. But Gracie didn't want to learn. She wanted to learn two-handed poker. The senator then made a token offer to the others to join, but both Port and Davy said no. So the senator taught Gracie the game, and she displayed a miraculous talent, winning respectable sums of money from him. Perhaps it was clear to him that she wasn't new at the game, but he let her win because he felt it was a way in which payment could be made delicately.

She and Port looked at each other now and then, but that was all that happened between them. There was no other choice.

When it got dark Port thought about Schenk, who had had a full day to find out what was behind that queer raid on Finkel, to find out perhaps where Canning was, to worry about Molnar and why nobody got to see him in the hospital.

But it occurred to Port that maybe Schenk hadn't found out anything yet, or else he would be here now. Or else he would have phoned at this point with instructions for Davy. Or else Schenk was simply playing it differently.

Whichever way, it got worse the longer Port sat. The card-riffling grated on him, and Davy was a strain on Port because he made no noise at all. When the phone rang in the dark hall Port was almost grateful.

"I'll get it," said Bainbeck, because Port had gotten up involuntarily. His movement alerted Davy, and Port wasn't allowed to make a move after that. He heard Bainbeck say in the hall, "Yes, Schenk. Everything's fine here," and then, "how about you?"

After that Bainbeck said very little.

Port sat in the dim room and sweated. He learned nothing from the phone conversation. He then began to concentrate on the plan he had saved for last, something without any finesse and good only because it might save his life.

He kept thinking how he would decide to go to the toilet—preferably to a very small bathroom—and there he would fight it out with Davy. Port, going over his plan detail by detail because he was very anxious now, didn't even catch what Bainbeck's part of the conversation could have told him.

"Why do you say that?" Bainbeck asked into the phone.

"Because, first of all, the cops they used for that raid were from the west side, so nobody in that group was getting ice. That alone makes it fishy," said Schenk.

"You mean there's more?"

"Damn right there's more. Look at it, Bainbeck—what did they raid? A game? A pay-off? A collection? Nothing! They busted in on a conversation!"

"Who's behind it?" Bainbeck wanted to know.

"You mean is Paducci behind it?"

"Yes. I mean that."

"I don't know," said Schenk.

Bainbeck thought about this, but said nothing. He stood in the dark hall with the phone close to his face, and if someone had been watching him they would have seen him as a different man now. He was not smiling, and he no longer looked like a ridiculous old man.

"And it wasn't Molnar," Schenk was saying. "I checked on that."

"Any ideas, Schenk?"

"Yes. Callo."

Bainbeck considered that, but said nothing. If he believed it, he might have been thinking of his own plans in such an event—and if he didn't believe Callo was stirring things up, he might have been waiting to hear how Schenk would act.

"He's moving in," said Schenk. "I been expecting it, you know that, and now he is. He must have got wind of something serious."

"Of that plan," said Bainbeck, because he couldn't talk freely.

"You mean the Port hit."

"Yes. That. How would that Finkel raid help him—I don't see it."

"I don't either, for Christ's sake, but there it is. There's been Callo men seen in town!"

"Are you certain?"

"Am I certain?" Bainbeck held the phone away from his ear, worried for a moment that Schenk's voice could be heard in the room. "I'm certain enough to take it serious, Bainbeck! I didn't see 'em, but I trust what I hear. All I know is I'm getting nervous. And when I get nervous, you know, I start to act."

"Of course. You know best," said Bainbeck.

"Right. Now listen. I'm coming over."

"Now?"

"Now. It's coming to a head, with Callo moving in. I'm coming over to get that Port thing finished off."

"Yes. I understand."

"Don't sound so weepy about it, for Christ's sake. Paducci is there, isn't he?"

"Of course."

"Well, you keep him there. That bastard's coming through now, or I'll know the reason why!"

"How long will it take you to get here?"

"Hour. Two hours. No more."

"Fine," said Bainbeck, and he sighed. Then he said good-by and hung up.

He came back into the room and turned on a reading lamp on the library table and a standing lamp near the couch. He looked like a housekeeper again, with his soft step and the officious stoop and smile.

"Well, my dear," he said to Gracie, "do you think you've won quite enough from me for the moment?"

"You don't want to play any more?"

"Perhaps later again, eh, my dear?" He was trying to be gallant.

"It's pretty late," said Gracie. She got up and yawned.

"That's what I mean," said Bainbeck. "And if you would like to freshen up for the evening, change into something else perhaps—"

"It's not that late," said Gracie, but she went upstairs. Bainbeck, it was clear, wanted her out of the way for the moment. Then he started on Davy.

"If you'd like to have another snack or something," he said to Davy, "why don't you go in the kitchen? I showed you where the beer is."

"I don't drink on the job," said Davy.

"You've done it so well I think you should relax for a little."

"I'm relaxed."

"Show Mr. Paducci into that little study across the hall," said Bainbeck, "because I can watch him better there."

"I'll watch him."

"There's just one small window and one door. You can see the door from the kitchen. And to be safe," said Bainbeck, "I'll take your gun."

"You know how?"

"Of course, Davy."

So Davy went into the kitchen and Port went into the study with Bainbeck.

It was a small room, and escaping from it would be hard to do. To make matters quite clear Bainbeck had Port sit on a couch, and he himself sat by the door holding the gun easily and well.

"If you worry me, Mr. Paducci," he said, "I'll shoot." He waited until Davy was well in the kitchen to say this, so there would be no doubt that Bainbeck meant it for Port.

"I'm not moving," said Port. "I'm listening."

"Yes," said Bainbeck, looking down at the gun he was holding. "Did you also listen to the phone conversation I had just now?"

"Not enough to know what you were talking about."

"I wish you could have, Mr. Paducci. Really."

Port knew that the call had been from Schenk, and in a way that was enough for him—especially now, with Bainbeck's new manner. Port sat quite still, but he kept his eyes on an upholstered chair that he could reach with his foot. With a fast move he could get the chair between himself and the gun, and from then on it would be a hassle.

"I tell you frankly," said Port, meaning it, "that I'm getting edgy. I've sat still for you and Schenk for a long while now, you know."

"You've been very patient," said Bainbeck, "but it'll be over soon."

"I don't want to guess any more, Mr. Bainbeck."

"The call," said Bainbeck, "was about you."

"Yes, I know. Schenk called from Cleveland?"

"Yes. But he'll be here in an hour or so."

It was clear to Port that Bainbeck wanted him to know that, wanted him to feel the pressure. In some way that was to serve a good purpose.

"Things are getting critical, Mr. Paducci. I don't know if you know Mr. Schenk very well, but when things get critical for him—"

"You needn't threaten me," said Port. "I react the same to pressure as Schenk does."

"I'm not threatening. I'm apprising you. Schenk's coming here and he'll want you to act."

"On what?" asked Port, wondering how much Bainbeck knew.

"On the Port thing, of course. You're here to kill Port, aren't you?"

Coming from Bainbeck it sounded peculiar. Even with Bainbeck sitting there and holding a gun it did not sound right.

"I'm here to kill Port," said Port. "Yes."

"Then please do, Mr. Paducci. Schenk won't take a no this time."

"On the surface," said Port, "you sound very nice, Senator. Almost as if you meant to save me some grief."

Bainbeck smiled. It seemed like a genuine one now, and even his topic became uncomplicated and open. "You know who I am, don't you, Mr. Paducci?"

"Senator Bainbeck."

"Of course. Public figure. And even the public knows that I'm involved with dark matters." He smiled at his choice of words. "But I don't mind, Mr. Paducci, and perhaps you'll understand that some day. I don't mind, basically, because I'm not an evil man. And I'm not a violent man. Even now." He nodded at Port. "You see?" Then he put down the gun.

Perhaps it was an invitation to rush him, but right then Port didn't take it. Perhaps it meant something else. It meant one thing, certainly—namely that Bainbeck was about to do something important.

"I'm glad we understand each other," said Bainbeck.

Port wasn't sure that he did understand.

"I know why you haven't revealed the whereabouts of our Daniel Port," said the senator.

Port stiffened. He hoped it wouldn't show.

"You do know where he is, don't you?" asked Bainbeck.

"Yes. Very well."

"Good. I believe you."

"Go on, Senator."

"So your only reason for holding back with the information, with the execution—" he looked down when he said that— "is your insistence to deal only with the head man."

"Like I've been saying."

"Would you trust me if I told you who the head man in this matter is?"

"You," said Port.

Bainbeck only laughed. It was such an effective dismissal of Port's remark that Port sat there and bit his lip.

"Is it Schenk?" he asked.

"I didn't say I would tell you *yet*," said Bainbeck.

"Then why are you wasting your breath?"

"Please. You must please respect my reasons as I respect yours, Mr. Paducci. For example, I have never questioned your reasons for insisting on the head man. Your insistence, under ordinary circumstances, doesn't make very much sense, but I haven't—"

"I always work that way," said Port.

"Yes. You have that trademark. But no matter." Bainbeck let it go. He said, "I'll tell you who the head man is as part of a bargain."

"Between you and me?"

"Between you and me only," said Bainbeck.

Now the double cross, thought Port. He already knew that the senator played both sides of the fence. O'Day had explained that. What Port wanted to know very badly now—was just how much Bainbeck knew about Port-

Paducci.

"The bargain is," said Bainbeck, "that you act on Port on my say-so."

The double cross was against Schenk! And that made Bainbeck the head man.

"I don't get it," said Port, hoping for more. Then he got more.

"Because Schenk and his associates are going too far," said Bainbeck. "They are no more important in this than I am, which is only of marginal importance. And I would like the balance to stay in balance."

"So help me," said Port, "I don't get it."

"Simply this—I want you to go now, on my say-so, and *not* kill Port until you hear from the head man."

Darkness fell again, and with a frustrating suddenness, as if the curtain had come down on a last scene before the punch line was said.

Bainbeck wasn't it, Schenk wasn't it, Molnar wasn't it. Or was Bainbeck with Callo? Or with O'Day?

"No," said Port. "I'm through playing footsie. There's too much in the dark." He was almost up off the couch when Bainbeck picked the gun off the floor. "You are in no position to argue with me, Mr. Paducci."

"But I will. Because I know where Port is, and nobody else does. Get that, Bainbeck."

"But you'll tell me if I tell you who's head man?" Bainbeck said that after looking at his watch.

Almost an hour had passed. Very soon now Schenk would show, which meant Bainbeck, whatever his game, would be out of luck.

"Yes," said Port. "Tell me."

"Very well." Bainbeck got up. He backed to the door and called down the hall. Davy came running, but to his disappointment he saw no emergency. Bainbeck said, "I'll get my coat on while you see that Mr. Paducci stays in this room. Then Mr. Paducci and I will leave the house for a while."

"You got my gun? Because you ain't leaving with him there and no gun between you."

"I have it," said Bainbeck from the hall. The light went on there, and Port could hear Bainbeck's grunts while he put on the overcoat. Davy stood in the door to the study, watching Port as he sat on the couch.

It was close now, thought Port, and then it would be over. Maybe they were going to see the top man. One thing was sure—Schenk wasn't it.

Then the door bell rang.

Bainbeck went to the door, opened it and said, "Good evening." A voice answered, "Good evening." Then Bainbeck stepped back.

The man had his hands in his pockets and wore a big-brimmed hat.

Chapter 12

Is Paducci here?" asked the man.

"Yes," said Bainbeck.

"I'd like to see him."

That's when Port appeared in the doorway. It was the first time that he had seen the man with the hat close up. He seemed very young. No effort of any kind showed in his face and even its blankness did not seem intentional. But he was holding too still. That took effort. When he saw Port he said, "Oh. There you are." Then he stepped back from the door, as if to make room.

"I don't think—" Bainbeck started, but the young man with the hat interrupted. He said, "That's all right." Then, "Out the door, Paducci."

It seemed as if nobody knew who the man was, because Bainbeck just gaped. Port hadn't moved, but Davy made a dash for the gun which the senator had left by the clothestree in the hall.

There was a crack like a rap on a box, and Davy fell down.

Port had heard that same sound before, at the Albany gas station, but then there was more than one silencer in the world. The man with the hat held the gun in his hand, and the tube on the end of the barrel made the gun look like something a plumber might use.

"Out," said the man. "You." He nodded the gun at Port.

It wasn't a question of deciding which was the worse of two evils—the known danger in Bainbeck's house, or the unexplained danger of the man with the gun. Port just went. The gun told him too.

Once they were in the dark the man with the gun showed some emotion. It turned out that he was very much in a hurry.

"While I hold this gun on you, Port—"

"*Port?* Who in hell—"

"Shut up. Just get in."

He nodded at the car which stood by the curb, its motor running with a fine purr. Then he grabbed Port by the arm and pulled him sideways. "You go with me and live," he said fast. "You give me trouble and die for sure. Either this way—" and he jabbed the silencer into Port—"or *that* way."

There was a quick glare of headlights as two cars turned into the village square. Then they came straight for the end of the street where Bainbeck's house stood.

"Schenk!" said Port.

"So which is it?"

Port ran with the man with the gun.

There was no time for them to head for the car and no time to go run for the street anywhere, so they lit out for the car shed next to the house. They ran in, stopped close behind the doorframe and watched. Outside the two cars stopped by the curb, and the headlights went off.

"What do you see?" said the man.

"Two in each car. Here comes Schenk, and he's in a hurry."

"The rest still in the cars?"

"They're all coming into the house."

"Both cars empty," said the man, and he started to move.

"Wait—Christ, stop pushing!" They held still by the doorframe. "One of them," said Port, "is staying outside by the door."

"The rest are in?" Then they heard the door close, and Port didn't need to answer.

The man drew Port back into the shed where they stood wedged next to Bainbeck's car. The chance for a run was gone. There was a lookout by the front door, and at any moment the rest would come out again.

"We sit it out here," the man said, and he nudged Port to the back of the shed.

Then it started. They heard the door of the house slap open, and they heard Schenk talking very intensely and cursing. Then there were footsteps, and the rattling of brush by the house.

"We stand on the bumper," said the man.

That wasn't easy. The car was a new model, which meant there was a great deal of grillwork but no decent bumper, only a built-in affair which made the front of the car look like fangs holding a bone. They each found a bump at the side of the grill and hung there like flies when the footsteps came toward them.

The man didn't come into the shed, thinking that unnecessary because of its small size. He had a flashlight which he shone into the back of the car, and then he squeezed by enough to open the driver's door. As he did that he made an explosive sound which was something like, "Got you!" While that brave statement gave the man courage to look into the empty front of the car it showed him nothing.

He didn't bother to close the door which meant he wasn't going to the front end of the car. Instead he went outside again, crouched and flashed the beam under the car. He was very nervous about it, having realized too late that if someone had been under the car, they could have grabbed his ankles and shot him in the foot.

He saw nobody under the car and nobody's feet anywhere. Glad of this, he left to chase around elsewhere.

"Jeesis," said Port. He got off the bumper and took a deep breath. "Jeesis. My fingernails—"

"Not so loud." There was a faint sound as the man next to Port eased the hammer of his gun back down.

They stood still for a while to calm their breathing and to listen to the sounds outside.

"Stay out of line of that window," said the man.

There was a small window in the side of the shed that looked toward the house. Port moved a little, and then they stood waiting again. They heard noises outside the house, which meant—most likely—that Davy, Bainbeck, and Gracie were still inside and that Schenk and his three men were outside, looking.

Then one came back and went indoors, then one more. Finally two more men came back, one of whom was Schenk who spoke to the other man when they got to the door. Only one of them went inside.

"That was Schenk," said the man, who had gone to the door again.

"And one at the outside, like before?"

"Same. But he's in line," he said and sighted along his gun. Then he took the silencer off to get a true bead on his target.

"Wait a minute," said Port.

The man lowered the gun and looked back into the shed. Port came towards him slowly and said, "Who are you?"

"Linden."

"Oh, Fine. You're Linden."

"You needn't sound that way," said Linden. "I'm helping you."

"Who's Linden?" said Port.

"Let's go back." Linden moved away from the door. "No good dropping him now. We'll wait."

"Do you know me from somewhere?" Port asked again.

"Never seen you. You're an assignment."

"Who assigned you?"

"The assignment isn't done, so don't ask, Port."

By this time the use of his own name irritated Port extremely. He said, "If you think—"

"I'm holding the gun," said Linden. "Don't forget it when you move like that. I don't want to talk now."

Port wasn't going to fool with him. Linden was too young to be either slow or lenient, and his face was too frozen for humor. Port, not knowing any more about the man, would do exactly as told and not rile him.

They looked out of the shed window into the lighted living room. Schenk was there, pacing around and sucking his cigarette, producing a trail of smoke every time he moved. Bainbeck was near the fireplace, and though his head was down most of the time he seemed to be talking with Schenk. Schenk was speaking now. One of the men that had come with him was in the room too, but he was just standing there. Davy, thought Port, was probably lying down somewhere.

"While we're standing here," said Port, "let me ask you again. I want to be sure I heard right."

"What?"

"Did you say you were here to help me?"

"I said that." Linden kept looking out of the window.

"Then why the gun now?"

"I don't know you."

"But I'm your assignment, you said."

Suddenly they saw the men in the living room turn in one direction. The missing one had showed up, and he was bringing Gracie. She stopped opposite Schenk.

Port froze. He felt more helpless now than he ever had since this race in the dark had started. He kept staring into the lighted living room as if that was the only way to hold on.

"Linden," he said, "listen to me. You got to tell me why you're here." No matter how inexpert it sounded, it was all Port could manage then.

"I'm here to keep you alive."

It sounded so novel at that particular moment that Port couldn't say a thing.

"Callo sent me," said Linden.

"*What?*"

"You don't think he can afford to have you killed, do you?"

The girl had no illusions about any of this. None about Donald, who was gone; none about Bainbeck, who was smiling gently; none about Schenk, who had asked for her because of one thing only.

"You got something to say," he told her. "Say it quick."

"Where is he?" she said. It wasn't a stall. It was pure fright. Schenk was banking on her a great deal now, and she was afraid to disappoint him. Where was Don Paducci? It would be good to hear that Paducci had left and that nobody, including Schenk, cared very much where he had gone. That was the only answer which could have eased her—that Paducci suddenly didn't matter.

"The son of a bitch got away," said Schenk. He dropped his cigarette because his hands were shaking, and then he stepped on it because he didn't care. He cared about only one thing.

"You were gonna tell me all about him. You remember?"

If Schenk smiled at her now perhaps that would make it easier, she thought. Then Schenk did smile, but in an ugly way.

"Or was that just a gag to get an introduction to him?" Schenk nodded in Bainbeck's direction.

The bastard, she thought. The evil, ugly bastard—and if she had been asked, she would have said that that meant everybody.

What had she left of herself now? Nothing—and when she felt that way she could do only one thing. So she turned stubborn.

"I've had it," she said, shutting out the meaning and the menace of the four men in the room. "You can go to hell, because I've had it."

"Now, one moment please—" Bainbeck had stepped away from the fireplace, and he made the real puzzlement he felt look like a gentle kind of pleading. It didn't really fit his face, but there it was. "You made a remark a moment ago, Schenk, about this young lady coming here—"

"To see you?" said Schenk. He hesitated to light a cigarette. Then he finished his statement with a lot of heat. "You can have her if you can do it, Bainbeck, but I doubt *she* will."

"Now— I must ask you—I'm going to insist—"

"Shut up a minute, will you?" Schenk, who had more important matters on his mind now than Bainbeck's feelings, felt annoyed. He looked at Gracie again, and he got mad. "But you know why you came here, girl! What about Paducci?"

"To hell with him."

"Answer me!" Schenk yelled.

"To hell with *you*."

Gracie felt shock when the man behind her grabbed her arms and jerked them back and more when Schenk grabbed her by the throat—then more pain when he slapped his knuckles across her face.

Port grabbed Linden by the arm. "Come on. Come on, move!"

Linden bored his gun into Port's middle.

"She knows my name!" said Port. "Does that make sense to you?" but when Linden didn't give, Port suddenly relaxed. Even his voice was softer. "You wouldn't shoot me, would you, Linden? That wouldn't make sense to Callo." Then Port pushed past the man and ran quickly out of the shed.

First the man at the front door, thought Port automatically. The hood by the front door was bending over with his hands close to his face, lighting a cigarette. He had the gun clamped under his arm. When he looked up, Port was there. The hood reached for a draw from a shoulder holster, but then he caught sight of the other one the big hat over his eyes and the gun as long as a club. Not that Port had counted on that. He was swinging already, and at the end of the first swing he rammed his elbow back, breaking through the man's involuntary guard and smashing his nose. When the man bounced back from the wall Port let him bounce, then cut him hard across the base of the neck. He scooped up the gun. Linden was at the door already.

Because those inside knew that their man was out there at the door they hardly looked up when the door opened. They were all looking at Gracie, wondering how she'd take the next one. Schenk was hauling his arm back to smack her.

"Hold it there," said Port. "Hold it there." Linden, because he was trained that way, shot the first man that moved.

That one dropped the way Davy had done and stayed on the floor. The rest waited where they were.

"Line up," said Linden, and they lined up fast. Port took their guns away from them, and then he told the men to file down to the basement. "Wait by the door," he told Gracie.

He couldn't find a padlock on the cellar door. He was glad that Linden wasn't there with him. Linden might have shot the lot of them because there was no padlock on the door. Port threw the bolt, hoping it would stay that way for long enough. Then he ran up the stairs, grabbed Gracie by the arm and ran down the hall where Linden was waiting at the door.

"Not my car," said Linden when they ran down the front steps. "The motor's off and the key's gone."

They all squeezed into Bainbeck's big car, and Linden took the wheel.

He was good and trained. He drove out of Hudson very slowly.

Port and the girl sat in back and hardly looked at each other. He did it, she kept thinking. He came back and did it. He came back and did it for me. He came back and did it because he was afraid I'd tell his name. He came back

"You see those lights?" said Linden.

Port saw the lights. Four lights, two cars, both going too fast.

Then Linden opened up and roared out of town. He remembered the Highway Patrol station down the bend and didn't go that way. He dipped the car into a screaming turn, bounced into a gravel drive and hit the gas again. But the gravel drive ended at a barn, and there was no place else to go.

"Around to the left," yelled Port. "Just do it."

Linden did it because he couldn't think of anything else to do.

"Behind the barn now, Linden. Behind the barn!"

The big car started to bog down in the soft sticky ground.

"Kill it behind the corner, between the fence and the barn."

Linden swung, but the wheels spun deeper.

"Not straight, damn it! Barn to fence, diagonal!"

Linden did it right. He knew what Port meant now and cut the lights immediately, let the motor choke itself. He jumped out of the car. Port tore the door open and pulled the girl after him. They had just enough time to huddle down between the car and the barn. Then the first car swung after them.

The headlights picked up Bainbeck's car at the last minute, but too late to stop a crash. The headlights went out with the impact. Bainbeck's car rocked as if it meant to turn over on its side, and the noise sounded like a ton of junk dropped by a drag line.

Then the next car hit. Its impact was bad, but nothing like the first because the lights stayed on.

And that's how Linden got such a perfect bead. Schenk came out, reeling, but holding on out of sheer rage. When he passed in front of the light Linden's gun cracked. Schenk spun and fell down dead.

Chapter 13

They left the two men who had come with Schenk there. One had knocked himself out on the dashboard, and the other got knocked out with Linden's gun. Then Linden started looking for his car key. He found it on Schenk's body. Linden was able to drive the rear car back into Hudson because nothing was wrong with it except a sprung radiator. It started to boil hard by the time they got back to Bainbeck's, but that didn't matter. They changed to Linden's car there. Inside Bainbeck's house a few lights were still on, but nothing moved.

It seemed a long drive back to Cleveland because Port and the girl sat in back without talking. Suddenly Gracie began to cry. She put her head down and cried while Port put her head on his chest and held her like that, rocking a little. In a while she went to sleep.

When they got back to the city they stopped at her place.

"Gracie," Port said. "Can you hear me?"

She nodded after a while and opened her eyes.

"You're home. I'm going to take you upstairs."

"Oh. Yes."

"Will you wait there for me?"

"Yes," she said.

She didn't ask him to stay when they were upstairs because she saw that he was not thinking of her now. She was glad for that in a way because she wanted to be alone for a while. Port covered her with a blanket and gave her a kiss. At that point she really thought he would come back.

Linden had the motor running, and Port sat down next to him. He lit a cigarette and offered one to Linden.

"I don't use them," said the gunman.

Port sat and watched the smoke spread against the windshield.

"Before we go," said Linden, "do you want to stop anywhere else?" He let the motor idle and watched the rear view mirror and the street in front. Port held his cigarette as if he'd forgotten about it.

"Before we go where?" he asked. "What did you have in mind?"

"Out of town. You're coming with me."

"Callo?"

"He wants you."

"I like you for saving me," said Port, "but that's all."

"I don't care. I'm just here to bring you."

"And he wants what?"

"He wants you alive, like I told you."

"Thank him for me."

"And a few things to talk about, like why you're here calling yourself Paducci. Why you're mixing in with that setup in town."

"You know about that setup in town?"

"No. Just that there is one. But Callo wants more. He wants those answers."

"Does he know who's behind things in this setup?"

"He's going to ask you that too."

"I think you shot him," said Port.

"The head man?"

"Schenk."

"You sure?"

"No," said Port. "I'm not sure." He threw his cigarette out of the window and said, "But I might be in a while."

"You want to stay in town a while longer?"

"For that reason."

"All right," said Linden, "we'll stay till you're ready."

There was only one thing worse than having an FBI man following him around at a time like this, and that was to be hailed by a Callo man. Port said, "Look, Linden. I'm not trying to shake you, but with the kind of work I'm doing down here I can't—"

"I don't care what you're doing down here," said Linden. "You can tell that to Callo."

"I know. But if you're seen with me here, I'll be a dead duck."

"Being with me," Linden said, giving it no inflection, "has kept you alive and killed one of them."

It would be hard to explain to Linden, if he would listen to explanations, without telling him about the entire Paducci masquerade. And that would really make Callo unfriendly.

"All right," said Port. "Let's go to the Sassafras."

Gracie's street, at ten in the evening, had been dark and deserted, but when Linden drove down Central it looked like a different town. Stores were open, signs blinked, cars lined the curbs on both sides, and in spite of the raw night there were crowds on the sidewalks. And in Hudson, thought Port, it looks sleepy and the trees are humming, with the wind—and just out of town behind an old barn lies a dead man next to a crumpled up car. Port was sure that Linden wasn't thinking about that, so he forgot it. They parked near the club and went inside.

There was a new act at the club. On the stage were three high school kids with their shirt collars turned up and with identical collarless jackets. A gold thread emblem was stitched on each jacket, a number three and a letter J. *The Three Jacks*, said the banner hanging over the stage.

They were singing something that made them move in mechanical unison, doing one kind of thing with the hips, something else with the elbows, and topped off by a strange shaking of the head. All that time they were singing in a ferocious monotone.

"We've been noticed," said Linden.

Then Port saw them—two waiters without trays or towels over their arms, who started angling around tables till they were able to close in from two sides. They didn't close in right away but just stood there.

"Are you known here?" Port asked Linden.

"I don't think so."

But it had to be Linden they were after. Port, at this point, was well enough known as Paducci, and nobody knew about Schenk yet.

But Port didn't worry about it.

"Here comes the one I want to see," said Port, and then he nodded at Leonard.

Leonard was in tuxedo again, with a wide tattersal cummerbund, and his bland smile changed just slightly when he saw Port. If anything, it got more professional.

"Mr. Paducci," he said and made a little bow.

"We'd like to see you," said Port.

"Nobody's using Molnar's office," said Leonard, but before Port could decide if there had been any special meaning in the way Leonard had said that, the Negro had turned and was walking toward the back.

The two waiters walked right behind Linden and Port, and followed them into the office.

Port didn't like them there. First he looked at them, and then he looked at Leonard, but Leonard was ahead of him.

"You needn't hang around," he said to the waiters.

He stood by the desk till the two waiters had left and the door was closed. Then there was a brief silence while everyone waited for somebody else to start. Linden had no intention of talking and stood there with his hands in his pockets. Leonard was wondering about Port, and Port was wondering about Leonard.

"It seems changed," said Port, "since the last time I was here."

"Yes. It does seem so," said Leonard. He leaned back on the desk and lit a cigarette. He didn't look at anyone while he did that.

"You know the latest change?" Port asked him.

"You don't mean the new act outside?"

It was the first time Port had heard the Negro say anything flippant.

"I mean Hudson."

"Hudson?"

"Schenk didn't give you my message when I went to Hudson?"

"I haven't seen him. He's out of town." It sounded as if Leonard was telling the truth. Then he said, "I don't know when he'll be back."

"He won't be," said Port.

"Pardon?"

"He's dead."

"Ah—" said Leonard. He looked down and flicked ashes into the tray on the desk. When he looked up he said, "Should I know more?"

"I don't know. I don't know where you fit, Leonard." Port meant that, in spite of the fact that the Negro was in with O'Day.

"Of course not," said Leonard, and when he smiled Port noticed for the first time that he hadn't worn his habitual expression since the door had closed on the waiters. "And right now," Leonard said, "I'm not sure myself." He walked around the desk once, and then he sat down on it again.

"But you see my problem," said Port, "don't you?"

"You got nobody to talk to," said Leonard.

"That's right. Or do you think my job's off?"

"Well, Mr. Paducci—" and in that way Leonard made it clear that he knew which job Port was talking about—"I'm not sure." He looked at Linden and said, "Especially since you seem to have more than one interest."

Since Port didn't seem to understand that, Leonard said, "I don't know the gentleman's name, but I know who he is."

"My name's Linden."

"And he is who?" Port wanted to know.

"You're a Callo man, aren't you, Mr. Linden?"

Linden said yes but didn't show much interest.

"What I mean," said Leonard, and he looked at Port again, "Mr. Linden couldn't have walked in here like this, let's say, two days ago, could he?"

"It would have been difficult."

"But it isn't now, is it?" Leonard rubbed his large hands together, looking at them, and then he said, "And now that the tide is turning or has turned, so it seems, here you are, Mr. Paducci, with the opposition."

"The reason I'm here," said Port, "is to ask you who's left now that Molnar and Schenk aren't functioning."

"As to the club, I'm managing that."

"As to the organization, I mean."

"Whom do you want, Mr. Paducci?"

"Same as before. The head man."

"I don't know who's running things now," said Leonard, and he shrugged.

"Can you find out for me? Because I'm still looking for that job."

"Of course. That job." Then Leonard sighed. "I'll drop a word for you here and there, Mr. Paducci, but not much more. My own interests—"

"Who is this guy?" Linden asked suddenly.

Port said that Leonard was the manager of this club and a functionary of a man named Molnar. "And now," said Port, "he seems to be telling us that he has no further function."

"Now that the tide is turning?" Linden asked Leonard.

"I intend turning with it," said Leonard.

"I got no standing," said Linden. "Go ask Callo himself, if you want a job."

That, thought Port, was that. Leonard was bowing out. There were Callo men in town, and Schenk was dead. So Leonard, with no place to go, fades to the other side.

To tell Port anything that he might know about Schenk's organization would only decrease Leonard's value. So he wouldn't talk. He said again, "I'll remark around about you Mr. Paducci; but beyond that I can't do you much good."

Port left after that and Linden went with him.

"Nice friends you got," said Linden when they walked to the car.

"He is," said Port. "He kept his mouth shut. Callo will like him."

The next visit, thought Port, would be more difficult. The next man he had to see wouldn't be likely to ask Linden for a job, though he might be happy to see him. The next one had to be O'Day.

Port said, "I don't know if you want to come along to the next one. I'm seeing the cops."

Linden had been about to open the door to his car, but he suddenly dropped his hand inside his pocket.

"I don't know why you're here," he said to Port, "or what you are doing. I told you I don't care. But I care when you do something like this while I'm around."

"Are you wanted here?"

"I did a job by a barn, a little while ago."

It was a shock to Port to have to be reminded of this by the killer. It had taken three days, just three days, to sink him back into the callousness which has to go with the kind of life he had led in the past. O'Day had been right, it struck Port—this was coming back to him easily.

"Let's sit in the car," he said. "I want to explain something to you."

They got into the car, and then Linden waited. He did not have his hands on the wheel but sat with them inside his pockets, as though he were still standing.

"The reason I'm alive," said Port, "the reason your man Callo will talk to me, for example, instead of sending you after me for a hit, is because I know how to keep my mouth shut."

Linden just nodded.

"When I tell you I'm going to visit the cops, Linden, it's not because I'm going to talk about you."

"You're asking me to do an awful lot of thinking, Port. That's not why I'm here."

"I guess you're not going to listen," said Port.

"No. But you're going—"

He didn't get any further because Port, sitting next to Linden, had swung out his hand flat, the edge of it cutting up under Linden's nose. It did not knock the man out but sent an icepick all the way through his skull freezing his muscles for a moment and giving Port enough time to yank out his right wrist.

Linden, as a gunman, was very good. He had, for instance, not pulled the trigger just because Port had hit him. It would have meant noise and at best a shot through his own foot. But now when the gun came clear he made an effort to point it—except by then Port had the barrel twisted up, and the little black hole was moving up closer and closer to Linden's own face.

"Take it," said Linden, and he let go of the gun. He would be no good dead, and he wasn't done with his job. When Port had the gun he crawled over the seat and got into the back. Then he clipped Linden so that the man's head sank onto the steering wheel.

By the time Port had moved him to the other side of the front seat, there was a lot of blood on Linden's coat from his bleeding nose. And by the time Port had started the car and had turned off Central, Linden had come to. He woke slowly but without a sound. He weaved up into a sitting position, and in a while he put his head down on the dashboard, cradling it with his arm. Then a very strange thing happened. Linden started to cry.

Perhaps he could not stand pain or blood or perhaps it was something else. He said nothing, explained nothing and did not hide his tears. He was not cold and bland now—though his emotion seemed strangely mechanical.

Port drove and did not interfere.

He drove past his hotel and stopped down the street.

"Linden. Can you walk?"

"Yes."

"I'm taking you into my hotel. We walk through the lobby and you're drunk. Understand?"

"I can walk," said Linden.

He wasn't too steady, which was good for the act, and Port got him up to his room. He sat him down on the bed and told him to lie down. Then he went into the bathroom for a wet towel.

Linden lay on the bed in his overcoat.

"Take this," said Port. "Put it over your face."

Linden held out his hand because he could not see very well. He took the towel and hid his face under it.

"Stay here"" said Port. "I'll be back."

"I know," said Linden.

There was an extra blanket under his feet, and when Port passed the end of the bed he had an impulse to pull out the blanket and put it over Linden. But he didn't do it because Linden was something he did not understand, and the episode in the car had not changed that.

To Port, O'Day was, first of all, like an antidote. He was a clear-cut and known entity. He was the law; he was ill-tempered because he had been called to the office at an odd hour; and he disliked Port, which was simple and permanent. He said nothing while Port walked toward his desk, and he had his attitude all set for the meeting. It would have meant nothing to him had he known what Port was thinking—that a lot of things would be easier if Linden were not what he was and if O'Day were not what he was.

"Where've you been?" O'Day began.

"You know where I've been," said Port, thinking of Leonard. It turned out that Port was right.

O'Day's face grew mottled, and at first Port thought it was because the man was angry for having been anticipated. But he didn't feel just angry, he felt righteous.

"You've come to tell me you're getting on with your mission? You walk in here and want to explain that killing a man, murdering Schenk, is an all-right piece of work because he's a crook maybe, and you're acting under the auspices of a legal agency?"

There was somebody else at the other end of the room, an agent doing paper work, and O'Day glanced at him to see if his voice had carried. O'Day wasn't through yet, but he lowered his voice now.

"Haven't I succeeded, Port, in conveying to you—"

Port, wanting to stop him as soon as possible, did it with the simple trick that the correctly accused often use.

"Killed Schenk? Who killed Schenk?"

"You!"

"Leonard said so?"

Leonard hadn't said so, and O'Day tried to let that pass. He became suddenly official.

"You're here, I assume, to tell me that Schenk is dead?"

"Yes. Schenk is dead."

"Who shot him?"

"I can't tell. I was only watching, and it was dark."

"Yeah. We'll handle that later. Where is he?"

"A few miles this side of Hudson. Behind a barn."

"And how come you were there?"

"Schenk had been holding me. My mistake. But he'd been holding me—"

"Where?"

"In Bainbeck's house."

"Bainbeck's?"

"Yes. Your friend."

O'Day pursed his mouth and looked at a wall. Then he said, "Don't tell me the senator was in on this shooting."

"Of course not," said Port. Not knowing much more which would make sense to O'Day, Port said nothing else on the subject.

Then O'Day did some phoning. He gave instructions to someone about the place where Schenk might be found, and he asked that Bainbeck be contacted. That's when he found out that Bainbeck had tried to get in touch with him.

Bainbeck had left a message. To clear up an upsetting series of events which had forced themselves upon him because of his service to the department, he would welcome an early visit from the FBI, the police, the whole works, because never before had his double role of crusader and infidel thrust him so dangerously close to the worst type of criminal element which he was, in reality, combatting. Something like that.

When Port heard this, he could well imagine the martyred look and pleading voice of the senator under the circumstances.

But Port's dislike of the man was drawing that picture. It was true that Bainbeck was not involved. It was also true, and much more important, that Bainbeck had tried to get him—meaning Paducci—away from Schenk. Why? He must have figured, it struck Port, that Schenk would get Paducci to go out and kill Port. And Bainbeck, as a man on the side of the law, would want to prevent that.

Port dropped it because he was back with nothing.

"The important thing," he said to O'Day, "is that I don't know where to go from here."

"That's right. You put two of them out of commission."

"Two of them *are* out of commission"" Port corrected. "Molnar getting beat and confined was a fluke. Schenk getting killed wasn't my doing."

"Whose was it?"

"I can't tell, I told you. There was shooting and chasing. Schenk was after me."

"I'll ask the senator."

"And ask him at the same time whether I had a gun."

"You didn't?"

"No, I didn't."

"Maybe your driver did."

Port just waited.

"What you're leaving out," said O'Day, "is that Callo character who's been following you. Remember you asked me to check out this guy in a big hat and so on?"

"You checked him out."

"Linden was his name. Then we lost him here in town during the evening. Then he turns up with you at the Sassafras. Leonard told me."

"And in between he was with me?"

"I'll ask the senator," said O'Day and dropped it because he was sure of himself.

O'Day made some notes, and Port sat quietly. He could have told O'Day half an hour's worth of new little items, all things O'Day knew nothing about. He could have told him about Leonard, who was quickly drifting in a double world of his own advantage; about Bainbeck, whose double life included identical smiles for Schenk, Paducci, O'Day, and Gracie; about Linden, sick on a bed because the emotion had been trained out of his killing.

But what would this mean to O'Day? Items to be used to condemn somebody—simple verdicts on very complicated matters. And in the end, how would telling O'Day any of this help Port to stay alive?

"Where's that Linden bastard?"

"I wouldn't tell you if I could."

"He's a killer. You know that."

"I hope you stop him," said Port. "I really do."

But O'Day didn't believe it. He said, "Just because he comes down here to save your life for Callo—"

"You learned a lot by trailing him for a few hours."

"We're an organization," said O'Day. "You keep forgetting that."

"No," said Port. "I made a foolish remark."

O'Day liked that. Any admission of a mistake was almost as good as a confession of weakness to him. He was now able to drop the subject and get more practical.

"A lot has happened, but we don't know a thing."

"And I'd like to hear what comes next."

"You'll have to stay put. You'll have to stay around the city till the organization gives you the call."

"And how long might that take?"

"If we knew that, I think we would know whom we're looking for."

Like at the start. Sit it out and wait for the call to go and kill Dan Port now. Same as in the beginning, as if nothing had happened since then.

"And another thing," said O'Day. "Since it's out of the question that Callo can have his man walk around here, handicapping our progress, you're going to get an FBI guard to look out for you. And as soon as Linden shows his face—"

"You pick him up, and Callo's going to get wind of more than he's ever hoped for. That your outfit is in on this thing."

"Leave that to us."

Most likely O'Day was right, and they could make the arrest look like something else. Port was tired.

"Just once more," he said and got up. "You pick up Linden while I'm still around, and it's bad. Please believe me, O'Day, very bad."

"Something personal?"

"Yes. Something personal. I'm involved."

"Honor among thieves?" O'Day wanted to know.

"This has nothing to do with the right side or the wrong side of the law, if you can understand that."

"All right," said O'Day. "We'll leave you entirely out of it."

"Don't use me to find him, or I don't move."

"I've said all right!"

"And I don't want your guard, like I told you in the beginning. I can't work that way."

"At this point, Port, you need a guard."

"No guard or I quit cold. Because I've had it."

"And let that plot on your life hang?"

"Let it hang. It doesn't look too potent to me any more."

He left, very tired. He went to his hotel hoping that Linden was no longer there.

Linden was still on the bed. There was dried blood on his face, and he lay there with both his hands on his stomach. He had to hold them close together because of the handcuffs.

There were two agents in the room, and they nodded at Port, making it look like they knew him.

"That him?"

Port didn't talk. He couldn't talk. He had the choice of coming out with hate for the two men and for O'Day who had sent them, or the choice of explaining to Linden. Both things were useless.

The agents helped Linden get off the bed and led him to the door. Port and the killer looked at each other when they passed.

"A long day," said Linden and walked by. He stopped at the door and looked back once more. "One thing, Port. Did you want to pull out that blanket that time and cover me? Just tell me."

"Yes."

Linden nodded at Port, then walked out.

Chapter 14

Port stayed in bed late the next day, lying awake most of the time. He went to the lunchroom downstairs and ate without tasting, preoccupied with something else. He was waiting. In the afternoon he took a slow walk across town, not knowing exactly why he was doing it. He ended up at the Sassafras Club without really wanting to be there. He was preoccupied with the thought that he had hit a dead end. Nothing had moved since the day before. No one had called him, looked him up, sent a message. It was as though he were surrounded by dead air.

At the Sassafras Club he looked for Leonard but didn't find him in. The bartender couldn't say where he was and didn't expect him till six, when the supper guests came.

Port went back to the hotel and sat by the window. He smoked and drank coffee, and some of the time he sat whistling the same tuneless phrase over and over.

He called Gracie once, and they talked for a while. He talked as if he were not alone in the room and didn't want to be overheard, and she talked to him the same way. Neither of them seemed to notice it.

"You're still in town," she said. Port thought that she said it with relief.

"Yes. I'm still in town," he said, feeling stupid.

"You sound like you wish you weren't, Don."

"I wish I weren't," he told her. "I wish you and me had met somewhere else."

His answer relieved her because she had asked her question with a doubt in her mind about Port. It bothered her that she needed to be sure about him—or about anyone. This had never been a problem to her before. She said, "Leonard called me. He says I could have my old job back."

"You didn't want it."

"I said I wouldn't take it."

"I didn't ask you that, Gracie."

"I know what you asked. No, I didn't tell him I didn't want it."

"Not sure?"

"I wish I could see you, Don."

"You will. I don't know when, but you will."

She wanted to change the subject.

"By the way," she said, "that old man called me up."

"Bainbeck?"

"Yes. He called."

"What did he want?"

"What do you think?"

"I'm surprised he's got time for games. He's in town?"

"No. He said he's staying in Hudson to be available to the authorities because of what happened. The reason he called me," she said, "was to tell me not to worry. He'll keep my name out of things."

"I can appreciate his motives," said Port.

"And anytime I wanted to pick up my overnight bag—I left that there that time we left—"

"It was only yesterday, Gracie."

"I keep thinking of it as if it had been a long time ago," she said.

"It helps."

Then they talked about nothing that really interested them, hating to talk on the phone, hating to hang up, getting almost formal with each other.

"Well," she said, "I'm glad you called."

"Yes. I just wanted to call you, Gracie."

"That was very nice."

"Are you resting?" Port asked her.

"Yes, thank you. In fact, I think I'll go to bed very early. I'm quite tired."

"Oh. I'm sorry. What I mean is, I don't want to keep you—" They finally said good-bye, glad it was over. It made them wish they were with each other.

It was getting dark early because of the weather, but the dark seemed wrong to Port because nothing had happened all day. He turned on the light in his room, hoping the lamps would increase the impression that the day was really over. He lay down on the bed, feeling sleepy. Then he slept with his clothes on.

All through his sleep he kept thinking of time passing with a solid, fast stride, and when he woke suddenly he looked first at the window.

It was dark outside. He looked at his watch and found he had slept thirty minutes.

To be doing something he took off his clothes and tossed them all in a pile. Clean clothes would feel good. First a shower, though—a long, strong shower. He went to the bathroom and turned on the faucets. He let them pelt the water out at full pressure and then he stepped into the stall. It hit him with a shock that he enjoyed. I can sleep half an hour, he said to himself, I can take a shower for half an hour.

But then it occurred to him that the phone might ring, and he wouldn't hear it. He got out of the shower and dried himself fast, as if it was necessary to be dry when the phone rang.

It didn't ring all the time he took to get dressed, and when he sat down again by the window to smoke he suddenly felt he would burst from the pressure. He left the hotel and walked.

He had forgotten his overcoat, and the cold wind from the lake pushed into his clothes and seemed to wrap itself into him. He walked faster, but without pleasure. It felt as though he were fighting his own muscles.

He spent twenty minutes in a bar which had tinny music piped in through the wall and thirty minutes in a movie which featured news films edited to please the whole family. It took several minutes to walk to the Terminal Tower and look at some train schedules which were of absolutely no interest and twenty minutes to walk past the Federal Building to the edge of the flats where he stood by a ramp and looked down into the blackness where a train was making an unending racket. It must be a very long train, thought Port, and then he started counting the cars, a unique effort because he couldn't see them. When this struck him he walked away in the middle of a number.

All right, he said. All right. One day of nothing. Fine. Better than ten minutes of what had gone on in the last two days in this town.

It was a lie, and it made him sullen. He looked back at the flats and could still see some of the bridges. There were so many of them they made Port think of a storeroom where bridges are kept for future use. A whole storeroom of bridges. There were two bridges crossing to the west side that looked like giants. They were the big, arched windows of the storeroom.

He looked away because the comparison was starting to bother him. They were beautiful bridges though, he thought.

After that he walked more easily. He walked back to Euclid, found a restaurant and ate a big meal. He called the hotel once and was told there had been no calls, but he didn't care so much any more. The day and the night which went with it were almost over. He liked that. And, liking the new feeling of no longer waiting so hard he went to another movie. This time he stayed through one-third of it, and when he knew what the end was going to be he got up and left.

He walked a great deal then and passed his hotel once, but he didn't go in. He wasn't cold any more and he didn't feel tired. He felt this way because he knew clearly that the last few days would not happen again. Even if he wasn't done with all this in the near future, what happened next would be something new. He wouldn't be going back into anything, he realized—he would be getting rid of it with each step he took. That was new.

He came to a wide terrace along one side of the street, beyond which there seemed to be nothing. There was no traffic here, and no lights except for street lamps. The big terrace was dimly lit, and at the end was a balustrade. Port stood there and felt the wind push him hard. Then he heard the lake, a faint sound, but echoing in the dark.

He turned his back to the sound after a while to light a cigarette. But then he didn't want it. He leaned on the balustrade with the dark lake just a sound behind him and the empty street very wide in front. Suddenly a newspaper truck came by, going like blazes. That makes the news important, he thought—it goes fast. Then a car rolled down the street slowly, looking alone. That makes it unimportant, going slow—

The car brought a new sound, singing of the tires, and out of nowhere Port suddenly felt he must scream with panic, leap with the fright that was uncoiling like a spring inside him.

The shot crashed at him and he hit the terrace floor.

He felt himself trembling, lying there.

Chapter 15

The big, dark space seemed to have swallowed everything, and then Port heard the faint lake sounds again. They had been there all the time, of course. The wind was still pushing over the balustrade, the car was gone very suddenly and it was almost like before. The cigarette which Port hadn't lit was lying close to his face, white and small.

He picked it up and broke it in two. Then he jumped up and ran all the way back to the hotel with no effort at all. He thanked his panic for his crazy jump, he thanked the black lake for having taken the bullet, he thanked singing tires and unlit cigarettes.

In the hotel he became quiet as a cat.

He closed his door, pulled a chair around to the phone and dialed the first number.

No answer.

He let it ring and ring.

"'Lo?" Gracie sounded very sleepy.

"Gracie? Port. This is Dan Port."

"What you say? You calling me?" and then suddenly, "Who did you say?" very much awake.

"It's Dan, Gracie."

"Oh—Danny!" He could see her smile.

"Gracie honey? Go back to sleep."

"What? I just— You just—"

"Go back to sleep. I'll explain when I see you." He hung up on her.

Then he called Leonard. Leonard wasn't at home. Then he called O'Day office. O'Day wasn't in.

"This is Medfink speaking," said the agent, "may I ask—"

"I'm Daniel Port. I must—"

"Yes, Mr. Port. I know who you are."

"Then can you get—"

"Perhaps I can help you. It's not yet six in the morning and Mr. O'Day won't be in till about noon."

"If you know this case, Medfink, I won't need O'Day."

"Please go ahead. Any new developments?"

"Brand new. I got shot at."

"Really! Are you all right?"

Port had to smile as he thought how O'Day might have answered this.

"They missed," he said. "I'm fine."

"Give me the details."

"No," said Port. "This is more important."

"Shoot."

"Where's Linden?" snapped Port.

"Police jail, Mr. Port."

"You're certain?"

"A break would have been reported to us immediately, and he's not getting out any other way."

"Now Leonard. Would you have any idea where he is?"

"Yes. It so happens I do. Some general questioning was being held at Mr. Bainbeck's house. The senator is confined to his bed there—shock, I guess, nothing serious—and O'Day took Leonard—"

"When was that?"

"Yesterday, late afternoon."

"He's been there ever since?"

"Yes. I talked to the senator, since O'Day was outside at the time, investigating something to do with tire marks. The senator said Leonard was going to stay the night, and so were the rest of them. He asked about Linden too, by the way."

"Nice of him."

"And he asked how you were, and I told him fine."

"Ah. And Molnar?"

"Same as before. Hospital, no visitors, no phone calls. He can't talk anyway, you know, the way his jaw is."

"Thank you, Medfink," said Port and hung up.

He felt wide awake.

The sun was fall-bright, and a strong wind kept the moisture out of the air. There were leaves driving through the street, and the big trees by the house thrashed frantically in the wind. Port parked and walked into the hall a little after eight.

They were all up—O'Day with a coffee cup, Leonard smoking, men in mufti and a stenographer. Bainbeck was walking around with his coffee pot.

They all looked at Port, a little surprised.

"Good morning," said Port.

"Good morning," said somebody, and most of them nodded.

Port walked into the room with the French windows and fireplace, and nobody said anything. It wasn't tense, it was just too early.

O'Day said, "Must be important."

"Will you have coffee?" asked the senator, and his smile was clearly anxious.

Port answered O'Day and said, "It's over." Then he nodded at Senator Bainbeck.

"We were done here," said O'Day. "You just caught us before going back."

"I'm glad," said Port, and to Bainbeck he said, "are you coming too?"

"If you'll pour your own coffee," said the senator to Port, handing the coffee pot to him, "I'll go up and get ready."

He looked down at his housecoat and smiled apologetically. It struck Port that the expression on his face wasn't fake.

The old man went upstairs, and everyone looked at their coffee or at the shaking trees outside. A branch from a tree near the house thumped on the roof overhead.

"Well, Port? What is it?" O'Day put his cup down quietly.

"He's it," said Port and jerked his head in the direction of the upper floor.

This time the silence meant shock.

O'Day said, "You better have more backing this up than your personal dislikes."

Port nodded. "They're all out. All the ones I could think of. Except him."

"Negative evidence."

"So far. Then you told me once, O'Day, that the senator didn't know such details as Paducci's function in Cleveland. That he didn't know anything about the Port murder affair."

"He did?"

"He did. He and Schenk talked about it freely, and the senator even offered his house for the job of holding me here, as Paducci, till I'd come around."

"I could have been misinformed."

"You were. You never knew how much he was on the syndicate side of the ledger."

"I still don't."

"Call your office in Cleveland," said Port, "and ask for Medfink."

O'Day called and got Medfink.

"Ask him," said Port, "if the senator spoke to him yesterday and asked about me."

"He did," said Medfink over the phone.

"What did he say, ask him."

"And how's Paducci? Something like that," Medfink told O'Day.

"Ask him, O'Day, what he answered that innocent question with."

Medfink said to O'Day, "I told him that Mr. Port was fine."

"You said what?" O'Day roared outraged into the telephone.

"I—I said very simply—I said, Mr. Port is fine. I kept all information to a minimum since—"

"Never mind!" yelled O'Day. He hung up the phone and the room grew suddenly quiet.

"So, yesterday in the late afternoon," Port said, "Bainbeck found out that Paducci was Port."

"I see that," said O'Day. "I can see that."

"And not too much later, O'Day, there was the second attempt on my life."

O'Day looked at his hands, then up at the ceiling. It was very quiet now, because the wind had died down. The trees were not shaking any more, and the leaves lay still on the street. Upstairs, there was still a soft, gentle thumping.

"Get him," said O'Day, and nodded at one of the men. "I want him to explain."

The man in mufti went upstairs and now they could hear his footsteps up there, intermingled with the other sound, the soft thump.

The footsteps drew nearer, and the man came down as far as the first landing. He leaned down and said, "He explained it."

"What?" O'Day interrupted.

"He hanged himself. Can't you hear it from where you are?"

The gentle thump was almost gone.

When she opened the door for him he just stood there and wouldn't come in.

"I brought your overnight bag," said Port in a gentle voice.

She looked at it and then at Port.

"I don't know if I want it," she said, "I was wishing you'd come, but I don't know… I don't really know …"

"I want you to come with me, Gracie. That's all *I* really know."

He came into the room and took her arm. She didn't move.

"Dan," she said. "I first have to know—" It was hard for her to talk about it clearly, and she stopped. She looked at Port once but then looked down again, staring at the floor.

"You don't know," he said, "whether you wouldn't have told them my name if Schenk had asked you to. Am I right."

She nodded.

"And I don't know for sure," he went on, "why I came into Bainback's house to interrupt you and Schenk. I don't know if I did it for you, to stop the beating—or for me, to keep you from telling him about me."

"It's hard," she said. "It's hard to live with it and never know for sure—"

"Come with me," he said. "That'll make it a little easier."

Then she came with him. They didn't forget their doubt, but it became unimportant.

THE END

Time Enough to Die

by Peter Rabe

Chapter 1

One wall of the house faced straight to the west and by the time the sun went down into the Pacific the wall was always very warm to the touch. He sat down there and leaned against the adobe, feeling the heat on his back and the sun on his face. Now and then he sipped from his glass and when the drink was gone he chewed on the ice. Then he smoked and looked down at the small bay where the village of Guanadera ribboned along the shore. It looked as if the jungle would soon push the houses into the water.

The thought didn't bother him very much because the weather was too hot to let you think. This was the main reason why he liked Guanadera, why he had found it and had stayed this long.

After a while the sun color moved toward red and the water in the bay became orange. The fishing boats turned dark blue because the sun was now behind them, and he turned his head to look at the road, where the colors did not hurt his eyes.

In that direction there was a lot of gray brush which seemed to creak in the heat. It was boring and two-dimensional after the view west, but he kept watching.

When she came around the bend he sat very still by the wall and grinned to himself. Maybe she wouldn't notice him until the last minute, when he would make some kind of a move to give her a start. Then she wouldn't know whether to laugh or to be angry, and all of it would show on her small face in quick, mobile changes.

When she passed him he made a noise in his throat. She kept walking. "Hey," he yelled. She kept walking.

"Maria—wait!" He scrambled up and ran after her.

When she stopped it wasn't because he had called but because she couldn't walk any more, laughing. She watched him come and said, "Hey, hey! Look at my lazy gringo. This is the fastest he has moved all day. All day? What am I saying—"

"That was very funny," he said. "Very, very funny," and kept a straight face.

She stopped laughing very suddenly and said, "Pooh. It's too hot to make fun of you."

"How soon did you see me?"

"You did the same thing only yesterday," she said. "And besides, gringos always sit in the hot sun. Look at you. A drop is running down to the tip of your nose."

He pursed his lips and blew at his nose, making the sweat jump off in a spray.

"You are nice and dark from the sun and your hair is black and shiny, and you don't look like a gringo at all," she went on. "So why don't you stay out of the sun, Danny? Soon your brains will cook away..."

"They have," he said. "I do all this to see you."

"Oh?" she said and made a face as if she were thinking. "And if you had brains?"

"I'd yell at you from the window. I wouldn't budge out of the shade but just yell at you to come up."

"I'd come," she said. She put her arm through his and he walked her back to the house.

"I'll have one glass of your beer and then I have to go."

"I know. All of Guanadera is extremely busy and you are the busiest. And I had to meet you."

"Well, there is this Rosita, this nice fat one, you know, who is dying to meet..."

"Talk, talk, talk," he said and gave her a small slap on the behind so she would go into the house.

The inside was a simple, tall cube with small windows and the tile of the roof showing under the ceiling. Like most Mexican houses, this one had no basement. Big slabs of stone made the floor. It was cool inside the room and the high-colored heat outside only showed in the view through the open door and through the deep windows.

"Aha," said the girl. "My lazy gringo made his bed all by himself this time."

"What makes you think, Maria, that you are the only one who..."

"Aha. So Rosita *was* here. The closest she ever gets to a bed is to change someone else's linens. But you, my night-life gringo..."

"Stop yammering about this Rosita," said Port. He went to the iron sink where he kept bottles of beer in a bucket of water. "I've never seen this Rosita. Is she ravishing?"

"Ha."

"Why else all this jealousy?" He grinned at the girl and gave her a bottle of beer.

They went out on the porch and sat on a wooden bench. The dry growth of shrubs came close to the house there, and beyond that they could see where the jungle started. Trees were denser and leaves were much larger. It was a restricted view, but there was a breeze on the porch.

"After the beer," said Port, "will you cook us something?"

"The old man is waiting. I won't have time."

Port mumbled something and drank beer. He put his elbow on the back of the bench and stroked the girl's arm. He stroked it on the inside where her skin was light and soft.

"This does not make me want to cook for you," she said and looked at the tops of the trees. But she sat where she was.

Port didn't answer. He just nodded. He drank beer and now and then he looked at the girl. She was fine-boned and small and very soft to the touch. The same softness showed in her walk because she had smooth, drifty movements and an effortless swing in her hips.

She put her bottle on the floor and Port said, "No more beer for you. You'll get drunk in the afternoon heat." He leaned over and kissed her on the mouth.

"And I might fall asleep," she said. "And you wouldn't want that."

They got up and went back into the house.

"I have beans," said Port, "and you could cook this sausage. Do you..."

"Danny," she said. "It takes too long." He put his hands under her elbows while she unbuttoned the front of her dress. Her skin had a dim sheen in the half light. "And there won't be time," she said.

"Talk, talk, talk," said Port into her hair. He ran his hands down her bare back and then he picked her up and laid her down on his bed....

She felt fresh and active after she got up, which Port could tell by the quick kiss she gave him and by the way she was humming when she put on her dress. But she wouldn't stay, because a fine time in bed during the afternoon didn't mean she would forget to do her work for the old man at the other end of the village. Port waved at her from the window when she walked down the road.

He yelled, "Hey, Maria," and when she turned, "I'm yelling at you from the window."

"It will do you no good this time," she called back. "All you want is to have me cook your beans." She waved as she walked through the bend.

He watched the way she was walking until she disappeared. Then he sighed and went to prepare something to eat. He ate some raw lettuce with too much oil, the sausage, which was still cold on the inside, and the beans, which were burnt and too hard. But he liked Guanadera.

The twilight was very short. He sat by his wall and watched the change very closely because it was the one moment of the day when there was excitement in the air. It was one moment when the speed of the change made you expectant. The Pacific sliced into the ball of the sun and the sun became purple. The daytime heat became quiet and the shapes which had been hard in the sunlight were suddenly fused. There was no sound from the insects. Then everything turned dark blue and the day was gone. Port could hear the surf as if it hadn't been there before. The growth near the house made dry rattles and he could hear little sounds from far back, where the jungle started.

As complete as the change had been, it did not seem finished. The suspense stayed. The night was complete too suddenly, while the senses had not yet caught up.

Port lit a cigarette and the flare from the match startled him. He could not sleep nights, and little things put him on edge. The days were peaceful, but the nights were like the nights up north, and he felt restless activity and a sense of danger. He hoped this would pass after a while. He believed that he needed nothing but daytime torpor, and that this was the place where he would find it.

When he could see again after the flare of the match, he looked down at the lights along the bay. Guanadera was a strange village. Even the lights in the night showed this. There were small square lights where the Mexicans had their houses; long, rectangular lights in the houses at the other end of the village. The shapes looked oddly modern.

The Japanese fishermen lived there. When the big waves of Nipponese poor had come across the Pacific they had hung on in the coastal towns along the California coast. Except for the fishermen. Their toehold on land hadn't been as eager and when the tuna struck farther south they had moved to the south, some as far as the west coast of Mexico. They didn't use nets in the bay, as the Mexicans did, but went far out after tuna, which they caught with poles where the schools were running. They learned enough Spanish to exchange greetings, they borrowed some habits, such as daytime sleep, and they lent some habits, such as using latine-type sails. The Mexican children borrowed that rig. The Japanese and Mexican children mingled. The adults just smiled at each other and sometimes said things about the heat.

If Maria is through working at ten, thought Port, and if she goes home right away and doesn't sit in the square licking ices, then she should pass here about half past the hour. "Or I might stay at his house because of work in the morning," she had said, "in which case, my night-time gringo, in which case you might have to go into town and look for Rosita. You can't miss her," she had explained. "She is very big here, here, oh—just everywhere, I should say, Danny, and you can also tell her by the beard. She has—" He had interrupted her at that point in one way or the other, though she had kept on laughing for a while.

A bug hit the wall next to him, giving Port a start. He was glad nobody had seen him, because being startled by a bug was ridiculous. He pressed his cigarette into the ground and got up. There was a night wind now, smelling of rot from the jungle. All the movements in the leaves seemed much greater now. He would look down at the ocean, walk across the road to the path that led to the beach and look at the shiny surf in the dark. He wished he had not let his watch run down so he could tell if the girl would be coming. He wished she were here.

"Danny?"

He turned the wrong way first because he thought she would come from the road to the village. But she came up the path from the beach, and seemed winded.

"Don't exhaust yourself," he was going to say, "because I'm not likely to move until you get up here," or some such remark, but she was up close then and he took her arms. "I've eaten," he told her and pulled her closer.

"I'm glad you're awake."

Port let go of the girl and tried to see her face in the dark. There had been no banter in her voice.

"You sounded so serious," he said, "as if you hadn't come to see me at all." He smiled at her when he said it but she didn't take up the tone.

"Danny," she said. "Would you come with me? I can't find Kiamoto."

"Who?"

"The old man."

"Oh. I never knew his name."

"Kiamoto, the old fisherman. Where I work."

"I know. And you can't find him." None of this interested Port. He was only wondering why the girl was so concerned. "Maybe his boat's just late."

"He doesn't fish any more. And his boat's in the bay."

"He's out drinking."

"He doesn't drink."

She was getting annoyed. She stepped away from him, annoyed more with her own helplessness than with Port's unconcerned questions. He saw this because she acted confused, unsure of what to say. He took her arm and said, "Come on. I'll go with you."

They took the path which wound through the brush down to the beach and then they walked where the sand was solid and moist, because that was the fastest way. Port would just as soon have taken the road which went through town. It was easier going. But the whole trip was to humor the girl, nothing else. Some old man, Kiamoto, hadn't come home to dinner. Perhaps it was a Japanese custom once a month. Or, being old, maybe he had fallen someplace and was dead.

They walked fast along the dark sand with the surf hissing at them each time the white line of foam came back to the beach. Maria walked ahead of Port, setting a fast pace, and in a while he began to feel the strain in the backs of his legs. But he still couldn't take the trip seriously.

"Maria, the road comes close to the beach up there. Let's take it through town and maybe the old man is there someplace, on the square."

"I've looked. Besides, he never goes."

"Maybe he'll be home by the time we get there, huh?"

"I hope so."

She wouldn't slow down and she never changed her mind about all this being something urgent. Port sighed, and then jogged a ways to catch up with her.

"I wish you'd explain to me why this is an emergency. A Japanese fisherman, retired, fails..."

She stopped abruptly and glared at him. "You are making fun of me? Or do you want to help me?"

"All right," said Port. "All right, all right." He turned her by the arm and they walked down the beach again.

"How well do you know him?" Port asked after a while.

"Not very well. I clean his house, I help in his garden, I cook."

"Oh."

Then she said, "Two weeks ago he went out with the boat, the time when the squall came through in the afternoon. He caught his foot in some painful way, the tiller hit him some way, and he hasn't left the house since then. He never leaves the house much," she added.

"You asked all the neighbors, of course."

Maria didn't bother to answer.

"Well," said Port, "I don't think you need to worry. In fact," and he sounded winded, "I don't see any of this. Don't worry."

But he hadn't said it right. She was suddenly angry. "I like him! When I like people I think about them and I do things for them!"

She glared at him so he wouldn't miss her meaning, and Port didn't miss it. He shut up after that and just walked. Let Maria have her old man. He was probably well mannered and kindly, he probably gave her gifts of food to take home, and perhaps he talked to her like a grandfather. Port had been at Maria's house once and he knew that she had little kindness there. She had no parents and lived with a bent little man whose name was Pepe—an uncle?—a small, morose man smelling of pulque and with a face like a headhunter's trophy.

They passed the village now, with adobe houses and mud huts coming down to the beach. Only the white church had a look of endurance. The beach looked dirty with use now; stretched nets, boats belly up, broken glass, some barrels of tar. Where the beach swung to complete the bay the jungle growth crept very close, as if this were the end of the village. In a way it was. Where the land was cleared again the huts were steeply gabled. The sides opened with sliding doors or showed half-beam work in the smooth mud walls. This was Guanadera, the Japanese village.

Maria left the beach where steps led up the bank. She took Port the length of a dirt street where all the houses had an un-Mexican touch.

"Past this garden," she said. "The small house under the trees."

"All the lights are on. Maybe..."

"I left them on," she said. "If he were home, he would have put out most of them."

There were two neat rooms, both empty. There were grass mats, a low table, a hearth. Past a delicate sliding door was a pallet, a clothes chest, and a calendar on the wall. The calendar was out of date but it had a too-colorful picture of Fujiyama across the top.

Port sat down on the chest. "Now what?" he said.

"I don't know—" She sounded anxious and kept blinking her eyes. "This is why I brought you, Danny. So I can ask you."

She could be very naive, thought Port. The old Kiamoto was her worry, which meant to her he would also be Port's as soon as she told him about it. After one look at two empty rooms the smart gringo would have a soothing answer.

"Turn off some of those lamps," said Port. "The place is getting too hot."

She left two lamps lighted and then came back to Port, who still sat on the chest. He had his hands between his knees and kept clapping them. To Maria this meant he was thinking.

"The place is pretty bare," said Port. "It's always like this?"

"He likes it this way."

"Yuh. Uh— How old is this Kiamoto?"

"I don't know, but he's old."

Port nodded at that, hoping it would look as if his mind was very busy. To his own surprise something did occur to him.

"An old man like him, does he walk with a stick, Maria?"

"Oh no. He is— Yes! Since he hurt his foot he has used a stick."

"And the stick is gone?" Port looked around and did not see a walking stick.

Maria went to the sliding door which led to the porch, went outside, stayed a short time. When she came back into the light she was holding an umbrella.

"He uses this," she said. "He left it on the porch."

For the first time it struck Port that old Kiamoto's absence might be a little peculiar and that Maria's worry was more than female agitation. After all, she knew the old man's habits, very regular habits most likely, and though he had a bad foot he had left the umbrella behind. Port said nothing for a while. The two lamps hissed and the warm night air from outside smelled of plant odors. The bare house seemed very small to Port and the jungle outside very large. And Kiamoto, whom Port had never seen, seemed especially absent.

"Is there more to his place?" Port asked. There was so little to look at in the two rooms.

"The garden, and the shed in the garden."

Port noticed that he was beginning to act as if he were looking for the Japanese and as if it were important. He shrugged and picked up one of the lamps. "I'll look in the shed," he said. "Show me where."

The shed stood at the end of the vegetable rows, where the wild growth started. The dull light from the lamp made the place look ancient.

"He doesn't use it any more," said Maria. "I don't think he's been in it since he stopped fishing."

"We'll see," said Port and opened the door.

A rat scampered across the floor and out through a board which had cracked open. A moment later the place looked completely still again, and unused. There was an old mast, with rigging wrapped around it, a pile of worn pullies, a stack of the thick poles used for tuna fishing. And there was a lot of old manila line which gave the small place the look of disorder.

"Looks dead," said Port. The girl frowned at him because he had said it in English, but then Port felt it was just as well not to translate for her.

There was one spot of color in sight, a bag full of glass floats which the Japanese use on their nets. They were yellow and blue.

"I thought these fishermen only use poles," Port said to the girl.

"The old ones use nets sometimes, when they can't handle tuna any more."

Good answer. For a moment Port had found himself interested, had started to look for the unusual, the little sign which did not jibe with the expected impression. First, there had been the umbrella. Was it usual for a Japanese in a Mexican jungle to carry an umbrella? A comic thought, but not necessarily meaningful. They used umbrellas in Japan, and almost everything in this settlement was imported, their habits most certainly. Then the floats. Why floats, and hidden in the back of the garden? But Maria had just explained that. A shame, thought Port. His brief curiosity seemed ridiculous now.

"Danny," said the girl. "Do you hear something?" She held the door ajar with one hand and with the other she touched his arm.

They held still for a moment and Port wished that the lamp wouldn't hiss so much.

"Somebody walking," he said. "Is that what you mean?"

"On the street."

"Limping?" and he strained to hear.

But then Maria dropped her hand from his arm and the gesture was so clearly disinterested that Port stopped listening.

"Kiamoto doesn't wear shoes like that," she said. "These people wear sandals."

The walking on the dark street on the other side of the house was making soft thuds, not like sandals.

"But I'll see who it is," she said, and ran across the garden.

Port stood alone in the shed for a moment, but the place meant nothing to him. After all, he was here only because Maria was upset, a very good reason to be here, of course, but not enough to worry about Kiamoto. A dull picture: Japanese fisherman, old, retired, uses umbrella, tried nets before he gave up fishing, wears sandals.

Port looked at the box with junk under the workbench and went over to look at it again before he knew why. There were boat nails on it, oakum, calking tools, a big cleat. There was also an old pair of sandals. He picked one of them up and now it struck him why the sandals had drawn his attention. He did not drop the sandal back into the box. Must ask Maria about this, she knows the old man and his habits— When he walked across the garden he started to whistle, just a blown rhythm mostly, which syncopated with his slow steps down the rows of lettuce.

When he walked up the porch he was slapping the sandal against his thigh, but suddenly he forgot that he had it in his hand, though he made the slap two or three times more. Maria was in the room, frightened, with four other people. They made an unfriendly picture.

Chapter 2

Guanadera, Port reminded himself, had no police force. The village had a policeman who sat on the square most of the day, in the shade, looking at his toes. He wore khaki pants, a big Mexican shirt. His revolver, which was a hot thing to wear because of the cartridge belt, usually hung on a nail in his office. This office was the corridor to the two cells where the same drunks slept every week end. Port knew this policeman by sight and he was not one of the men in the room.

There were two policemen, carrying army rifles, besides a police captain and a civilian in a white linen suit.

"Close the door behind him," said the civilian to one of the policemen.

"Immediately!" said the captain.

The one they were talking to double-timed to the door while he carried his rifle at port arms. The man looked very earnest and was full of a concentration that did justice to his uniform. It was starched, khaki, very new, and it pinched him in several places. His face was round and he had thick lips, and he gave a blown-up balloon kind of impression because of the very tight collar.

"You slide it, idiot!" yelled the captain. "From one side to the other!"

While the man worked with the sliding door, Port almost laughed. But then he looked at the civilian and his mood was no longer humorous. The civilian was slight and gave an impression of precise details; the fine nose, the very black eyes, the thin fingers, the carefully pressed white suit.

"Who are you?" said Port.

"Alphonso Maria Juan d'Ortega," said the man, and another detail struck Port. D'Ortega's Spanish was almost Castilian. D'Ortega was Mexican but he affected the speech. Port did not find the man likable.

"I notice," said d'Ortega, "that I wasn't mistaken about you, Señor Port." He made enough of a smile to show his teeth, but that didn't make his smile any friendlier. He walked up to Port and held out his hand. "May I have it?" he said.

All Port was holding in his hand was Kiamoto's sandal. "You mean this?" he said, and when he held it out d'Ortega took it away from him.

That wasn't Port's chief worry at the moment. He let d'Ortega take the sandal and tried to think of what to ask first.

"How come you knew..."

"A tourist in this little town," said d'Ortega, and he shrugged. "Naturally your name would be known."

This was pure evasion, Port knew, and explained nothing.

"Why are you here? And with an army."

"To arrest you," said d'Ortega.

This now, thought Port, was much more to the point, though it still explained nothing. And then, when d'Ortega saw that Port was getting irritable, he nodded his head and said, "We'll discuss it later."

The nod had been for the captain and the captain yelled, "Surround him!" which the two men with the rifles took literally, because they went to stand right and left of Port and held out their guns so he couldn't pass.

"Crap," said Port and pushed.

They stumbled back and one of them dropped his rifle, but that was the end of the comedy.

"Uh-uh, Señor," said the captain and then he said it again, and even though it might have been comical because of the way he talked through his mustache and the way he looked apologetic, it was now serious business. He had his gun out of the holster with a fast draw and by the time it pointed at Port the hammer was back, making a ratchety sound.

"Will you come?" he asked, "or do I ask them to hit you with the butts?"

The two cops with the rifles lifted the weapons and waited for the word. Port had no doubts about them. They would do as the captain said.

"Where are we going?" Port said.

"To the station." The captain jerked his head at the men so they would let Port through.

With a primitive respect for the uniform, Maria hadn't dared move through it all, but when Port turned to the door she suddenly started to scream. She tried to explain why she was here, why Port was here, that Kiamoto was missing, and if the police would only listen—

"Quiet," said d'Ortega.

"But he has done nothing! He has..."

What stopped her short was d'Ortega's gesture. He was going to slap her across the face. Port saw it, but the gun was still on him, and the captain saw it, and Port thought that the man looked shocked. But then d'Ortega didn't hit the girl. All he wanted, it seemed, was to stop her from screaming. If she screamed enough there would be a crowd outside the house. Too much attention seemed to concern d'Ortega a lot.

He said, "And before we go, Señorita, I'll explain to you that this is a matter of murder."

"My God! You mean Kiamoto—"

"Perhaps. I mention it for two reasons. One, so you know that this is not a matter to talk about, after we're gone. And two, so that you keep your ears open."

"But Señor Port didn't know the old man! Señor Port couldn't have anything to do..."

"That's why you should keep your ears open," said d'Ortega, "since Señor Port may not be the one. And if he is not the one, perhaps there is someone else. You understand?" and he looked at her so she would be frightened. "You understand why you should be quiet?"

Maria understood what he wanted her to understand. She would keep quiet and she would look around. Port understood something quite different.

They left the girl behind. Port looked at her when he went through the door, wanting to say something comforting, but Maria was too scared now to see anything clearly. She barely looked at Port and while he went out she rubbed at a spot on the table next to her.

Port thought that she'd be all right for a while. If she had nothing to do with any of this—whatever any of this might be—then she would be all right because d'Ortega was not staying behind. And if she was part of this thing, she would certainly be all right now that he, Port, was leaving.

They walked down the dark street, avoiding the board walk along the gardens, because that way their shoes made less noise. There was no one outdoors. Japanese in Guanadera, unlike the Mexicans, were not in the habit of strolling in the night air or sitting on the front stoop.

At the end of the street was an old sedan. One of the cops opened the rear door for Port. D'Ortega and one of the cops sat in front, Port sat in back, between the captain and the second man with the rifle.

This was fine. Port was interested in the captain. There had been that brief moment when the captain had shown his surprise at d'Ortega, the shock that a man should threaten to beat a woman, or perhaps—if he must—that he should do it in public. For one thing it meant that the captain did not know d'Ortega too well; for another, that he had an imperfect idea of what was involved in this business. That, thought Port, put the captain and himself in somewhat the same position. Not to mention that the captain might be a nice person.

"Your man is passing the jail," said Port. The car was going through the square.

"Oh? Ah, yes. I'm not stationed in Guanadera," said the captain.

"You're taking me—" Port made it a question and waited politely.

"Ciudad de Miguel," said the captain. "A much finer jail," and he smiled.

And a much bigger town, thought Port. Busy enough and big enough to allow for more irregularities.

"I'm glad," said Port. "I am confident that your establishment is of finer caliber than the local one."

"Oh yes. Of course."

"Cigarette?" said Port.

The captain was happy to take one, and said so. He was happy to learn, through the offer of the cigarette, that Port hadn't talked facetiously, but from true appreciation. And Port was glad to see that the captain was the kind of man who would take it that way. They smiled at each other and smoked.

"A long trip," said Port. He exhaled and then, with polite anxiety, waved at the smoke so it wouldn't drift into the captain's face.

"Ah, yes. But the road isn't bad." When the captain exhaled he waved at the smoke the way Port had done. They were building a nice relationship.

"A minor matter," said Port. "The convenience of your jail is what counts. A long trip is nothing in view of that prospect."

The captain said something equally flattering and a few grateful things concerning Port's manners. "The prisoner in general," he said, "lacks the refinement, the manners, if you follow my meaning, which allows for the relationship, retains the relationship, if you follow my meaning, between two human beings. Not two enemies, but two human beings." He exhaled and waved at the smoke, automatically now. "But you, Señor Port, I am happy to note..."

"Please," said Port. "Please. You flatter me."

And this was the time, thought Port, to take the captain up on this business of two polite human beings. "I wonder," he said, "since we are passing my house—"

"Yes, Señor Port?"

"I wonder if protocol would permit you to stop there, just for a moment, you understand, and with me under guard at all times, naturally—"

"You need something from your home?"

"A few little necessities. Soap, some money for cigarettes—"

"Ah, yes. Where is your house?"

"The one you are approaching."

"Stop!" yelled the captain. "Stop at that house."

D'Ortega might not have been listening, or after having listened for a while had become bored with the small talk, but when the car stopped suddenly he was concerned again. He swiveled around to the captain and talked very sharply, like an employer to an underling from whom he expects better.

"What are you doing? Are you forgetting yourself?"

"It will take just a moment," said the captain. "I thought I made clear to you..."

Just like an employer, thought Port.

"Señor Port made a simple request and is a gentleman. I will accompany him myself."

The captain did not give way, because he cherished the human relationship. He had none with d'Ortega, Port noted, and their relationship was therefore most certainly financial.

The captain and Port went into the house, where Port lit an oil lamp and went to the sink. He picked up a cake of soap, showed it to the captain, and the two men smiled at each other. Then Port went to the closet, pulled out his suitcase, offered to let the captain examine it.

"No, thank you," said the captain. "We understand each other."

Of course. He was still holding the gun. He was holding it down and it wasn't cocked, but Port remembered how fast the man was. Soap him a little bit more? It might work, something casual with dropping the lamp, something quick in the dark— But the chances were that d'Ortega would get away. And d'Ortega hadn't declared himself yet. Once that had happened Port would know what to do.

He opened the suitcase and moved a few things with slow care, so the captain could follow. There was a zipper pocket, which Port opened, where he kept money.

He put a large amount in his pocket. Port smiled and the captain smiled.

"Shall we go?" said Port.

"If you are done, Señor Port."

"I'm done here."

They went back to the car and took the rest of the trip in silence, expectant like two seducers who were keeping their obvious secret.

They reached Ciudad de Miguel around midnight, which was not late in this climate but a sociable time in the streets. Coffee bars were open, some shops were open, and the restaurants used part of the streets for their tables. Nobody looked at the car because the town was of civilized size. Ciudad de Miguel was a railway center. Trains and trucks made a noise in the night.

The jail was very quiet and cool. From the outside it looked like a Spanish mission, and the inside was antiseptically bare. It seemed prearranged that they should use a side entrance, and the little room with a table and two chairs seemed prearranged too. They left Port there with one of the men who was holding a rifle. When d'Ortega had closed the door the jail was very quiet again.

Port leaned by the wall and looked at the policeman. The man seemed in dull suffering because of the tight shirt, but he took it like a soldier. His face, like a pinched balloon, showed nothing. There was nothing, Port decided. He lit a cigarette and started to smoke. Then he let the cigarette burn by itself.

D'Ortega and the captain were still in the corridor and now were angry enough so Port could hear.

"...concludes our agreement, Señor," the captain was saying, and his firmness was hardly polite now.

"But where is Capo? How do you expect me to manage my affair..."

"It is your affair and Capo is your man," said the captain, "and for that matter, the less I know about Capo the better. This is, after all," and he put reprimand into his voice, "an official establishment."

"Your service is only as good as..."

"You were interrupting me, Señor d'Ortega. I was going to say that an arrest is something I can do officially. What you and your Capo have in mind is not—er —official."

Then d'Ortega started to curse. His man Capo was gone, said somebody's voice; he had been bored waiting, he was probably drinking beer somewhere in town—all of which made d'Ortega feel pressed for time.

"I can give you until tomorrow morning," the captain insisted, "as we arranged." And then, "No, Señor, your money insults me."

The dumb son of a bitch, thought Port. The stupid bastard was pressing d'Ortega too much. This would make d'Ortega worse, Port was sure, something he did not like to think about. And with pressure, maybe they would find Capo that much sooner, since d'Ortega was so anxious to have his muscle man back.

The door opened and d'Ortega came in. He said over his shoulder, "When he comes, send him in," and then he jerked his head at the rifle man, who left the room immediately.

D'Ortega was in an evil mood. He was still holding Kiamoto's old sandal and he tossed it on the table, where it made a sharp smack.

"Sit down, Señor Port. We will discuss this."

"Without Capo?" Port came over and sat down at the table.

At first d'Ortega said nothing, but then he thought he might play it like Port did. He smiled, showing his teeth. "You insist on him?"

"Oh no."

"Then please talk to me."

"I don't even know why I'm here," said Port.

More of that strange humor, d'Ortega thought. The North American grins under stress. He sat opposite Port and toyed with a strap on the sandal.

"Where is he?" He pushed at the sandal.

"Where is who? Kiamoto?"

"Well?"

"I have no idea. Never saw him in my life."

"But you were concerned enough to interest yourself in his shoe. Careless of him, wasn't it? Leaving it there."

"It's pretty old," said Port, waiting.

"Yes. Old enough so he forgot it. And such a careful man."

"Doesn't seem very important."

"Where is he, Señor Port?"

"I'm barely interested," said Port.

D'Ortega took that with a cold face. Then he picked up the sandal just slightly, dropped it again.

"But enough," he said. "Like this, eh, Mister Port? This was interesting to you, wasn't it?"

The sandal had thongs which passed over the feet. The thongs went back and forth in a pattern. With a foot in the sandal they would cover the instep, and there was no strap which would pass between the toes. Japanese sandals have one strap which passes between the first toe and the second.

"You know," said d'Ortega, "as I know, that—Kiamoto, was it?—that he isn't Kiamoto, and that he is *Chinese*."

When they had interrupted him at the house, Port had been about to ask Maria. He had wondered why her Japanese fisherman didn't wear Japanese sandals. He still didn't know who Kiamoto was, but he was no poor fisherman, in spite of the studied conformity of his bare house. D'Ortega knew that. He seemed to be after something big.

"Tell me," said Port, acting impatient, "what makes you think I know what you're talking about?"

"Because you are here."

"I'm here because you bought yourself an arrest, d'Ortega, and if you think..."

"And you are here because you are interested."

I was there because of the peace and quiet and the hot sun and then Maria, Port was thinking.

"You don't think for a moment, Señor Port," d'Ortega was saying, "that your act of a stray tourist in Guanadera did anything but attract my attention? There are no stray tourists in Guanadera. It has no hotel, no swimming pool, and no air-conditioning. But you, Señor Port," and d'Ortega laughed, "you, of all people, show up there!"

"What?"

"I inquired about you. *The* Mister Port of syndicate fame. The young man who made a great deal of money and when he had enough broke the organization to pieces so he could walk out. And walked out. And has done nothing since those exciting days. But perhaps your money is running low, Señor Port? Perhaps your special talents for clandestine action have just been dormant for too long?" It wasn't meant as a question, because d'Ortega finished off, "Which explains your presence to me, Señor Port, which makes it clear why you, especially you, show up in Guanadera."

D'Ortega was wrong all the way down the line, about Port's coming to the village, about most of the background. But the way d'Ortega was acting, there was no point in explaining all this. He wouldn't believe it. Port hadn't left the Stoker mob because he was rich enough to turn to more legal ways. Money hadn't been part of the move, just disgust. He'd been sick of the jungle life with the tricks of the worst in civilization. Nor was he looking for money, not right now, anyway, or in Guanadera.

But what reminded him of the time he had broken out of the syndicate was another thing: he was starting to feel just as cramped now, and just as unpleasant. Though d'Ortega did not know that yet.

"And you?" Port asked. "Who are you?" A reasonable question, nothing ominous.

"My name..."

"Means nothing to me."

Oh?" D'Ortega seemed offended. "But Pan-Continental, surely you've heard..."

"Pan-Continental Industries?"

D'Ortega just smiled, thinking that Port was still playing his game. Then he stopped smiling and looked at his watch.

"Your manner of ignorance, Señor Port, will come to an end now. Either now, as you and I talk, or shortly, when Capo returns. Most certainly when Capo returns."

But the threat had no time to develop. The door opened and Capo came in.

Chapter 3

Port still knew nothing; what made Kiamoto important, who d'Ortega was, what he, Port, was supposed to be after. There would now be no chance to find out more. Capo looked tough. He was short, like most Indians from the interior, and in his case, too, the Western clothes made him appear swollen.

But with Capo it seemed to be muscle. Even his face was muscular. There was a round bulge over his eyes, his cheeks were tight and shiny, his thick mouth was like muscle. With this strength in his face there was room for nothing else. No emotion, no doubt, no interest.

He walked up to the table and stumbled.

"Pig!" d'Ortega yelled, and jumped up from his chair. "You are drunk!"

Port almost laughed.

Capo licked one lip. When he talked his voice was like his face. "Yes," he said. "So what?"

"So what? How do you expect..." d'Ortega started to say, when Capo waved his hand so that d'Ortega should stop talking. Then he said, "Like this."

He slammed his knuckles across Port's face.

It hurt like hell. The blow had been sloppy, more a slap than anything else, but the pain raced up Port's nose, into his eyes, around and around in his skull. He fell back in his chair and then he let himself fall on the floor. This gave him time and distance, the best he could do for the moment.

But nothing else happened. It had been a demonstration. Capo and d'Ortega were arguing, d'Ortega mostly, because he was having nothing but bad luck that night. First the captain, now his muscle man, and of course Port himself. But d'Ortega seemed to have some prestige. He told Capo, and it sounded a lot like a reminder, that if there were any more of this crap then he, Capo, would end up where he legally should and he, d'Ortega, was not a lawyer for nothing.

So while Port sat on the floor he found out two more things: that Capo was a thug with a pending sentence, and that d'Ortega was somebody's lawyer. If any of this had a bearing on Kiamoto, Port didn't see it yet. Nor did he keep thinking about it. He took a slow breath and started to move. He'd had it.

"You want to ask questions in this room?" Capo was saying. "I could hear you talking, from the corridor."

"Do you have to be noisy?"

"Not me," said Capo. "But he will." He nodded at Port.

Both men watched while Port helped himself off the floor with the chair. He was pulling himself up by the chair like a dying man, ready to make his move.

D'Ortega went to the door and said, "I'll arrange for a different room," which he hardly got finished because Capo coughed.

That's all he did, cough, though Port knew how the pain must have felt.

With Capo drunk Port knew of one advantage, speed. Capo might be as strong as deer, but he was slow. Port's first move showed this, because Capo had not been able to get out of the way of the chair and the chair had sailed smartly into his shins. And the second move. Capo had been slow enough so that Port could reach out and pull back the chair. By then the pain in the shins had pulled Capo over, and the clear advantage kept Port going.

He cracked the chair down on Capo's head. Nothing happened. He did it again and this time the chair came apart. Capo started to straighten up and Port reached out with his left. Capo fell over and sighed. He stayed down.

"Don't open the door," said Port.

D'Ortega took his hand from the knob. "Why don't you try to leave?" he said.

"Spoken like a lawyer. I think I'm still under arrest."

"Try to leave, Señor Port, and you will be sure."

D'Ortega would like that. There was a suspicion-of-murder charge over Port, or something similar, and walking out now would add just a little charge. Maybe resisting arrest. But the little charge would be much more substantial because there'd be nothing drummed up about it.

Port wouldn't do him the favor. He was sick of d'Ortega and the confusion that went with the man, and the best way out was to pay his way out. Port was no longer curious, just angry.

"Take the drunk and get out," he said.

"If you think that delaying this interview will be of any advantage to you..."

"If you leave him here," said Port and nodded at Capo, "I'll fix it so he won't wake up for twenty-four hours."

"Why don't you stop bluffing?" said d'Ortega. Then he had meant to take up his questions again. In the middle of that, if Port talked long enough, Capo would wake up and then—

"I'm not bluffing," said Port.

He went over to Capo, turned him with his foot, bent over and clipped him hard on the side of the head. It was an unpleasant thing, hitting a man who was unconscious. But it impressed d'Ortega.

D'Ortega looked for a moment longer, because of the way Capo's head lolled to one side; he could still hear the flat impact of the blow. This Daniel Port, d'Ortega considered, would be a dangerous man. D'Ortega would need a different approach, less simple, most likely, than he had planned. This Daniel Port was not simple. D'Ortega would watch it. He was not through.

Chapter 4

One guard helped to move Capo out and one guard stayed with Port, and after a decent interval the door opened again and the captain came in.

"They are gone, Señor."

"Good."

"Uh—to be back in the morning." He nodded at the guard and waited till the man had left the room. "Are you ready to go to your cell, Señor Port?"

"It is polite of you to ask me," said Port. "I'm tired," he added, which was true.

For a moment the captain was confused. He frowned. Could he have been mistaken, thinking that this was a gentleman? He coughed, straightened his face. He would put this matter to the test.

"I will see to it," he said, "that you have a clean blanket. In your cell," he said with emphasis.

Then he waited. But what Port said next made the picture even less clear.

"For consideration," said Port very politely, "I would appreciate a few other things."

"Uh—yes?"

"There's an airport in this town, isn't there?"

"Uh—yes."

"I would like to know when I can catch a plane to Mexico City, sometime in the morning."

"Er—in the morning. Yes. There is one in the morning," said the captain. And then he started to add, "And as I was saying, Señor d'Ortega will also be back in the morning," but Port interrupted him.

"I would like to know just when the plane leaves, I would like a ticket, and besides the clean blanket, captain, I would appreciate shaving things and a towel. I brought soap," he added, and put it on the table.

"Er—yes," said the captain.

The soap lay there, wrapped in the bills Port had brought.

Port thought a moment, not looking at the captain. The captain was looking at the soap. Port thought of the rank of the captain, the size of Ciudad de Miguel, the possible worth of d'Ortega, and then he put the soap back in his pocket. He left, out on the table, one thousand pesos.

It was less than a hundred dollars but more, Port was hoping, than d'Ortega's offering.

"Will this cover my flight?" he asked.

"Most certainly," said the captain.

"Round trip?"

"Uh—no," and the captain smiled like a gentleman, but one who knew limits. "However," he said, "I will buy your ticket myself, so there will be absolutely no mistake."

"You are kind," said Port. "And there will also be no mistake about an undisturbed sleep, undisturbed awakening in time for the plane, and my undisturbed, clean record with the police?"

"Señor," said the captain, "you and I are assuredly two gentlemen," and he put the one thousand pesos into his pocket.

Port reached Mexico City in the afternoon. The switch was wrenching; the large streets, the fantastic traffic, the entirely Western tempo. The night before he had slept in the jail of a provincial town, and before that he had slept in an improbable village which sat on a margin of jungle and ocean. He felt interrupted, but he did not think the interruption would last very long.

The American Embassy was large and cool, and while Port sat waiting it occurred to him that he wasn't dressed for the place. He was still wearing khaki pants and an open shirt and he had to put his hand to his face to make sure he was shaved. And what would he say to the man, the undersecretary of something or other who might then send him to the sub-consul or something, and from there to a department clerk in charge of complaints from the provinces? By that time his repeated story would be so ridiculous, they might advise him to go back to jail, for the sake of his own conscience and in order to stabilize international tensions between Mexico City and Guanadera.

Port bit his lip when he caught himself in these idiot thoughts, and patted himself for a cigarette. He didn't have any.

"Take one of mine," said the girl who was typing at a desk opposite him.

Port thanked her, took a cigarette, thanked her again.

"Out of money?" she asked him.

"Huh?"

"They come in every day," said the girl. "Though most of 'em aren't even shaved."

"Yes," said Port. He blew smoke and sat down again. "They lent me a razor in jail this morning."

"Really?" She typed something quickly because she didn't know what to say next. But she felt she should say something nice to a citizen. And it should also show something of her international knowledge. "I know they have very progressive jails in this country. Didn't you find them so?"

"Oh, certainly. You wouldn't believe it if I told you what a fine, human relationship I established with the jail commandant."

A light blinked on her desk and the girl was sorry that they had been interrupted. "Go right in, Mister Port," she said. "And we're happy to have you back."

This remark surprised both of them, but Port was halfway through the door at this point, and glad of it.

The assistant to someone or other who waited for Port behind the desk looked and behaved according to Port's worst expectations. The young man looked like a football player with a benevolent face, so that one quality cancelled out the other and only blandness was left. The young man smiled at Port with the same cast to his face that anyone might use when smiling at a large group of people. He asked name, age, residence, former residence, permanent residence, length of local stay.

Then he said, "Well now, Danny, what seems to be the trouble?"

"It's a complaint. Last night I was arrested..."

"Local police?"

"Yes. Mexican. I was..."

"You know, Danny, we don't make it a policy—and this comes straight from the top, top echelon Washington, State Department—of interfering with the internal affairs of a friendly nation. That's what's meant by friendly—haha—in contrast to belligerent, where we'd go right in with all we've got. You get what I mean? Were you in the war, Danny?"

"Yes."

"Second doubleyoo doubleyoo? Musta been, by the wrinkles. Time does fly, haha. Now then, did they treat you bad?"

"Who?"

"Local cops. That's why you're here, isn't it?"

It would have been easy to forget completely why he was here, because Port already had a defeated feeling. It was hard to remember the point of this visit.

"Let me just tell it," he said. "May I please?"

"Sure, Danny. Sure, sure."

"I went to Guanadera..."

"Wait a minute, wait a minute. Have I got that down here?" and the young man looked at his sheet.

"You must have written it down," Port said with a very controlled voice, "when you asked me for one of my residences. Under last residence, for instance."

"Yessir, here it is. Go on, Danny."

"I got involved with a man by the name of Alphonso Maria Juan..."

"Wait a minute, wait a minute—"

"No," said Port. "You don't have that down there because this is the first chance I've had to mention it. Alphonso Maria Juan d'Ortega."

"Funny how they use female names here, huh?" and the young man wrote it down.

"Ready again?"

"Sure, Danny, sure. Go ahead."

"D'Ortega, I gathered, is connected with Pan-Continental Industries."

"Big outfit. Let me just..."

"Go ahead. Write it down," said Port and lit a cigarette. He struck the match with a vicious snap of the wrist.

"Go ahead, Danny. Just tell it in your own words."

"Yes." Port blew smoke and tried to think of a way to tell it without any names in it. Then he said, "This concerns false arrest, mistaken identity, bribery, and illegal use of force."

"Hey, Betty?" the young man said into his intercom.

He smiled at Port and urged him to just go on talking. But the typist girl came in then and Port saw no point in talking. The young man gave the girl the sheet he'd been writing on. Betty should be a good girl and type that up in quadruplicate and not forget to shoot one copy down to Jack right quick. Then he asked Betty why she never wore the pink blouse any more, the one with the little things on it, and while Port didn't know what the girl answered he heard when she closed the door. He opened his eyes then and found the young man gazing at him.

"Go right ahead, Danny."

"The point is this," said Port. He had to take a deep breath then and when he talked again his voice sounded quite good and normal. "The point is that I came here for a vacation, not a work-out."

"I envy you. Haha."

"I was arrested in Guanadera by the police from Ciudad de Miguel on suspicion of murder, I think they called it." Port knew that the young man would now want to write down that new name, and closed his eyes. He only opened them when he heard the other one talking again.

"Danny, I've been thinking about this and I honestly think you should talk to Jack about it. Let me ask you this. Have you got any money?"

"Money? Yes."

"I thought so. I mostly handle destitutes in my department, you understand?"

Port understood that he himself was beginning to feel severely destitute, money or no money, but that it would be foolish to say so to the young man.

"Guys that come down here and end up without any money to go back home to the U. S."

"I understand what you mean," said Port.

"When you get out there where Betty is, ask her to show you to the place where Jack holds down, okay, Danny?" He stood up and held out his hand.

It was just as well, thought Port, and just as well that he hadn't had a chance to tell his story to this one, because he would naturally have to tell it again to the next one.

Jack's office had more files. He looked a great deal like the other young man, but Port had expected that. Also the long walk from one office to the other had helped. It had given Port time to shake off the effects of the first young man's benevolent indifference, so that now Port knew the point of his visit again and he'd get that into the conversation before anything else.

"My name's, Pierce," said Jack. "Can I help you?" He didn't pick up a pencil immediately but seemed to be listening.

"The point of my visit is that I got sucked in on somebody's business, getting sucked in by some kind of mistake, and what I want from you, Mister Pierce, is some manner of very strong statement to the cops involved in this thing, to lay off in the future and leave me alone."

"You're going back to Guanadera?"

Pierce, it seemed, had gotten his copy from the typist girl in the meantime.

"Yes. To lie in the sun and not be bothered."

Port noticed that Pierce had turned out to be a good listener, or a normal listener at any rate. Also, he didn't smile as much as the first young man had and looked as if he wanted to know more.

"I came to you," said Port, "because I felt that a word from the top would make the best impression down there—maybe just your letterhead might do the trick—because my main interest is that this business should stop right here." Port stopped, and it struck him that all this would be very vague to Pierce and he'd better hold the man's attention with the real details.

"Do you know d'Ortega well?" Pierce asked.

He had not only read the copy from Betty but remembered the names without looking them up. Port didn't feel that Pierce was rushing him, but it was almost as if Pierce had interests which had nothing to do with Port's story. Port had, in fact, not told his story yet.

"I don't know him from Adam," said Port and then he detailed the whole thing as it had happened, from the time of going to Kiamoto's house, and why, to the night in the captain's jail.

Pierce nodded and said that was certainly interesting and something would certainly have to be done. And would Mister Port mind if he'd take down some personal data, a little bit of background material.

"I don't see what bearing that has on my complaint," said Port.

Pierce smiled and said that this was a safeguard to the department, that it established the veracity of the complainant, so to speak, giving the department more confidence in their efforts to defend the rights of an injured party.

"You doubt my story?"

"No, the fact is I don't," said Pierce. After he had waited a moment and seen that Port was getting hostile instead of compliant he gave a little shrug and said, "In a sense it's unnecessary. Just a rule for guidance, asking these questions, but I personally am satisfied. Excuse me a minute?" and he actually waited for Port to say yes.

Then he went out of the door. He stopped at his secretary's desk and used the phone to ask if Briggs was there. When he got Briggs he said, "That thing you're on, have you got the name Port in it?"

"No," said Briggs. "As you know, I got just about nothing."

"The name is Daniel Port. Guanadera at present."

"What else?"

"I have to get back inside, but I'll send you what I got," and he hung up.

He told his secretary to take the Port form over to Briggs, the form Betty had sent, and then he went back into his office.

"I've never been in Guanadera," he said when he sat down again. "How did you ever find it?"

"By chance. I looked at the map and saw how it got greener and greener going up the coast, so I tried it."

"That's a fine way of traveling," said Pierce. "I'd like that. Did you know about the Japanese settlement there, when you picked Guanadera?"

"No. I was surprised."

"Nobody knows about it, I mean in detail. The most a tourist will know is that there are Japanese fishermen somewhere along the Pacific."

"I hadn't even known that. About Mexico, I mean."

"Are there any Chinese up there?" Pierce wanted to know.

"Only what I told you," said Port, "about Kiamoto maybe being Chinese."

"Queer, isn't it," said Pierce. Then he looked at his wristwatch and started to move things on his desk. When he had moved papers in certain ways he picked up a pencil and wrote something down.

The silence started to feel like a stall to Port, though he couldn't be sure. It could also be his impatience with the slow creak of officialdom, with having told them his story and having been given no answer.

"Now that I've made my complaint," said Port, "what can you do for me?"

Pierce looked up and said, "Oh, we'll help you." Then he looked down again and wrote a few things.

"How?" said Port.

"Uh—I'm sorry. I wasn't listening. But go ahead."

"You're starting to sound like that idiot boy I was with before I got to you," said Port. "You know whom I'm talking about?"

"Oh yes," and Pierce laughed. "He is sort of an idiot boy. That's why he gets to do just that one form." He laughed again.

"And you, Mister Pierce?"

"Except for lapses, I just listen."

"There's nothing else to listen to, Mister Pierce. How will you help me?"

"The reason we're sitting around here with you not getting an answer, Mister Port, is to wait for word from another office. We have a file of complaints, used for collating and so forth, and with that in back of us we decide how to deal with new incidents. If there's been more than one complaint from the same area, we deal with it one way. If there's been..."

"I get it," said Port.

It was a long explanation, using more time. But the man had explained what the time was for, and there was no reason for Port to feel edgy. Also it made the small talk a natural thing.

"And about how long do you think you'll be staying there?"

"I hadn't thought about that," said Port.

"Till you get sunburned, huh?" and Pierce laughed politely. "You have no idea how many tourists go by that criterion."

"I don't expect to get burned," said Port.

"Of course not."

"I would just like to be sure that there'll be no further involvements."

"Or else?" said Pierce.

Port shrugged. He didn't know Pierce at all and he thought this was getting to be more than small talk. Then he said, "Do you know this Pan-Continental Industries outfit?"

"Oh yes. Our government deals with them."

"Who are they?"

"One of those combines, those international combines, with industrialists of a number of nations forming a cooperative working agreement on manufacture, distribution, and so forth."

"Sounds pretty vague. And important."

"Nothing mysterious, really. Like I. G. Farben, you know? Or like United Fruit Company, that sort of thing."

"They deal in fruit?"

"Uh, no. It's mining, smelting, shipping."

"No manufacture?"

"That too. Machinery, munitions," and then Pierce started scribbling again.

Port wanted to ask who d'Ortega was in all this, but the phone on the desk rang. Pierce mostly listened and it didn't take long. He said, "Okay. It's okay? Okay," and hung up.

"Well, Mister Port, you can leave now with my assurance that you won't be bothered again. Yours isn't the first complaint and via the proper Mexican department we're sending a strong warning to the officials in the Ciudad de Miguel area."

"Ah," said Port. "Good." He got up.

"If you're harassed again, of course, let us know, though I doubt it will happen." He got up and shook hands with Port. He held on to the hand and said, "Are you returning today?"

"I hope to get a plane to Ciudad."

"Well, let me help you," said Pierce, and let go of Port's hand to scribble a note. "Let me arrange for a reservation for you and if you want, we can even arrange for the ticket."

"For nothing?"

Pierce laughed and said, "The secretary outside will tell you where you pay your money, and we'll have the ticket waiting for you at the airport. One of our services." He smiled.

Then Port left and Pierce stopped smiling. It was good to be certain on which plane Port would be, but that was really minor. Compared to the rest of it, this was so minor that Pierce forgot about that little success by the time he was halfway across his office. He went down the corridor to the door which had just a number, and after he had said hello to Briggs he watched the older man so he wouldn't miss anything.

"Boy," said Briggs. "I think we hit pay dirt!"

Chapter 5

Briggs rubbed the gray stubble on his head and said, "First of all, this guy has a background that could curl your toes."

"Daniel Port? He seemed so—sort of quiet."

"So would you be." Briggs rattled a teletype sheet but didn't have to look at it while he was talking. "High man in a syndicate set-up, dough from rackets, politics, state appointments. Next he decides to cut out, and *makes* it. This he does over the ruins of the organization; he broke them up like old cement and every Tom, Dick, and Harry ends up with indictments. But not Danny Port. If he gets rubbed out, he lets it be known, he'll take care of the very big management posthumously. So then comes a time of no known activity, he bums around, then comes and turns up here."

"You suspect what—the bumming around?"

"Listen, Pierce, we got nothing on Port; he's too clever. Once, after his break, he even did a short stint on something with the Washington office. Because of his background."

"Informer?"

"Uh—not really. We kind of had to push him a little."

"None of that means he's in on this."

"He sounds like a tourist to you?" said Briggs.

"How come you got all this so fast?"

"Because of that recent stint he did, for the office. Just the dry statistics here," and he rattled the paper, "but I remembered our man. Look. He's used to activity, and dough. He bums around a few years and it looks as if he didn't do anything then. Next he shows up here. I don't know how yet, but he smelled money. He's used to it big."

Briggs sat back and smiled. "Wouldn't you say, Pierce, that one million dollars in cash is big money?"

This required no answer, and while Briggs pulled a folder over, Pierce sat down and lit a cigarette. He might still have been thinking about the million, because when he exhaled it sounded like a sigh.

Briggs opened his folder; on top of the pile of sheets was a clipping. It was part of the dossier and more than a year old.

"A million people read this," said Briggs, "but it's almost forgotten now. No publicity, the way it was handled. But a sharp nose like Port's, this must have kept teasing him."

The clipping read: "The Nationalist Chinese Government, through a local representative, jointly with the Government of the United States of America, have filed suit against General Hoi Kio of the Chinese Nationalist Army, Bureau of Procurement and Arms, for embezzlement of one and a half million dollars in cash and securities. General Hoi Kio had arrived in this country as official representative of his government in order to negotiate purchase of fighter planes and infantry equipment. The money in his possession constituted down payment on his prospective purchases and was part of a sixteen-million-dollar loan recently awarded the Formosa government by the United States. At present General Hoi Kio's whereabouts is not known."

"At present," Briggs paraphrased, "Hoi Kio's whereabouts is maybe just about established."

"Kiamoto?" said Pierce.

"Look at it. Where can an Oriental hide? Among Orientals. And he picks the most out-of-the-way place, where money doesn't matter, where the news of the day doesn't matter, where nothing but siesta and fishing matter."

"But if anybody is going to spot a Chinese among Japanese, it's going to be a Japanese."

"Kiamoto comes originally from Manchuria, and the mixing of Chinese-Japanese culture and genes would be in his favor."

"So now," said Pierce, putting out his cigarette, "Port is this close to the loot, and what does he do? He comes here and draws official attention to it. You mean to tell me. . ."

"I don't know why he did it," said Briggs, "but I do know from way back what a fox this man is. I figure this. We know, and Port knows, that d'Ortega is in on this thing. As a matter of fact, d'Ortega, representing Pan-Continental, has a legitimate interest in that million bucks, and we know for a long time they've been looking for Kio. They prepared a big order of ammunitions and the stuff is still sitting around, waiting for payment. So this Port runs into d'Ortega, kind of hard the way I understand it, and he's now got to shake the competition. Maybe," said Briggs, "he's pulling us in to play us and d'Ortega against each other. It's got to be something like that." Briggs got up.

"You going alone?" asked Pierce.

"Me and Sanchez."

"You look neither Mexican nor Japanese," said Pierce.

"That's okay. He'll never know we're around."

Port had none of the fancy suspicions and motives which Briggs was reading into him. There was a strange note here and there, when Port thought back to his embassy visit, but none of that fit anywhere, nor was he interested. There had been that odd wait in Pierce's office, some odd questions by Pierce, relating to nothing, and then that bit with the plane, as if to make sure Pierce would know when and how Port was leaving. Bureaucrats, he was thinking, and then he dropped the whole thing.

Except there was this Kiamoto, who was really somebody else—

The bus from Ciudad de Miguel to Guanadera must be the oldest bus in the world because, Port reasoned, it still had square wheels. It was dark outside, which made the trip that much worse, because there was nothing to look at. There was only the hard movement and the squeak of the bus. It didn't even bounce or lurch, because there were no springs. This bus slapped and crashed all the way from Ciudad to Guanadera.

Port got off at his house and watched the taillight of the bus shaking itself to pieces. At one point he was even sure that the taillight had jumped off and bounced to the side of the road. But it had been the whole bus making that motion. Then it disappeared at the bend in the road.

It was almost like the night before, very quiet and warm, when Port had waited for Maria to come down the dark road or up from the beach where the surf made a sucking noise. There was no reason to expect her now. She didn't even know where he was. He would look for her, surprise her. He went into his house, took the soap out of his pocket and laid it back on the sink, put the bills he had left back in the suitcase. Then he washed a little and changed his clothes.

Maria might be at home, with old Pepe, or on the square, because that was the custom, or at Kiamoto's place, which would mean that the old man was back. That would be the best thing all around, and Maria would no longer be worried. So Port went to the end of the village where the Japanese houses were.

Kiamoto's house was dark. There was a Japanese on the street, carrying poles, and Port asked him if Kiamoto was back.

"*Salud*," said the fisherman. Then he kept walking along.

Port went back to the square and didn't see Maria anywhere. He asked the policeman if he had seen her, but he hadn't.

"Ask Rosita," he said. "She might know. You see the big one over there, with all the hair?"

Port didn't want to talk to Rosita. He went to the other end of the village where Pepe's adobe house was.

There was a light in the house and the front door was open, for the breeze. Pepe was on the small porch, with a pulque bottle next to his chair. The bottle was lying on its side.

"Is Maria home?" Port asked.

After a while Pepe nodded. He just nodded and pointed to the door.

Maria was on the bed. One eye was closed and the other one slitted. One cheek was blue, glistening like an eggplant. There was a little dried blood on her lips.

"Daniel—" she said. It was low, and she tried raising herself on one arm. "You're alive!"

Chapter 6

There was an oil lamp near the bed throwing the kind of soft light which can erase small imperfections and make everything smooth and mysterious. It did the opposite for Maria, because there was so much bad in her face and what was left of the good parts was so small. The light made her whole face a bruise.

Port made a painful sound. He wanted to go to Maria and touch her and was afraid; he wanted to run out on the porch and yell at the old drunk and maybe beat him up for the sight on the bed there. He had no idea how long this state lasted, but then he went to the bed and touched the girl's arm.

"You stay there," he said. "I'll help you."

He took a large bucket which was full of corn and dumped all the ears on the floor. Then he went out to the well and got water. It was good and cool and would stay that way for a while in the large bucket. He put it down next to the bed and Maria pointed to show him where he would find rags.

"Now every time you feel it get warm on your face, take it off and I'll give you a new one," he said. Then he covered her face with the wet cloth.

At first the cold made her start, but then she relaxed and breathed evenly.

"Are you hurt anywhere else?"

"No. Just my tongue."

"Swollen?"

"No. A small cut only."

Port lit a cigarette and looked at the wall over the bed. Then he said, "Who did it?"

Maria started to say something but there was a catch in her throat.

"Was it Pepe?"

She made a sound as if she were laughing. "No. Not him."

"D'Ortega?" Port waited.

"No. He watched."

Port looked at the ash on his cigarette. It was long. He dropped it into the palm of his hand and then he powdered it into dust with his fingers. He did this till there was no grit to it any more, but felt slippery.

He no longer remembered that he had come back to Guanadera to start over again, as if nothing had happened. Nothing was over now. He flipped the cigarette out of the door and made a sound as if spitting a small piece of tobacco. There was no question of his being done with d'Ortega. He was just starting.

He changed the compress on Maria's face. The bruises were not so vivid any more. He said, "They came back to ask you where Kiamoto was. And you didn't know."

"If I didn't tell them, d'Ortega said, they'd kill you," she said. "And I could tell them nothing." Her hands curled into the cloth of her skirt and held on very hard there. After a while she let go. "I would have," she said. "I would have told them, if I had known."

Port didn't ask her why.

"Was the other one, the one that did it, was he called Capo?"

"Yes. The one with the bandage."

Port remembered about hitting the man with the chair. Capo would need more than a bandage before this was over.

"When was this, Maria?"

"They came here. Around noon."

And in a fine state, after finding that Port had left the jail.

"Was Pepe here?"

"Yes. He knows nothing."

Port went out to the porch and stood by one of the posts. He looked down at Pepe and didn't say anything for a while. Should he blame him for standing by when they beat her? For sitting there in dull indifference while the girl was on the bed?

"How much did you have today, Pepe?" Port asked. The old man looked up and scratched his thin whiskers. His face looked ruined, and the only life in it were the lines down his cheeks, which gave him a resentful expression. Like a resentful bug.

"This one here," he said and kicked the bottle, "and the one they brought me."

"They brought you a bottle?"

"Yes. A gift."

"That's why you didn't help Maria?"

Pepe shrugged, but it wasn't indifference. He did it as if he were shaking off something annoying.

"I left," he said. "I didn't drink here."

There was nothing to say to the man, nothing Port could have done that would have made any difference. Port turned away and stared into the dark street. There was a house opposite with the tall door showing light and an iron grill over the door, the kind that locks up the house but lets in the air, and behind that were a man and a woman at a table, eating. Port barely noticed.

They still didn't have Kiamoto, or they wouldn't have come back. And where was this man, Maria's fisherman, d'Ortega's Chinese, the U.S. embassy's—what? Pierce had asked about Kiamoto several times.

There were three ways out of Guanadera for Kiamoto, by boat, on foot, by bus. One more way, by truck. There was a truck that picked up fish from the icehouse. Port went back into the room and sat down next to the bed.

"How is it, Maria?"

She lifted the wet rag off her face and looked at Port.

"Better, Danny. I'll be fine. And you'll have to promise me something, Danny. Please promise me..."

"They won't harm me," he said. "Believe me."

She didn't believe him. She also saw that Port wasn't going to listen, and her face hurt badly and she felt feverish. She put the rag back on her face so he couldn't see how she felt.

"They were here at noon, you said. Are you listening, Maria?"

"I'm listening. Yes."

"Did you see Kiamoto's boat in the bay? Just by chance, did you perhaps look that way any time today. . ."

"In the morning. I went to his house in the morning and saw his boat in the bay when I walked back."

No good. Conceivably the old man could have left while d'Ortega had been with Maria, and after that time she hadn't looked for the boat.

"Perhaps Pepe knows," said Maria. "He was at the icehouse in the afternoon."

"You were thinking the way I was," said Port. He got up and went out to ask Pepe.

Pepe hadn't noticed. He hadn't looked that way. Then Port asked him who else might know if the boat were still there and it took a while for Pepe to think clearly about this. Only patience would do, and Port tried to keep calm. In a while Pepe said Jimenez might know, he worked at the icehouse. He nodded down the street.

"Go ask him," said Port. "Now. Hurry!"

The old man went and Port watched him for a moment. He stood and thought that it might be easier to find d'Ortega than a Japanese who had disappeared and was really Chinese, but finding Kiamoto might explain more than any meeting with Capo and d'Ortega. Not that Kiamoto would be friendly to start with—

He went back inside.

"Maria, is there a way by land, on foot, that a man could leave Guanadera?"

"He could leave," she said, "but I don't think he could go anywhere. Ask Pepe. He knows a lot about the country where the jungle is and the hills."

It was almost midnight and a slow wind came in from the Pacific. It wasn't a wind that made a sound or would lift a curtain, but you could feel it on your skin. The air cooled. The girl on the bed felt it and curled her legs.

"Do you think you could sleep, Maria?"

She reached over and took his hand and didn't let go. "If you'll stay here with me, Danny, I could go to sleep now, and then in the morning..."

"Maria, please listen to me—"

For a moment she kept holding his hand, hard, and then suddenly she let go.

"Maria, if I don't find..."

"Go," she said. "Go," and turned away from him. Port explained to her that he would be back in a short while, and would stand guard all night, and that she should lock the house in the meantime. He explained about men so crazy as to beat up a woman and how that meant he couldn't just sit and be glad it was over; how with that kind of men nothing is over—

She didn't answer and perhaps she hadn't listened. Perhaps he should also have said that something in all this was getting ominous and more complicated than a Japanese fisherman missing, but she might not have understood that either. What he did not want to explain for sure was that Kiamoto wasn't the first one to look for. First things first. And he had an idea where he might find Capo.

Pepe came back, looked inside, stayed on the porch. When Port got there the old man was sitting down.

"Jimenez saw it," he said. "He left the icehouse at seven and Kiamoto's boat was still there, where it always is."

That was good. There were still three other ways out.

"The bus leaves once a day, is that right, Pepe?"

"In the morning to Ciudad, in the evening back here."

That left two, because d'Ortega would hardly let the bus leave the village without checking if Kiamoto was on it.

"Can you walk out of Guanadera? Some back way?"

"There is just the jungle. You can't walk far on the beach. The rocks go far out after a while."

"There are paths in the woods."

"Yes. Several. But they no longer go anywhere. Just jungle." That left one.

Port didn't have to ask Pepe about this one because he knew that the fish truck left town once every twenty-four hours. The boats came in during late afternoon, the haul was weighed, sorted, and packed until late at night, and around two in the morning the truck pulled out. It would barrel through the streets and out to the highway, water streaming out of the back, nonstop to Ciudad.

Before Port left he brought fresh water for Maria and then covered her with a light blanket. She said thank you, very low, but nothing else. Port bolted the wooden door in back and locked the grill in the front, then he tossed the key on the bed inside so that even Pepe couldn't get in.

Chapter 7

Most of the electric lights in Guanadera were in and around the icehouse. There was a high bulb over the gate for the truck, a lot of bulbs inside, over the cleaning tables, and several lights on the pier side, where the boats tied up. The clapboard building looked solid enough where it sat on the ground, but the walls weren't plumb and the roof had a sag where the building stuck out over the water. Because the tide had a range of twelve feet, the posts of the building were very tall.

Port walked up slowly and then he stayed in the shadows, before the ring of light by the house. The big door was open, showing workers inside, and the truck and the empty pier on the other side.

Somewhere here were d'Ortega, or Capo, or maybe a third man. It had to be that way, because d'Ortega was after the old Chinese.

Port didn't see d'Ortega, or Capo, or anyone else he knew.

The women stood at the long tables, gutting fish. Men dragged boxes, shoveled ice, carried slop to the pier and let it splash into the water. The women hardly talked, working fast, and the men with the boxes didn't talk because everything had to go at uncommon speed. Ice melted everywhere. There was a fine fog in the air, making halos around the light bulbs.

The women and the workers with the boxes would be of no help, Port thought. They were too busy to watch, and they all seemed local.

There were maybe four or five men not so busy: the young driver who was smoking a cigarette; an inspector, or a buyer perhaps, who looked beefy in a loose, rumpled suit and didn't seem to be Mexican; a Mexican with the clean clothes of an office worker, who was making marks on a check list. Then Port found another man, on the pier, but he was asleep and reeked of liquor.

Could be faked, thought Port. The man sat on a box, leaning. Port made him lean more. When the man fell off the box he gave a start and a grunt, but just that. He lay there and slept again.

Port walked into the building. There was a big fan by the door blowing the sharp fish odor and the cold air around. It was cold and damp in the high building. Port stopped near the door, showing interest in the fish and the packing, but he stayed by the door and sat down on a box.

It looked as if there were four men, any one of whom could be d'Ortega's man, checking to see if Kiamoto were trying to leave town on the truck. They were the four who did most of the standing around: the beefy inspector, the truck driver, the checker with the clipboard, and an Indian in a big serape, who sat on his heels.

Port sat and started his whistle, a low sound which didn't carry far, a slow beat with no melody. Then the driver came over. He came slowly, smiling all the time.

"A place to keep cool, huh?" He squatted down next to Port.

"It is. And you've got the best job, watching them work."

"I do. I just wait and then drive." He smiled, enjoying the thought of his job. "Except for the odor," he said.

"Don't you get used to it?"

"Why should I? It smells bad to me."

Port nodded and then said, "Why isn't the Indian working, the one with the serape?"

"His wife is working," and the driver nodded toward one of the tables. "He brings her to work, watches that no harm comes to her, then takes her home."

"Ah," said Port. The Indian didn't sound like a d'Ortega man. The driver?

"Tell me," said Port. "Sometimes I have to go into Ciudad de Miguel, and I was wondering if you'd take me for the ride. Do you..."

"No," said the driver. "Not very likely."

"Oh? I'd pay you."

"That's good of you, but the company is against it. You see the fat one there, with the gray hair? He is from the company. He was just telling me not to do this sort of thing any more, or no more job."

"You took somebody?" Port said.

"Oh yes. Sometimes. Just for the company."

"When?"

"Huh?"

"When was the last time you took somebody—that they should warn you so often?"

"Months ago," said the driver. "I don't do it often."

It didn't sound as if Kiamoto had gone this way.

"You could pick company up on the way," said Port. "Then they wouldn't know."

"Never," said the driver. "I go too fast to stop."

The company man waved at the driver, and the conversation was over. The driver left, went to the office with the gray-haired man. So Port kept watching the clerk.

He watched him because it suddenly struck Port that the man was doing a lousy job.

Three cases were swung into the truck while the clerk craned his neck to see where the company man was going. When he looked back to his clipboard he made one line there for the one case of fish which happened to pass him then.

Maybe it didn't matter. Maybe they had a system which wasn't obvious.

There was a delay at the cleaning table while the men with the buckets shoveled the slop away. It made a delay in the whole line—the weighers, the icers, the boxers stopped—and the clerk walked toward Port and stood in the door. He breathed deeply a few times and looked around. Then he looked at Port, nodded at him, and asked if he could bum a cigarette. Port gave him one.

"You're new here," said Port, guessing.

"How did you know?" The man smiled and held the cigarette in his teeth. His teeth were nice and white and his black hair was wavy.

"Because I've never seen you here before."

"Yes," said the clerk. He had a soft smile which stayed on his face all the time. "I started today."

Why should he lie, Port thought. If he thinks I'm familiar around here he would do best by telling the truth.

The company man came back with the driver and the two of them stopped for a minute, to say something about shipping lists. Then the company man took out a cheroot, leaned down to the clerk for a light, then groaned and straightened up again. The company man and the driver went back to the truck.

They were loading boxes again and the clerk kept sitting with Port.

"You can't be very important here," Port said and nodded at the men loading the boxes.

"Huh? Oh, this," and he held up his board. "I can count them when they are loaded. You know, I multiply the tiers. It's much simpler."

It made sense. But then why was he standing around with his clipboard? It also struck Port as peculiar that the man should be wearing his jacket. Perhaps he was not used to the cool air inside the building?

"It's no way of keeping your job," said Port. He shifted his weight a little, moved on his box.

"I don't care. I don't like the smell and the wet air. I will quit anyway."

"You're not from town?"

"This town? No," and he laughed. Then he became very earnest. He said, "It's a peculiar town, though, you know? I have never seen Japanese fishermen before."

Port nodded. He moved on the box a little, patted it. "Sit here," he said. "It's better than squatting."

"Thank you," said the clerk. He sat down and thought for a moment, and Port waited. If he starts on the Japanese again—if he makes one more innocent-sounding remark about that and then asks a question—

"I notice," said the clerk, "that none of them work here."

Port leaned a little, feeling the clerk next to him.

Then he drew back and dropped his cigarette. The clerk was asking whether any of the Japanese ever came down here for scraps, why none of them came to get the fish scraps to make chum, but Port was no longer interested. Not in the talk.

He said, "I guess they don't do any bottom fishing," and got up. "I need some fresh air. Want another cigarette?"

"Why—yes," said the clerk. "But I'll have to stay close," and then he followed Port out to the open.

Port went along the side of the building and where the light got dim he turned around with the cigarette in his hand. The turn was abrupt and the clerk almost bumped into Port, but he smiled and reached for the cigarette. That's when Port hit the man in the stomach, with a short, heavy punch.

There was a stack of pilings where the light didn't reach, with tall weeds around it and smelling of creosote. Port dropped the man there and opened his jacket.

The clerk had a small belt holster on and a gun was in it. Port put the gun into his own pocket and started to curse. He knelt next to the man and cursed while the clerk was getting his breath back.

"All right," said Port. "You can hear me. And not so loud."

"Madre—" the man groaned. "What did I do—"

"Where's d'Ortega?"

"Madre—"

Port clipped him.

"Where's d'Ortega?"

"Where? My God, I don't know. Who is he?"

"And who's the clerk that's been here one day, doesn't check his boxes, and wears a jacket so the gun doesn't show? Huh?" and Port shook the man.

But d'Ortega had picked his man well. The clerk said nothing, he even stopped pleading when he saw how Port felt. Perhaps he knew who Port was and what Capo had done to the girl.

"I'll bleed it out of you," said Port. "Believe me. I'll twist it out of you so it hurts like hell. Where is he?" and Port hit him again.

"I don't know— So help me, I don't know where he went. Please—"

A little while ago, Port remembered, it had been, "I don't know d'Ortega." Now it was, "I don't know where he went."

He was getting close. Port grabbed the man's arm and swung it around for a twist. Then he pushed the man's face into the ground so the screams wouldn't carry.

For a moment the sight of the man under him, twisted and sick, emptied the strength out of Port. Then he thought of Maria and how she had looked, because he wanted his will back and the cruelty. But he never got that far.

There was sharp kick into his side, a loud voice yelling curses, and when Port looked up there was just time to get out of the way of the fist.

It rammed past his head and the face of the beefy man seemed very dark. He was cursing in English. When Port had rolled out of reach the company man turned to the clerk to see how much damage there was. Port thought this was his chance and reached into his pocket. The company man showed Port his revolver. He wasn't angry, but highly annoyed. And he was very efficient and seemed to mean every word he said.

"Get your hand out of there very slowly, bud, and if I think you're moving too fast I'll shoot you in the gut. Understand?"

"I understand," said Port.

"And don't try to get up just yet, bud."

"I won't."

Port held still and watched how the beefy man turned the clerk over. He did it with one hand, the gun looking at Port all the time. When the man saw the clerk's face he started cursing again, but angrily this time, and he looked at Port with a new expression. If this were all he knows about me, Port thought, it would be all right. He'd be very careful and keep his distance, and he might even pay more attention to the clerk than he had before. Except that these two knew much more.

D'Ortega had more of a crew than Port had expected—one more, to be exact. Beating up the one who was waiting to see if Kiamoto would come had turned out to be a rotten idea. He had flubbed, and the two d'Ortega men would be happy to bring Port to d'Ortega. And d'Ortega would be happy again.

"Can you stand up?" said the big man.

"Sure," said Port, and started to do so, but the whole pitch was silly to start with and the big man treated it that way.

"I wasn't talking to you," he said.

The gun was still aimed at Port's middle, and he held still. The clerk turned over painfully. His face looked a mess, with blood, discolored skin, and dirt from the ground. It was no longer a matter of comparing this to the way Maria had looked, because, having beaten the man, Port was no longer angry. He looked at the face and felt lousy about it.

But just for a moment. When the clerk was up the older man kicked Port's shoe.

"Come up slow," he said. "Stand by the pilings there."

Port stood and tried to think how he might influence them. So far they were only concerned with the comfort of the man who had gotten the beating. Next they'd turn their minds to taking it out on the one who had done it. After that, after a good job of that, they'd remember about d'Ortega's interests and take Port to him. Port felt that only the last point might distract them.

"Wait a minute," said the clerk. He was breathing hard. "Let me sit a minute. My stomach—"

"He hit you in the stomach too?"

"*Madre díos*," said the clerk. He doubled over and retched.

And after that, thought Port, they'd be good and ready for the next step, and to hell with what d'Ortega would think about the shape in which they'd deliver him. If he was going to distract them, he'd have to do it soon.

"And while you're holding his hand," said Port, "you don't worry about the other one at all, do you?"

"What?"

"Forget it," said Port.

But the clerk was done retching and the other man was standing up now, with the gun like before.

"Who?" he said. "Who else?"

"Kiamoto. I mention it because the truck's ready to go."

The driver was slamming the door and then the whole truck rocked when the motor turned over. It made a big roar when it caught.

"You want him too, don't you?" said the company man, and he smiled suddenly as if this gave him great satisfaction.

"He asked me," said the clerk, "where d'Ortega was."

The two men looked at each other, puzzled, but that might have been the light making them look that way, or just a signal they were passing between each other. At any rate, it didn't last.

The whole icehouse was rumbling with the truck inside and then the truck started to move.

"He's got my gun," said the clerk. "I think you better. . ."

The other man was already patting Port's side. Just when he pulled the gun out of the pocket, Port got stiff. The company man noticed and jumped back.

"There," said. Port. "Don't you see him? To the left of the gate!"

There was a man half in shadow and neither Port nor the two men with him knew who it was or could see him clearly. Then the truck came moving out of the gate, the man ran toward it as the truck passed from the lit icehouse into shadow, and the truck slowed.

"Can you see him?" said the clerk. He was getting up. "Is it him?"

"Christ," said the big man, "I can't see through the truck. Hurry up, here—" and he turned to hand one of the guns to the clerk.

The truck had stopped and the driver was opening the cab. The big man, for just one moment, was turned away from Port to give the clerk one of the guns.

Then Port knocked the gun out of his hand and kicked him in the back. He saw the two men fall into each other—any moment the big one would whirl and fire—so he ran.

The only clear space left was toward the water.

Port kept running. He heard one more thing, the big man yelling, "The truck—the Chinaman's more important." Then Port came to the pier and a dead end.

The water looked black and oily. There were things floating in it and there were splashes, little flips and wet sounds where something was milling under the water, gobbling the slop which had been dumped out of the icehouse.

If the man in the shadow had been Kiamoto, then the best thing would be to go back! It would clear up everything, whatever there was in the whole affair. And if it wasn't Kiamoto—

There was hard breathing behind Port. He couldn't see who it was yet but it must be the clerk, he thought, coming slowly and painfully, but with the gun.

"Sanchez! You got him?" That was the big man, yelling from the truck.

Sanchez, with the pain in his stomach, didn't want to waste his breath yelling. He kept going toward Port. Port could see him now, and to wait any longer would kill every chance.

If the water weren't so black—If he knew what was under the water, milling—If he knew what kind of fish came into the bay—

Sanchez raised the gun and said, "Stay where you are!"

Port jumped.

Chapter 8

If the black water had not roared all around his face and the panic had not strangled his senses Port might have heard the truck again, pulling away, or he might have been aware that Sanchez, now at the edge of the pier, wasn't shooting.

Port was fighting with a known fear and an unknown fear, with the gun behind him and the black water in front, heaving gently, reflecting the lights from the icehouse, showing swirls exaggerated by the reflections, making sucking sounds under the pilings—A dead mass touched his hand and Port almost choked on his scream. He held the scream, the fear being that it would tear all the strength out of him, all the strength he would need for the black water and the little flops there making phosphorescent sprays. And if they had Kiamoto, he should go back!

The man who had stopped the truck to exchange a word with the driver, to look into the cab for a moment, knowing already that nobody was in the back of the truck, had been the one whom d'Ortega had sent. As Port had figured, d'Ortega would send a man to watch if Kiamoto would go with the truck.

The beefy company man, whose name was Briggs, had been disappointed to find a Mexican talking to the driver, and not talking about anything in particular either. Then the Mexican had gone back into the shadows, the truck had pulled away, Briggs had run to the pier. The Mexican had not known Port when he had seen him in the icehouse, and he had no further interest when the truck left without Kiamoto.

Port didn't know that Kiamoto had not been at the truck—nor that Briggs and Sanchez were from the embassy. He only knew that the two men would be in a mood for murder.

First he had gone under the pier, between the pilings. He could hear the footsteps above, and the lighted cracks overhead showed like bright lines.

"He's under the pier—he's out that way—must be under the pier—get the boat—the light over here—"

They were handling it like an accident, like a man having fallen into the water by accident, and everyone in the icehouse would soon come out, to help and to look.

"Jump in," said somebody. "I think that splash under here must have been him. Take this line and I'll lower you—"

"No, never, Señor. Not I."

The man was afraid to come into the water. The water was warm and cloying, but suddenly Port froze with cold.

Moray eels don't hang around pilings. They live in the rocks. There were rocks where the buildings rested on the land—And 'cuda strike so fast, going sixty miles an hour when they strike, that they rip out your flesh without any pain— And sharks are scavengers and go after dead things or something that's bleeding. If they shot him in the water or if he cut himself on the barnacles crusting the pilings— He bumped into the piling with a swell of the water and felt the little knives dig into his arm.

He almost screamed again. Then he was sure that he hadn't been cut, had to feel sure that he hadn't been cut, because to think otherwise would have been full panic.

"Take the ladder down," somebody said.

Port dove.

If he didn't splash and stayed away from the surface, then a shark wouldn't be likely to strike at all—

He swam underwater, as much to exhaust himself as to get away. Then he felt that his chest would burst, his neck, then his head—he held out as long as he could—and came up like an explosion.

The pier was farther away than he had thought. He could see men there, black against the light, some standing and looking down. They had gotten a boat.

Port breathed like a pump. It made him lightheaded. No one was looking in his direction and it struck him how frightful the fish in the water must be, because nobody thought he was way out here. With a crazy twist the thought now exhilarated him and he felt like laughing. He might swim out of the bay and really give them a run for their money— Or take one of the fishing boats—

Kiamoto's boat, Pepe had said, was the one opposite the icehouse.

It was big and black from water level. It wasn't far. Port swam. When he got closer to the tall hull he saw another boat lying off to the left, then another one behind that. They were nodding slowly, moving up and down with the swell.

And the closer he got the more urgency came into him again; the black water was his enemy and the safe boat too far to reach—"I can afford the panic now," he said to himself, but the joke didn't work. What if this weren't Kiamoto's boat, but the one to the left was the one he wanted? What if a man were on board, somebody who'd yell when he saw Port? Or what if Kiamoto were there, the man Port didn't know, with a long fish knife, with nothing to lose over a quiet murder—

Port touched the mooring line and his impulse was to push away to some other boat, but then his hands clamped and he couldn't have let go had he wanted to. The one concrete thing now was to hold on to the mooring line and to drag himself out of the water.

The bow looked very high and pointed, too high— But he was already climbing. His hands were past the slippery part where the algae were growing on the hemp and his grip was good now, and automatic. He went up the rope and all that concerned him for the moment was the water running out of his clothes and prattling into the bay.

When he touched the prow the boat had moved so that the mooring line was now hanging straight down with his weight. He was suddenly exhausted. To drag himself up the rest of the line and over the gunwale was now more impossible than to swim in the gray scum by the pier. His fingers ached and the ache went the length of his arms and into his shoulders. He slipped a little.

He looked down at the water below, which threw no reflections here but seemed bottomless. If he had had the strength he would have groaned. Then the boat gave a tug, as if trying to leave him— Port made it over the gunwale and fell down on the deck.

He felt like sleeping, and perhaps he did for a moment, because when he sat up again he did not remember the moments just before. He could see the lit pier like a miniature and a rowboat in front of it with a man who was holding a flashlight. The beam fingered over the pilings and into the blackness under the icehouse. With a strange feeling of being invisible Port almost lay down again in order to sleep.

"I'm on Kiamoto's boat," he said to himself, "and the next thing that will happen is they'll come out here."

He took a deep breath and got up. The water slapped the hull now and then and there was a slow motion. The wind felt cold through his wet shirt. Move, he said to himself. Move and get this done.

He walked down the slant of the deck toward the beam. Then it struck him that nothing creaked. A masted boat and no sounds from the rigging? He saw that the boom had been taken off the mast and the running rig that must have been there was all taken off. A pile of line was lying next to the wheel house. Kiamoto's boat for sure. The man was retired and the boat was stripped.

There was a tiny cabin below, with table and bunk; there was a small engine which straddled the bilges, and the rest was a large hold. It smelled of oil where the engine sat and the hold smelled of fish and moist wood.

There was no one on board. Port went over the boat again, saw the lines on the deck, in coils which had slipped over; checked the table top in the cabin and there was dust; opened the water tank and found it empty.

Kiamoto hadn't been here in some time, nor was the boat fitted to take him anyplace. The abandoned feel of the place made Port think that there might not even be a Kiamoto, that all of this affair would be over and done if everyone in it would just look at this unused boat.

He had to get back to Maria. The empty boat, its abandoned air, seemed to push Port away now. He would even have swum back to shore without the painful reluctance he had felt before.

There was a small, double-ended rowboat on top of the hatch, and Port upended it to the gunwale, lowered it down to the water. There was one oar which fitted into a saddle in the stern of the boat. Port had never sculled before, but at least the method wouldn't splash, the way rowing might.

There was water in the boat, because of the way he had lowered it, but his feet were wet anyway and the boat rode steady. He sculled slowly, watching the lights from the icehouse. They should not be able to see him. He sculled and looked back, to check his progress, and then he saw the wild phosphorescence where the oar churned the water. Every push and pull of the oar made a glittering sparkle and a short trail of light in the water.

"Señor," someone yelled on the pier. "There is a big fish coming, breaking water—"

Port let the boat drift. They could not possibly see him. He held the oar out of the water so it would not make a streak.

"Now! See it? It's an oar, see the flash?"

His wet oar had caught a reflection from the pier and the boat there was turning now, the flashlight zigzagging his way. The beam didn't reach him yet but until they knew who was in the boat they wouldn't let up.

He sculled as fast as he could, splashing water, twisting the boat back and forth unnecessarily, but they were watching the sparks in the water now and coming his way.

Port almost wished they would catch him. The work on the oar wasn't enough to take care of his anger now. He was thinking how it would be, how he would brain the first one with the oar, how he'd kill the second one with his bare hands, how he'd drown the next one in the water— His bow bumped the shore. He jumped out and ran. Once across the pebbles, by the edge of the brush, he stopped and looked back, but then he gave up ideas of revenge. He'd meet them again for sure, the way things had been going, but better the next time and not running.

He ran now, knowing they could never find him in the dark, and because he had to get back to Maria. There were too many d'Ortega men in the village.

The dirt street looked as before, only there were fewer lights. There was the same light from Maria's house, and Pepe was on the porch.

And the tall grill at the front door was open.

Port ran to the house. He saw that Pepe was sleeping, but didn't stop to talk to him. He rushed into the lighted room, saw the bucket next to the bed and one of the rags making a dark spot on the wrinkled sheets. The bed was empty.

Port grabbed Pepe by the front and hauled him up. "Where is she? Wake up, you sonofabitch!" and he smacked the drunk into the wall. It made a loud crash. "Where? Why's she gone?"

"He took her," Pepe managed to say. "Please, he just..."

"The same ones? Wake up and talk, damn you!"

"No. He was alone, came alone here. Suddenly he came on the porch and..."

"And made you drunk again. How did..."

"No," said Pepe. "I swear. He brought nothing."

Good old d'Ortega saving his liquor. Why waste it on nothing?

"How did he get in, for heaven's sake?"

"She opened for him. Maria opened the lock for him."

"Was she out of her mind? She didn't see who it was?"

"She did, so she opened. It was Kiamoto."

Chapter 9

He had come very quietly, without Pepe's hearing him, even though he had been wearing heavy boots. And there had been dark stains on his pants. "Those brown stains," Pepe said, "and wearing those boots, that's why I say he had been in the jungle. The stains are from the damp ground and he wore the boots because of the thorns and snakes."

Port changed his mind a little about Pepe. He was not as dull as he seemed.

Port had boiled coffee for the old man and himself and they sat in the room with the lights out. If there were going to be any more visitors, Port would see them first.

"And he asked her to come along and she just did?"

"Yes. Why not? He said he did not want her to come to any more harm and he would see to that, if she came with him."

"Where to?"

"I don't know. Back where he came from, I think."

"Does he have a car? Or a donkey? Maybe they took the road. Or maybe he's here in town."

"He told her to wear good shoes."

Port sipped his coffee. Then he kept holding the cup close to his face, smelling the burnt odor. Now and then, in the silence, it seemed to Pepe that the other one was almost whistling.

"How did Kiamoto know about Maria, that she was hurt?"

"He said he had been watching and was sorry to be late."

"Late for what?"

"Too late to stop the beating."

"Did he watch that too?"

"He didn't say."

"How do you figure," said Port, "he can watch all these goings on and nobody sees him?"

"The village is narrow, Señor. On the other side of the street, behind those houses, it is wild already."

"And you have no idea where he went?"

There were footsteps outside and the two men didn't talk. Port moved to the grill and looked out and saw there were two people walking, very close to each other, whispering and holding back their laughter.

"The jungle, I think. He must know some of it," said Pepe, "because sometimes he would be gone for a while. Maria told me that sometimes he went through his garden and on to the back where the jungle starts and would be gone all day."

Port nodded in the dark and then he lit a cigarette. The sudden light showed Pepe's face, a shut monkey face, perhaps tired. The old man sat and answered questions and did not ask any himself. His lack of interest was genuine and it was something which Port could not understand. As if Pepe lived by rules which no one else knew, and these rules made ordinary events meaningless to him. That's how he had taken Port's treatment. He had not understood it, and so he did not think about it.

"You know the jungle," said Port. "Take me in."

"No."

"Maria said..."

"I know the jungle," said Pepe. "It is therefore that I say no."

"Listen, Pepe. Your own niece, Maria..."

"It is no good at night. I can't see. I can't tell the way. And the mosquitoes are bad then."

"Kiamoto went at night. If he can..."

"He knew where he was going. I would have to find the way."

It made sense. For a moment Port had thought that offering liquor, buying the man a whole bottle and giving it to him, would do the trick, but Pepe had explained it well. There was no point in going now.

"But you will take me in the morning," said Port.

"If you want."

It would solve a great many things. It would show whether Maria was safe, it would show Kiamoto that he, Port, had nothing to do with any of this. He went to sleep hoping that this was true.

They left the house at four in the morning, when it was still cool. Pepe wore his white pants and shirt and a serape over that. He gave Port one, to wear over his shirt, because of the thorns, he explained. And the old man took a machete along.

Pepe had been right about the jungle. It started almost immediately on the other side of the road, and what was more surprising, it was as wild and humid after five minutes as it was one hour later.

Pepe followed what he called a trail, which meant that the thickest vines didn't grow there and the trees had no branches there until six feet up. The rest, Port saw, was impenetrable. Even where he followed Pepe the leaves snapped, branches grabbed out, the twigs snapped at them, and roots in the soft ground seemed live and purposeful.

Pepe never stumbled, and often he waited for Port. Once he stopped to hack at a snake and the two parts of it coiled and trembled when Port walked by. The heat was like a thick mist after a while and the darker the shadow the worse the air. Then Pepe stopped. He stood in the green light and the moist growth close around him, and looked. Port wiped his face and sat down.

"Do not sit. The ants," said Pepe.

"All right. Let's go then."

"I was able to follow him this far," said Pepe, "but from here he did not follow the path."

Port said nothing. Anything he might have said would have been foolish. He did not have the faintest idea of where to go.

"There is one parallel," said Pepe. "Perhaps he crossed to it."

"Yuh. And why would he do that?"

"It leads somewhere else."

"Yuh," said Port. "Of course." And then, "Why do you think he didn't like this path?"

"It starts to rise more in a while, up the large hill."

Port hadn't been aware of the rise in the path, and there was no steep hill to see. There was no sky to see either, or simple, solid ground, for that matter.

"And the other path, I suppose, goes downhill and is much easier."

"Much easier," said Pepe. Then he struck out into the solid foliage. "We cross here," he said.

After five minutes Pepe was still hacking and they hadn't moved an inch.

"Why not find the place where Kiamoto crossed over," said Port. "He must have cut a way through this stuff."

"But I don't know where. He did not cut until he was into the thicket."

"Maybe you weren't looking at the time," Port said. "Maybe when you killed the snake you were distracted."

"We can try," said Pepe, and they went back.

In a while Pepe stopped again and looked around. Port looked for the two halves of the snake, but they weren't there.

"Something carried it off," Pepe explained. "Here are the tracks."

Port saw no tracks but he nodded. He slapped a mosquito and closed his eyes. When he would open them again he hoped to see a path going off to one side, (something like a garden path, was his image) and at the end of it maybe a clearing covered with grass and an old Japanese—a Chinese, rather—sitting by a campfire with Maria beside him stirring a pot.

When he opened his eyes he saw only foliage. Not even Pepe was there any more.

For a moment it felt like the time in the water, when he had first jumped into the dark and into fright. He was as blind here in the forest as he had been then.

"Come, Señor. This way."

The voice seemed next to him, and then, by the movement of foliage, Port saw where Pepe was. They could have reached each other by stretching hands.

"He went through here," said Pepe. "He was careful not to break anything where it showed, but I smelled it."

"You did what?"

"You cut the leaf of this plant and the sour smell goes into the air. Back here— No, you must crawl under here, and then it is easier."

After, pushing his way through the solid growth, where big blossoms powdered their pollen into his face, Port could see the hacked plants. Kiamoto had cut his way across just the way Pepe had said he must.

After an hour it got easier. The land seemed to rise again and with less moisture the growth was less tangled and the trees looked more like trees. Then they went down again, which made the sun disappear over the roof of leaves and the soggy air became like a weight. Now and then their footsteps squeezed water out of the ground.

"How much more, Pepe? Where are they?"

"Soon. In the valley, I think," and the small man never stopped pushing ahead.

It was a strange transformation, thought Port. The sullen drunk, the small, wasted man who sat on the porch and looked at a dusty street, was a strong man here in the jungle. He understood everything here, and that made him feel right. What he does here means something to him and has a purpose; what he does in the village means nothing—

"How far are we from the valley?" Port asked after a while.

"Not far. Perhaps half a mile.

"I don't know how well sound carries here," said Port, "but if we're getting close to Kiamoto, maybe you should stop hacking."

"Sound doesn't carry here," said Pepe.

They didn't talk for a while and for a stretch Port used the machete, giving Pepe a rest.

"You have an idea where in the valley? Where he might be?"

"The ruin. It makes sense for him to be there."

Port wondered how much sense it made. If there was such a landmark and Pepe could find it, then d'Ortega, with some help, would be able to find it too. And Kiamoto would know that. But then, Port had no clear idea what Pepe might mean by ruin; Pepe also had called this trek through the solid vegetation a path.

When Pepe said that they were in the valley they were walking in something that was almost a swamp. The ground sucked at their shoes, the air seemed brown with the odor of rot, and the mosquitoes made singing clouds. But it was possible to see farther now because the growth became shorter. Pepe stopped hacking and they mostly climbed through the dark green plants. Then a rise, a rim of tall trees, and Pepe followed that line. There were rocks underfoot now.

"There," said Pepe. "You see it?"

Port didn't. The gloom was intense after the open. The trees made a woven roof and the light was blue-green underneath.

"We go quietly now, if you are worried."

Port was too tired to worry. He had only the strength for one intent, to see Kiamoto finally, and to find Maria.

The trees were big and old now and the creepers did not reach to the ground, but an undergrowth survived in the shadows which kept Port from seeing where they were going until the last moment.

His first sight of anything manmade in this forest was impressive; a black gate made of stone. Vines covered part of it and dark, moss-like patches, but there was a tall gate, empty to both sides, leading from jungle to jungle. The wall of which the gateway had been a part had started to sink. Blocks of stone had slid off and the lower blocks came out of the ground at an angle.

"Earthquake?" Port asked.

"No. The swamp is creeping."

The rocky rise they had passed after the swamp ended here. The ground went down again and was moist.

"You want to follow the wall," Pepe asked, "or cross the court?"

It had looked like the same jungle again on the other side of the black gate, but passing the arch now Port saw the clearing. There were no trees, no vines, few low bushes. The clearing was paved with large slabs of dark stone.

The prospect was irresistible. No matter who might see him, Port would walk on the even ground and at least for a moment forget about snaking through roots and leaves.

"If he's here," said Port, "maybe he'll see us and come out. Kiamoto knows who you are?"

"Yes. I've seen him."

"Good. Walk next to me," and they entered the court. The whole thing slanted and some of the slabs had sunk away. They didn't head for the surrounding trees but cut across to the rest of the ruins: a terrace, raised several feet, a square-headed idol with wild convolutions surrounding the face. That slanted too.

"The gringos know this place?"

"Yes. Many years ago they were here."

"I'm surprised they left anything."

"They took a few things, small carvings. They tried hard with the rest, but the jungle wouldn't let them." The idol had claws held to its breast, resting there. The stone gaze too looked very still. It did not have a defined expression. Whatever you felt, the face returned it—

So it happened that Port saw the figure long before he reacted to it. The man stood very still. He had short legs, thick in their wrappings, feet heavy in boots, a square torso. His face repeated the idol's expression; still, rather smooth, and suggesting whatever you read into it. Kiamoto, standing wide-legged, did not look like an old man.

"Come closer," he said. He held a large automatic in his hand, letting it hang. "Climb over here." He waved with the gun.

"He speaks Spanish well," said Pepe. "I had not noticed."

They climbed up to the terrace where Kiamoto was waiting. Port thought that to speak bad Spanish was in character for Kiamoto when he was in the village, but that matters had changed now and he didn't need the pretense. The thought was not reassuring. "Don't come closer," said Kiamoto.

He nodded at Pepe, recognizing him, and then he looked at Port. The look was bland and then Kiamoto put the gun in his pocket.

"Why are you here?" he asked.

Once, in the Pacific, when Port and his outfit had hit their third island, they had crept through the jungle, not knowing what was ahead, and a native had stepped in their way. The man next to Port had carried a flame thrower and he had hit the trigger immediately. It had scorched a tree and a vine had smoked. The native had stood there, wide-eyed. "Why?" he had said. "Why are you here?"

Kiamoto's manner had reminded Port, and for a moment he felt the same lack of an answer. He got rid of the feeling with an anger that surprised him.

"You're Kiamoto?" Port asked.

The man didn't answer.

Port was closer now and saw how much older the man looked. There were many fine wrinkles around his eyes and the skin under his chin looked tired.

"Where is Maria?" Port asked.

"Don't come closer."

"Where is she?"

"She is safe." Kiamoto raised a hand slowly and said, "I don't know you. Don't come closer."

"You listen to me. I can jump you from here before you get a chance at that gun, and I'm fed up to the ears..."

"Don't," said Kiamoto when Port moved again.

Perhaps it was the indifference in the man's voice, or the gesture with the hand, something half-interested only, disregarding everything that had made Port move for the last twenty-four hours.

Port barely thought about it, but hit.

He did not feel the jolt of the impact and he had no idea how it happened, but he gasped for breath suddenly and heard the thud. He lay very still for a moment and looked up at Kiamoto. The old man had not moved.

"Jeesis," said Port.

"What?" Kiamoto bent his head slightly.

"Judo," said Port to explain things to himself.

"No. Jiu jitsu."

"Of course. You're Chinese."

"I am sorry you know that," said Kiamoto.

Then he stepped back to let Port get up.

When Port brushed himself off and looked at the Chinese again, the impression was as confusing as when he suddenly found he had been tossed on the floor. When Port had never seen the old man whom Maria had described the impression had been simpler; a retired fisherman, kind to the girl, living in a bare, uninteresting house. The only odd note was the sandal.

Then it got worse. The Japanese was Chinese and d'Ortega, a lawyer working for Pan-Continental Industries, had a determined interest in the man. But even that hadn't been too confusing, and it became plausible by assuming that the fisherman was somebody else. But to see the man in the flesh, a man showing no age from a distance, looking old from close up, and suggesting whatever you liked with a face mostly empty, holding a gun he did not bother to use, but quick as a snake and better in action than a man half his age—

"I just want one thing," said Port. Maybe this would settle his thinking. "I want to know where Maria is and if she is well."

"She is well. Are you an American?"

Port nodded. He was beginning to notice that he always gave Kiamoto more information than he got back.

"Then you are Dan Port. The girl mentioned your name."

"Good. Maybe that'll make you less suspicious."

Kiamoto smiled very slightly and said, "I would welcome such a luxury, I would cherish it." He said it in English. He spoke with a British accent, very sure of the language, the un-English intonation slight.

That made at least four languages, Port was thinking. The myth of the simple fisherman was now entirely gone.

"But the trouble is," said Kiamoto, "that I can't afford it. I now can afford neither your presence, nor your absence."

"Call Maria."

"She loves you, I think. What she says about you would be useless to me."

"I came unarmed," said Port. "I came openly."

"Perhaps you are very clever."

Port got off the ground, watching Kiamoto to see if the older man meant to object. But Kiamoto just stood at a little distance and waited.

"I'm so clever," said Port, "that I end up sucked into your affairs to the ears. Do you know why I'm here? Why I came here? To lie in the sun, you stupid fool! To meet Maria and make love to her! That sounds so romantic and simple, doesn't it, Kiamoto, I bet you now think I'm especially clever to dream up an explanation like that, huh?"

Port was starting to talk fast with excitement. "And I also tell you," he went on, "that I'm rarely this simple or romantic ever. I'm from up North. Big towns and big times. And the bigger they are the more the detail shows in them and the detail of all those big times is puny and petty. So I came down here, Kiamoto, for the contrast, to be in something smaller and simpler. You follow me? Because that makes a great deal of sense to me."

Port stopped and then he made a disgusted sound in his throat, as if angry for having talked this much, as if embarrassed, because Kiamoto's face showed no reaction.

"And?" said Kiamoto.

"And this. I went to your house without knowing you, simply because Maria had asked me. She was worried about you." He gave the Chinese a mean look. "Or maybe she wasn't worried about you either? Maybe you know better and she did it just to steal your Fujijama calendar off the wall?"

Kiamoto smiled and said, "A very unattractive print, isn't it?"

But Port didn't have the leisure for small talk. "So that was the first time you struck me as fishy. I found your sandals. A Japanese, name of Kiamoto, wearing Chinese sandals? Maybe, maybe not."

"I'm Chinese," said Kiamoto. "You're right."

"So what?" Port didn't take it up and he didn't notice that Kiamoto was watching with interest. Port just kept on. "You've got a bastard by the name of d'Ortega on your neck and you're something big enough to be involved with Pan-Continental who dig coal, make tin cans, and who knows what else. I don't know you except as a man with a fake name and with personal problems. All I want..."

Port stopped because Kiamoto had started to laugh. It was a slow laugh which hesitated coming out of his belly, but genuine nevertheless. "Personal problems—" he said, "—with *personal* problems," and he laughed again with no mirth showing on his face, which made his reaction seem almost macabre.

When he was done he and Port looked at each other without saying anything. Then Port said, "I don't think I want to hang around you. Show me Maria and I'll leave."

Kiamoto didn't say yes or no. He turned and let Port follow him. Pepe followed Port.

There was a roofless room toward the back of the ruin, the floor of grass, a high arch in one wall, the tops of the walls garlanded with creepers pushing in from the jungle. Maria was on a blanket, sleeping. Port could not see her face. It was covered with dark green leaves.

"Ah," said Pepe. "I should have remembered—"

"What?" said Port.

"The plant," and he nodded at Maria. "I'd forgotten."

He looked as if he meant to say more, that he too knew about healing plants and was sorry not to have thought of it, the pulque preventing him. But he just shrugged and looked out of the arch at the jungle. Then he squatted down.

Kiamoto touched the girl on the shoulder and she woke up. She sat up and Kiamoto pulled the leaves off her face, wiping the sticky juice from it.

When her face was clean there was no swelling, no dark color, no bruises. Some small marks were still there, like scratches, but it was Maria's face again.

"Daniel!" she said. "Daniel, you're here!"

Port went to her and held her hand. He was afraid to touch her more but Maria was happy and put her arms around his neck and said how good it was to see him whole and alive, and to have him come for her was a sweet thing.

Then she looked from Port to Kiamoto and said, "You did come for me, didn't you, Danny?"

"So he says," Kiamoto told her.

"Oh?"

"Your friend Kiamoto," said Port, "is very suspicious, but Pepe and I came only for you."

She looked at Pepe and smiled at him and Pepe nodded.

"It hardly matters," said Kiamoto.

"It hardly matters?" Maria sat up and watched the old man.

"I told you I was in some danger," Kiamoto said. He spoke kindly to her and with some patience. But the tone, thought Port, would make little difference in Kiamoto's decisions.

"Yes, you told me," said Maria. "I don't know why, but I believe you."

"Therefore Pepe should not have brought this man."

Maria frowned and Port said nothing.

"What did he do wrong?"

Kiamoto looked at Pepe and it was strange to see how both men seemed so unimpressed with each other; because of strength in one of them and because of withdrawal in the other.

"I asked you," said Kiamoto, "to stay away, that Maria would be all right."

"I remember," said Pepe.

"Why didn't you listen to him?" said Maria. She talked to Pepe as if she were the older one.

"Because I forgot."

"But there is something dangerous here, some danger to Kiamoto," Maria went on, "and he asked you..."

"I don't have to listen to you," said Pepe. His monkey face became shut and if there had been a bottle of pulque now, he would have drunk from it.

"Did Mister Port pay you?" Kiamoto put in, and perhaps that was more of an offense to Pepe than Maria's tone, because Pepe got up and turned his back.

"I didn't pay him," said Port, "and it isn't Pepe's fault that I'm here. I asked him. I was worried about Maria." He looked at Kiamoto and said, "And I don't give a damn about you, by the way. Take it or leave it," and then he held out his hand so that Maria would get up.

"If you don't know why I'm here," said Kiamoto, "then you must take my word for it that it is important. I cannot let..."

"Let go of my arm," said Port.

Kiamoto stepped back.

"Pepe," said Maria. "Wait."

But Pepe had gone very quickly. He had gone through the arch in the wall, some leaves nodded, and that was all.

Kiamoto had spun around and run after him but it had been pointless. The jungle was too thick and Pepe knew it too well. The Chinese and Port looked at each other with dislike and Maria looked puzzled and helpless. These three were now alone.

Chapter 10

For a short while Pepe could see Kiamoto quite closely, but that hardly bothered him and he only watched the fisherman and the ruins behind him because he felt dull in his anger and without pressure for action. Then he went home.

He went fast most of the way, because the path was well hacked by now and because Port wasn't slowing him up. He did not go fast because he felt rushed to get out of the jungle, but only because he had nothing else to do. And with nothing else to do, in a while, he started to think.

Pepe's thinking was mostly feeling. He felt angry about the way Maria had talked to him but in time he felt only sullen about it and churlish. But that feeling did not leave. He wished it would, but it kept eating at him. He wished he had a drink. He cursed himself for his lack of peace, but it didn't help. Instead, it became like a conversation, one Pepe talking, injured and insulted, the other Pepe a man of great strength.

Why does she talk like that to me? Did I beat her? Did I ever make demands?

The ungrateful bitch lives in my house, uses my furniture, tells *me* what to do! Let her rot with her crazy friends in the jungle.

Did I ask to raise her? Did I tell her parents to lie down and be sick and to die so I could raise her in my house?

I raised her! A difficult chore in any event, but *her!* A hard, restless creature, just like her father!

I deserve a brother like that? A child like that to disrupt my life? Did I ask her to make a friend of that foreigner, that slit-eyed fisherman who is old but looks like a baby?

She deserves what she gets! She gets beaten up by a brute who comes to my house, a friend of that foreigner most likely, she gets beaten while I'm not even there—I should feel badly?

Why blame me for the friends of a silly woman? Does she obey me? Does she buy the provisions I need in the house?

That Kiamoto! He's made her the slut that she is! An old man who looks like a baby and moves like a cat—and pays her money.

Does she give me the money? Does she say kind words to me because I raised her under my roof, gave her freedom to roam all over the village, to the Japanese houses, even—

Pepe licked his lips and tasted the sweat there. He was not sweating from the fast walk. It was the thinking, the useless excitement of thinking about the wrong—Maria—and the right—himself. And the thought of what they were saying about him now, back in the ruin, taking Maria's side and cursing him for allowing her own friends to beat her while he, Pepe, had not even been in the house!

He wished that he had a drink. Another hour of walking—and why did he have to wait another hour? Because of his love for Maria who no doubt would feel lost and alone with that crazy fisherman in the jungle and was anxious to have that other crazy one with her, that gringo with the motionless eyes—

Pepe felt almost touched to tears at the thought of his painful trek into the jungle, that long trek to bring Maria her friend. And then gratitude? Hah!

He stayed with this theme for all the time it took him to get back to the village, where he turned right, toward the square, and not to the left where his house was. He went to the square and to the grocery store where the cheap pulque was sold.

Did he ask for tequila? No. For the fine, expensive pulque? Not he. For the cheap, hot, throat-biting, gut-eating junk he asked! A modest, a humble request!

"I'm sorry, Pepe," said the grocer. "Maria said she would pay for no more."

And the fat, button-eyed pig was an Indian like himself, but how different, how wrong!

"I'll bring you the money when they pay me at the icehouse, Luis. They pay..."

"Only if you work, they pay, Pepe. And you haven't."

Argue with a pig?

Now the anger was biting him the same as the pulque should have been biting his insides. But was it the same? Not the same! The injustice was ruining it, was ruining his mood, spoiling the anger even, and Pepe could have wept.

He stopped at his house, breathing hard, staring into the dim room without seeing it, because what was there to see? A chair, an empty bed, a sack of cheap flour, a table—what was there in an empty house to comfort him?

He stopped in the door and looked at the table. Then his face puckered up and a helpless feeling took hold of his throat, because to whom should he be grateful? Who was his friend?

On the table stood a bottle of pulque.

"Now?" asked Capo.

D'Ortega shook his head. "Let him finish half, anyway."

"He's almost finished all of it."

"Oh? Now, in that case."

D'Ortega and Capo came in through the back door and Pepe did not act surprised. Nothing surprised him at this point.

"My dear Pepe," said d'Ortega. "You look well."

Pepe shrugged. He felt well, but why tell this one?

"I am glad you enjoyed the gift, Pepe," and d'Ortega sat down at the table. "Are you enjoying it?"

The tone made Pepe suspicious. He put one hand on the bottle and said, "There is little left. Hardly enough to offer..."

"No, no. You misunderstand. Finish all of it, Pepe." The old man did. He had hoped to save the rest for a slow hour or so, but he now poured the rest of the pulque down his throat, though it felt as if the fire might kill him.

D'Ortega frowned at the old man, marveling at his strength and endurance.

"Can you hear what I'm saying, Pepe?"

"What have you said?"

The answer made Capo grin at d'Ortega, but that had been the wrong thing to do. D'Ortega became mean.

"Go to the car and get him another bottle," he said.

"But the car is all the way..."

"Go. The walk will sweat fat off you."

"But he's drunk enough of the poison to make..."

"Now," said d'Ortega. "And come back fast."

Pepe sat still and looked sober. Only his vision seemed ruined. He could see very little and of course he was not thinking at all. There were violent shapes which drew his attention. Then an icy slap hit his face.

"Do you hear me now?" he heard. He heard it several times, and each time the voice was much clearer.

His face was wet and the front of his shirt was wet and cold. D'Ortega stood by the table, holding an empty bucket.

"I told you when you drink this too fast, especially this very cheap..."

"Shut up, Capo."

Capo sat down on the bed—Pepe could hear this—and then d'Ortega sat down at the table.

"Pepe. Are you listening?"

"What have you said?"

"I'm sorry about the water," said d'Ortega, "but you looked sick."

"I'm fine. I see you."

He saw very clearly now, and felt clearly. It was too bad he had finished the bottle so quickly, leaving nothing, and especially he should have remembered about the very bad effects of drinking too quickly on a hot day, the cheap stuff especially, which produced ugly pictures and painful sensations. He could feel the needle pain in his skull even now, more often lately than usual, and if there were just a drop left in the bottle...

"Capo brought you this," said d'Ortega, "thinking you might like just a swallow to clear your head."

What unbelievable luck. There was an entirely full, fresh bottle and this well-dressed gentleman—d'Ortega?—was pushing it across the table.

Pepe took one careful swallow. The needle pain jumped in his brain, but that would soon go away.

"Tell me, Pepe. Where is your niece?"

"Maria?"

"Yes. The girl."

Pepe took another swallow. Easy now, or else the pain and the shapes might go out of control.

"I don't know," he said, feeling sad. "I don't know from one moment to the next, Señor, where that girl is."

"When did you see her last?"

"When I was at the ruin." He reached for the bottle but suddenly grabbed air.

"Where did you say?" D'Ortega was holding the bottle.

"The ruin, Señor. In the jungle. Please—"

"What was she doing there?"

"Leaves on her face. Where you beat her."

"Dammit, make sense!"

"Please—"

Capo got up and looked at d'Ortega. Then he sat down again when d'Ortega shook his head.

"Here's your bottle."

Pepe drank. It was no longer necessary to sip carefully. The shapes were gone—they only came in the beginning—and just the needle pain was in his brain. If it were not for the strange, ominous pressure—a pressure like fear looking at him—then the pain in the skull would also mean nothing.

"I'm asking," said d'Ortega, "not because I want your niece, Pepe. I mean her no harm."

"I know that."

"I'm asking to find out where her friend is, the Japanese fisherman."

"Kiamoto."

"Yes. Him."

"Ruin."

"Did you say ruin?"

"You spilled from the bottle," said Pepe. "Please, don't spill—"

D'Ortega put the bottle back within reach and waited.

"He remembered about the leaves and the paste," said Pepe. "I should have remembered about boiling the paste out of the leaves because—"

His voice drifted off, with surprise at first, then with breathlessness, because Capo was holding his arm from behind and it cracked badly inside his shoulder and hurt. Then the pain was a terrible flash.

"You saw Kiamoto?"

"My God, my God!"

"Let him go, you idiot," said d'Ortega. "How can he talk with that arm doubled over?"

Capo let go of the arm, which produced another pain. "Where is Kiamoto?"

"But I told you! I told you, the ruin!"

D'Ortega looked at Capo and Capo shrugged. "You shouldn't have given him so much," he said. "It's poison."

"He is hiding there with a gun, and my Maria is with him because she is afraid, she thinks he will help her to keep you..."

"Kiamoto and Maria," said d'Ortega, "are at this ruin. Is that true?"

"I swear!"

"And the ruin is where, Pepe?"

"I swear I saw them no more than..."

D'Ortega nodded and Capo hit the old man across the face. It cut Pepe's lip and a little blood got smeared on his cheek.

"Where is the ruin?"

"There. In the jungle."

Then Pepe started to cry.

D'Ortega waited a while, then gave Pepe the bottle, then waited a little bit longer because Pepe kept crying right through the drink.

"I told you," said Capo, "that stuff makes queer..."

"Shut up."

Pepe thought the remark had been for him and stopped crying. The feeling stayed, the sense of hurt and injustice, but he stopped crying and licked his cut lip.

"Dear Pepe," said d'Ortega. "We must find this Kiamoto. He's bad."

"I know," said Pepe.

"Ah. Then you know. Then you understand we must find him."

"He threatened me with the gun."

"Very bad. Will you take us there, Pepe?"

"Maria will be back. In spite of everything, Señor, I love her, you know, and therefore trust her, to come back."

D'Ortega nodded and Capo made the cut in Pepe's lip larger and much more bloody.

"Pepe," said d'Ortega, "please take us there."

Contending with the strange stubbornness of a drunk who was now badly glazed by the pulque poison, it took a while longer before they made Pepe get up and convinced him that he had to take them back where he had seen Kiamoto. Then they did not hurt him any more and did not give him pulque any more until later, because he took them into the jungle and only needed to drink now and then when the shaking got very bad.

It went slowly and now and then Capo had to hack with the machete because Pepe was getting weak. He lost his way once, which they never noticed, but then he found the direction again and led the way without protest. He hardly knew why he was taking them, except that d'Ortega was carrying the bottle and the big one, Capo, was cruel without reason. Maybe he could cause Capo to get lost in the swamp later, but that would be later and took some thought. Later, perhaps, it would be easier to think about this—

Chapter 11

After midnight the lights in the icehouse went off. One light stayed on in the office where the safe stood, but that was of no importance because the light did not reach to the pier or the water.

"You understand," said Kiamoto, "you stay close and don't move suddenly."

"I understand nothing," said Port. "But I'm staying." He reached for Maria's hand in the dark and held it.

Then they did not talk any more and cowered in the dark where the stiff grass made small, rubbing noises and where they could see the dirty beach drop away in front of them. The mosquitoes sang in their ears and the water licked back and forth over the pebbles.

They waited almost an hour, because the tide wasn't right. When the dark band showed faintly along the water, and they could smell the algae that covered the stones, Kiamoto stood up.

"To the left, slowly," he said, and took Maria's arm.

She pulled it away but said nothing.

The boat was half out of the water and made a loud, grinding sound when they pushed it afloat. But nobody stopped them. Nobody saw them. Kiamoto sculled away from the beach into the very dark bay. Port didn't know how they found Kiamoto's fishing boat but it was there suddenly, very close and big. Port went up first, then he helped Maria, and then Kiamoto came over the side with the gun in his belt and the painter in his teeth so that the boat wouldn't drift away.

I could hit him over the head right now, Port thought, and he would either drown or he would manage to live. He would probably manage to live, but in either event nothing would be gained. There was now no short cut to get out of this business.

"I am glad to see you stepped back," said Kiamoto. He swung himself over the side like a young man.

He did not ask Port to help with anything, but readied the boat by himself. He primed the engine but did not start it. He cast off the mooring and then ran to the stern, where he stood with a long pole. In a short while they swung alongside a fishing boat and then another, and Kiamoto used the pole to keep himself clear. The tide pulled them through to the mouth of the bay.

There was a rip where the open water started. It swung the boat hard about while Kiamoto stood to starboard, dipping the pole nervously and cocking his head for sounds. Then the pole hit bottom and Kiamoto strained terribly hard trying to give the boat some direction. He must have gotten his way, because the boat kept on floating free. To starboard a faint line of beach swung past and then was gone. The boat started swaggering in the beam and the bow nodded. They were out of the bay.

The engine caught on the second try, sounding low and heavy and in good shape. The wind became clammy. In the wheel house they could see the faint binnacle light and Kiamoto's face over it. His face looked very smooth and asleep.

"Come in here," he said. "It's warmer."

Maria stayed close to Port as they went into the wheel house. Kiamoto looked at them without speaking and then watched the compass again. It was not warm in the small room and a thin draft worried the backs of their heads. Once Kiamoto shivered.

"You're wet," said Port. "Your shirt is all dark on the back."

"It will dry."

The way he had worked that pole, Port thought, no wonder he's sweating.

"Do you want a blanket?" Port asked him.

Kiamoto shook his head.

There was a stool in the wheel house and Maria pushed it over so Kiamoto could sit. He saw her do it and smiled at her, but he didn't sit down. He's afraid he'll get too sleepy, Port thought. And if he goes to sleep what good would it do? I have no idea where he's heading, how the coastline runs, how much gas he carries, how any of this will solve anything—

"We will be together a little while," Kiamoto said. He said it away from Port, at the blank window which reflected his face. "And if you think of it that way, Mister Port, perhaps we can make it a little easier living together."

"You've got the gun," said Port.

But it wasn't the right answer and Port was sorry he had said it. Kiamoto, he remembered, hardly needed a gun. But that wasn't it either. Kiamoto was an old man cold with his own sweat, driven hard by something and that much harder for not sharing it with anyone here, and his voice had been tired when he had made the remark. He looked at Port now as if he too wished that Port had said something else.

"All right," said Port. "We can try."

"Yes," said Maria. "And let me bring you a blanket."

But Kiamoto didn't take it up. He watched the compass and then he said, "Do you think you can hold it on this reading, Mister Port?"

"Steer the boat?"

"Just for a short while."

Port nodded and took the wheel. He overshot immediately and then did the same thing the other way, while Kiamoto was still there.

"It doesn't matter too much," Kiamoto said. "Just stay close." Then he left the wheel house and Port could not see where he was going.

"You have a very strange friend there," said Port.

Maria stood next to him, as if for warmth.

"I don't always understand him," she said, "but he's never done any harm."

"You mean he never threw you over his shoulder, slamming you flat on your back?"

"He was afraid then, Daniel. He thought you had come to do something to him."

"He never looked less afraid in his life, girl."

"I don't always understand him," she said again.

"Do you know why this trip?"

"To keep us with him."

"I don't mean that. I mean, do you know what all this is about?"

"There are men after him who want to kill him, he told me."

"And you believed him and left it at that."

"Doesn't he act like it?"

"Yes," said Port. "He does." Then he tried to get the boat back on course.

"I want to thank you," she said, "for coming after me, Daniel."

Everything was very simple to Maria. Kiamoto was kind to her; Port was kind to her; and this trip, tantamount to kidnaping, was simply something she did not entirely understand. Not that she was stupid, but this way of thinking was possible for her because she trusted Kiamoto. Port didn't know whether he trusted the man. It was hard to have a simple reaction to the Chinese.

It was time to question the man. Where had Kiamoto gone and what was he doing right now, for instance? Port was sure he had not just gone to get a blanket.

The door to the wheel house opened and a wet gust blew into the small room. Kiamoto left the door open and took the wheel from Port.

"If you look out there," he said, and pointed out of the door, "you see a small light. No. Down there. The door to the cabin."

Port saw a small yellow light where the steps led down to the cabin.

"Once you're outside you will be able to find your way," Kiamoto said. "The moon is coming up."

"And?" Port watched Kiamoto's face, trying to understand.

"Walk slowly, because the deck is moist, and go to the cabin."

"So that I can't watch your compass heading?" Port said.

"It is late. I thought you might want to sleep."

Kiamoto said nothing else and Port didn't know what else there was to say. For that matter, Kiamoto probably knew that seeing the compass heading wouldn't mean a thing to Port. It made Port angry that Kiamoto was being so kind.

Tomorrow, thought Port. To hell with all this tonight, but tomorrow—

He took Maria's arm and they went outside. Port closed the door of the wheel house, thinking that it would cut the wind and leave only the draft on the back of Kiamoto's head, which at any rate was some gesture of friendliness. But to hell with Kiamoto, who didn't care one way or the other about drafts on the head. For that matter, the cabin would not be any better.

The cabin lamp was electric. The weak bulb made a yellow glow, warm and friendly, and once Port had shut the door he noticed the real warmth in the cabin. Kiamoto had lit a fire in the small coal stove, a pot was on top of it with water simmering, and he had left a coffee tin and a can of beans on the table. The table was not dusty, the way Port remembered it, and there was a blanket in the bunk. It was pleasant in the cabin.

The bunk was very narrow, so when Port woke up he was not able to move with Maria so close to him. For a moment the waking was easy and pleasant with the girl warm against him and with her head under his chin so that he could smell her hair. He lay very still for a while.

"I know you're awake," she said. "Don't try to fool me," and punched his ribs.

There was nowhere for him to go and he bumped his head on the bunk post.

"If you make me fall out," he said, "you'll roll out with me."

"Then hold on tight."

"And I'll fall on top of you because you're softer than me."

"You're a goat," she said. "You would act like a goat even while lying on top of a fence post," and this time she pinched him hard so that he did fall out of bed.

"Ah, well," he said. "You can't get away. Miles and miles of deep ocean."

They laughed about it but that was the end of it, because this was Kiamoto's boat, it might as well be Kiamoto's ocean for all the good it would do them, and Kiamoto's time.

Port got off the floor and rubbed the back of his neck. Maria got up and patted her wrinkled dress; ran her fingers through her hair. The electric bulb swung on its cord and Port could hear the faint slosh in the bilges. This sound made all the rest of the world very quiet.

There were no windows in the cabin, just a door at the top of the steps, and a small window in the door showing white against the sky.

"How quiet it is," said Maria. She looked around, as if the cabin was frightening her.

"I just noticed. The motor is off."

"And the bulb," she said. "it doesn't swing enough. Do you notice, Daniel?"

He clambered up the well and kicked open the door.

The sun was very hot. Something creaked in the rigging, but just faintly, and the ocean stretched very far, glistening like oil. Without looking more, Port raced to the wheel house. The wheel moved one way a little, then back, the way an unsecured wheel might move when a boat is not under way.

"The bastard. The double-faced bastard—" Port said.

He looked at the painful reflections on the wide ocean and suddenly he knew that Kiamoto was not on the boat any more. The bow rose a little, and tugged.

Anchored?

Having thought they were far out and adrift, it came as a shock to Port when he finally looked to the other side and saw the trees over the gunwale. They were clearly defined in the sun, they were very close, and the view out of the wheel house was suddenly like a garden view from a small cabin.

Port's anger turned into something sheepish and useless.

"The rowboat's gone," said Maria from the stern. "Wasn't it tied here, in the back?"

"I'm sure it's gone," said Port. "It's the only thing I'm sure of right now."

They were in a small bay and the land was an island. The bay was in the lee of the island, so that trees grew near the water, but what they could see of the rest of the island was mostly rock.

"Maybe he'll come back," said Maria. "I can see the rowboat."

It lay pulled up on the small beach. The long sculling oar wasn't there.

Port stood at the gunwale and looked down into the water. It was still and clear, very deep, but the bottom was visible. A spotted ray floated across the green rocks. His wings made wave motions.

"Will you swim across?" Maria asked.

"I don't know yet. I don't know what goes on," said Port.

It was true that Kiamoto had been kind to them the night before, but Port found it just as plausible that he would shoot Port while swimming in the water, watch him struggle there in a cloud of blood, watch him die when the sharks came. It was as plausible as a Chinese fisherman who spoke with a cultured accent, knew four languages, was in his late sixties, could break your back with a flip of the hand, lent you his blanket while he shivered in the wet wind, needed no sleep, explained nothing, not even his kindness—

Port looked at the boat on the beach and then the tracks in the sand. They went to the rocks on one side and disappeared. Then they came back from the rocks. On the other side of the rocks might be more water, thought Port, the way they cut off the beach and formed a skyline. There was something on the other side of the rocks, but then the tracks came back and went to the edge of the sand where the trees started. There they stopped.

"Kiamoto!" Maria called out. "Kiamoto!"

It was too late to stop her from calling. Kiamoto was lying in the shade but he sat up immediately. He sleeps like an animal, thought Port; he wakes up without any transition. And like a very smart human, he was sleeping with his face toward the fishing boat and was probably watching it all the time he was asleep.

Kiamoto got up, moved his shoulders. He looked up at the sun and then he walked down to the water. He stopped where he was closest to the fishing boat.

"Stay there," he called across. "I'll be back." Then he turned toward the rocks. He stopped once more and said to Maria, "Don't worry, child. Just stay there."

As usual, he had said the minimum. Port was getting used to it. He was also learning to read it better.

There had been no point in that last remark to Maria, unless it was meant like a good-bye. There had been no point in sleeping there on the beach until they woke him up, unless he, Kiamoto, had overslept. There was no point in having taken the sculling oar out of the boat, unless it was to be used elsewhere.

He had been weak with tiredness and now, when he had said he'd be back, he had been lying.

"Wait," said Port, and when Kiamoto stopped, "at least you can tell us where we are."

It was exactly the kind of underplayed remark which Kiamoto would understand. It said everything with the least effort; that Port knew Kiamoto was leaving, that the practical question to Port was how to get out off, here, that he was thinking of that first and perhaps not at all about how to detain Kiamoto.

"You can stay here," said Kiamoto, "and wait. I will see to it that you are found."

"There's just one can of beans on the boat," said Port. "And no water in the big tank."

"There is a canister by the stove," said Kiamoto. Then he said, "or you can take the boat back. Do you think you can take it back?"

It surprised Port, because he did not think Kiamoto would have left the boat shipshape.

"The mainland is that way," and Kiamoto pointed. "You have enough gas. There is no distributor cap on the motor, but you will be able to find it. I left it on the boat."

That sounded much more like Kiamoto. But not enough. Port was sure there would be more, to make everything even safer.

"If you try and follow me now," Kiamoto said, "I will shoot you while you swim across."

Of course. Port didn't doubt it for a moment. And what else? What final provision?

Kiamoto was at the rowboat, leaned down, took out the rusty tin can which was in there for bailing. He came back along the beach with it while Port watched. Though all this might well be a matter of life and death, Kiamoto's quiet manner, his quiet purpose in everything, kept Port at the railing, fascinated. He watched Kiamoto not because he was an enemy, but because he was strange to watch.

"And I do not want you to follow," said the Chinese, "as soon as I've passed the rocks. Will you promise that, Mister Port?"

"No."

Kiamoto just nodded. He was not surprised. Even Port's honesty did not surprise him.

He took a knife out of his pocket, held it away from himself, let it snap open. Then, very swiftly, he gashed his arm. He held the gash over the tin can and allowed the blood to drip down, and after he had clasped his knife and put it back into his pocket he squeezed the wound to get more blood.

No one talked. The water made smacking sounds on the hull of the boat and Kiamoto kneeled on the beach dripping his blood into the old can. All this is really happening, Port said to himself. Perhaps in the long view it will look insane, but right now it is happening and is therefore real. Like Maria, he just stood and watched.

Kiamoto got up, shook his arm, licked the cut. Then he walked into the water. He kept walking until it was up to his thighs, when he stopped and heaved the can toward the boat. It plopped on its side, sucked water immediately, and spiraled slowly toward the bottom. A dark plume of blood, smokelike, spread in the water.

Kiamoto walked back to the beach.

"They will come soon," he said. "They can smell it for miles, I believe. You will then be able to see the sharks from where you stand, Mister Port, and you would be a fool to swim across."

Kiamoto stood a while longer while all of them watched the water in the bay and the water farther out in the ocean.

It took only five minutes. The stiff fin came veering back and forth, making a neat V of a bow wave. Then a flop, and the fin was gone.

The fish looked beautiful under the water, a large blue shark with needle nose, spread-finned like a plane, the whole body a hydrafoil which belonged in motion and would look as if it were in motion even when still. The shark curved and wheeled, finding nothing. It passed through the cloud of blood and kept hunting the bay.

Kiamoto left. He was crossing the rocks before Port had noticed.

"I'm afraid," said Maria. "I'm terribly afraid."

Port put his hand on her arm, maybe to comfort her, but then he forgot. He was biting his lip and watching Kiamoto. If that old man leaves and I never see him again I'll go out of my mind with not knowing, went through his head. The bastard. He plays everything in his own rhythm and I don't know what it means, but I dance to it.

Port wasn't thinking of the chance he would take steering the boat back to the mainland alone across the open water; he wasn't thinking about the chance they would take staying here, waiting for Kiamoto to send someone after them; it was nothing practical of that sort. He thought of Kiamoto getting away, remaining an enigma.

"Daniel, you are out of your mind!"

Maria gaped at him, didn't believe him.

He pulled off his shirt, dropped his pants, kicked his shoes across the hot deck.

"Take the pole," he said. "There, up forward. Take it and splash the pole in the water."

"The shark, Daniel! The shark is lying there on the bottom!"

"Don't argue," said Port.

She saw him drop a line over the side and then she almost ran up to him, to hold him by the arm, claw him if necessary, scream at him so he'd look at her, but she saw that she would not be able to tell him a thing. He was not entirely sane, she thought. But if she splashed the pole, as he had said, then he would be safe. She ran away from the look on his face, grabbed the pole, started swirling it in the water.

The shark rose a little and floated in a wide arc, like a long lazy drop.

Port lowered himself into the water.

If he stayed away from the blood, made no splashes, swam under water, the chances were good. Blue sharks were not like the Mako, which was known to strike at large shapes, like a human. And sharks favor the sick, the fish splashing half dead on the surface and bleeding.

Port sank under, maybe five feet. Then he swam.

The shark passed through the blood, which was faint now and spreading in all directions. There was no current in the bay. The far arc of its pass took it so close to Port that Maria stopped breathing. She beat the pole on the water. She beat and beat and smacked it down in a frenzy.

The shark flipped, showing the silver belly. It shot through the foam where Maria was beating, so that she could have poked the long belly with the pole.

Port broke water close to the beach. He looked once and saw Maria point down by the hull. He dove again, swam till he scraped his chest, then stood up and ran.

On the other side of the rocks was the windward beach of the island, a narrow strip of rough pebbles. Surf slanted along the beach, the small breakers racing into the land at an angle. There was a ketch in the breakers. The boat reared every time the spray shot by.

Kiamoto was still on land. He was bending down for the big sculling oar, and his back was turned.

The wind made a noise in Port's ears, and the same would be true for Kiamoto. And the Chinese was closer to the water, hearing the surf more.

But it was too long a run. Would Kiamoto shoot a naked man running along the beach? Port didn't bother to answer himself. Kiamoto might not shoot. He might just stand there and wait till Port was within range and then brain him with the sculling oar. Or there was still that other trick, the one he did with the wrist or what-ever—

He hefted the oar over his shoulder and straightened up. Fifteen feet away? Twenty? If he did not turn, if Port could be sure he would not turn—

Then he didn't think any more. He jumped down the rocks, reached into the crevice where a nest of driftwood had caught itself, pulled up a short log.

Make out it's like baseball. No. Make out it's like life and death.

The wood spun through the air, straight and hard, and if it hits flat on his back it'll knock the wind out of him, and if it jams endwise into his back maybe something will break—

Port heard Kiamoto's involuntary grunt. Then he saw him stagger.

Kiamoto was just turning painfully, because he had fallen with his face into the water, when Port was all over him. He was not really all over him, being much too cautious of Kiamoto, but he gave a vicious twist to one foot, doubling the leg over, spinning the body belly down again, making Kiamoto's face hit the water. There was only one thing for Kiamoto to do now, struggle for air. He had no room and no time for anything else.

Port reached for the gun in Kiamoto's belt, pulled it out, and let go of the foot. He jumped back and waited. At first Kiamoto hardly moved. He was up on his arms, to be clear of the water, and he just tried to breathe. The log that had hit him in the back was floating next to his body, bumping him with each slap of the surf. Kiamoto did not notice. He fought for breath and then crawled very slowly away from the water.

I won't touch him, Port said to himself. He'll strike like a snake, or he'll bite the barrel off this gun, or maybe, if I grab him, he'll suddenly turn into a real old man, weak and bleeding and needing help.

Port sat away from him, cowered on his heels like a native, and cursed to himself. He didn't know why. First he cursed to himself and then he started to whistle. He made sure not to whistle in the same rhythm as Kiamoto's slow crawling, but he watched the old man all the time.

Then Kiamoto lay down on his back. He did it slowly and with purpose. He had to favor a spot on his back, favor his left foot and his left arm. The cut was bleeding again and probably burned from the salt water. In a while he took a deep breath and turned his head toward Port. He did not look at the gun in Port's hand, just at his face.

"What would you have done if the wood had missed?"

"I don't want to think about it."

"Had you planned this long?"

"No."

"It doesn't look like it."

"Does it matter?"

Kiamoto waited a moment and then he said, "Yes. It shows your motive. Or rather, it doesn't. You puzzle me."

Port felt like laughing.

"And now?" Kiamoto asked. "How will you make me talk?"

Port frowned. He did not think they were on the same subject.

"I'm an old man," said Kiamoto, "and in many ways, I'm done, I don't think there is any way to force me."

Port shifted his weight and then he blinked at the sun. "I don't know any real good tortures," he said. "You're quite right."

Kiamoto said nothing for a while. He didn't know what to think.

Then he said, "Why did you stop me?"

For a moment the question baffled Port. Why? Because Kiamoto had been leaving without explaining anything; because he had, in some way, sucked Port into his affairs and Port didn't know what they were. He said, "Why? Dammit, because I want to know why I can't be left alone!"

Kiamoto closed his eyes. Either a pain bothered him or he was thinking.

"What if I give you the money?" he asked quietly.

"Money? What money?"

Then Port got up. He took a few steps, cowered down again. "Listen," he said. "Let me explain this again."

"You don't have to," said Kiamoto. "You just did." He tried to raise himself up but couldn't make it.

"If I put the gun down," said Port, "will you jump me if I come close?"

"No," said Kiamoto. "I wouldn't."

Couldn't, thought Port. I'll risk it. He put one arm under the man and raised him into a sitting position. Kiamoto breathed hard. He felt hot and moist.

"How's your back?"

"All right, when I keep it straight."

Port let go and then he put his hand on Kiamoto's forehead. The old man was burning up.

"How long have you had that fever?"

"Just the night. You can let go now."

Port let go and didn't know what to do next. Maria would know. She would have no conflicts about this.

"I'm taking you back," said Port. "You're sick."

Kiamoto was holding his lip in his teeth. It tensed his face, but then, when he let go, his face seemed to fall and looked older than ever before.

"If you will help me up," he said, "and into the boat—Please, Mister Port."

It was hard to remember the trouble Kiamoto had caused. But had he? What had he done intentionally? He had held a gun on Port. Because he had been afraid, Maria had said. Maybe he had cause. Maybe he was the kind of a bastard who by the end of his life had to be afraid of almost everything. And he wore a bland face to hide all that.

"I'm taking you back, Kiamoto."

The old man put his head down, tired, and looked at his hands.

"Why do you keep calling me Kiamoto? You know I'm Chinese."

"I don't know your other name. Hold on now. I'm going to heft you up so..."

"Wait. Please wait."

Port let go of him and tried to see the man's face.

"Hoi Kio," said the Chinese. "You know the name?"

Port waited. He couldn't remember.

"General Hoi Kio," said the Chinese. "The army of Nationalist China. Do you remember a few years ago there was..."

"Jeesis!" said Port. "Jeesis Christ! You came to the U.S. to buy planes and small arms and then you took off with a million bucks!"

"Yes," said Kiamoto. "You remember."

He blinked his eyes because the fever was blurring his vision. Then he shook his head so the dullness would leave.

"Lie down," said Port. "You're going to faint." He helped Kiamoto lie down and the old man didn't resist.

Port remembered about him and how for a short time the news was big in the papers. Then suddenly nothing. It had been too big. And since that time Kiamoto—or General Hoi Kio of the Formosa government—had been a complete success. Nationalist China was after him to get back their million bucks; the U.S. was after him because the one million was part of lend-lease, a conditional gift to be spent in the States; Pan-Continental was after him because they stood to lose the biggest slice of the Formosa order; Communist China had been after him because the one million bucks was to buy defenses against them.

But he'd been a success. It had brought him to a hard pebble beach on a bare island, a man with a painful back, a bad foot, and a fever.

"You don't look like you've been spending it, Kiamoto," said Port.

"It was too much money."

"And you didn't think of that ahead of time?" Port asked him.

Kiamoto looked up. "You think I stole it to spend?"

"I would," said Port.

"You're young. I'm near seventy."

Even now, looking at Kiamoto, it was hard to believe his age.

"By that time," said Kiamoto, "loyalties are well-established."

"You stole it for your loyalties. Country, honor, family."

"Honor," said Kiamoto, "is a fixed commodity only, if you forget about everything else. I've lived a long time and remember a great many things. It makes honor flexible, and therefore nothing."

"Country," said Port.

"What country? China? Which China?"

Port said nothing.

"The conflict narrows your loyalty," said Kiamoto. "What is left, to a man of my training, is family."

"Weren't you from Manchuria?" Port asked.

"Yes. A long time ago."

"So the Reds got to you and pulled the old saw: if you want your family sane and safe, don't deliver the war purchases."

"Yes. It is particularly effective with a Chinese. An old Chinese. Particularly one like me, with no honor or country."

"You're a clever man," said Port. "Why did you handle this thing so stupidly?"

"You mean run away with the money?"

"Yes. Something that's almost impossible. You could have arranged a grand theft, a fire destroying the cash, a purchase arrangement which could have stalled, you could have railroaded the arms transaction. A thousand things like that to leave you in the clear."

Kiamoto sat up without help this time. He did it slowly, carefully, but when he sat up he did not seem to suffer. He looked at Port and the bland face assumed an expression. It was the last thing Port expected, because Kiamoto started to smile, a sure smile without effort or conflict.

"It was my first deed of independent conviction," he said. "It was time for that, since I'm old."

Port, not for the first time, got the impression that Kiamoto did not always think by the rules.

"In your dramatic press," said Kiamoto, "I was sometimes described as a war lord. You know what that is, Mister Port? I am born, raised, and trained to hold everything that is mine inviolate. This produces one thing, Mister Port: the war lord. The act of force. Do you follow me? The act of force becomes law. This law makes order of chaos. I hope you follow me," said Kiamoto, "because I'm describing to you the flaw."

Port nodded, so that Kiamoto would go on.

"For a great part of my life I would wonder about this," said Kiamoto, "about the act of force making order of chaos. After all, why was I a military? To make order."

Kiamoto shrugged very slightly. His voice became low.

"I have never seen it to succeed. I have never seen the act of force—an act which I perform with some skill—create order. Did you follow me, Mister Port?"

"So you chucked one million dollars of force."

"Yes. My first deed of independent conviction."

Kiamoto reached for the sculling oar, propped it up, and started to raise himself. He groaned a little, but then he stood.

"Did you destroy the money?" Port asked him.

"Would you believe me if I said yes?"

"I don't know."

"So the question is pointless."

Port got up and looked at the gun he was holding. He was wearing no clothes and didn't know where to put the gun.

"What makes my act meaningful," said Kiamoto, "is to run as if I had something to hide. It makes the loss of the money meaningful to those who would want it, Mister Port."

"Yes?"

"Will you let me go?" Kiamoto, using the oar for balance, stood close to the water. The ketch was bobbing in the surf.

"Yes," said Port.

He watched the old man wade out into the water.

When Kiamoto was by the boat he turned once to call back.

"You can make the mainland in five hours. The distributor cap is under the bunk."

He threw the oar into the ketch and climbed after it.

Chapter 12

You didn't hear it," said Briggs, "because he drifted out with the tide. That's the only explanation."

"I don't get it." Sanchez shook his head nervously and didn't look at Briggs.

"What's the difference whether you get it or don't get it? The boat's gone!"

Briggs sounded angrier than he had intended. He tried to cover with a cough, and then he gave Sanchez a pat. "All right. Let's get to business."

They climbed down the steps of the pier and into the motor boat. The motor boat was all business too. It was twenty foot long, without a cabin, but a lot of room was taken up by the motor. The motor was inboard, decked over, and a small canopy made shade for the pilot.

"Cast off those lines," said Briggs, "and then I'll punch this button."

When he punched the starter button the boat roared like a truck. They sliced off, the boat curling a big, white wave up its bow.

Having said that he was now ready for business, Briggs didn't talk any more and had stopped worrying about Kiamoto's boat having slipped out. Being ready for business didn't mean that Briggs was grim, tight lipped, or tense. It simply meant he had no thought of failure and that he wouldn't stop till he had his man.

But Sanchez was younger, and he had slipped up twice.

He had let the fishing boat slip away, and before that he had let Port jump him. Sanchez was still shaky from that and disturbed about everything. Sudden violence left him upset, especially if it happened without anger. Sanchez did not think that Port had been angry.

"We had this wrong," he said. "I say Port wasn't looking for the Chinese.

I say he had him already."

"They're together in this?"

"I don't mean friendship, but if we find that boat—"

"*When* we find that boat, Sanchez."

"When we find that boat, there's going to be the Chinese general on it and that Port."

"Could be. First he shows up at the icehouse, checking around—"

"And beating my brains out," said Sanchez.

"Yes. And the next thing, the boat disappears. Maybe," said Briggs, "there'll be just Port on that boat."

"Which means that he's done with Hoi Kio."

"Yeah," said Briggs. Then he didn't say any more.

They had figured out that the best way to hunt the fishing boat was to trail the fleet. Since all the boats always went into the same general area, it would look less odd if Hoi Kio's boat went there too. From the fishing grounds, which were not very far out, it would then be an easy run to disappear toward shore, to run for Quesada, for instance, where there were roads. Something like that.

"Watch the shoal at the mouth here," said Sanchez.

There was no cause for concern because the tide was in, but Sanchez didn't feel calm like Briggs. As soon as they were out of the bay and angling toward the fishing grounds, Sanchez picked up the binoculars and started looking at nothing. First he looked at the shoreline and then he looked at the ocean.

"He wouldn't be here," said Briggs. "Not yet."

"Sure." Sanchez kept looking.

"Come under the roof here," said Briggs. "That sun's going to shrivel you up."

"I can't see from there. Too much salt on those windows."

He kept squatting in the stern, the glasses up to his eyes, and when his head started pounding it could have been from the squinting, from the sun boring into him, or from the thought of Port. Briggs said nothing else, not wanting Sanchez to get any more irritated.

"Did Hoi Kio's boat have a sail?" Sanchez asked.

"He had a mast."

"I know he had a mast," said Sanchez. "What I asked was, did he..."

"I don't think so," said Briggs. He almost asked Sanchez why in hell he didn't remember, having watched the boat most of the day and the night, but he let that go because he didn't want to be irritating. Once they met the boat, if they met the boat, it would be no good to have Sanchez jumpy.

"I know he had a mast and no sail up when he was in the bay," said Sanchez. "What I'm asking is, did he have the boom on or off, which is important to know because if it was off he couldn't hoist sail if he wanted to, but if the boom was still on..."

"I don't remember if the cotton pickin' boom was on, Sanchez."

"Cotton picking?" said Sanchez. His English didn't include all the colloquialisms.

"Come on out of the sun," said Briggs. "You're sweating like a pig."

Sanchez didn't budge but kept looking through the field glasses. He's going to be ready to jump out of his skin, thought Briggs, in about ten more minutes. Nothing to do about it. He's the type that can't operate without emotion. He craves it to fire himself up. If Port is out there someplace, he'd better watch out, and more power to Sanchez.

"I'm asking," said Sanchez, "because there's a boat out there under power and with no sail."

"Huh? Where?"

"Just keep going the way you are," said Sanchez. "Will you?"

He didn't want to make a mistake again. One mistake was enough—and he'd made two mistakes already. He was going to be damned to hell if he made another one and said there was a boat out there, Hoi Kio's boat, and then it wasn't.

"Just tell me where, Sanchez."

"You're almost heading for him. He's more to the left, but don't bother heading there any more than you are."

"If it isn't him," said Briggs, "don't worry about it. We're just checking."

"I know we're just checking."

"So relax."

Then Briggs started to curse under his breath. Sanchez wasn't cursing or saying anything but sat crouched in the stern and looking. He was holding it in. Briggs cursed to himself because he was worried now.

"You know," said Sanchez, "he's heading toward shore."

"Toward us?"

"That's what I said."

"Kind of unusual," said Briggs.

It was not unusual to Sanchez, because he was convinced by now that the boat he saw was Hoi Kio's boat. He had to think that or explode. And Hoi Kio's boat would be doing the unusual thing, such as heading toward Guanadera in the forenoon—

"Why in hell would he be heading toward shore, toward town?" said Briggs.

"Ah," said Sanchez. "I know why."

"Hoi Kio would be an idiot..."

"Because the Chinese isn't running the boat, you understand. This Port is running the boat!"

Briggs didn't get it, but he felt that Sanchez had to think this or go nuts with not knowing.

"I see him now," said Briggs. "Right in the damn sun."

"He hasn't changed course."

"If he does," said Briggs, "we can be sure this is fishy."

Ten minutes later the fishing boat still hadn't changed course, but more important to Sanchez, this was clearly the boat he was after.

He put the glasses down because he could see well enough without the binoculars now.

"There's somebody at the rail," said Briggs. "You see him?

"It's a woman."

"Woman? What in hell is a woman doing there?"

"I have no idea," said Sanchez. "I have no idea how the mind of someone like this Port might work at any given time."

Oh Christ, thought Briggs. Now he's getting formal. He's getting mean—

They were close now. Sanchez was standing and hitching his pants. Briggs throttled back a little and the nose of the motor boat settled down.

"Sanchez? Come here a minute."

Sanchez went under the canopy. He kept looking at the fishing boat all the time Briggs was talking.

"We play it cool now, Sanchez. Understand?"

"Of course."

"We're the packing company. Supervisor, that sort of crap, and looking for the fleet. Just checking up."

"Nothing unusual."

"We play it cool. Remember that, Sanchez."

"I'm sure Hoi Kio isn't running that boat," Sanchez said. "He would not come back like this, showing no suspicion."

"Are you listening to me, Sanchez?"

"It must be Port. Not that he isn't suspicious right this very moment, but I wouldn't attempt to guess what goes on in that man's mind. Look. The woman is going to that little cabin."

"The wheel house."

"I wonder why—"

"I wouldn't attempt to guess," said Briggs. Then he added, "Now hold on. I'm letting him pass and then make a swivel alongside. Here we go."

Briggs gunned the motor and made a fine, splashy arc. The fishing boat kept plodding along.

"Sanchez."

"Yes."

"Remember, we're not a boarding party."

"We wave, we say hello, we ask where the fleet is."

"Yes."

"Just to see who's aboard. The pinch comes later."

"Yes. Yes."

They were alongside now, matching speed. Maybe twenty feet off.

There were two people in the small wheel house and then one of them came out.

"That's Port!" said Sanchez.

Say something light, thought Briggs. Sanchez is tight as a wire.

"If he asks again where d'Ortega is," and Briggs manufactured a chuckle, "we'll just explain..."

He didn't get any farther. A gun cracked and the slug ripped into the deck that covered the motor.

"All right, you bastards!" They could hear it loud and clear. "Where's d'Ortega? He aboard there?"

Sanchez giggled from nervousness. "Very funny," he said. "Just like you said."

The next moment he had his revolver whipped out and was no longer giggling.

The gunwale of the fishing boat wasn't high but Port had disappeared. He was flat on the deck and sighting at them through the scuppers.

"Next shot I cut up your gut!" he yelled. "Now ease over your boat."

"I'm going to do it," Briggs said to Sanchez. "Hide that cotton pickin' gun, for god's sake!"

"He can't hit at that distance, Briggs! Don't..."

"Shut up. I want to talk to him."

Port saw the motor boat ease over and then he turned to wave up at Maria. When she saw this she cut the motor. Port stayed by the scuppers. He felt the warm deck under his belly and smelled the caulking. Then he forgot about it.

"I'm gonna toss down a line," he yelled, "and all the while I've got this gun on you bastards. Now tie up!"

He watched the younger one tie up the line. The two boats bumped hard and the young guy almost fell over. Let him drown. Let the sharks tear his legs off, and it would even be better if this were d'Ortega. Meanwhile these two would have to do. He thought about Kiamoto and what had happened between them on the beach.

"You! The thin one! You come up first!"

Sanchez came over the side. He looked almost too eager.

"You still carry that gun in the little belt holster?" Port asked him.

Sanchez unbuttoned his jacket.

"And while you pull it out," said Port, "I'll kill you twice before you can aim it. *Sabe?*"

"*Sabe.*"

Sanchez tossed out the gun.

"Now you, Dad!" Port yelled through the scuppers.

The gray-haired man waved up, to show his agreement, and then climbed over the gunwale. Port got up and out of the way so the man wouldn't step on him.

"And the gun," said Port. "I'm sure you've got a gun."

"Mister Port," said Briggs, "before this misunderstanding goes any further..."

"On the two count I shoot off your hand," said Port. When he was through saying "one" Briggs dropped the revolver on the deck and kept his hands in sight.

"You both stand by the gunwale," said Port. "With your backs to the water."

"Mister Port. My name is Peter Briggs and this is Fernando Sanchez..."

"He and I've met."

"Lieutenant Sanchez is special agent..."

"Oh crap," said Port.

"And I am with the Federal Bureau of Investigation, special assignment out of our embassy in Mexico City."

"Glad to meet you," said Port. "I am Baron von Unterhosen, special dick with Intergalactic Security Squad, Sector Nova Lunacy. Now, move to the hold."

There was a short silence while neither of them moved. Then Briggs laughed. It came out a cackly sound but he was determined to laugh because he did not want to lose his temper. He wanted to talk to Port, who was not the important one Briggs was after.

"Lemme make something clear," he said to Port, and he was so determined to play it his way that he paid attention neither to Port's mood nor to Sanchez's.

"The hold is that way," said Port, and went close enough to poke Briggs with the gun barrel.

Briggs gave up his idea of a talk and went down the deck. He pushed

Sanchez ahead of him, which meant Port couldn't see the other man. He saw Maria up at the wheel house, watching quietly, with her hand near her throat. Suddenly she flung out her arm.

"Watch him!" she screamed, and then again, "Watch—" which Port didn't hear any more.

He had jumped back fast. He caught Sanchez's movement and threw himself back and if he hadn't stumbled either Briggs or the other one would have been dead. But his bare foot had stepped on one of the guns on the deck, so that Port's shot went wild and the knife Sanchez was throwing buzzed through the air.

When Port hit the planks he banged his knuckles with his own gun and Sanchez kicked it out of his hand. Sanchez and Port went at each other bare handed.

It was different from the time at the icehouse. Both men were angry. Port was on the bottom and Sanchez, like a cat, was all over him. He took a knee in the chest but clipped Port hard on the side of the head. He hit his hand on the planks when Port swiveled out of the way, but landed one on the ear so Port's head was ringing. He could feel Port's bare foot working up his leg but he jumped free just before the toes dug into his groin.

Briggs didn't make it to the guns in time. There were three guns on the deck, behind Port, but Sanchez knocked Briggs out of the way. Or perhaps it was the screaming that stopped him, because he looked so startled. Maria had jumped down from the wheel house, screaming like a wild animal, cursing the two men, cursing all men, and then she scooped up a gun. She threw it.

She threw it at Briggs, who was too surprised to duck, and the hard metal caught him flush on the side of the head. He ducked then, because she threw the second gun.

"Don't!" yelled Port. "For heaven's sake don't throw any more!"

Sanchez and Briggs didn't move. She's holding the third one on them, thought Port, she *must* be holding the third one on them. But he was almost afraid to look.

He jumped up and backed toward the girl. She was holding Kiamoto's gun on them. She was holding it right and was squeezing the grip. She was squeezing it several times, but her finger wasn't on the trigger.

"Gimme that," he said in her ear. "For Chrissakes let go and give it to me."

Briggs was bleeding on the side of his face and Sanchez looked winded. Port had a sore hand and his head was roaring.

None of them felt like fighting any more. It had been quick, intense, and now it was over.

"In the hold," said Port. "Like I said two minutes ago."

He made them jump down through the hatch, locked them in, wiped the sweat off his face. Then he looked for the other two guns, but only found one of them.

"It fell in the water," said Maria. "The one that missed him."

"Don't worry," said Port. "You're a good shot. You clipped him good."

He found Sanchez's knife, which had dug itself into the mast.

Then he started the engine and found the Guanadera bay one hour later. The fleet was out and there was only a kid in a boat, sailing for pleasure.

Chapter 13

It took him a little while to figure out what to do with the fishing boat, because he was sure he would crash into the piling or beach the boat by mistake. On a slow turn he almost ran over the motor boat which Briggs and Sanchez had brought, because it was tied with only one line and had drifted off when Port made his arc. He would go ashore in the motor boat and leave the big one at anchor.

He cut the motor, raced down to the bow, and threw the anchor overboard. Then he decided about Sanchez and Briggs. He would check that they were locked in good and solid and leave them in the hold to fend for themselves. Someone would hear them after a while, or in a day or so he might even come for them himself.

Port had left too much slack in the anchor line. The fishing boat had swung into the wind and the stern was now backed up close to the wharf. Port could look down on the wharf.

"Daniel," said Maria. "Daniel, look." Her voice was frightened and she took his arm.

There were two men coming down the wharf. They walked slowly, as if surprised by the sight, but then they came faster. D'Ortega was first, and then Capo.

"Finally," said Port. "Finally."

He could appreciate d'Ortega's emotions. He was close to his quarry, and perhaps hardly believing it, and all that puzzled him now was that he only saw Port.

"You stay here," said Port to the girl. "Right here, by the gunwale. If those two pigs try to board, you yell good and loud."

"I will, Danny."

"And I'll be right back."

Then he ran to the hatch and threw it open.

Briggs and Sanchez came into the sun and couldn't see very well. They smelled a little bit musty and a lot like fish.

"You walk toward the girl," he told them. "You can see the girl up ahead. And when I say stop you stop by the rail."

They thought Port had the gun on them, though they couldn't be sure. He was holding it low and the sun was very sharp in their eyes.

What d'Ortega saw was Briggs, Sanchez, and Port, all by the rail. They were all looking down at him and he didn't know what to make of it.

"D'Ortega," Port called down to him. "Listen good, you bastard."

D'Ortega blinked.

"I've got these two now, d'Ortega, and I'm going to explain to you what happens next."

He stopped talking because d'Ortega wasn't paying attention. Capo had stepped up to him and was hissing into his ear. D'Ortega stared straight ahead. Then he looked up at Port and smiled at everybody. His cultured voice was a little hesitant, but polite.

"I am pleased to make your acquaintance," he said.

Port was sure it was meant for Sanchez and Briggs. D'Ortega nodded at them and made a small bow.

"And I hope your trip has been successful."

"You will never find him," said Maria. She was spitting her words. "Kiamoto is safe. He is not here."

D'Ortega bowed and backed away. He turned then and walked down the wharf quickly. Capo had to jog to keep up.

"I'll be damned," said Port. "What was that?"

"I will explain it to you," said Sanchez. He turned toward Port, ignoring the gun.

"Shut up and stay there," said Port.

"You will want to know this," said Sanchez. "D'Ortega was running from us."

"Your own boss?" and Port swore something in English.

"We're not with d'Ortega," said Briggs. "I've been trying to tell you."

"You saw the stocky one whisper to d'Ortega?"

Port remembered that, because it had interrupted his play.

"The stocky one is called Capo," Sanchez explained, "and he recognized me. He and I have had dealings together."

"I don't doubt it," said Port.

"Because he is a criminal and I am with the police."

That same tack again. It was starting to sound stupid to Port, unless it was true.

"I can show you my credentials," said Briggs.

Briggs had claimed to be FBI. Then Port remembered their guns. They were both .38 Smith and Wessons and both men had worn them in small belt holsters. An official touch.

"Show me," said Port.

Briggs threw over his billfold and there was the card with his picture, Briggs, FBI.

Sanchez had a card from the Mexican government.

"Jeesis," said Port. He stuck the gun in his pocket and said "jeesis" again.

In a way this was good. He had two less enemies and he had scared off d'Ortega, who thought now that Port was with the cops.

"It's a shame," said Briggs, "that this young woman explained to them that Kiamoto was not on the boat."

"A shame?"

"D'Ortega will look elsewhere. I'm sure it's too late to find him in town."

Port hadn't thought about that. Nor was he interested.

"And you, Port," Briggs went on, "better explain where Kiamoto is."

"To hell with that."

"What makes you think," Briggs explained, "that you're any less under suspicion now?"

Port hadn't thought about that.

"Perhaps the young lady will tell us?" asked Briggs. He was lighting a cigarette, but sounded like business. He no longer felt like a prisoner.

Maria said the same kind of thing that Port had told them.

Briggs sat down on the gunwale and blew out smoke. He watched it dissolve and then he looked up.

"I've got a case against you, Dan Port. The way you behaved at the icehouse, the way you treated us here, the fact that you came back with Kiamoto's boat, the fact of no Kiamoto—all that and your background, Dan Port—"

"You're not thinking of shooting us, are you?" said Sanchez.

Port said, "Don't be an idiot," and chewed his lip.

It didn't look good for him. Five minutes ago he had been out of it. Now he was back in, and deep.

"Where is Kiamoto?"

"So help me," said Port, "I don't know."

"Is he alive?"

"I didn't kill him. I haven't even been after him." He looked at the men's faces but didn't see much understanding there. "It's a long story," he said. It came out lame.

"If you and I," said Briggs, "could find Kiamoto, do you think he could clear this up for you?"

Kiamoto could. No question. And then the cops would nab Kiamoto—

"Don't you think it's better that we should find him than for instance d'Ortega?"

Briggs had made a convincing suggestion. Port looked at Maria.

"Kiamoto will help you," she said. "He is a good man."

Port nodded and gave her a smile. Of course, Maria didn't know who Kiamoto was.

"Or you'll be under arrest within twenty-four hours," said Briggs. "I can make it heavy."

Port sat still and looked at the two men. He sat and hated their guts.

He would stick with them, so he wouldn't be railroaded. And he'd stick with them so he would be around when they found Kiamoto. The old man might need help.

"All right," said Port. "All right."

Except he had no idea where to look for Kiamoto.

"He'll go out of his head again," said Capo. "You gave him too much."

"Drive and watch the road," said d'Ortega. Then he handed the bottle to Pepe. "He doesn't talk unless he drinks."

"You will kill him with the pulque," said Capo. "You can give him something else to stay drunk."

"Pulque is cheaper," said d'Ortega. "Pull off the road."

Capo slowed down and bumped the car into a lane which went toward the water. The Pacific glistened along the rocks and the road ended there. They stopped next to a shack. It had only part of a roof, but it was useful enough. They had used it before.

Pepe stopped at the door because he would have liked to sit in the sun for a while. He felt he wanted to sweat and then sleep. Capo gave him a push and they all went into the shack. D'Ortega was holding the bottle.

"You hear me, Pepe?"

"Sure. I do." His eyes looked bad and the stubble on his face made his wrinkles look sharp and deep. Pepe stooped more than usual.

"Sit down on the floor," said d'Ortega. Then he stood by a wall and looked through a crack in the boards where he could see the ocean.

"Maybe," said Capo, "we should have stayed to see if Kiamoto came off the boat."

"No need. The girl wouldn't lie."

"Oh no?"

"Keep quiet," said d'Ortega. "I'm thinking."

He thought about the time when Kiamoto's boat must have slipped out of the harbor—ebb tide during the night, most likely, since they hadn't heard the motor—and when the boat had come back. Port hadn't taken her out, because d'Ortega was sure he couldn't have managed it. Not the way he had maneuvered around coming back. And besides, would he know where to go in the night? D'Ortega didn't think that Port knew the waters, or the coast, well enough.

Kiamoto had done all that. And the way Maria had sounded, shouting at them that Kiamoto was safe, Kiamoto had gotten off, leaving the boat to them.

Then there was Briggs and Sanchez. D'Ortega wasn't too clear about this, but they had come in the motor boat—maybe Port and the girl had come that way too—and then had found the fishing boat and Kiamoto gone. Something like that.

Where had Kiamoto left the boat?

D'Ortega turned back to Pepe.

"Wake him up," he said to Capo.

Capo kicked Pepe in the side of the ribs.

"I don't like the way he is," said Capo. "I've seen it before. He hardly feels anything."

"Maybe he just doesn't tell you," said d'Ortega.

He felt vicious. He looked at the wreck cowering on the floor and his dislike for the man was like an itch. How much longer this closeness to this bug of a man? And how much longer Capo, for that matter?

But for one million in cash, American money, it was possible to use them for a while.

He stood over Pepe and let the bottle hang by the neck. "Kiamoto left with his boat last night. You hear me, Pepe?"

"Yes."

"And maybe he never was in that jungle, at that ruin where you dragged us yesterday."

"He was there. Before we came to it he was there."

"We found the leaves he had torn off for the girl, don't you remember, d'Ortega?" said Capo.

"Shut your mouth." Then d'Ortega talked to Pepe again. "And maybe, when you led us through that swamp, Pepe, maybe you did that to give him time to escape, eh, Pepe?"

"He did that to me," said Capo. "He did that to drown me," and he kicked at the old man again.

Pepe felt it, but the way d'Ortega had put it, he didn't tell anyone. He didn't yell, or groan, or tell anyone because he no longer cared. The last time he had cared about anything had been in the swamp. It had been a brief luxury and it hadn't worked, but at first, crossing into the swamp below the ruin, he had only thought how he hated that Capo. An Indian like himself, but so bad.

Pepe had taken them across the mat of roots, with the soft ground and water underneath, and he had jumped very cleverly. And Capo, the heaviest one, had fallen through. D'Ortega had been wet to the knees, ruining his suit, but only Capo had fallen through, stuck up to the chest.

But d'Ortega had forced him to help Capo out. He had stood there with a gun. Later, he had stood there with the gun while Capo had beaten him. It had been so bad that Pepe hadn't cared after that.

"I'm just reminding you," d'Ortega was saying, "so you remember what happened then."

"He remembers, all right," said Capo.

"So don't play any more tricks," d'Ortega finished.

All the threats and the kicking, all the useless things they were doing, thought Pepe. Why? I have never lied. I have always answered. And they, always insulting him and his truthfulness. Only the pulque helped. It was a strange thing how one and the same man, this d'Ortega, could be so evil and then so kind. He always gave him the pulque.

"I am hot and dry," said Pepe.

D'Ortega gave him the bottle.

"How far can a fishing boat go," asked d'Ortega, "which is gone for maybe ten hours?"

It could go far away from Guanadera, straight out into the ocean where the waves became smooth and deep and—

"Pepe!"

"Ah," he said. "Far."

"Listen to it this way," said d'Ortega. "You take the boat out in the middle of the night and you get there at daybreak. Where is that?"

"It could be up the coast, if you knew where to stay away from the rocks, or it could be down the coast, if you knew where the jungle water ran down into the ocean and the mud fish would bite anything. If only they tasted better—"

Capo tore the bottle out of his hand, spilling some pulque.

"You go up the coast until morning," said d'Ortega, "and you get where?"

Pepe tried to talk but he had a cramp in his throat. Then Capo gave him the bottle back.

"The rocks are steep there," said Pepe. "I couldn't land there."

"If you land there, where could you go?"

"You could die on the rocks before going anywhere. And after the rocks is nothing."

"What town is there? Where do the roads go?"

"No town. It takes all day to the next town, with a motor. With a sail, I once tried it. The trip is useless. I was dry like old wood in the sun and the deep water was smiling at me, telling me to kill myself quickly—"

He was remembering a thing that happened years ago, maybe twenty years ago, when he only drank pulque on Saturday night and worked his boat all week. D'Ortega was not interested in that. He spat into his hand and rubbed the spit on a stain which he had discovered on the sleeve of his suit.

"Fine," he said. "Very good. And now, Pepe, you go down the coast from Guanadera. You leave in the middle of the night..."

"I wouldn't go that way," said Pepe. "They bite good but taste like brown water."

"Take the bottle away from him."

Capo took the bottle away from him and kept slapping the belly of it into the palm of his hand. Each time he made the sound Pepe winced.

"You go down the coast—"

"Nothing is there. I am telling you!"

"Hit him."

"Nothing is there except jungle coming close down to the shore," Pepe said quickly, and then he waited for the hit, but nothing came.

"Give him the bottle."

That Señor d'Ortega was strange, thought Pepe. Such sudden kindness. Why would he want to go down the coast?

"If I land there, in the morning, how long do I have to walk before I get to the road?"

"You would die before you get to the road. There is no road."

"You mean you would die, if you walked there?"

"I? Oh no. I can live in the jungle. I once lived deep in the hill country, where the trees and leaves are matted close, like..."

"How long could you live there?"

"Long? As long as I like." Pepe drank and wiped his nose. His eyes hurt and his nose was itching. "But I would not get anywhere," he said. "You asked me where could I go."

"Yes?"

"Nowhere. There is nowhere to go. Only to get lost. The time I lived in the back hills, the time I was thinking of, that time I was lost. I went nowhere."

Maybe Capo had been right, thought d'Ortega. Maybe it was past the point when the pulque could help. According to all this, Kiamoto would not go up the coast, would not go down the coast, and could only have gone out straight into the west. Perhaps Port took him there and cut him up for the sharks? But for that, why go out for ten hours?

"If I wanted to go to Lupe," the old man said suddenly, "I'd go past the islands."

Capo started to say something but d'Ortega waved him off. "Lupe? Who's Lupe?"

"The town," said Pepe.

There was a town down the coast, halfway between Guanadera and Ciudad de Miguel, which was called Lupe and had roads leading out of it. One inland, to Ciudad, one south, to the resorts, others—

"What islands, Pepe?"

"I'd go there because of the way the coast curves around. I would therefore go straight out to the west toward the islands. I once did, because of the wind."

"What islands, damn you?"

"They have no name. I take half a day with my boat, because of the wind."

"With a boat that has a motor, Pepe, how long?"

"You said five hours."

"He's not making sense," said Capo. "The way he talks about going to Lupe, he goes around a corner instead of straight."

"Because of the wind," said Pepe. Then he drank.

Then d'Ortega got it. Because of the wind: Pepe was talking of sailing. To sail to Lupe—

"Can you sail from the islands to Lupe?"

"It is the only way."

"Can you sail in the other direction?"

"Against the wind?" said Pepe. "It always blows toward Lupe. Except in the fall."

This wasn't fall. This was where Kiamoto had gone: out to those islands, and from there, under sail, down to Lupe.

"He can be there before night," said Pepe. "I've done it."

"Or maybe he's out there on the islands," said Capo.

If he were, he would be there tomorrow. If he weren't, he would be in and out of Lupe by night.

D'Ortega did not think he would need Pepe much longer. He let him keep the bottle for the whole drive toward Lupe. It wasn't a question of kindness, because d'Ortega was very excited now and thinking of other things, but it kept Pepe from talking nonsense, kept him sitting quietly in his seat, allowing d'Ortega to concentrate.

His plans for Kiamoto needed no further thought. That had all been worked out a long time ago. But now, on the drive down the coast, d'Ortega wanted no distractions. The other two men in the car left him alone and d'Ortega kept watching the water. He did this all afternoon and especially when they came close to Lupe. He watched till his eyes were burning and even while the low sun melted everything into a red haze—the sky, the water, the inside of d'Ortega's head—he watched all that time, with his eyes hot and runny.

Small torture for one million, American. His stomach rolling over inside him was worse, and his heart pounding all the way up in his throat. But then there was relief. At one point d'Ortega yelled. It surprised Capo, and even Pepe looked up. D'Ortega, beside himself, gave that one yell when he saw the boat with the sail bearing down on Lupe. He did not know that it was a ketch, but it was smaller than the fishing boats and it was running before the wind. Behind it, the sun was just going under.

Chapter 14

It took d'Ortega a few hours to figure out that Kiamoto had sailed off from the island. It took Briggs only a minute or so to learn the same thing from Port. But after that Briggs and Port didn't do so well. They knew nothing about the coastline, north and south, they didn't know about the prevailing winds out by the island, and though Port had seen how the wind blew there he didn't know enough to think about it. And even if they had known all that, they didn't know a broad reach from a close tack, and had no notion that Kiamoto might reach the town of Lupe by that same evening.

"How big a boat was it?" Briggs wanted to know.

"How long is your motor boat?" Port asked.

"Twenty feet, I think."

"That ketch was bigger. Maybe twenty-five."

"Ketch?"

"That's the sailboat. One mast, pretty well in line with the beam, a sail with a stick on top—"

"Gaff."

"All right. Gaff. And a jib in the front."

"You don't know a thing like a gaff, how come you know the boat was a ketch?"

"From the dictionary. When I was a kid I used to..."

"Never mind," said Briggs. "We're out of our depth."

Then they went for help. They sent Maria home, to rest, and Sanchez to go with her and see that she would not be disturbed, and then Briggs and Port went to the icehouse. It had the only phone in Guanadera.

Briggs called the embassy in Mexico City and explained to Jack that he should find a map, a marine map which covered the coastal stretch around Guanadera, so they could get a picture of things. There wasn't a marine map anywhere in the embassy, but there was a nice topographic map which Jack found in a travel book. According to that source there were no tourist attractions or even roads anywhere up or down the coast, that is to say, not till Lupe.

"What's Lupe?" Briggs yelled into the phone. He had to do this to get through the static.

"A town," yelled Jack.

"Around? Around where, and who?"

"T-o-w-n."

Then Briggs understood what was meant by Lupe, but he had his doubts about the map information. Next Jack suggested he ask Major Gimbel, who was military attaché at the embassy and had once made a study of the country's west coast. "When there was this question of Jap submarine landings, you remember, that's when Major Gimbel ..."

"Just ask him," yelled Briggs. "About roads and so forth."

When Jack came back he said, "Submarine approaches to the coast around Guanadera impractical. There are numerous ..."

"Never mind that! How about a ketch?"

"You mean fish? What kind of catch? I didn't ask him about that."

"Oh sainted patience," murmured Briggs. "Abandon me not."

"I can't hear you," Jack shouted.

In a while the two got together again and there was more information from Major Gimbel.

"Survival possibilities in the jungle are fair, if troops are equipped with water purification tablets, army standard manual on edible plants in the tropical zone of the Western..."

"Never MIND," said Briggs. "Are there roads? R-O-A-D-S!"

"One road down the Guanadera coast. I told you that when I checked this little map in the travel..."

"What does Gimbel say?"

"Lousy road," he said. "There is no place to go, therefore no good road."

"What I need to know, Jack— Are you there?"

"No. But Gimbel has been there, on this survival research, and if you don't waste your energy trying to cut yourself out of that jungle, he says, then you can maintain your weight pretty good on these certain worms you find there, an edible toad which abounds..."

"Jack? J-A-C-K!"

"Yes?"

"Can you land there and walk to civilization, away from Guanadera, that is?"

"No."

"Ahh—" said Briggs, and sank back in his chair.

Jack started explaining again but Briggs interrupted him, loud but controlled, saying he did not want to hear any more about the toads.

It seemed improbable that Kiamoto would land anywhere except maybe in Lupe, and if Briggs had asked any one of the icehouse laborers who were outside of the office, he could have learned the same thing in a matter of minutes.

"About the marine map," Jack was saying, "Major Gimbel suggests you call Ciudad de Miguel where..."

"They are fifty miles inland!"

"Yes. But they have a good telephone exchange and you should be able to hear them much better than Lupe. You should call Ciudad and ask the operator to inquire in Lupe, harbor master in Lupe, and if they can get you connected with Atlantis."

Briggs heard all this but, no longer trusting his ears, he waited a second or two before shouting back. "Atlantis? Do you mean the lost continent of Atlantis? Are you and I, Jack, still talking about the same thing?"

"*Atlantis*. Name of the geodetic survey ship which is right now anchored off Lupe. They should be able to tell you just about anything you care to hear about the global sector from latitude..."

"I need that," said Briggs and hung up.

Port watched Briggs sit for a while and then he offered him a cigarette. "Doing any good?"

"Shut up," said Briggs.

Port kept still because it was all right with him if Briggs sat around and didn't find Kiamoto. Port thought Kiamoto would be safer that way.

"What's geodetic?" Briggs asked suddenly.

"Measuring the surface of the earth," said Port. "Shape and size of it."

"Huh?"

"From the dictionary," said Port. "When I was a kid ..."

"Just shut up," said Briggs.

But at any rate, thought Briggs, it's a geodetic boat. They must know something about the water out here and where a ketch might go.

They had, as a matter of fact, an amazing amount of information. The telephone connection to the *Atlantis*, including a ship-to-shore relay, was surprisingly good, but the discussion took just as long as the talk with Jack had.

Briggs learned a lot about the contours of the ocean bed, distribution of silt versus rock, permanent currents, seasonal currents, and water temperature data. When he managed to clarify that he wanted to know how long a ketch would take from there to the next town up or down the coast, the oceanographer at the other end of the line thought a moment, excused himself, left the phone to walk down to the galley.

There was a young Mexican there, washing pots, and the oceanographer said, "Isn't your father a fisherman, Luis?"

"And so am I, Señor. And when I'm fifteen my father will give me my own boat."

"That's wonderful, Luis. Uh, what I meant to ask you, do you know those small islands off Guanadera?"

"Oh, yes. They are very hard to get to."

"Really?" The oceanographer thought of his charts and remembered for certain that there was no adverse current preventing good passage from Lupe to the islands. "Why do you say that, Luis? Even an outboard motor should have no..."

"I sail, Señor. I don't have a motor."

"Oh. That's a shame, Luis."

"And the wind is always in the other direction."

"I see," said the oceanographer. "Ah— I see," and he went back to the ship-to-shore phone.

So it was an hour after he had started his call that Briggs found out there was only one sensible course for a ketch which was leaving the islands: to the bay of Lupe. Any other way would mean sailing into the wind, sailing back to Guanadera, or sailing five thousand miles across the Pacific.

If Briggs had asked one of the fishermen who were sitting outside of the icehouse, he would learned the same thing in a matter of minutes.

Briggs hung up, sat a while, then asked Port for another cigarette.

"And now I'm going to ask you something," he said to Port. "What makes you think this Kiamoto isn't holed up on one of those islands?"

"Think?" said Port. "You're the one who's doing the thinking."

Briggs looked at Port with dislike but didn't say anything. When the icehouse foreman came back into the office, Briggs got up from the chair, put his cigarette out, and said, "Anyway, to sail from those islands out there back to civilization, not counting here, is going to take days. We're taking a trip out there."

"The deserted ones?" asked the foreman.

"Yeah. Out that way."

"It is a pleasant trip. And from there you can make Lupe in half a day. Even with nothing but sail."

Briggs stared. Even this information he could have gotten hours ago. He waved at Port to come on and then ran out of the icehouse.

Chapter 15

Maria was up, with her hair combed and wearing a fresh dress, and Sanchez was eating a rice soup she had made. The sight was calm and domestic, but then it broke up.

"He's going to hit Lupe tonight," said Briggs.

"This night, you mean?" Sanchez put his spoon down.

"We can make it, if we drive like hell."

"How did you figure that out so fast?"

"Don't ask," said Briggs. "And stop eating. We got to go."

Sanchez got up and Briggs waited for him at the door. But Port hadn't moved.

"One of us stays behind," he said. "I'm not leaving Maria alone."

"Don't be an idiot, Port." Briggs was shouting again. "If I know d'Ortega, he knows the same thing we do, only he knew it sooner, and nobody's going to bother the girl. "

"I'm not taking that chance," said Port. "I have no idea where d'Ortega is and what he's doing."

"He's after Kiamoto," Briggs yelled. "Don't you know that by now?"

"All I know is he's a lawyer for Pan-Continental and he once beat up Maria."

"Listen to me, Port. He's not after the girl, he's after the money. D'Ortega is a lawyer for Pan-Continental all right, but on a contingent basis. He gets a percentage for what he delivers. Now how much of that money he's after do you think he's going to deliver, huh? He's a crook, with a crook for a partner. He's not going to..."

"Let Sanchez stay here, if you want me along."

"You're damn right I want you along, bucko! And I want Sanchez along because I don't trust you alone with me, seeing I expect to be very busy. Now move, Port."

"If the girl stays, I stay."

"You forgetting I can tie you up in jail for a very long time?"

"Not without some time and effort," said Port. "And you're in a hurry."

They took Maria along. It was not what Port had wanted, but it was better than leaving her.

The trip was hot and rough. They first had to drive inland, where the highway was cut through the jungle. Then when they reached higher ground, like a rocky plateau with short, scrubby growth, the road angled back toward the ocean. They could see it glisten, now and then, but they were still far from Lupe.

"Did you call ahead?" Sanchez asked.

Briggs started to curse heavily. In his haste he had forgotten that. The road passed two or three villages, but not the kind which had telephones. Briggs made a detour at one point, away from Lupe, so he could reach a settlement where a railroad went through and the station had a telegraph line. While Briggs ran into the office, the rest stood by a pump and ran water over their wrists. It was late afternoon and the country was boiling. Then Briggs came back.

"You reach anybody?" asked Sanchez.

"Yeah. Come on, let's get in the car."

In the car, when they were driving again, Briggs said that he had reached Lupe and the police there would watch for a ketch.

"They said they already knew about it and I shouldn't worry."

"What's that?" said Sanchez.

"They got the same request a few hours ago. I shouldn't worry, they said, they've been watching ever since."

"D'Ortega?"

"Who else?" said Briggs.

The dust blew into the open windows with the hot air. It bit their eyes and itched on their skin. It turned into warm mud and kept their sweat from running. "Did you explain to them they should ignore..."

"How could I, by wire? They don't know me from Adam." Briggs was hoarse, coughing the grit in his throat. He wiped the back of his neck and then wiped his wet hand over his face. It gave him a moment of coolness.

"A phone would have been better," said Port. He felt nasty. "It's so much easier, isn't it, Briggs, to pass information by phone."

Briggs was driving and he had a mind to run into the ditch intentionally. Kill everybody.

Nobody talked and it seemed to make the heat worse. Port sat in back with Maria and they kept far apart. They sat carefully on the edge of the seat, because the upholstery felt like hot nettles.

When they came to the road leading to Lupe, they could see the Pacific all the time. It looked like soft pitch to them, with sharp flecks of gold on it. Then the flecks turned red, because the sun was setting.

"It'll be dark when we get there," said Sanchez.

The thought of the dark, without sun, could have been good, except by now they all hated each other. They hated the sound of each other's voices and Port, sitting in back, hated the sight of the necks in front. Sanchez's black hair had formed wet licks, like soaked feathers, and the short stubble on Brigg's head was a dark, matted cap. Maria had turned to the window, but she could not lean out because the metal was hot.

The sudden dark was no pleasure. Briggs did not slow down the car, their sweat dried now and itched like insects on the skin, and Lupe was a string of lights along the black water. Unless the police had seen the ketch, they would not find the boat until morning. If then. And if they did, would Kiamoto wait, even if d'Ortega hadn't gotten there first?

If Briggs had thought that racing through town would attract a policeman, he was wrong, and he went fast enough so that in a short while he was leaving Lupe on the other side. They turned back and found the police station, a fine stucco building which reminded you of a church. They stopped in front of it and a policeman got off the steps. He came over to the car, smiled warmly, and asked if anyone was drunk.

"Where's the commandant?" Briggs asked him. He jumped out of the car and asked it again.

"You won't need the commandant," said the policeman. "I can take you inside. Come," he said and took Briggs's arm. "It is nice and cool inside."

Port let out a guffaw and Briggs spun around, looking like murder.

But to do what he had in mind, to do anything now, would make everything worse. It would convince the policeman that this drunk was also dangerous, and Briggs would spend part of his mission in jail.

With the smiling policeman steering his arm, he went into the station. There was a uniformed man at a desk, large book open, pencil poised.

"My name's Briggs. I called in the afternoon about the ketch coming in."

"He's drunk," said the policeman who was holding his arm. "But nice about it."

"Listen to me," Briggs bellowed. "I telegraphed that I was coming...."

He could see the entry in the book, a slow, careful hand, first his name, then the word drunk.

It was a good thing Sanchez came in. Sanchez spoke in a normal voice, but with an official edge to the sound, and he produced his credentials. They were Mexican, from a main bureau, and the policemen were impressed. They nodded and agreed that Lieutenant Sanchez should by all means keep his important prisoner. And, "Yes," said the one with the book, "we showed your other gentleman where we saw this boat."

"Where?" said Briggs, and "When?" asked Sanchez.

"It came in with a very fine wind— It dies down after dark, but you should have seen..."

"When?"

"A while ago, when the sun was just..."

"Two hours!" said Briggs. "Dammit to hell."

"But it was another hour until she made land."

"Where?"

"Not the harbor. We have a very adequate harbor, but the boat ..."

"Say it!" Briggs shouted. "Where?"

"There is a low spit of land, as you leave this way," the policeman pointed to the side of the harbor, "and one of our force," he said, "took your other gentleman there."

"Who?" said Sanchez.

"The *other* one," said Briggs. "Don't you remember, Lieutenant?"

Sanchez nodded. He looked calm and official, but he was sweating again.

"Can we find that land tongue by driving along the harbor and turning right, toward the water, where the installations end?"

"That is one way," said the one with the book. "The best way is to follow the highway out and when you come to the old mission ..."

"It has no roof," said the other one.

"There you turn toward the water. The road will take your car."

"It is the dry season," said the other one.

They had not seen d'Ortega since, and they had not watched or been there when d'Ortega had gone out to the boat.

Briggs and Sanchez ran back to the car.

"When you left Kiamoto," Briggs asked Port, "out there on that beach, did you give back his gun to him?" Briggs was driving fast again.

"No," said Port. "I've got it right here in my pocket."

"Damn it all from cotton pickin' hell to cotton pickin' heaven," Briggs said.

"I shot at you with it," Port added, "Don't you remember?"

Briggs just cursed and drove faster. Then Port got the sense of the question, and he too felt the pressure now, about being late.

"And I don't think," he said, "Kiamoto had another one."

They turned at the ruined mission building and ran the car down a road with two ruts. The grass between the two ruts kept whisking the underside of the car with a rattle like paper. They met no one. The moon was up now and Briggs turned off the lights. It slowed him for a moment but then they could see far, the gray, scrubby land flattening down toward the water and the Pacific lying still on all sides.

"Tide's out," said Sanchez.

"Down there. Half right," said Port. "See it?"

They all saw the boat. It lay on the wet flats and the stubby keel kept the boat at an angle. The boat's belly looked like a big egg in the moonlight. The boom had swung out and was stuck in the sand. The sail was lowered but there had been no time to furl it. It was a limp pile on the deck. Some of it had slipped down to the sand.

Briggs slowed and it was very quiet. Sanchez looked at his hands, which were in the dark, making small, clicking noises. He was checking his gun.

They stopped the car and Briggs opened the door. They all stood on the hard road and looked down where the boat was lying in the faint light. The odor of kelp was all over and something flopped on the flats. There were no other sounds, with the water way out, except a small smack now and then and a wet flop.

"You have your gun," Briggs whispered. He stood close to Port. "You can stay here with the girl."

"It looks as if it's over," said Port, and looked at the boat leaning there, rolled to one side as if it were dead. The moon made a shine on the belly.

Then there was a terrible scream.

It screamed like a beast and wouldn't stop, and it kept on till they were half way to the boat, running across the wet flats. When it stopped suddenly they all slowed down, as if the scream had been their propellant. Without that sharp sound pushing them, they felt suddenly wary. Somebody moved a little, making a squishing sound with his foot.

"All right," said Briggs. "Keep apart." Then he ran ahead.

They went over the low side of the boat and it teetered a little. Briggs slipped on the wet deck, cursing, and Port gave him a push.

The deck was a mess of lines, but otherwise empty, and the cabin door hung open, showing blackness inside.

Briggs and Sanchez went in. They had a flashlight. Port saw the beam go on inside the cabin, and then the screams started again.

Port held Maria around the shoulders and kept her outside. She stood by the leaning boat and he crouched on the deck, listening.

Something scuffled inside the cabin—or perhaps it was awkward footsteps, because of the tilt in the boat—and then the screams, sliding a little bit, became laughter.

Sanchez stuck his head out of the door. "They're gone," he said. "But there's a crazy man in here."

"Drunk?"

"Maybe that too. Small and wrinkled—"

"Pepe," said Port, and moved up the deck.

Briggs had the small man in the flashlight's beam. The sight was wild; the cabin stood on edge, a bolted table stood at a fixed angle, the floor was no longer a floor and the wall, meeting it, formed an angle where blankets, pots, and cans of food made a lumpy pile which had climbed up under the bunk.

Pepe stood in that angle holding a kitchen knife. He was still laughing—what had sounded like laughing—except now, with the sight of him, the sound made no sense. His swollen lip had cracked open, there was a scratch down his throat, and his eyes were rolling around in a useless way.

"Put the beam down," said Port, "so he can see you."

"You hold it," said Briggs. "I'll put on the lamp."

There was an oil lamp hanging from the ceiling. It was the only thing upright in the cabin, and it looked out of place. When the lamp was lit Port cut the beam.

"It's me," said Port. "You remember me, Pepe?"

Pepe wasn't looking at Port. He looked down at his feet, squeezed himself back as far as he could, and then started to jab his foot into the litter. He kicked and stomped and spat down at his feet. The effort made him groan. Then he screamed a few times, and each time hacked the knife into the cans at his feet. They jumped and spun and one of them started oozing soup.

Pepe dropped the knife when he cut himself, and covered his eyes. Balancing on floor and wall, Port went to him, took the knife, tried to raise Pepe's head by the chin. Pepe didn't move.

"You know him?" said Briggs.

"He brought d'Ortega down here, I think."

Briggs pushed Port out of the way, crouched down in front of Pepe, and talked into his face from close up.

"When did they leave? You saw Kiamoto? He went with the others? Pepe! Open your lousy mouth!"

When Briggs shook the man, Pepe gave a gasp.

"Wait," said Port. "He's hurt somewhere."

Under his shirt they saw where the ribs were broken. A thick, dark swelling covered the edges, but the ribs were cracked and were bent too much.

"Jeesis—how's he stand it—"

"Pulque," said Port.

And then, as if he were in no pain at all, Pepe started to bellow again. He had seen Maria. She climbed into the cabin with Sanchez helping her and the closer she came to Pepe—one hand out and saying things to calm the old man—the more he acted like an animal.

"Get her the hell out of here," said Briggs. "I've got to talk to this man."

Port got her out. He told her how they had made Pepe sick with the puique and now that he didn't have any, he was getting sicker.

"But we've got to help him—" She kept saying this while they stood on the crazy deck, and Port tried to explain how it was hard to move a man in his shape. "And his ribs are broken. If he twists around too much, wild like this—"

Inside the cabin, Briggs wasn't getting anywhere. Port and Maria could hear him and Pepe, who kept saying that Maria's face would heal soon if he could get the right leaves.

"The D.T.'s," Briggs was saying. "How in hell am I going to get him to talk?"

"Briggs," Port called from the door.

Briggs stuck his head out, breathing fresh air.

"The way he is," said Port, "we can't move him. We got to get him more poison."

"Pulque?"

"I can't think of any other way."

They sent Sanchez off with the car and kept Maria outside the cabin. Pepe was sitting now, shivering.

"Was she my own?" he was saying. "She was never my own. That's how I forgot about the leaves and the juice. Why can't she understand that, coming in here, pointing her finger, looking the way she does—"

"Maria's going to help you," said Port. "She's well now and is going to help you, Pepe. Sit still."

"He'll puncture his lousy lung," Briggs was saying. "If I didn't need him to talk, so help me, I'd knock him in the head."

"Oh?" said Pepe. "Oh. That again. No matter. I don't hurt any more. No matter. I only hurt when I laugh. Then why laugh? Ah!" and he pointed at nothing. "Did I laugh when they got him here—"

"I'm going straight out of my mind," said Briggs. "Shut up. He's telling us."

"—laugh because they thought he'd do nothing because they were two. First one, wham!" and Pepe slammed down his hand, "then two, crack!" he did it again.

"D'Ortega and Capo?" Port asked.

"But he slipped on the deck, and the sand had saved Capo. Wham. Like you, Señor Port," and Pepe laughed.

"Maybe Kiamoto got away?" Briggs said.

There was a little blood on Pepe's lip and they thought it was from his cut.

"Shot him in the hand. That little one in the white suit, all wet and sandy, he had a gun too. Shot him right through the hand."

"They got Kiamoto?"

"Then, because I laughed, they did this to me. Why laugh?"

Pepe was suddenly quiet and Maria came back into the cabin. Pepe sat with his eyes closed and only his breathing was wrong. It made a sound and then more blood came out of his mouth.

"Pepe," she said, "dear old Pepe," and that made him open his eyes.

He jerked his head away from her hands and screamed obscenities.

"Did I beat you? Did I see them beat you? Did I ask to raise you all these years and still never beat you once—"

"You did, Pepe, you were very kind all that time, Pepe."

"Like a beast," he said. "You ask a beast to walk on hind legs and live in a house in a town, then what? It goes sick. I'm sick. I can tell by the pain which is now outside my head. They are nibbling at me; holy mother, why are they doing this—"

"I hear the car," said Port. "He's back."

Sanchez had brought two bottles. They gave one to Maria so she could give it to Pepe. He didn't take it at first, suspecting her, but she kept holding it out to him so he would catch the smell. When he had taken the bottle from her she went back to the door. She covered her face and breathed hard, as if she were exhausted from crying.

"We're killing him," she said. "You know that, Daniel?"

"You might be right."

Pepe knew how good it would be in a moment, and after two swallows he sat and waited. He spat old blood out of his mouth and then took another swallow.

"Is she all right?" he asked after a while.

"Maria?"

"Is she all right?"

"Yes. She's here."

"I don't want to see her. I just want to know—"

"She's all right. She'll take you home, Pepe."

Then Briggs leaned forward. He was sweating again, even though it was no longer hot.

"Pepe, do you hear me?"

"You have said nothing." Then he blinked at Briggs and said, "You look different. Where is your hair?"

"Did they take Kiamoto?"

"The only reason I laughed," said Pepe, "was because nothing had changed. Close to him, yes. They even had him by the arms. But nothing had changed. Nobody catches Kiamoto. Like me. Same manner of thing. Would you like to hit me?" he said to Briggs. "Hit. Nothing changes." He drank more and seemed sleepy.

"Pepe. When did they leave?"

"After shooting his hand."

Briggs wiped his hand over his face and groaned. "Pepe," said Sanchez. "Where was the sun when they left?"

"Blue."

"What?"

"He means down," said Maria.

"That could have been three hours ago."

"Pepe," Sanchez said again. "When they walked away, did they walk through the water?"

"Splash, splash," and then he made another sound which was exactly like mud sucking a shoe.

Sanchez turned to Briggs and said, "The way it's flat here, the tide would run out very fast. Maybe three feet at high tide, by the marks where the rocks come down, and the tide changed only two hours ago. I'll say one hour. They waded out of here about one hour ago."

"So what?" said Briggs. "So what? What's all this geodetic crap? I got to know *where* they went, understand my problem? Where?" and Briggs sat down on the slanting wall, cursing in a hoarse voice.

Pepe was looking at Maria.

"Can you remember, chiquita, when you cut your knee and I made it good?"

"You did?" she said, and smiled at him to say more.

"I wish you had remembered that," he said. "I so wish you had." Then he drank more.

"Pepe," said Maria. "I remember a lot of lovely things, when you and I..."

"Please," said Briggs. "Just hold it a minute, will you, for chrissakes?"

It was a cruel scene. Port held his lip in his teeth and did not know what to do.

"Pepe," said Briggs. "Where did they go?"

"To the road. Dry, dusty road where the car was steaming."

"And from there, Pepe. Did they say? Did any of them say anything?

"Curses, and Kiamoto very quiet. He and I..."

"What did d'Ortega say?"

It went on like that for a while and Port had his own struggle. Should he help them so they could catch Kiamoto? Or would Kiamoto need no assistance and would sicking Briggs on him only double his problem? And should he let them delay while Pepe was killing himself?

He sat down next to the old man and said, "Where is your serape?"

"For god's sake, Port, will you please refrain from constantly interfering with..."

Port waved his hand at Briggs to shut up.

"Where is it, Pepe?"

"He and I are much the same, do you believe me?"

"I think you're right, Pepe. I do."

"We die, perhaps, but we don't come apart. Pain? Nothing."

"I know. Don't drink any more, Pepe."

"Why not? I just explained to you."

"You're right. I'm sorry."

"He's killing himself," said Maria, and all the men looked at her, knowing she was right. But it was not such a horrible thing, Port said to himself. Not the way Pepe had spoken of it—

"The serape," said the old man, "is now his."

"Kiamoto?"

Pepe nodded. He swilled the pulque around in the bottle but did not drink any more. There was not much left.

"Did Kiamoto ask for it?" Port wanted to know.

"Of course. He and I know it is needed for protection. And I won't need it any more."

He lifted the bottle and let the small amount of liquid run out.

Port stood up. His legs felt cramped and he worked his hands over them. Then he talked to Briggs. "I think Kiamoto is taking them to the money."

"Kiamoto? Just like that?" said Briggs.

Port shrugged. "Perhaps he is not taking them to the money, but I think he told them he would."

"I didn't hear any of this," said Briggs. "I was sitting right here..."

"He asked Pepe to lend him the serape. That's because he will take them into the jungle. The thorns and the flies..."

"Where? He tell you that too?"

"No, but I think it will be back in Guanadera. It's the jungle Kiamoto knows. I don't think it's likely he knows any other parts, but he knows the terrain back of Guanadera as well as one of the Indians does. I don't think Kiamoto will give them the money because his thinking of a little thing like that serape sounds to me as if he means to come back. They wouldn't let him, once they had the cash. And that's another reason why I think he's guiding them back to Guanadera. He can find his way out of those woods, but he might not anywhere else."

There was a moment's silence and then Briggs slapped his legs. "Come on," he said and got up. "We're going back."

He scrambled out of the cabin and Sanchez started to follow him. Port hadn't moved.

"We're not leaving Pepe," he said.

Briggs stopped in the cabinway and turned his head. His face was suddenly thick with blood.

"Get moving, you son of a bitch, or I'll shoot you lame on the spot. You got that clear, Port?"

"We're not leaving him," said Port. "That's all."

"I'm sending help," roared Briggs. "But I'll have no more delays. And not out of you, you two-faced hood, not out of you in particular!"

All the delays and the half starts had piled up on Briggs, and he was giving way under it. He had come back into the cabin, kicking things out of the way, red eyed and sweating hard.

What kept the clash from happening was Pepe. He got up, balanced himself toward the cabin door. He did not act drunk but he was so quiet in everything, it was clear there was a cloud of the poison holding him up.

"Before the creatures come back," he said very reasonably, and he took the full pulque bottle out of Sanchez's hand. Then he cracked the bottle over the edge of the table and did not even watch how the stuff ran down.

"Maria," he said to the girl at the door, "will you remember the time I helped..."

"I remember it! Of course I remember it now, Pepe." She said more, but when he had patted her arm he walked past her and out on the deck.

"All right," said Briggs. "He can move, you can move, Port. Now!"

The two men didn't look at each other when Port passed close. They all went out on the deck, one by one, slid down to the low side of the boat, and stood on the wet sand.

"Where's Pepe?" "I just saw—"

They did not see him right away because the moonlight made more shadows than brightness on the flats and there was water standing in puddles, which distracted the eye. When they saw him they wasted time shouting to him, to come back, this way, drunken bastard, what's gotten into him, Pepe, please come back—

He was running, which was hard to believe considering his condition, but he was running with purpose because they could hear the sound he made when the water got deep.

Because of the light they could not tell if there was blood in the water when they pulled him out, but they thought there might be. Port did not think it mattered. Pepe had meant to die anyway.

Chapter 16

A sense of exhaustion came over them all. The moon became a large, quiet eye, the flats were very quiet, and the ocean made sounds as if too tired for anything else. Maria did not cry very long because everything that was going to happen had happened already and there wouldn't be anything else, either good or bad.

They took Pepe back to the road where they had left the car, and on the way past the ketch they took a blanket and wrapped it around him. The blanket was soggy and smelled. But it was better with the blanket around him, because it turned out Pepe had lost a great deal of blood which the water had washed all over him.

They put him in the trunk of the car and Briggs drove back slowly. He turned his head a few times and asked if everything was all right. Once he asked if he should slow down.

"No," said Maria. "It's all right now. At least, he's not bumping around any more."

Port thought she was too calm, or there was too much hardness with the calm and she was only this quiet to save her strength. Port was glad that they would drop Maria off in Guanadera and that she would not have to see Capo and d'Ortega again.

They had wasted a great deal of time, but if Port's guess about Kiamoto was right then there was no real need to rush. With the strain of the last few days behind them they all wanted to feel this way. They were certain it wouldn't be long now before it was over. They would get the three men in the car ahead of them, and they might as well save their strength for that. It would happen. Nothing worse could happen.

They left the body in Lupe, with the police, and Port arranged for it to get back to Guanadera in a good coffin. Then they went to a cantina and ate something hot.

Briggs had mostly coffee.

"I'm sorry about back there in the boat," he said to Port.

Somebody else's death makes everybody mellow, thought Port.

"We can forget it now, Briggs," Port said.

"And if you want a good night's rest," Briggs said to Maria, "I can set it up for you to sleep here in Lupe and tomorrow..."

"I want to go back to Guanadera," she said. "I don't want to wait."

It struck Port that she hadn't said she wanted to go home. It would have been simpler and more to the point. Unless that hadn't been her point.

"Well," said Briggs. "What do you say we go—"

They went back to the car. Sanchez drove.

They drove back the same way they had come but the trip was different. Something had gone out of it and nothing was added. Perhaps their tiredness did it. Time was no longer important and the landmarks seemed changed. There would now be nothing between here and Guanadera, and to Port it was almost like going home.

Briggs slept in the front seat and Maria was curled up in her corner. Port did not think she was asleep. Her stillness seemed wakeful. Port asked Sanchez for a match, lit his cigarette, passed the box back to Sanchez, who was humming something and kept his head to the front.

"If you're tired," said Port, "I'll take it for a while."

"No, thank you. I'm all right."

"You sound tired. Let me know when you're ready."

Sanchez didn't answer but just nodded, and then Port closed his eyes. He had stayed that way for a while when Sanchez said, "Looks like a wreck."

Briggs kept sleeping.

"Where?" said Port. Maria sat up and looked too.

"There's a bend here. I lost it for a moment. We should..."

"I see it," said Port.

There was a black car farther ahead, leaning where the road dipped toward the ditch, and one door was open. Perhaps it was sprung.

"Is it burning?" said Sanchez. "Did you see the smoke?"

"Steam," said Port. "I think it's steam."

They slowed when they came closer, and they saw the white steam pour out of the hood. The hood was not all the way open, which made the steam boil out of the seams and pushed clouds of it under the car.

"I think I'll stop," said Sanchez.

"You see anyone?"

"No. Maybe he's walking ahead."

"Didn't Pepe say their car was steaming?"

Briggs woke up when the car stopped moving and Sanchez explained why they were here.

"Chance to stretch the legs, anyway," said Briggs.

Then they all got out.

There was nobody in the car. Once Sanchez called into the dark but got no answer.

"Might have been standing here a while now," said Briggs.

Port was at the hood and flipped it open. The metal was very hot.

"I don't think so," he said. "The steam is still thick."

It billowed out when the hood was up and there was a strong, hissing jet of it pushing out of the radiator. The cap was still on.

"Let it boil," said Briggs and walked back to the car.

Maria came back and said, "I think there is blood on the seat there."

Nobody said anything for a moment. It wasn't alone what Maria had said, but the cold way she had said it. Then they all moved.

Sanchez ducked to his driver's seat and cut off the lights. Briggs ran to the steaming car and was yanking his flashlight out of his pocket. Port drew Maria away, so they stood in the open door of their own car.

There was just the invisible hiss from the steam now and then the brief flash of Briggs's light. He cut the light immediately and they heard him come back.

"It *is* blood."

"Fresh?" asked Sanchez.

"Sticky."

"Kiamoto's hand had a bullet through it."

They didn't move. They all waited for Briggs to decide. "You go right," he said to Sanchez, "and I cut through here. Don't use a light any more."

"Wait," said Port. "They wouldn't be forcing their way up this rock slope, not with Kiamoto to push along. If they're near, they're likelier down that way, toward the ocean."

The Pacific was not far from the road. It was black except for the silver flashes where the moon was reflected.

Briggs crossed the road and told Sanchez to stay. In a short while they couldn't see Briggs any more but could hear the crackle where he went through the brush.

"Can you hear me?" he called back.

"Yes," said Sanchez.

"Come on this way. There's a stretch of big rocks by the beach. Better give me a hand."

If somebody was down there, hiding, he would have heard Briggs, but Briggs figured it would not be important. If somebody was down there, he would know by now anyway that he was being followed.

Sanchez left the road and made little noises when he walked through the dark.

The steam had died down. It rumbled inside the machine and sounded thin and hot now.

They heard Sanchez say, "Where are you?"

Briggs gave a brief flash with his light and perhaps he also said something, though Port didn't hear it. But he heard the shot belt out and then the smack of the slug not very far away.

Briggs must have been holding his gun cocked and ready because he answered immediately, twice, three times, with the muzzle fire hidden from Port's view.

Port had seen the other gun flash where Briggs had said the rocks were on the beach.

Then Sanchez fired too. Port could hear the two men running.

"Come on," said Maria. She sounded hoarse. "Come on! They must be near, Daniel," and she ran away from him, across the road.

She ran toward the sounds of feet on pebbles and the new shots.

"Maria! Damn it, come back here." But she didn't hear him or didn't want to.

Port wasn't sure what had gotten into her, but he knew she had changed. He had no time to think about it but ran into the dark, trying to find her. Maybe she wants to see Kiamoto saved. Maybe she wants to see somebody killed—

He caught up with her where the rocks started. They looked black and ugly in the night light and farther down by the water they glistened. This was not really a beach; it was a wild field of rocks. The water line swung away opposite where a low neck of land reached far into the water.

They had stopped firing. They had flushed each other out with the shots and now they were running. Port saw two figures close to the water where the stones were not so big; a small man, yelling and cursing—that was d'Ortega—and a big, lumpy shape. Capo? It was Capo carrying a man, carrying Kiamoto most likely. Was Kiamato dead, badly hurt? Capo must be strong as a bull.

Briggs and Sanchez were coming at them from two angles. They kept the two others close to the water and when d'Ortega came to the neck reaching out into the water he could only run there.

Maria didn't watch very long. She saw where the men were heading and raced over the stones like a goat. She caught up with Briggs and Sanchez when the two men came to the neck. There was no time for Port to argue with her. He had his gun out and ran along.

The neck reached far out and then split, like a forked tongue. One end was low to the water and curved away, the other was a steep pole of rock. Capo, because of his burden, ran where it was easiest. They could see him and his lump as if he were running on water.

When the four came to the split d'Ortega turned and fired, making them stop.

"We're higher than he. He can see us plainly." Briggs waved them back.

"The rock," said Sanchez. "I think we can cover them there."

"No!" Port yelled. "Don't! Not the tongue. We can—"

But nobody listened. D'Ortega fired again and the ricochet sang past their knees. They ran down the tongue where the rock lifted out of the water and Port had to follow.

They lay high up and could see the other tongue curve away. There were three shapes on it. They had gone as far as they could.

"Got them bottled," said Briggs. "Look at them," and he started to laugh. "With their cotton pickin' backs to the sea."

"It's lousy," said Port. "The way it is now...."

"You don't like it?"

"He said so when we started up here," said Sanchez. "Why did you?"

Port safetied his gun and stuck it back in his pocket. Then he said, "Can you reach them from here with your fire?"

Briggs squinted down to the end of the low tongue. Then he looked at his rock going steep down to the water.

"No," he said: "Their tip and this one are too far apart. But they can't leave! I can pepper the fork, where the tongues come apart. Notice that?"

"They can do the same thing to us, Briggs. You notice that, don't you?"

Chapter 17

They sat still, as if it were the end of the world, with their guns which didn't reach. This kept them apart and safe. Now and then Port could hear d'Ortega and Capo talking, brief things which he couldn't catch, and then one of them lay down for a while and then they changed, with the other one sleeping. Kiamoto sat. He didn't move or talk, but he seemed to be alive.

On the rock, nothing happened either. Briggs stretched out for a while, but it wasn't comfortable. Then he sat next to Port and smoked a cigarette. Then Sanchez lay down. He took his gun and his knife out and put them on the rock because they poked into him when he lay on his side. Only Maria seemed awake without any discomfort. She said no when Port asked her if she wanted to rest and after a while she moved away, to a spot where the rock went down. She sat there and did nothing.

Port let her be. He did not think there was anything he could say to her now that she would listen to. Maybe later. Maybe in the morning. She wanted her distance, and perhaps she needed it.

Briggs crawled down toward the fork, but not too far, and cowered there with his gun. Sanchez was sleeping.

Then Port realized he had slept too.

"...you take it?" he heard and somebody was shaking his arm, so that his head hit the rock a few times.

"Port, you hear me?" said Sanchez.

Port jumped up, the sudden wakefulness like a pain.

"My knife!"

"Was next to you," said Briggs. He had crawled back up to the top.

Port didn't answer them. He looked around and seemed to know where the knife was before he was able to focus.

"Where's Maria?"

She was not where she had been sitting before and she wasn't anyplace else where they looked.

"She didn't pass me," said Briggs. "Not down this way."

They looked across to the other spit of land but all they saw was the three figures. One of them stood up—Capo. He was trying to listen to the talk from the rock.

The waves were uneven and sparkled a little because of the moon. The water made a moving impression with nothing to focus on.

"See her?" Briggs was whispering now.

"No. But the best we can do is shut up so he stops looking this way," Port said.

They said nothing else about it. They were sure that Maria was in the water.

"I'm going to draw fire," said Port. "I'm going down to the fork."

They didn't argue. They watched him go and Briggs went down with him part of the way.

If he sits down again now, thought Maria, I'll swim closer. If they stop talking up on the rock, worrying about their knife, then he'll walk back again and watch Kiamoto.

Then I go closer. Then I kill him in the back. In the throat, maybe— She kept very low in the water, feeling how cold it was down by her feet. She had the knife in her mouth and only worried that the water, which slapped into her now and then might make her cough.

Or perhaps, she thought, I swim toward Kiamoto. He sits closer to the water. I cut his hands free and give him the knife into his hands— But that way,

I would not be the one who did this. Then Kiamoto would have to do it for me. The way Pepe was left all alone— But he isn't like Pepe, like Pepe was. Only their age is close—No. More. He is like Pepe could have been. Then she swam again, because Capo had turned away and was walking a few steps before sitting down. He sat down with his back to her, facing Kiamoto, who was at the end of the spit.

If she's killed herself, Port thought. If she drowned—

He saw nothing, heard nothing, and he filled all that blankness with the worst he could think of. He held the gun very tightly, as if that would make the gun stronger. He was almost down at the fork, where the rock wouldn't hide him any more. He would walk straight so he could be seen—

A curse, more like fright than anger, and then her screaming. Port ran.

He could see two, rolling on the sand, and the other one, d'Ortega, up now and shooting immediately. Kiamoto sat.

With the second shot d'Ortega knew what he was aiming at. The bullet kicked up sand close enough so that Port got stung by the spray.

"Come closer," d'Ortega yelled. "Try and come closer!" When Port moved d'Ortega yelled again. "And I kill the girl now!"

When the east turned gray and then bright blue it was still the same. They could see each other now over the safe distance, and nothing moved. Port was on the rock between the two men because they didn't trust him. He held his gun, which was useless, and he didn't move except for his breathing. He could have been running, the way he breathed.

They hadn't tied Maria up, because they didn't have any rope. She looked cold in her wet dress. They had ropes on Kiamoto, a clever job. They had his wrists, his ankles, and they had him around the neck. That way Kiamoto say very still and he seemed to be sleeping. Port remembered that the old man couldn't have had any sleep for over two days.

And they sat.

The sun came up and got hot and the tide came in, making the sand spit smaller and climbing up the side of the rock. A wind blew in from the water and after a while the salt dried their lips and the sun dried into them and made them crack.

"If you can't think of anything better than sitting here," said Port, "let me rush them."

"Let them go off their rockers first," said Briggs. And then, "Maybe the tide's going to get them."

"It's as high as it'll go."

Nothing. They could think of nothing. They could not move across the fork unless they wanted to get shot, and if it came into d'Ortega's head that they shouldn't move at all, not even a finger, he might have managed that too by holding his gun to Maria's head.

But he didn't think of it. He was going frantic with the sun biting into him and the shrinking sand, and the only reason he didn't show it was because he was going crazy with something else. One million, American, and so close, so close— He walked to the edge of the water where he faced the mainland. He walked around there like a caged beast, like a thin-legged ocelot moving back and forth at the bars, smelling the other side.

"In a pinch," said Sanchez, "they could swim it."

"Then they couldn't shoot and we'd make it to the beach before they do."

"I tell you what I'm going to do," Port said, and Briggs told him to shut up.

Port shut up because he had no clear idea what he wanted to do. He had no thoughts at all, just a million pressures. He watched d'Ortega, pacing back and forth near the water, and knew how the man felt.

D'Ortega went over to Capo and they could see that the two men were talking. The words didn't carry enough and their eyes told nothing. Maria sat, Kiamoto sat, Capo sat, d'Ortega was standing.

"But I can't swim!" Capo shouted. "I told you!"

D'Ortega said more and Capo shook his head. They could hear Capo again a few times, but only obscenities. D'Ortega looked at his watch, paced, then sat down. Every so often he looked at the sun.

"I think they're going to sit it out till the tide goes down. Maybe then they can walk it."

Maybe. Meanwhile nothing.

Once Sanchez went down to the fork and got shot at very accurately. The bullet tore through his pants.

Capo went to sleep. They watched Capo carefully as if this sleeping were important.

After an hour Capo got up. He stretched and they could hear his grunt. He walked to the water and splashed it over his head and his neck. They heard his sound again, a sound as if he was bored.

The rock under Port seemed to get harder and the sun was like another rock, pressing down on him. And the two men next to him, why sit so close? They were too close even feet apart. The thought alone made Port sweat. The sweat stung out of his skin like quills.

"I've got to close my eyes or look at something else," he said under his breath, but he only blinked and kept looking across at the tongue. The sight became miniature and meaningless. An old man sitting and a young girl sitting and a small man smoking by the water and a big one walking.

The sun was like a spike going into Port's skull and he wondered how the two men with him could sit so still. Didn't they feel their skin all around them as if it meant to split?

A meaningless miniature. The big man sitting down and now there were three sitting. The thin one still standing and blowing smoke. Three? Two only. No, three. Two of them were sitting close together.

Port shook his head. It made things worse, because for a long time everything outside his head had been spinning around and then his head was spinning too.

"Take it easy," said Briggs. "You take it easy."

Why? Why say that?

Two were close together and they were Capo and Maria. Her head was back and Capo's arm on her back kept her from falling. Their heads were close together. Port could not see Capo's other hand.

"I said, take it easy." Briggs put a rough hand on Port, pulling him.

That was all. They all stopped.

"You see it?" Capo yelled up at them. Port could see clearly, even the grin on Capo's face.

"Now," d'Ortega yelled, "now I ask you. Just once."

He paused and the three men on the rock held still under the silence.

"I ask: do we walk off, or don't you care?" and he jerked his head at Maria.

"I promise you something," Port screamed across. "I'll see you die for twenty-four hours straight if you force that girl! I'll ..."

"That's enough," said Briggs. He was like a machine suddenly. He smacked Port's gun out of his hand, tripped him hard, watched him fall back on the rock. "I need your lousy love interest like I need a fever. I run this and you hold still!"

He nodded at Sanchez to hold the gun on Port and then he turned back to the tongue.

"Give up," he called across. "We got you tight."

"You are confused from the sun," d'Ortega said.

Port couldn't see far. He could only see Sanchez over him and the back of Briggs, and he couldn't see that so good because the gun was close to his face.

Would they kill him? What was it with Briggs, a sudden leadership urge? Port bit his lip to help himself concentrate. He could taste the blood where his lip was cracked. Not leadership, business. Briggs didn't trust Port and never had. He'd shoot an ex-hood, or would have him shot, if he felt stopped in his business of one million, American and three prisoners on a small spit of land.

There had been no sound from anyone for quite a while. There was just a low sound from Briggs—he was still looking across—a sound like a cut-off groan.

Port sat up slowly. He did not want to frighten Sanchez with the gun, he just wanted to sit up and know why there was silence. Sanchez moved back a little but did not turn away from Port, and kept holding the gun.

Over the edge of the rock Port saw the miniature again, sharp and clear. First Kiamoto. He must have fallen over because he was on his side, lying down. Then d'Ortega, still by the water. D'Ortega was smoking. Then the rag. Rag? The dress! It was lying on the sand like a rag.

Maria's skin looked very brown on the sand, but Port could not see much of her because Capo was so big.

"Christ—" said Port. "He doesn't even have to hold her down—" Then he jumped up, the sound of his own voice in his ears, screaming something he did not understand.

Briggs whirled around and they didn't shoot him. Briggs cracked his gun over Port's skull and then Sanchez caught Port as best he could, grabbed his head, so it wouldn't cut open on the rock.

Chapter 18

When Port saw everything again the sun was much lower and the sand spit was bigger, because the tide was out. He saw that Maria was sitting again and wearing her dress. She leaned on one arm, looking down, and she was making lines in the sand with one finger. Capo was there with his gun on Kiamoto because Kiamoto was no longer tied. Just his hands were tied now and he stood moving his feet. He stamped them as if they were cold.

D'Ortega was in the water. He was walking there with the water up to his chest.

"Moving day," said Port. He felt cool and cold; his feelings were cool and his thinking was cold. And he felt flip and ugly. "But that will pass," he said to himself. "Once I move that will pass and just the cool and the cold will stay. The heat will come later."

"How's your head?" Briggs asked him.

"Hurts here."

"Can't be helped."

"I know." Port stood up and stretched carefully. Then he exhaled and asked, "Why are you standing around?"

"Right now they're testing," said Sanchez. "D'Ortega just walked through the deepest part. He's coming back."

"Then he goes with Kiamoto, and with Capo standing rear guard," said Port.

"Looks like it. When d'Ortega is ashore where he can cover the land tongue, then Capo goes."

"We need three for this," said Briggs. "Are you in?"

Port nodded and said, "Gimme my gun back."

Briggs gave him the gun.

"I'm going to swim the way the girl did it. When Capo is alone on the spit."

"With the girl."

"She doesn't count. What counts is to draw his fire."

"I swim better than you," said Port. "I swim good and I'm especially anxious to draw his fire."

Briggs frowned at Port but then he let it go.

"Then Sanchez and I will run the fork. He can't hit both of us."

"Just run fast enough so you get to the beach before d'Ortega does."

"Don't worry," said Briggs. "Don't worry."

They saw d'Ortega come out of the water and talk to Capo. The two men were talking and pointing.

"It looks like a close thing," said Sanchez, "getting to that beach before he does. That spit curves toward the land."

"If we don't make it in time— Port, you listening?" said Briggs.

Port had been listening. He had been taking off his shoes and his pants. Then he took off the shirt. "Go ahead," he said.

"If it looks close, his making the beach, then you got to cover him from the end of the tongue. You could shoot across there and hit him."

"Cover him in the water," said Sanchez, "If he's still in the water, it's a sure thing."

They didn't discuss how Port might manage this with Capo still there.

Port climbed down the cliff to the water before anything had changed on the spit. They were talking. Maybe they were arguing about the girl or about how to time this thing right, or perhaps Capo was suspicious or worried that he might be left behind.

Port wasn't worried about that part. He was not even thinking about it. It was all settled.

He had brought his shirt along and when he stood in the water he tied it around his head with the knot under his chin. Then he slipped the gun under the cloth where it crossed the top of his head.

He couldn't see Sanchez and Briggs any more, but Capo showed him where they were. The movements on the spit were now fast and nervous. Capo was especially nervous. He kept looking toward the fork and once he raised his gun, to show the two men there he was aiming. But they hadn't come out all the way. Or Capo was saving the rest of his ammunition.

They hadn't seen Port climb down to the water and with any luck they wouldn't see him until he shot or until he was on the sand. He swam low and nobody looked his way. D'Ortega had Kiamoto by a rope that went to his hands, and those two were going into the water. They were walking away from Port, toward the land side. And Capo kept watching the fork. Then he shot.

"Save them!" said d'Ortega. He said it with a sharp hiss and quite low.

Port could hear it well. Off the rock now and swimming, he caught the voice perfectly.

"Give me some of yours," Capo was saying, but d'Ortega kept walking into the water. "I need them more than you!" It sounded tense, getting angry.

"I have only four," said d'Ortega. "You have a full cylinder," and he walked away.

It was time now for Port to show himself. Fire now, even if it doesn't hit, so that Capo knows he's got two fronts. That way Briggs and Sanchez would get through. That way they would get through in time to get D'Ortega on the beach before he could cut them off.

Or don't show. Let the two men by the fork get more desperate and goad Capo into shooting more often. That would be good. Kill him barehanded. He had five bullets left—

Four bullets.

Briggs must be getting anxious, thought Port. Briggs could see d'Ortega walk toward the beach. He should know about Capo's four bullets.

Three bullets.

Briggs was yelling. He was screaming curses and calling to Port that he should start firing. He was shouting in English and Capo didn't understand. Good, thought Port. Good. He still doesn't know where I am. I hope they don't get hurt on the fork.

Two bullets.

Maria wasn't sitting in the sand any more. She walked toward Capo. When he turned around, checking her, she still kept walking, slow now, like a stroll, but then Capo yelled at her. She sat down on the sand and Capo turned back to the fork immediately.

One bullet.

But he had been late. Port could see Sanchez sprint over the fork while Briggs laid a cover for him. He shot three times, driving Capo back. Port could see all this now. He was close. He touched bottom, swam, walked, swam, walked—ran.

Last bullet!

It chased after Briggs, who was running now, but only Capo and Port knew that this had been the last bullet.

No. And Maria!

Port was afraid to call to her, to stop her crazy sprint at Capo, because the sooner Capo turned back to the girl the worse for her. Port ran out of the water and yanked the gun out of the shirt. But shoot whom? Capo? Maria? They were both in line, they now faced each other. Capo's muscles were hunching him over, his lower teeth showed, he said something filthy— What did she expect to do with her crazy run and her crazy anger, scratch him to death?

"Maria! Duck!"

But she never stopped. Only Capo paid attention, looked up and saw Port with the gun.

But then Capo still had a way. He opened his arms for her and she ran into him.

She would shield him. He would hold her that way and the gun in Port's hand or the rage in his hands wouldn't do any good. Capo could stand there and break her in two with his arms. He was holding her tight, like a bear— like a lover—a drunk—

Maria stepped aside and Capo fell down on his face. Then he rolled over. The knife was still in his belly.

Chapter 19

There was firing from the land side but Port didn't pay attention. He took Maria by the arms, thinking she would come to him, needing him close, but she didn't. She only nodded her head a few times, slowly, and squeezed Port's hand.

He said, "I was going to kill him. I was going to do it for you."

She looked at Port for a moment and then she said, "For me?"

Port didn't know what to answer.

"You think that was for me?" and she pointed where Capo was dead with the knife in his belly. "No." She put her hands on her thighs and said, "This was nothing. What he did here was only like an animal." Then she dropped her hands and looked away. "The other things, though, they were not like that. They were Capo enjoying it, causing pain." She took a deep breath, then blew it out slowly. "To kick an old man to death," she said, "because he laughs—"

"Yes," said Port.

Then they walked to the road.

Until they got back to the car Port had felt finished: the act on the sand, what Maria had said, all of it. But it wasn't finished yet.

There was only Briggs and Sanchez on the road. Sanchez had his head under the hood of the car.

"D'Ortega made it," said Briggs. "We didn't." He kept staring at Port as if there was an answer.

"And Kiamoto just went with him?" asked Port. Nothing else came into his mind for the moment. "He just sat down in the car?"

"In the trunk, Port. At gunpoint he was forced into the trunk. And *my* car," said Briggs. There was a clear menace in his voice now.

Port looked at the car on the road and remembered that there was no water in the radiator.

"You mean you left the keys in the car?" It sounded foolish as soon as it was out.

"He just jumped the wires," Briggs roared. "He was that far ahead of us so he had time to jump the wires! You know why? You know why, Port? He jumped the wires because you jumped the gun! You were swimming out there and that's all you were doing out there, swimming! Nice swim?" Briggs bellowed. "Nice private swim, was it, you dirty hood bastard?"

It had been private all right, for all private reasons.

"Kick something else," said Port. "I'm getting sick of you."

That didn't finish anything either. Sanchez interrupted after a while, stopping them from going further, but that didn't settle anything either.

"I'm going to get salt water," said Sanchez. "It'll be better than nothing."

"Get salt water. I don't care if we burn out the whole rotten guts of it," and Briggs slammed a car door shut, just for the noise.

"Did you leave my clothes back there?" Port asked Sanchez.

"I'll bring them."

"Thanks. I'd hate to walk over those rocks again barefoot."

"Let him get his own damn clothes," said Briggs.

"I'll get them," said Maria and walked off with Sanchez.

Briggs and Port looked at each other once, when they were left behind, but did nothing else. The unfinished feeling in Port wasn't just Briggs doing his worst; it had started before. Port remembered racing up on the sand, sure of the finish, and then Maria had done it her way. And beating up Briggs, would that help?

"You and me got one more stint, Port, before we're done."

"I was just thinking of some plans of my own for you."

"That'll have to wait," said Briggs, "till I'm done with you."

Beating up Briggs, thought Port, might help.

"You're going to show me where Kiamoto went."

"In the trunk," said Port. "You just told me."

But that remark didn't help either. It only made the irritation much worse.

"In the jungle," said Briggs. "Where that ruin is."

And if Port didn't, there were those plans Briggs had for him, those blown-up charges he had mentioned once before.

"You thinking about it, Port?"

He was thinking about it and that it might finish the thing. It would be good to get d'Ortega for everything, and it would be good to help Kiamoto.

"I'll take you," said Port. "To finish all this."

They drove the car into the ground. The salt water held out longer than they had thought and when they came through the first village they didn't even bother to change it. They added fresh water and then they drove like hell again.

It boiled out before they saw Guanadera and the bearings started to knock when they were driving in. They rolled into the square where Guanadera's policeman was sitting in the shade.

Yes, he had seen the car, very large and beautiful. Yes, it must still be there, since it had not been back. "Visiting Kiamoto," said the policeman. "It's in front of his house."

The car was there but the house was empty. In back of the house, past the garden, they found the path where Kiamoto had led the way into the jungle.

"Sanchez stays here," said Briggs, "in case either of them comes back."

Whichever way, they did not think both of them would come back out.

"And the girl can stay with him," said Briggs, "for protection."

Port thought about the man with the knife in his belly and how strange it seemed that Maria needed protecting. But he said nothing.

"You'll be careful?" she said to him.

"I'll be back."

"And Kiamoto?"

"Maybe," he said. Then he smiled good-bye.

Briggs wanted to cross into the woods behind Kiamoto's house but Port didn't trust himself to find anything that way. He let Briggs curse but took him back through the village and to the point where Pepe had gone into the jungle; once with Port, once with d'Ortega. The cut path should still be plain.

They went by the broken branches and cut vines. They stayed far apart so that Briggs, who walked second, would still be with a landmark if Port, going first, should lose his bearings. It was easier than Port had expected but it took a very long time. The green shadows became very dark after a while and the day could have been sunless. Only the heat stayed the same.

"After we cross the swamp," said Port, "we climb up there. Then we start watching it."

"They're up there?"

"I don't know," said Port. "The ruin is under those trees."

It turned daylight again when they crossed through the swamp, but the sun was low. The twilight would be short. They walked through swarms of mosquitoes which bit right through their shirts. Port wished he had brought a serape.

"Now," he said. "Start listening."

It got dark again and the black gate was there. No sound. Just leaves rubbing.

Then they heard the breathing. It was hard and straining, like torture.

They had their guns in their hands and didn't dare move.

"It doesn't sound close," Briggs whispered.

"I can't judge it. But I think it's human."

They crossed the open court because the sound was on the other side. They passed the idol which leaned with a heavy tilt. The sound was still farther.

It wasn't in any place where Port had been before. The harsh sound got rhythmic, making no sense at all, rhythmic and painfully heavy.

"I think down again," said Port. "There's more swamp—"

An overgrown wall tilted down the incline and where the ground became wetter there was another terrace. It had broken and some of it had sunk away and there were massive steps which led out of nothing to nothing. They ended up in the air and on the other side was the place where the swamp drained away. The growth around the water was thick and the water was moving. It was one of the outlets that went to the sea.

"Something moved," said Briggs.

Port nodded. He had seen where the green water had rippled.

"There," said Briggs, "on that wall."

There was a wall next to the water, thick like a quay, and a ruined arch. There was a man in the arch, standing still, watching.

Kiamoto.

They could not see what he was watching.

Then he moved his head, showing no surprise, and looked over at Port. Kiamoto's hands were still tied. He nodded at them with a deliberate turn of his head.

"He signaling us?" said Briggs.

"Must be. He means this way."

They crawled back down the steps and then followed the terrace. It took them along the water but kept them out of the thicket. Then they saw the arch from another angle. They saw Kiamoto again, standing there, and d'Ortega.

He was making the sounds. He groaned and gasped with effort, trying to move a slab.

There was a stone pedestal with the idol lying next to it. The platform where it had been was the slab d'Ortega was trying to move.

He stopped and struggled for breath.

"If you're lying," he said. He was too breathless to say any more.

"I can do nothing to you," said Kiamoto. "I can't even help you," and he moved his hands.

"You'd like that, huh? If I were to untie your hands."

"You want the money," said Kiamoto. "I don't."

Then d'Ortega struggled again, trying to move the slab. It was his pure greed which gave him the strength after a while. The slab tilted, balanced, then slid off with a thud.

"Inside," said Kiamoto. "At the bottom of the steps."

With the slab off, the pedestal was a square, hollow chamber.

"I told you there would be the steps," said Kiamoto.

D'Ortega was looking down into the pedestal.

"It's at the bottom."

"But there's water at the bottom."

"Not deep," said Kiamoto. "You reach into the water and feel for the handle."

D'Ortega showed his conflict; to leave Kiamoto out of sight, to go down and get the money, to untie Kiamoto and make him go down— Right down there, at the bottom of the steps. A minute. One minute and one million dollars.

He looked around like a thief but he hardly saw anything. He was with the one million at the bottom of the steps. He had one leg over the pedestal, and then he stopped. He showed the fear in his face, and the confusion.

"Under water? Why would you hide money under water?"

"The chamber was dry when I hid the money there," said Kiamoto. "But the swamp moved."

Then d'Ortega started to screech. "And you left the money there? You knew the water was seeping in and you left paper bills, one million paper bills..."

"I packed them well," said Kiamoto. "And besides, I didn't want them. You do."

D'Ortega couldn't wait any longer. He could doubt more, question Kiamoto's explanation, he could show how he trembled with fear—but he couldn't wait any longer.

He climbed into the well and Port could hear the footsteps going down on stone.

Kiamoto looked at them again and nodded his head.

From close up he looked just as bland as before, but the wear was showing. He was cut and bruised, there were dark shadows under his eyes, and perhaps he had lost weight. But none of that interfered with his expression.

Port cut the ropes on his hands and Briggs looked down into the well. The stone steps angled off and the bottom just showed under an arch. It was like a basement, with water in it. Then Briggs pulled his head back. D'Ortega was moving down there, grunting and moving.

Briggs looked at Kiamoto and pulled out his wallet. Then he showed his I.D. card and the badge.

Kiamoto was rubbing his wrists. He looked at everything and made a slight bow.

"You are under arrest," said Briggs.

Kiamoto made a slight bow.

There was a loud yell from the hole and then d'Ortega was jabbering. He cursed, laughed, said silly things, threatened an invisible audience, harangued them for doubting him, spat in their faces, and he did all that while he panted back up the steps.

Port moved back and Briggs moved out of the way.

He threw the box out of the hole. It was like a small trunk and after it hit, with a hard sound it lay there on the stones next to the pedestal, running water.

Then d'Ortega jumped out. His arms had green slime on them and his pants were soaked brown. "Open it," he yelled. "How do you open it?" If he had a gun in his pocket he had forgotten about it.

"I'm sure it's rusted," said Kiamoto.

D'Ortega was yanking and pulling. His voice kept blathering nonsense.

"Perhaps use the flat of your hand," said Kiamoto, "or your knuckles. The way you did to Maria."

The other one didn't answer. He used his flat hand and then his fist.

"Perhaps use the gun in your pocket," said Kiamoto. "With the butt. The way you did it with me."

The other one yanked out his gun, ruined it pounding the box.

"Or kick it," said Kiamoto. "Kick hard. The way it was done to Pepe."

D'Ortega stopped, exhausted. He stood up and looked at Kiamoto. He held the gun as if it could still work.

"Open it," he said. "Damn you, Hoi Kio, open it!"

Kiamoto bent down to the box, hefted it over his head, and smashed it down. D'Ortega was so absorbed he never questioned why Kiamoto's hands were no longer tied.

It splashed water and cracked open.

"Now," said Briggs, and stepped out.

D'Ortega saw Briggs and then Port, but he had no time to grasp their presence. He looked at them very briefly, like a little distraction might make him look, and then he looked back at the broken box. His mouth hung open.

"But the money—" he said. "One million in money. The crime—"

It was a crime. It was still one million—the big block of bills showed—but a block of solid pulp.

"I said I would show it to you." Kiamoto shrugged.

D'Ortega put his hands into the pile, very carefully, and came up with a handful of soggy pulp.

"A million," he said, and then again, over and over, with the rage splitting his voice.

"A worthless million," said Kiamoto. "Let me see you throw it away."

A bill stuck to d'Ortega's hand. It was still whole.

"Throw it away," said Kiamoto. "Here. So. And so." He took handfuls of pulp, shredded it, threw it into the water.

Some of it sank, some of it drifted, and something snapped at it from underneath.

Then d'Ortega went berserk. Kiamoto stepped away from him, avoiding the man, so d'Ortega turned and saw Port. He grabbed him and pounded his fist on Port.

"Where is it? Where is the money? Where is the real, the one million dollars of real money? I'll kill you for less, I demand..."

"Get back," said Port. "Get away from me."

Port gave the man a push to be free of him. It didn't move d'Ortega very far. He came back and raked his gun over Port's chin, and when Port jerked out of the way the other one kept swinging and cursing.

The disgust was almost too much. Thin, crazy d'Ortega was too much to take but not enough to hit.

"Here," said Port. "Here, yours, all yours, jump for it, rat man," and he threw handfuls of pulp and torn bills into the water.

The shreds and the lumps moved away quickly with a swirling mot

D'Ortega stood at the edge of the stone, wanting to jump, afraid to ju seeing one million, American, drift down a green jungle stream, When P reached down to get more, d'Ortega kicked at his head, missed, and scream his curses again. Then he spat at Briggs and at Port.

He had to touch him once, Port felt. Just once and be done.

"Get it!" he said. "Jump and get it, d'Ortega," and he kicked the man in the back so he flew into the water.

He hardly looked after that. D'Ortega was spinning around in the canal, reaching for bills, squeezing the pulp, following it and screaming. Once his scream got very shrill. He was half hidden around a bend.

Briggs stepped to the edge of the wall and said, "What was that?"

"It is better if you don't go into the water," said Kiamoto.

They ran along the edge of the water as far as the tangle would let them. But they didn't see d'Ortega again.

And they didn't see Kiamoto again. They looked for a while, but it was useless. It was darker now, almost brown under the trees, and they knew only one way through the jungle. Kiamoto, like Pepe had shown Port once before, could be anywhere here and be invisible.

They didn't leave that night. It was suddenly dark. They stayed by the pedestal and waited for morning.

"You're going to look for him?" Port asked.

"I don't know. I myself wouldn't." Briggs folded his arms and felt damp.

"At least you got all that money," said Port.

"Enough to show what there was. I was worried you'd throw all of it into that stinking stream there."

"You didn't stop me."

"It seemed—ridiculous," Briggs said. He felt unofficial and didn't say any more.

Port thought about Kiamoto for a while and then he went to sleep. Kiamoto had been the strangest of them and the most distant.

When Port woke in the morning he found that he was covered with an old serape.

"Will he come back?" Maria asked.

Port shrugged. He put the serape in Maria's lap and said, "I don't think so. He left this."

THE END

337

on,
np,
ort
ed